Bump, Set, Sparks

Also by Jennifer Moffatt

Flirty Dancing

THE FALLING HARD TRILOGY

A Hard Sell

A Hard Fit

A Hard Note

Bump, Set, Sparks

A NOVEL

Jennifer Moffatt

ST. MARTIN'S GRIFFIN
NEW YORK

This is a work of fiction. All of the names, characters, organizations, places, and events portrayed in this work are either products of the author's imagination or used fictitiously.

First published in the United States by St. Martin's Griffin, an imprint of St. Martin's Publishing Group

EU Representative: Macmillan Publishers Ireland Ltd, 1st Floor, The Liffey Trust Centre, 117–126 Sheriff Street Upper, Dublin 1, D01 YC43

 Printed in the United States of America. For information, address St. Martin's Publishing Group, 120 Broadway, New York, NY 10271.

www.stmartins.com

Designed by Meryl Sussman Levavi

Volleyball image © Net Vector/Shutterstock

The Library of Congress Cataloging-in-Publication Data is available upon request.

ISBN 978-1-250-37930-6 (trade paperback)
ISBN 978-1-250-37931-3 (ebook)

First Edition: 2026

10 9 8 7 6 5 4 3 2 1

To my dad, Dennis,
the first and best coach I ever had

A handful of sand contains about 10,000 grains, more than the number of stars we can see with the naked eye on a clear night. But the number of stars we can see is only the tiniest fraction of the number of stars that are. What we see at night is the merest smattering of the nearest stars. Meanwhile the Cosmos is rich beyond measure: the total number of stars in the universe is greater than all the grains of sand on all the beaches of the planet Earth.

—Carl Sagan, ***Cosmos***

Bump, Set, Sparks

1

Wins: 3
Losses: 9

> ***Carry*: When setting, the volleyball must be played with fingertips only, and not caught or thrown in any way. A ball that is lifted or held too long is a "carry." The referee should call this fault, but there is a measure of subjectivity involved, i.e., sometimes they fuck it up.**

There was something about the heat and the sweat. Down in the sand, feet sinking and dragging, extra effort was required to overcome that friction to make the play. Every stride slower. Every jump harder. Beach volleyball was about overcoming not just the body's limitations in muscle, tendon, and stamina—physical and mental—but the environment. The sun and the sand, the wind—gusts blown in from the vast, unyielding ocean, an uncaring product of climate and currents—none of that gave a fuck about the athletes or the game. . . . The team who overcame it, though . . . they won.

"Are you fucking kidding me?" Jess cried, trying not to yell directly at the referee. "That was such a carry!" She wiped the sand from her uniform while the other team celebrated their tying point with high fives.

"Jess." Tania, her levelheaded and long-suffering partner, gave her a low warning.

"But . . ." Jess trailed off. The ref was glaring at her, hand twitching in the direction of the red card. It was lucky Jess hadn't gotten a card already this match, to be honest. Other refs would have had her and her chirpy ass in the locker room by now. Jess bit her lip and swallowed any further words about the missed call.

Tania gave her a low five. "We need a pass now. Come on, refocus."

"Yeah. Okay." Jess tucked a sweaty strand of hair that had escaped her ponytail behind her ear and brushed the sand from her butt. She turned to face the server, hands on her knees, the California sun hot on her back.

They hadn't lost to this team since early last season, and she certainly wasn't planning on starting today. But her head hadn't been in the game, and it was tied at fourteen in the third and final set. Time to dig in.

Her opponent and off-court friend, Chrissy, hammered a serve, but it was right at Jess. She passed it easily to Tania, who gave her a beauty of a set. Jess tore in for a hit, arm winding up . . . and cranked the ball out the back of the court. The few hundred spectators cheering for the other team hooted their approval from the stands. Jess and Tania's fans offered encouraging shouts.

"Fuck," Jess growled while Chrissy and her partner pumped their fists at her error.

"Jess." Tania took her hand and gave it a tug so Jess looked at her. "It's fine. We've got this. Give me another pass like that one, then swing away. Yeah?"

"Yeah." Jess's heart thudded in her ears. Fourteen to fifteen. Match point. No time-outs left.

Chrissy paused at the back line before the whistle, gaze

flicking between Jess and Tania. Another tough serve, this time a couple feet to Jess's left. She stepped into it and gave Tania another great pass, which got her another beauty set. *Don't blow it, Jess.* She eyed her crosscourt shot, knowing she could get it past the block . . . but another unforced error at match point was unacceptable. She took some heat off her swing—too much—and lobbed an easy ball at them. Chrissy got there no problem and dug it up for her partner.

Jess settled at the net and waited for Chrissy's attack, aware of the sweat on her temples and her tired legs, then jumped in time with her for a block. The ball brushed Jess's fingers and continued into the court behind her. "Touch!" Jess yelped, peeling back and ready for the third hit. Tania chased the touch deep into the court and brought it back high enough for Jess to attack. The ball approached at an awkward angle, lost for a second in the sun over the open-air pavilion, so she had to give them another easy shot. Chrissy popped it up, then went hard on her attack.

Jess jumped, reaching her hands over the net. She got a few fingers on the ball, but the hit went off her block and flew far out of bounds.

They lost.

"Fuck," Jess spat. "*Fuck.*" The familiar feeling of failure curdled in her gut and made her heart race, prickling her skin with shame.

Chrissy and her partner whooped and hopped around the court in their hug while their fans cheered.

Jess watched them, hands on hips and trying not to scowl. Tania gave her a brief hug and slapped her butt. "Good game, Button."

"No, it wasn't," Jess grumbled, the cutesy yet pointed nickname Tania had given her last season even more irritating now. "Not from me, anyway."

"You played great," Tania said. "We can't win 'em all."

"I played like crap. And I'd settle for winning half." Jess sighed and followed Tania to the net. "Good game," she said to Chrissy. "Nice serves," she added, even though the loss rankled.

Chrissy grinned and shook her hand. "Thought you had me on that last block."

"I had nothing but air, I guess."

Once the score sheet was signed, Chrissy tugged her hair elastic out. "You guys heading over to Maggie's?" Her red hair spilled over her shoulders as she scrubbed at it.

Jess's tastebuds watered at the thought of a nice cold beer. "Can't. I'm working today." She didn't normally work on Sundays but she had picked up a shift after the morning game. With summer approaching, the amusement park was getting busier, so extra hours were usually available if she wanted them.

"Okay, cool. Maybe later, then?"

"Maybe."

The four of them signed a few autographs for the kids hanging around and Chrissy gave a quote to the local sports reporter, then Jess and Tania stopped to chat with Tania's mamá, tías, and assorted cousins.

"Come for dinner soon!" Tía Diana said when she hugged Jess. Jess's first hug from Tía Diana had come after she and Tania won their first match together and now Jess melted into the comforting softness of each one. "It's been too long, mija."

"I will, I will." Jess squeezed her back extra tight. "Just let me know when."

After a few more hugs for some cousins and promises for a visit, Jess and Tania rinsed off at the outdoor shower near the locker room, then headed in for a proper cleanup. The cool quiet of the locker room was welcoming after the late spring heat and rumble of the crowd in the bleachers. The shower spray on her tired muscles and scent of her lavender shower gel soothed her, but Jess couldn't stop replaying that last failed block in her mind. If she had just jumped a bit higher . . . reached a little farther . . .

Jess wrapped herself in her towel when she was done and was heading back to her locker when a voice cut through the chatter.

That voice. Low and judgmental. Smooth and haughty. "Ugh, who got all this sand everywhere?"

The voice that crawled down Jess's spine like the most unwelcome of insects. There was no mistaking it.

Jess rounded the corner, clutching her towel, hair dripping, and yup, there she was.

Vivienne Morris. Perfect and petite—for a beach volleyball player anyway, one of the smallest women in the league—with shining black hair, golden tanned skin, and features so tidy and delicate they looked painted on with the tiniest of brushes. Vivienne and her partner, Lee, were locked into the top spot in the league, undefeated so far this season.

Jess hated her. Even more than she hated losing, which was a lot. Everything came easy to Vivienne, and she looked down on people who had to work for it, the ones who showed the effort with mess and imperfection.

And Jess was nothing if not a mess.

Their eyes met as Vivienne looked up, curling her plump lips into their usual condescending grimace. "Oh." Vivienne raised an immaculately groomed eyebrow, then looked pointedly down at the sandy floor again.

Jess tried to keep the scowl off her face. "That wasn't me," she said, aware she sounded like a petulant five-year-old. "I rinsed off."

"Mmm." Vivienne shared a look with Lee, who struggled to hide a smirk.

The heat rose in Jess's cheeks, her chest tightening in anger. She bit back the repeated denial that gathered in her throat and instead breezed past Vivienne to get to her locker.

Vivienne stood and slid her fingers into the bottom of her swimsuit to snap the elastics into place. She and Lee were playing in the next match so were in their new one-shouldered bikinis—black with gold accents. Sleek and expensive-looking—all the glamour of the bad guys in a sports movie . . . aside from Lee's old, gross, sweat-stained "lucky visor."

"How did your match go, Jess?" Vivienne asked with wide eyes.

The absolute bitch. She knew exactly how it had gone. "Fine," Jess snapped.

"Did you win?" Vivienne's face was blank and innocent.

Tania joined the crowd at their lockers. "We'll get 'em next time." Tania was on the smaller side too, but with prominent curves and still taller than Vivienne. Jess delighted in the way Tania patted Vivienne's head as she passed by.

"I'm sure you will." Vivienne glared at Tania and smoothed her hair, not that she needed to. Vivienne always had the most impossibly perfect ponytail. It hardly even budged after a long match. Her fingernails were gold this week. Most of the athletes in the league didn't wear nail polish, but Vivienne always had her nails done—short, but glossy and immaculate.

"Good luck today," Tania said cheerfully. She dropped her towel and started pulling on her underwear.

Jess followed suit. "Yeah, good luck. Being undefeated must be a lot of pressure, hey?"

Vivienne's placid expression wavered. "No, I wouldn't say it's a lot of pressure."

"No? I mean, you've got to lose one day, right? Might be today!"

Vivienne pressed her lips together. "If I need advice on how to deal with losing, I'll be sure to ask you."

Lee snickered, and the other pair getting ready smothered their giggles.

"Oh, just teasing," Vivienne said in a sugary sweet purr.

So sweet it made Jess sick.

"Vivienne Morris is such a bitch," Jess spat to Tania on their way out. "God, I can't stand her."

"I know," Tania said.

"Those new uniforms of theirs, like, please. Black? Who wants to wear black in the sun?"

"They look good, though."

"Not really," Jess grumbled, even though they both knew that Vivienne and Lee looked amazing.

They were passing by the courts when Jess noticed the Sunside Cable cameras. "They're televising this one?" Not many games in their league were shown on TV. Aside from winning the state championship and getting an invite to join the pros, a televised game was as good as it got.

"Looks like it," Tania said wistfully.

Vivienne and Lee were on the court warming up like clockwork—dig, set, hit, dig, set, hit . . . almost boring in its efficiency. That was the way Vivienne played. Straight-faced, little emotion, smooth and steady. The exact opposite of Jess.

"You want to watch for a bit?" Tania asked.

"Gotta get to work." Technically speaking, Jess had a few minutes to spare, but she was not in the mood.

"Oh, right. Maggie's after then?"

"I'll see how I feel."

"I know 'I'll see' usually means no, so consider this my formal request for you to please come."

Jess hugged her, a smile playing at the corner of her mouth. "Okay. Fine. I'll come."

Tania squeezed her back. "Love you."

The amusement park was not far down the boardwalk from the volleyball pavilion. Jess enjoyed the walk, flip-flops slapping on the sandy slats while gulls wheeled overhead, their cries mingling with the steady roar of the surf. The sun on her shoulders and smell of the salt in the air was a balm to her wounded ego. She could almost forget about losing . . . almost.

From the employee entrance she made her way to the staff locker room—a cramped space with an aroma of stale popcorn and disinfectant with a slight undernote of sour sweat. Sometimes it seemed like she spent half her waking hours in locker rooms, and they all smelled bad. Jess pulled out her uniform—although "uniform" was an insult to all other uniforms. It was a neon-green T-shirt with an orange vest and bow tie sewn onto it. Clearly, whoever had designed it had a sick sense of humor, or maybe some sort of early-childhood cotton-candy trauma that they enjoyed taking out on amusement park employees.

Jess had recently earned the title of "manager" for the midway games, but so far that meant only a bit more money and a lot more problems to solve. It wasn't a long-term career plan, but as long as she was playing in the Southern California Beach Volleyball League from April to October, it was perfect. Only steps apart, she could schedule her shifts around her games, and nothing on the midway was too taxing, mentally or physically. And maybe one day . . . maybe . . . she could leave it all behind for the pros.

During a lull in the line, she leaned on the ring toss counter, thoughts drifting back to that last losing point. In her mind, she stuffed the ball back in Chrissy's face. The crowd roared. Scouts from the pro league happened to be there, nodding and making notes on their clipboards. That hardly ever actually happened, of course. Scouts weren't in the habit of plucking players from the obscurity of the SoCal VL and bringing them up to the Pacific Beach League. The only sure way to earn a spot in the pro circuit was to win the state championship. She and Tania had almost made it to the finals their first season together, Jess new to the league and the two of them fast friends, but finished near the bottom last year. Vivienne and Lee, meanwhile, were a new team last season and had come *so* close to earning the pro invite when they won the SoCal league, but had fallen just short in the state final.

Speaking of Vivienne . . . Jess swiveled her gaze to the lifeguard station that was visible not far down the beach. Vivienne wasn't there, of course, she was playing right now, but Jess had grown used to seeing her perched high on her chair, looking down at the world, much like the way she looked down on Jess and just about everyone else.

The second time they ever spoke, Jess had been wandering along the shore, head down, collecting a pocketful of seashells. She had just uncovered a particularly beautiful one—the inside shimmering pearlescent in the fading evening sun—when Vivienne's snooty voice floated down from the lifeguard chair. "You're not supposed to take seashells."

Jess blinked at her, recognizing Vivienne instantly, but needing a second to figure out why she was eight feet up in the air. "Excuse me?"

Vivienne had lifted her sunglasses and was examining Jess intently. "I'm just telling you. It's illegal."

Jess's hackles went up. "Why do you care?"

"I don't, really. But beach patrol would love to give you a big fat ticket." Vivienne crossed one gleaming leg over the other.

Jess clenched her fist around the shell, Vivienne's haughty tone making her want to throw the shell right at her head. "I'm not worried about it."

Vivienne shrugged and leaned back, flicking her sunglasses into place. "Suit yourself."

"'Suit yourself,'" Jess had muttered, stomping away. "How about 'go fuck yourself'?"

Jess sighed. Vivienne hadn't changed a bit in the year since.

After an uneventful shift—not so busy that she felt discombobulated, but not so slow that she had to resort to counting the minutes until her escape—Jess trudged to the locker room and changed out of her hideous uniform and back into her gray tank top. She tried to do something with her limp brown hair but it proved futile so she left it down, lifeless and flat. Her gaze rested on the magazine page she had taped up in her locker. . . . Bianca Collazo, star of the professional Pacific Beach League. Bianca had played in the SoCal VL four years ago and won the state title, and was now a bona fide celebrity—endorsement deals with major brands, guest appearances on sitcoms . . . Bianca had it all. And she had been right where Jess was today.

So Jess dreamed.

Maggie's wasn't too packed, since peak tourist season had yet to arrive. The old bar's entrance was off the boardwalk, with the other side open to the beach, a faded deck extending onto the sand, usually humming with live music and women who liked women. The name came from the owner's love of Dame Maggie Smith, and photographs of Maggie in her most iconic roles were featured throughout, mixed with portraits of the VL stars who had made it to the pros, like Bianca. Right next to the volleyball pavilion, the bar was the main hangout for the athletes in the league. Anytime Jess popped in, she was sure to recognize some friends . . . or foes.

Like Vivienne Morris, sitting at Jess's favorite table with Lee, Chrissy, and a few other players.

Jess let out what could only be described as a growl.

"To our winning streak!" Lee shouted as Jess approached, raising a shot glass.

Vivienne toasted her partner.

Lee swallowed her shot and pointed at Vivienne. "See, my lucky visor is working. You wanted me to get a new one to match our uniforms but I told you, it has magical powers."

Vivienne shook her head and smiled at her teammate.

And the smile turned her into a dazzling beauty. Which made Jess hate her even more. Jess had always considered herself plain-looking. And while her height and broad shoulders were advantageous on the volleyball court, they were not so useful growing up, and certainly didn't help her meet conventional beauty standards now. But Vivienne was effortlessly beautiful, as she was effortlessly everything else.

Jess slumped into a chair at the other end of the table.

Chrissy saw her and leaned over to greet her above the hubbub of the bar. "Hey, how was work?"

"Fine."

"Did you catch any of the game? Viv and Lee crushed it. Viv actually—"

Jess lurched back to her feet. "Sorry, you know what? Hold that thought. I really need a drink." She abandoned Chrissy and her fawning and made her way to the bar.

A bachelorette party was in the way. A cluster of partygoers blocked her path, screeching and passing shots around. They were obviously not from Southern California—most of them clearly hadn't seen the sun in months. The bride-to-be wore a wedding veil and a glittering pink bachelorette sash labeled BRIDE #1, but it was the woman next to her in a pale yellow sundress who caught Jess's attention. Sultry and curvy, flowing dark brown hair, wide eyes, and an alluring vibe that pulled Jess in.

Even if Jess wasn't a dazzling beauty herself, on occasions such as these, she reminded herself that she was in excellent shape and her boobs looked good in a tank top. And sometimes women were really into her size. She could pick most of them right up, in fact—a fun party trick. But the question now was whether the woman in the yellow dress liked women.

Jess edged through the crowd, passing right by Yellow Dress. Their arms brushed and Yellow turned. She smiled when their eyes met. Jess smiled back, cheeks warming. Once she got to the bar, she waved down the bartender and ordered a Corona. Yellow continued to watch her.

Go talk to her, Jess said to herself, sipping her beer. *She's looking at you.* But she didn't even have a chance to chicken out as usual, because Yellow approached.

"Hi."

Jess tried not to stare at her cleavage . . . her very lovely cleavage. "Hi."

"I saw you come in."

"Oh, yeah?" Jess gulped and tucked her hair behind her ear.

"Yeah. You were sitting over there, right?" Yellow nodded at the table of volleyball girls.

"Yup." Jess resisted the urge to tug at the hem of her tank top and prepared herself for what was coming next . . . the usual comments she got, something about her height or exceptional tan.

"What's the deal with her?" Now Yellow pointed at the table.

"Uh . . ." Jess blinked. "Sorry?"

"The little one there on the end with black hair? Is she into women?"

Jess turned to look. The little one on the end . . . ?

Vivienne.

Vivienne fucking Morris.

2

Wins: 3
Losses: 10

> ***Leg day*: Volleyball players must have both foundational strength and explosive power in their legs. Dead lifts, lunges, box jumps, Bulgarian split squats . . . there is all manner of torture to be found in the gym when it's time to focus on legs.**

"Oh, that's . . ." Jess tried to swallow, mouth dry. "That's Vivienne." Of course. Of course Yellow wasn't actually interested in her.

"And? Is she straight?" Yellow's eyes were bright . . . eager.

Yes, Jess wanted to say. *Totally straight. Don't bother.* But . . . "I . . . I actually don't know," she replied truthfully. Now into their second season together in the league, Jess had never seen Vivienne with a romantic partner, or even heard her talk about one. Of course, Jess suspected, Vivienne's heart was probably a series of gears, humming at peak efficiency and incapable of love. Jess took a big swallow of her beer.

"Oh." Yellow shifted and stuck out her lower lip. "She's hot."

Keeping her expression polite and noncommittal, Jess clutched her bottle and pondered her choices—return to shark-infested waters, or stay there getting battered by the tide.

"'Kay, well . . . I've gotta . . ." Jess pointed vaguely with her beer and hauled anchor. She abandoned Yellow and swam back to the sharks, cheeks burning in humiliation. All she wanted to do was sit and drink her beer and try to salvage whatever dignity she had remaining. But as she approached their table, Vivienne stood. Their eyes met. Her face was soft for a moment, unguarded, then Lee stood behind her and whispered into her ear. Vivienne curled her mouth in amusement as her gaze swept up and down Jess's body.

Jess faltered for half a second, then took a sharp turn toward the bathrooms. Nope. There was no dignity to be found here tonight. She left her beer on a ledge and went out the back door.

Mercifully, Jess's tiny apartment was only three blocks from the beach. And "tiny" was not an exaggeration—the only reason she could afford to live within walking distance of the tourist hub, the home of both her jobs, was that the building used to be a motel, and her apartment was an actual ex-motel room . . . fortunately free of seedy motel-room classics, like suspicious stains on the walls or a lingering smell of cigarette smoke. And if she stood at her one big window and craned her neck, she could catch a glimpse of the Pacific Ocean. Bright white walls reflected the California sunlight, and every inch was covered in plants, woven wall hangings Tía Diana had made for her, beachy knickknacks, and an odd mix of romance and astronomy books, plus a telescope in the corner that she carried up to the roof on clear nights. Aside from a volleyball court, her apartment was her favorite place in the world. A safe retreat from the struggles of life.

One of the best parts about living there was taking her morning tea out onto the covered walkway outside her door and sitting in a metal chair from Goodwill—the ornate kind you might find in a Parisian café, aside from the flaking white paint. She would cradle her mug and smell the ocean while the sun crept toward her feet—the sunshine she had craved her whole life. Born in Seattle, she grew up in rainy Vancouver, British Columbia, a dual citizen, thanks to an American mom and a Canadian dad. Desperate to escape the rain by the end of high school, Jess went to USC on a volleyball scholarship while earning a degree in sports management, then captured a spot in the SoCal VL after graduation. It was an amateur league but provided a stipend, so between that and the amusement park, she was able to make the perfect motel apartment only three blocks from the sun-soaked beach a reality . . . without relying on her parents for financial support.

Jess trudged up the steps to the second floor, but before she could retreat to her cocoon and nurse her bruised ego, she had to pick up Fleming. She knocked on her neighbor's door. It cracked open and a wriggling short-haired dachshund threw himself at her legs.

"Hi, baby, did you miss me?" Jess cooed, scooping him up.

A handsome bald Black man followed the dog. "A little, but I got through it okay." Nelson leaned against his doorframe, pulling his silk robe tight.

"Oh, stop it." Jess burrowed her face into Fleming's fur. It was impossible to be sad or angry with the sweetest pup in history in her arms.

Nelson pulled a tube of lip gloss from his pocket and applied a shimmer to his lips as he spoke. "Your little baby there wouldn't stop growling at my gentleman caller."

"Hmm. Maybe Fleming is getting a bad vibe. Might be best to let that one go."

The wiener panted his agreement.

Nelson scratched the dog's head. "Fleming growls at everyone and licks his own crotch. What does he know? Also, I got you some of that eye cream I was telling you about." He fished in his other pocket.

"Nelson, I don't—"

He held up the jar. "Girl, let me tell you. You are out in the sun all day and you won't be twenty-five forever."

"I'm twenty-four."

He raised an eyebrow. "I rest my case."

"Oh, give me the fucking cream."

Nelson grinned and handed it to her. "Add it to my bill."

Jess leaned over to kiss his cheek. "You're the best."

"I know. See you tomorrow."

Nelson, a computer whiz of some sort who worked from home, refused money of any kind for helping out with Fleming, but accepted banana bread and cookies when Jess delivered them fresh from the oven. The day Jess came home with Fleming, shortly after she moved in, Nelson had scooped him up and declared him the best boy in the entire world, and they had been friends ever since.

Jess set Fleming down and he trotted behind her on their way to their apartment.

She hung up her keys and bag by the door, then went

over to a shelf by the window. She took a seashell out of the "win" jar and put it into the "loss" jar. "Another one," she sighed. The season started with sixty shells in the "win" jar. Six weeks in and already ten losses out of thirteen matches.

Fleming settled into his dog bed and looked up at her with big eyes.

"I know," Jess replied. "Just gotta keep going."

On that note, she retrieved her phone from her bag so she could confirm a workout with Tania for tomorrow and discovered she had actually missed a text from her partner over an hour ago. **Workout tomorrow?** Tania had asked.

You bet. 10:00?

Tania's reply came right away. **Yup, see you then.**

How was the rest of your day?

Good. George and I went to the market. Got some of those peaches you were raving about. You? Tania was straight and lived with her boyfriend, but Jess tried not to hold that against her. George was a decent guy anyway—a chef at a fancy French restaurant who loved to cook at home for Tania, too.

Fine, Jess replied. **Work wasn't too busy.** She left out the part about how the woman she was checking out bypassed her plain looks and big nose for Vivienne instead. **See you tomorrow!**

Jess changed from her jean shorts and tank top into thin cotton pajama bottoms and a camisole. She spread her long legs out on the one bit of floor space where she fit—ignoring the fact that half her leg was under the bed and at least one pile of books got knocked over in the process—and did a few quick stretches, then she made a cup of tea and curled up in bed with a book.

Her current read was *Queen in Shining Armor,* a steamy

sapphic romance by her favorite author, Veronica Doyle. Queen Andromeda, unhappy and trapped in her royal life, disguised herself as a knight and ran off to battle, but upon spotting the queen of the enemy country, fell instantly in love. Jess envied Queen Andromeda, so confident in herself that she would risk it all after only a glimpse of what she wanted. Veronica Doyle had the best main characters—Jess's gay realization had come courtesy of Cleo, the protagonist of *Constellation Prize*, the first Veronica Doyle book she'd ever read. Cleo was swoon-worthy: a tough but kind adventurer who learned magic to explore the stars.

Jess, sweaty after already jogging four miles, arrived at the pavilion the next morning. She found Tania in the gym doing weighted squats. It was leg day.

"Hey, Button," Tania said on an exhale.

"Hey." Jess refilled her water bottle at the fountain.

"How was your run?"

"Painful." Jess hated everything about running, except the feeling of it ending, which was enough to keep her going. "You're early." It was more a question than a statement. Tania was not a morning person.

"I had to get out of there. George suddenly wanted to reorganize the garage. You know men once they get a house project in mind."

Jess took another drink. "Not really."

"Oh, right." Tania racked her weight and shook her legs out. "My bad. So . . . we play that team from North Bay on Wednesday."

"Yup." They played Sunside pairs most of the time, but teams sometimes traveled between North Bay and Horn

Beach. There were no VL matches Mondays or Tuesdays, and then usually one Wednesday or Thursday night, and another one, maybe two, on the weekend. "They're off to a bumpy start too, so we really need to capitalize and get this win."

Tania stretched her quads. "Both of them are huge, bigger than you. Chrissy said we want to serve to Reese, the blonde one."

They chitchatted about their game plan as Jess began her workout. She was just getting into a rhythm when they were joined by another team in the gym. The last team Jess wanted to see.

Vivienne and Lee strode in like they owned the place.

Jess shared a look with Tania. *Well, fuck.* Their Monday-morning-workout routine had been going so well.

Vivienne and Lee flashed them hollow smiles on their way to the weights. And did they really have to look so put together for a workout, in matching sports bras and everything? Jess's gym vibe was more sweaty cave troll in stretched-out sweats.

"Ladies," Tania said, pausing between sets.

"Hey." Jess barely managed to force the syllable out.

"Oh, hey." Vivienne flipped her perfect braid over her shoulder.

Jess's brain flashed back to last season, when she and Vivienne first met across the net before Vivienne and Lee's debut match.

"Hey, I'm Jess." She had extended her hand under the net, stomach swirling, taken with Vivienne's hand-painted features and natural beauty.

But Vivienne remained cool, closed off, and she returned an unenthusiastic shake back. "Vivienne."

"Welcome to the league," Jess said, unsure why she felt the need to be the fucking Welcome Wagon.

Vivienne raised an eyebrow and shared a look with Lee. "Thanks?"

Jess flushed, old feelings of being awkward and perpetually uncool flooding her cheeks. She put her head down, mumbled "Good luck," then went back to serve and blew it so badly she nearly took the ref's head off. The crowd "oohed" over the near miss, and, in case she wasn't embarrassed enough, she caught Vivienne starting to laugh, then swallowing it quickly under her hand.

You are such a loser, Jessica, she had told herself, tears stinging her eyes as she tried to smile through the embarrassment.

And that feeling around Vivienne had never gone away. Pushing back in advance of scorn, keeping her brittle shell up, was her only defense.

Vivienne sat on the weight bench next to Jess. "How's it going? Big game for you guys Wednesday." Her voice was low and breathy, like she was trying to impress someone.

Jess frowned. "What do you mean?" The North Bay team wasn't anything especially scary. Jess and Tania had beaten them their first game of the season, in fact.

"Well . . ." Vivienne regarded her reflection in the mirror. "It's just that you've lost your last three, and they've won their last three. They're only a point behind you in the standings now. Once they pass you, you'll be second to last."

Jess could hardly believe Vivienne was explaining this to her like she was stupid. She worked her jaw, trying to find a response that was appropriately cool but wouldn't get her in trouble.

But Tania chimed in first, voice heavy with sarcasm. "That's *really* helpful, Viv. Thanks so much for pointing that out."

Vivienne flipped her braid to her other shoulder. Happy with her appearance in the mirror now, she began her bicep curls. "I was just making conversation."

"We're trying to work out here, thanks," Jess snapped.

Vivienne pretended she was wounded. "Sorry for existing."

"We know the standings," Jess had to add, the frustration hot in her throat.

Vivienne rolled her eyes. "Relax. I said I was sorry."

Another retort jumped onto Jess's tongue, but Tania put a calming hand on her forearm and squeezed. Jess swallowed it down, fuming. But Tania was right. No sense arguing with someone who thought she was perfect.

Their workouts continued in uncomfortable silence, until Lee started giggling over something on her phone. "Viv, look at the video Toni sent me." The two of them hunched over Lee's phone, laughing.

Jess had to get out of there. "You good?" she asked Tania loudly. "I'm done."

Tania knew they had a set left, but she nodded and wiped her brow with a towel. "I'm good."

The moment they were through the door, Jess shuddered. "Ugh. I cannot stand her."

"I know."

"And we play them next week."

"I know."

"*Ugh.*"

Tania lurched to a halt. "Are you okay?"

Jess stopped, too. "Am I okay?"

"You heard me."

"What do you mean?"

Tania shrugged and squinted up for a second. "You just seem . . . a little cranky . . . er than normal." She softened it with a wink and a small smile.

"Yeah, I'm fine. Sorry, it's just . . . I hate losing."

"I know that, too."

"And I'm so in my head about it. Then Vivienne has to walk in—"

"Jess. Forget about Vivienne. She is irrelevant to us. To what we're trying to do."

"She's not really irrelevant—we have to play her."

"Sure, we play her a handful of times throughout the season. But she only matters in terms of what she can do with a volleyball. She doesn't matter to what's inside us."

If only Jess's brain believed that. "I know, I know. You're right." Jess hugged her. "I'm sorry."

Tania squeezed her back. "You don't need to be sorry. You just need to stay focused and keep working your butt off. We can do this. Right?"

"Right."

"Come on. Let's head to the courts for a few drills before you have to get to work."

"Yeah." Jess exhaled. "Let's do it." She had a job to do, and it did not involve letting Vivienne's attitude ruin her day.

"Great try," Jess said flatly without even looking at the bottles. She knew the kid's ring wouldn't have been even close. "You get one more."

The boy, maybe seven years old, scrunched his face up, tongue sticking out, and chucked his last ring.

"Oh, almost," Jess said with as much enthusiasm as she could muster. "Better luck next time."

The boy looked like he was going to cry, red-stained lips quivering. The mom glared at Jess as she gathered him up and marched off.

Jess fought off a sigh as another customer approached, but it turned into a smile when she saw who it was—a customer she actually liked to see. Troy, a young Black man and assistant to the SoCal league manager, came by a lot because his girlfriend worked in the park, too. He'd stop and shoot the shit with Jess and had, over time, developed the habit of buying a handful of rings to throw, with an eye on winning the giant teddy bear hanging from the roof for Sunny. It was perhaps the most precious teddy bear Jess had ever seen—the color of toasted marshmallow and impossibly soft, with an expression that said *I'm here for you.*

"Hey, Troy!" Jess handed him his standard allotment of rings before he even put the five on the counter.

"Hey, Jess. How's it going?" Troy, always smiling, seemed to love his job at the VL, and took a genuine interest in all of the athletes.

They chitchatted about the growing tourist crowds while he studied the waiting bottles, then with a practiced hand, tossed the first ring. It landed on the center bottle.

"Winner!" Jess cheered. Troy was coming in hot today.

"So . . . close game yesterday?" Troy asked. He chucked another one. It ringed a bottle in the second circle.

"Nice one." Jess shifted her weight. "Yeah, close but . . . we lost."

"Hmm." Troy didn't look at her, eyes narrowing at his next target.

"I don't know, we won the first set and things were going fine in the second, then I missed a serve, then I missed a hit and . . . I blew it in the third."

He ringed two more while she spoke. "Hey, none of that 'I blew it' talk. Mistakes happen. It's volleyball. Have I ever told you about that time I accidentally spiked the coach in the face while trying out for my college team?" He smiled winningly at her, then landed another ring.

He had, many times. Jess shrugged. She didn't want to interrupt his focus. He hardly ever scored with all ten. "We *have* to win on Wednesday. If we lose that, we'll drop a spot in the rankings. We'll be second from the bottom."

He missed one. She winced.

"And if you win?" He ringed the center bottle again.

"Well, then we won't drop a spot . . . for now."

"Focus on the positive outcomes, Jess. Energy flows where thoughts flow. I really believe that." He tossed the final three in rapid succession and scored with each one.

"Nice work! That's twenty points." He already knew that. "Prize or ticket?" And she already knew the answer. He could have chosen a cheap prize for his twenty points—a whistle or an eraser or some crap like that—or he could collect the points to save them up. She handed him the ticket as he was answering.

"Thank you." Troy, as always, tucked the ticket into the back pocket of his khakis. "Good luck on Wednesday."

"Thanks. Hey, how many points do you have now?"

Troy shrugged, face turned toward the waft of grease from the concession. "Not sure."

"But how do you know when you'll have enough for the big guy?"

"I'll count 'em up one day, but it'll probably take me another ten years."

Jess laughed and waved. "Probably. See you later."

"Later, Jess."

No other customers approached, so she snuck a peek at her phone when it buzzed. Technically, she wasn't supposed to look at her phone when she was behind the counter, but there had to be some perks to being a manager.

She had a text from Tania. **Hey, what time are you done? Just ran into Chrissy. It's her birthday and a bunch of them are hanging out on the beach right now and are going to Maggie's later. You up for it?**

Jess's head swiveled on instinct to the lifeguard chair. Yup, there was Vivienne, high on her throne. **I don't know,** Jess replied. **I left Fleming with Nelson all day yesterday, too.**

I'm sure he'll be fine with it. Come on, George has D&D tonight and I actually want to go out.

Jess rubbed her forehead. It did sound like fun, and Nelson probably wouldn't care. Fleming would certainly be thrilled about it, anyway. Nelson's place was packed with toys and treats—basically puppy paradise. And Vivienne was still at work, so . . . **Sure,** she texted back. **I'm in.** She wanted to add *As long as Vivienne's not there,* but she didn't, because she wasn't worrying about Vivienne.

3

Wins: 3
Losses: 10

***Shank*: When the pass goes horribly, horribly wrong.**

"Jess!" Chrissy jumped up from the sand and gave her a hug. "You look so cute!" Ice-cold liquid sloshed from her plastic tumbler onto Jess's bare back.

"Not really, I— Ooh!" Jess squeaked. "You got me . . . What is that, margarita?"

"Oh, absolutely not!" Chrissy turned Jess around and wiped at the spill with a warm hand. "I would never consume alcohol on a public beach. It's just water with lime." Her loose limbs and wide smile said otherwise.

"Well, happy birthday." Jess hugged her again. "Let me buy you a drink later."

"Imma hold you to that." Chrissy kissed her cheek, windblown hair tickling Jess's skin.

Jess said hi to the others—Tania, Lee, Chrissy's teammate, Shay . . . no Vivienne—and laid out her towel. An emergency bikini lived in her locker for occasions such as these, and as her tan deepened with the season, she looked even better in forest green. Still, she always lathered on the sunscreen, Nelson's skin-care admonishments loud in her head.

Tania propped herself up on an elbow and looked at Jess with a squint in the sun. "How was work?"

"Oh, you know . . ." Jess settled on her towel. "You've seen one kid miss all his rings and throw a tantrum, you've seen them all. At least no one dumped their slushie on the counter today."

She sank into the sand, tension draining out of her as the sun kissed her bare skin. A draft of warm air tickled loose strands of hair while ranchera music blared from a tent down the way. With a wiggle of her toes, a happy sigh slipped out.

"You want a drink, Jess?"

Jess cracked open an eye. The red halo of Chrissy's hair framed the shadowed face hovering over her. "Sure, thanks."

Chrissy handed her a "water with lime."

"Cheers." Jess bumped their cups together.

The other girls chatted idly about their lives—one of Tania's cousins was having trouble at school, Chrissy's mom had a new biker boyfriend—until Lee sat up straight and pushed her short, spiky hair back off her forehead. "So . . . I actually have some news that I've been dying to share. . . ." She was nearly vibrating with excitement. "Toni and I are expecting! We're due the beginning of December."

"That's amazing!" Chrissy squealed, tackling Lee for a hug. "You guys have been saving up for IVF for so long!"

Everyone else crowded around to hug Lee too, so Jess joined in, even though it felt weird hugging Vivienne's partner. Lee had never bothered to say much to Jess, and seemed to think Vivienne's snarky comments were highly amusing. But Jess mentally declared a brief Lee truce for this occasion. For the baby's sake.

The chatter resumed, words pooling around her as the sun dipped toward the horizon, until Lee spoke again, a wave of cold water shattering Jess's tranquility.

"Here comes Viv!" she chirped.

Jess looked up, the tension that had drained into the sand flooding back in an instant.

There she was in her red lifeguard one-piece, long, tanned legs gleaming in the low-angled light. Somehow she seemed to be walking in slo-mo, like a character on *Baywatch,* hair down, black tendrils dancing around her face in the ocean breeze.

Jess's stomach clenched. Why did she have to show up and ruin everything?

"Hey, Viv," Chrissy called. "You made it!"

Vivienne stopped and posed like a beauty pageant contestant. "Ugh, I just had the most heinous day at work," she announced.

Jess was not able to contain her eye roll. "Tough day of tanning, was it? Did you run out of sunscreen?"

An awkward silence fell over the group.

Jess pressed her lips together, trying not to look chagrined. *Okay, that was a little mean.*

But Vivienne didn't look upset. In fact, her eyes glittered with triumph.

That was not good.

"No," Vivienne said in a low, measured tone, waiting before she delivered the death blow. "But I did have to reapply after I dragged a kid out of a riptide."

"What? You did? What happened?" The other girls burst into a flurry of exclamations and questions while Jess sat there, a huge asshole.

Vivienne raked her hair back and told the story with

plenty of dramatic pauses and a false modesty that made Jess's skin itch. And, *please,* it wasn't even a riptide. The kid just swam a bit too far out and his dad wasn't paying attention.

"Wow," Chrissy breathed when Vivienne had completed her tale. "I can't believe you saved a child's *life* today and I . . . only sat here drinking."

Vivienne brushed nonexistent sand from her suit. "It's all part of the job." Her gaze flicked over to Jess for a split second. "Usually I just work on my tan, of course."

Jess pressed her lips together, fuming.

Chrissy popped up. "Well, I'm going for a swim! Promise you'll save me too, Viv?"

The other girls laughed and stood to join her. Jess did not.

"You're not coming, Jess?" Chrissy asked.

Jess gripped her drink, feeling the need to have about twelve more of them. "No, thanks."

"Oh, come on!" Chrissy held out her hand, pleading.

"Jess is afraid of the ocean," Tania reminded them.

Jess sighed. Apparently, she had to explain it every time. "It's not that I'm *afraid* of the ocean, it's that I . . . don't feel *comfortable* in it."

"'Don't feel comfortable'?" Lee raised an eyebrow. "What, like you're socially awkward around kelp or something?"

Chrissy patted Jess's head. "Don't be afraid, Jess. Viv would rescue you, too."

Jess looked at Vivienne without meaning to. *Oh . . . God.* "No, I, er . . ."

Vivienne's dark eyes met hers. She raised her eyebrow in challenge.

Jess stammered. "I—I doubt you could haul me out of the water."

Vivienne put her hands on her hips. "What are you saying? That I'm not a good lifeguard?"

"No." Jess's cheeks flushed. "It's just that I have, like, six inches on you and probably a hundred pounds."

Vivienne leaned back and slowly dragged her eyes up and down Jess's body. "First of all, not even close. Try four inches and *maybe* twenty pounds."

Jess scoffed, alarmed to feel her face heating further. The way Vivienne's eyes explored her body . . . It made her feel . . . exposed.

"Second, I've pulled huge, fully grown men out of there. I'm properly trained and all muscle."

Jess's eyes flicked over those muscles—the curve of her biceps, the ridges of her calves. . . . "I'm sure you're fully qualified. . . ." Her face burned in irritation. "I just . . . I prefer the sand, thanks."

"Okay, well," Vivienne said, snapping her strap into place, "if you need me to rescue you later, you let me know." She winked before turning to stroll down to the water. The others followed her, laughing and leaping toward the waves.

Jess bit back what she wanted to say as Vivienne retreated—something about *Hope your huge head doesn't drag you under.*

Tania sighed. "You're missing out. The water feels so nice."

Jess raised her cup. "I'll be fine."

"I know you will." Tania turned, chuckling, to join the others.

Jess glowered at the group splashing in the surf. Vivienne

dove under a breaking wave, her sleek black head emerging on the other side, powerful strokes pulling her deeper into the rolling gray swells.

"Show-off," Jess muttered. She reached for Chrissy's cooler to refill her drink.

They came back from the water glistening like mermaids, ocean drops on their skin, hair wet and slicked back, giggling at something Vivienne said. Jess brushed the sand from her towel, determined not to let Vivienne's dark cloud hang over the rest of the day.

Vivienne flipped her head over, rubbing a towel in her hair, then tossed her mane back again like she was in a fucking shampoo commercial.

Another drink might help.

Once they had dried off and the sun dipped below the horizon, they hit Maggie's, just adding shorts to their bikinis and striding into the place like they owned it. Men and women alike stopped and stared at the pack of tall, fit, tanned volleyball players. Jess always found the attention amusing, even though she knew she was not nearly as pretty as the others and only adjacent to the admiration.

Another handful of people from their league were waiting at a group of tables near the stage and they whooped at their arrival. The pack scattered from there—bathroom, dance floor, bar, a flock of exotic birds fluttering off into the jungle.

Jess followed Tania to the table.

"You want a Corona?" Tania asked her as she signaled to the server.

Jess nodded, wiping some clinging sand off her thigh.

Tania placed their order with April, working her regular Monday night shift, who returned with their beers only a minute later.

"How you ladies doing?" April asked. April was the best server—she'd played volleyball back in her day, knew all their names, and even came to their games sometimes. She was in her forties and powered around Maggie's like a bulldozer, but was known to offer hugs and tissues, and, if it was really bad, a free beer when her girls needed some comfort.

"We're good, thanks," Tania replied. "How are you?"

"Oh, better without any bachelorette parties! Let me know when you need your next one."

"Thanks, April."

Jess's gaze wandered around the bar as they sipped and chatted, drifting over the VL athletes and a few other faces she recognized, friends and partners, mixed with tourists and other random locals. Her eyes stopped when they landed on Vivienne.

She was leaning back on the bar with both elbows on the polished wood, smiling, then she turned to face the woman next to her. It took Jess a second to realize that the woman was Yellow, in aquamarine this time. Vivienne said something. Yellow laughed and scooted closer—so close their chests were touching. The tension between them was palpable from Jess's table. She could almost taste it, feel the heated air between them. . . . Then Vivienne closed the gap between them and kissed Yellow. It was soft, lips gentle, short and sweet, then they leaned apart and smiled at each other. Yellow pushed a piece of Vivienne's hair behind her ear, hooked a finger into her jean shorts, and pulled her closer for another kiss. This one was not short. Flashes of Vivienne's pink tongue were visible as the kiss deepened.

"Night's going well for Viv," Tania's voice interrupted.

Jess jolted, mortified to realize she had been staring. "I guess," she muttered.

"I didn't know she was queer."

Jess took a swig of her beer. "Me neither. Not that I care."

Tania paused, like she was considering saying something. "Why do you hate her so much?" she asked after a beat.

Jess shrugged. "She's too perfect, and she knows it. She's so smug. She actually . . ." Jess frowned as another thought came to her. . . . One she had pushed away many times before.

"She actually what?"

Jess fiddled with her bottle, unsure if she wanted to finish that sentence out loud. But it was Tania, and she'd had a few. "She reminds me of my first girlfriend."

"Oh?" Tania raised an eyebrow and waved at April for another round. "Do tell."

So Jess told her. "In high school I was basically confused and closeted, but the first time I saw Phoenix in the USC gym . . . I just knew. I knew that I loved her."

"Aw." Tania rested her chin on her hand.

"Yeah, well . . ." Jess smiled through the tears prickling the backs of her eyes. "She was already on the team, a junior, and we did everything together—practiced, trained, studied. . . . She used to braid my hair while I quizzed her on organic compounds."

April dropped off their next round. Tania didn't move. "And?"

"And it was all so good. Phoenix was a starter and I rode the bench my first year, but I was so happy to cheer her on. I honestly couldn't believe someone as cool and confident as her even noticed I existed. It was a dream."

Tania reached for her beer and slid Jess's over, too. "But?"

"Yeah. But." Jess drained her first bottle and picked up the next one. "But Phoenix graduated at the end of my sophomore year. We had talked about getting an apartment together while she tried out for the VL and looked for a job and stuff . . . And then . . . on the last day of classes she told me . . . she had found a dream job and was moving to Florida where her grandparents lived. And . . . it was over between us."

"Oh my God."

"I remember standing on the sidewalk outside her residence. She kissed my forehead and told me she'd always remember me." That was the last time Jess ever saw her.

Tania clutched her heart. "Jesus, Jess. I'm sorry. That's so brutal."

Jess cleared her lungs, then sucked in a fresh breath. "Yup." She took a long pull from her bottle.

"I mean, *damn*."

Jess shrugged. "She was my first everything. First kiss, first girlfriend . . . first heartbreak."

"And Vivienne reminds you of her?"

Jess blinked. Right. She had forgotten they'd been talking about her. "Yeah. Dark hair, beautiful, but it's more the confidence, the smoothness, like life has always been easy for them."

Tania quirked an eyebrow. "How do you know things have been easy for Vivienne?"

Jess swiveled her head to take in the escalating make-out

session by the bar. Yellow had a leg between Vivienne's. "Have you ever seen anything be difficult for her?"

They lost to the team from North Bay on Wednesday.

It had started off well. Despite the butterflies in Jess's stomach, they came out strong. The other team was indeed "huge," both of them taller than Jess, and while that was an advantage for them at the net, it was more of a liability when it came to moving around the rest of the court. Jess and Tania's carefully placed roll shots—deep corners, or sharp and short crosscourt—had been effective . . . until the other team adjusted their game plan in response. They started to dig everything up, and that, plus the wall they put up at the net. . . . Errors crept in on Jess's side. They lost the first game 19–21. So close but, as her clenched stomach reminded her, close didn't matter.

If we lose this, Jess thought to herself while waiting to pass a serve early in the second set, *that makes four in a row going into our next match.* She shanked the ball into the crowd. She shook her head and tried to refocus. *I cannot face Vivienne and Lee on a four-game losing streak.* She shanked the next one the other way.

They lost in two straight sets.

"Fuck!" Jess chucked her towel at the bench in the locker room, then sat and yanked her hair tie out. "At this rate, we won't even make playoffs."

Tania sat next to her and wiped her forehead. "Jess, it's early still. It's only May."

"Almost June, which is practically July, and then before you know it, it's October. Besides, what teams do you know who make playoffs that have a win percentage anywhere near as bad as ours?" She sighed and rubbed her scalp. "What are we doing wrong?"

"I don't think we're doing anything wrong. Sometimes things don't go your way and you just have to keep going."

"Mm-hmm. Maybe we need to ramp up our workouts."

"Sure, Jess." Tania sounded very tired all of a sudden. "We can do that."

"Let's hit the gym hard and talk strategy. Do you have some time now?"

"Yeah, sure. Now's fine."

"Great. I am *not* losing to Vivienne and Lee on Saturday."

They worked hard that week. Strength training Thursday, cardio Friday, some yoga Saturday morning before the game. Jess made sure to hit her protein target and get lots of sleep. Well, she tried to get lots. She had some trouble falling asleep, so she read the next chapter of *Queen in Shining Armor.* Queen Andromeda had a chance to kill the enemy queen, but instead she helped her escape from the battle.

Late night romantasy adventures aside, when Jess arrived at the pavilion on Saturday, she felt ready.

Jess and Tania typically showed up well ahead of their start time, but this time Jess got there even earlier because she wanted to be sure she didn't run into Vivienne in the locker room.

Uniform in place, hair tied back tightly, her lucky stud earrings in—sparkling suns that her parents gave her before she left Vancouver—she was ready to hit the court for warm-up.

But on her way out of the locker room, she ran into Vivienne. Almost literally—Jess just about threw out her back wrenching to a halt before she crashed into the person hurrying around the corner on their way in. She got a whiff of vanilla before Vivienne drew away, scowling.

"Sorry," Jess forced herself to mumble.

"It's fine." Vivienne's hair was already pulled back in a perfect pony. Her eyes traveled up and down Jess's body so quickly Jess almost missed it. "Good luck today." Her lips quirked in a smirk.

Jess rolled her eyes. She didn't want luck from Vivienne Morris. She flounced past her without a word, brushing Vivienne's shoulder with her arm on the way.

She could have sworn she heard Vivienne chuckle under her breath.

Jess clenched her teeth. *Vivienne Morris is going down.*

4

Wins: 3
Losses: 11 . . . and well on the way to 12

Seam: **The empty space between two players on the same team . . . where things get missed.**

Stuff block: **When you block someone so hard they regret their life choices.**

Tania called a time-out when they were down 0–5. "Jess. I need you to take a deep breath."

Jess's heart hammered as she patted her face with a cool towel. "I'm fine."

"Are you?"

"Yes." She took a swig of water.

"You signaled you were blocking Vivienne down the line and then you blocked her crosscourt."

"She was swinging cross. I thought I could get her."

"Jess." Tania seemed almost at a loss for words. "That's not how this works. I can't dig around your block if you move it."

Irritation flared in Jess's gut, mostly because she knew Tania was right. "It's just—"

"Listen." The ref blew the whistle to get them back to the game. Tania ignored it. "I don't know what's going on with you, but Vivienne is just a person. She doesn't have superpowers, okay? Let's stick with our game plan."

"I know. I'm fine."

Tania sighed. "All right. Let's go." They high-fived each other and went back to get ready for Lee's next serve.

Lee served to Tania, who gave Jess a great pass, then rolled her hit deep to the corner.

Vivienne chased after it and dove, body stretching long. She managed to just catch a piece of the ball, but not enough. The ball glanced off her fist and continued on its way out the back of the court.

They finally had a point.

"Let's go!" Tania whooped.

"Yes!" Jess cheered. They slapped hands. "Great shot, T."

The linesperson tossed the ball to Jess for her serve.

Tania nodded at her. "You've got this."

Jess exhaled and smacked the ball logo twice, like she did before every serve. She looked at Vivienne for a second, then at Lee. Both were waiting, hands on their knees. Lee's visor put her eyes in shade, but Vivienne's gaze was clear. Vivienne smiled at her, taunting.

Their game plan was to serve to Vivienne anyway, since Lee was a more effective attacker, given her height, but Vivienne was a phenomenal passer, and still a solid attacker, which explained why they had won the league last year and were currently in the top spot.

All Jess and Tania could do on defense was hope Jess cut off most of the court with her block, and Tania dug up the rest.

Jess jump-served, aiming for Vivienne's right, toying with the out-of-bounds line. Vivienne stepped into it and passed it easily enough to Lee, who set up Vivienne's attack.

Jess studied Vivienne's shoulders, expecting her to

swing cross but, at the last second, she turned and crushed one down the line, past Jess's hands and landing on the rope. The crowd cheered along with Vivienne and Lee. 1–6.

"Woo!" Lee high-fived Vivienne with gusto, then smacked her butt. "Sweet hit, bitch!"

The embarrassment swirled in Jess's gut at the way Vivienne had so easily hit right past her block. Jess sucked in a breath, not quite able to get it into the depths of her lungs. "Sorry," she muttered to Tania in their huddle. "I've got her."

Tania wiped sand off her legs. "I thought you were blocking her line?"

"I was. I am. I guess I drifted a bit, I don't know."

"Just go harder line. I'll dig the rest."

"Yeah." They slapped hands while Vivienne went back to serve.

Vivienne stood at the back line, ball in hand. Her gold nails glimmered in the light. She tossed the ball high and hammered a jump serve right between Jess and Tania. Jess took a step toward it, but so did Tania, so she stopped, then so did Tania. The ball's velocity tickled the hairs on her arm before it slammed into the sand.

Jess straightened and adjusted her pony. "Fuck. Sorry."

Tania's head dropped. "Come on. We know better. You got the seam."

"Yeah." Tania was very nicely reminding her that Jess should be the one passing those middle balls, because that meant that she would be the hitter. It was more basic team play that, for some reason, Jess was completely forgetting. And now they were down 1–7, the possibility of a comeback quickly slipping out of their hands. Jess's heart was beating too fast.

On her next serve, Vivienne sent the ball to the same spot. "Fuck you," Jess muttered under her breath as she passed it. She gave Tania a decent ball and got a decent bump set in return. Jess wound up, loading the spring as she jumped, the sand giving way under her feet, and imagined smashing the ball into Vivienne's face.

It hit the sand on Vivienne's side instead.

Almost as good.

"Yes!" Jess pumped her fist.

Tania hugged her. "There you go. Few more of those. We've got this, Button."

Goddamn, a kill felt so good. Not as good as a stuff block, but pretty fucking good.

But Vivienne looked almost bored. It didn't even faze her. They were still up 2–7. She and Lee slapped hands and turned their backs to the net to have a quick strategy talk.

Jess and Tania gave up the next point and the one after that. They managed to put a few good plays together here and there, but they lost the first set 10–21 . . . and the second 11–21.

Another loss.

Jess couldn't bring herself to meet Vivienne's eyes when they shook hands. She knew it was bad sportsmanship, but she couldn't do it. She couldn't handle whatever she might see there from Vivienne—triumph, derision, contempt, or maybe, even worse, pity.

Tania was quiet after the match as they trudged to the locker room. She didn't even stop to talk to her family, only offering them a halfhearted wave on their way by. Jess beat herself up for the length of her shower.

"Sorry," Jess said to Tania when they met again at their lockers.

"Don't be sorry." Tania toweled off her legs.

Jess sat on the bench, rivulets of water running down her back. "I don't know why I got so tense. . . . I felt like I was panicking every second of that match."

Tania dug into her locker for her underwear, still avoiding eye contact. "At least we don't play those two again for a few weeks."

"Yeah." Jess's body was heavy. She couldn't muster the energy to find her own clothing.

Tania pulled on her top. "And Wednesday is the road trip to Horny Beach. That'll be fun." Some of the Sunside teams would be busing to Horn Beach—affectionately nicknamed "Horny Beach," known for its "what happens on the road, stays on the road" vibes—for league matches next week.

"Yeah." Maybe the change of scenery would help shake her out of this funk.

Or at least Jess really hoped it would.

After her shift on Tuesday, Jess stopped by Nelson's apartment. "Hi, sweet puppy." She tucked Fleming under her chin for a snuggle as he licked her face. "Thanks, Nelson. Hope he wasn't too much trouble today."

Nelson waved his hand. "Nah. I got you, girl. And thank you again for the banana bread this morning. It was—" Nelson kissed his fingers.

"You're welcome. Cookies next week."

Nelson sighed. "My girlish figure . . ."

Jess scoffed. "Please. You look amazing."

Nelson pretended to fluff his nonexistent hair. "I know I do, just wanted to hear you say it."

"How are things going with your gentleman caller?"

"Oh, you know, you know. A lady must maintain some mystery." He waggled his eyebrows suggestively.

Jess snickered. "Yes, keep your secrets."

Nelson patted Fleming's head. "You're dropping him off again tomorrow morning for the night, right?"

"Yup. At about eight, if that works?"

"Sounds great. I got a shit ton of code to comb through and Fleming is the perfect reason to pry myself away from my keyboard from time to time. Where's your game?"

"Horn Beach."

"Horny Beach, hey? You gonna get some?" Apparently, Horn Beach had a reputation that extended beyond the SoCal VL.

Jess laughed. "I wish. Not with these pores."

Nelson ignored her joke. "As if you couldn't pull a hottie."

"The evidence suggests otherwise." Fleming wiggled enough that Jess had to put him down. "Okay, this guy needs a walk. I'll see you tomorrow."

"All right, miss. You have a good night, Jess."

Jess clipped on Fleming's leash and headed for the stairs, his nails clicking on the cement behind her, then she scooped him up for the trip down. Mrs. Horowitz was on her way up, flowered blue caftan blowing in the breeze. "Hello, Mrs. Horowitz," Jess said, subtly switching Fleming to her other side to keep him farther away from her. It didn't matter. He started growling.

Mrs. Horowitz glared at him like she wanted to growl, too.

"I'm so sorry. He growls at everyone," Jess explained for the thousandth time. "It's just for show, he's really so sweet. . . ."

"Mm-hmm," Mrs. Horowitz muttered as she huffed up the stairs. "That dog . . ."

Fleming looked up at Jess like it was hilarious, tongue lolling.

"I'm really sorry!" Jess called again to her. Once they got to the bottom, Jess set him down and scolded her pup. "Why you gotta be such a tough guy?"

She swore he would have chuckled, if dogs could do such a thing. Instead, he sniffed the patch of grass at the bottom of the stairs and lifted a leg.

When they got home, Jess gave him a scoop of his favorite kibble, watered her plants, and warmed up some leftover chili for dinner. She wasn't huge on cooking, but she sometimes made big-batch dishes, like chili or stew, then froze them in individual portions. As she stirred, her brain replayed points she'd lost to Vivienne—visions of balls hitting the sand, brushing her fingertips and soaring out of bounds, or ricocheting off her forearms in the wrong direction. She shook her head and opened her book to read while she ate, to drown out the mistakes of the day.

Once she had packed most of her bag for tomorrow's trip, Jess looked at the clock. She should probably be heading to bed, but . . . it wasn't that late.

Jess pulled on an old USC sweatshirt—the cuffs were frayed but it fit perfectly—and headed up to the roof. She propped open the gate behind her and settled into an old lawn chair on the side of the building where the streetlight was out. The night was warm, almost too hot for a sweatshirt. Jess set up her telescope, running her hands affectionately over the black casing. The night was clear, and Venus and Mars were side by side. Sunside was far enough away from the big city lights that the stargazing was decent.

Before she looked through the lens, Jess tipped her head back and examined the sky with her naked eye. The sight gave her a thrill every time. Hundreds of pinpricks of light . . . or thousands, even, more and more the longer she gazed, looking back in time billions of years. How many of those stars were gone now, their last rays of light still traveling across the unending blackness of space to this pale blue dot? It made her feel insignificant but also in awe of the gift she had been given—a life, however brief, however tiny, a particular arrangement of atoms that allowed her to be here for a few breaths.

She put her eye to the lens.

And lost herself in the stars.

Jess dreamed of stars and planets, a spaceship adrift in the cosmos, desperate to reach home, all but lost to the infinite nothingness. The cockpit buttons beeped and flashed at her. She slapped at the controls, trying to make it stop. The beeping grew louder and more incessant.

She jolted awake and fumbled with her sleeping mask, squinting against the white light of her room.

She looked at her phone. Twelve texts. *Oh shit.* Horn Beach. The bus. *Fuck.*

Ten messages from Tania—**Are you almost here?**

Jess.

Jess???

Jess!!! Where the fuck are you?

Seriously, the bus leaves in five!

Hurry up!

The bus is leaving, Jess.

You're not dead, right???

Winston says you'll have to get a ride with Vivienne. She's driving separately.

Jess!! TEXT ME BACK!

Jess's brain spun. The bus had left half an hour ago. And she had to get a ride . . . with *Vivienne*? Oh *hell* no. Horn Beach was three hours away. Maybe more with traffic. Three-plus hours trapped in a car with Vivienne was a cruel and unusual punishment for sleeping in.

She also had a text from Winston—the league manager—confirming the plan, then another from a number she didn't know.

This is Vivienne. Apparently I'm picking you up. What's your address?

Jess stared at the message, dread building in her belly. This had to be a bad dream. She closed her eyes, willing herself back to the spaceship. It didn't work.

She replied to Tania. **I cannot sit in a car with her for three hours!**

Well, you kind of have to . . . unless you rent a car and drive yourself but a) I don't think you can afford that and b) it would look a little insane.

Only a little, though?

Jess. It'll be fine. Just pretend to sleep or something.

Jess frowned. Not a bad idea, actually. . . .

Tell me how you missed the bus??? Is everything okay?

Uggggh. So stupid. I slept through my alarm.

Were you at least up late having amazing sex or something?

Ummm yes?

Making love to your telescope doesn't count.

Another text from Vivienne interrupted her snarky reply for Tania. **Hello?? We need to hit the road. Traffic is going to be a bitch.**

Jess fired back her address then replied to Tania. **I gotta get moving.**

See you in Horny Beach, space girl.

Vivienne replied. **Can you be ready in fifteen minutes?**

Jess chewed her lip. **I need at least thirty.**

I'll be there in twenty.

Jess rolled her eyes. How was this happening? How could the universe play such a cruel trick on her? *Ugh.* Unfortunately, it was true that renting her own car would be insane. There was nothing to do but get ready. Vivienne would undoubtedly be there in twenty minutes. Nineteen now.

She sniffed her armpits. A shower would be ideal, but a fresh coat of deodorant would have to do the job. Served Vivienne right for rushing her anyway. Jess brushed her teeth, threw the rest of her things in her duffel, filled up her water bottle, tucked some banana bread into her tote bag, and scooped up Fleming.

"I thought you said eight?" Nelson said by way of a greeting.

"I did. I'm late." Jess placed Fleming at Nelson's feet. "Okay, you be good for Nelson, do you hear me? When I get back I don't want—" She turned as a person approached them from behind. It was Vivienne. Her hair was loose and extra shiny, swinging in time with her steps and her jaw working a piece of gum. Her romper was adorable, tie-dyed pink, her hands in the pockets, and lips and sunglasses a matching glossy pink. She strutted along the walkway with the confidence of a runway model. Jess suddenly felt like a cave troll again, hair up in a messy bun, wearing the shorts she had slept in, makeup free.

"Uh, hi," Jess said, wishing she had at least brushed her hair.

Vivienne stopped. "Hi."

"What are you doing here?"

"Picking you up?" Vivienne said, like Jess was slow.

"I know that. Why are you here, like . . . up *here* by my door?"

"What, was I going to honk from the street? I saw you come outside so I just . . . came to pick you up."

Nelson looked back and forth between them, brows raised in amusement.

Jess shot him a warning look.

"And who is this gorgeous thing?" Nelson asked anyway.

"This is, uh . . . Vivienne."

"Oh, *Vivienne*," Nelson said, as if that was profoundly interesting. "You haven't mentioned Vivienne before. And you two are . . . ?" He waggled his eyebrows.

"Vivienne plays in the league," Jess said quickly before Nelson could get any other ideas. "I missed the bus this morning so she's giving me a ride."

"Nice to meet you . . . ?" Vivienne extended a businesslike hand to shake.

"Nelson. Neighbor and dog nanny. Girl, what moisturizer do you use? Your skin is glowing."

Vivienne tilted her head. "That would be telling, wouldn't it."

Nelson studied her some more, face blank, but eyes glimmering. "You know what, I respect that."

"And who's this?" Vivienne crouched to pet Fleming, tossing her hair on the way down.

"Careful, he doesn't like strangers. . . ." Jess started to

warn, but Fleming wagged his tail and sniffed her hand like they were old friends. "Traitor," Jess murmured.

"He's precious." Vivienne looked up. "What's his name?"

"Fleming."

"Hi, Fleming." She gave him another head scratch. This time he licked her hand.

Jess frowned at him.

"I always wanted a dog growing up, but my sister was allergic."

"Why don't you have one now?" Jess wondered.

Vivienne shrugged and straightened. "I don't know. I'm never home, he'd just be sitting alone all d—" She stopped. "I mean, I don't think any of my neighbors are as helpful as Nelson."

Jess's throat tightened. Vivienne had to show up at her *home* now and criticize her pet ownership? "We should go," she said stiffly. She turned to Nelson. "Thanks so much. We'll be back by dinnertime tomorrow. I'll text you when we're on our way." She picked up Fleming for one more snuggle. "Be good. No growling." She kissed his head and passed him to Nelson, negligent-pet-owner guilt clogging up her throat, then hefted her duffel and marched toward the stairs.

"Nice to meet you, Nelson," Vivienne said. "Fleming."

Jess's skin crawled. They could not get to Horn Beach fast enough.

5

Wins: 3
Losses: 12

> ***Pepper*: A basic two-person volleyball warm-up where the partners send the ball back and forth in a "bump, set, and hit" sequence repeated over and over. And over.**

Vivienne led her to a gleaming midnight-blue Mercedes parked at the curb. Jess's eyes bulged. She was not a car person and normally didn't notice these details—she couldn't even say what kind of car Tania drove—but she knew enough to appreciate that this was an impressive ride—new and expensive.

Vivienne popped the trunk. Jess added her duffel to Vivienne's luggage, which seemed excessive, and got in the passenger side. The creamy beige interior even smelled new, with a hint of vanilla underneath. One thing Jess knew for sure was she was not going to eat her banana bread in that car. Vivienne would probably murder her if she got so much as a crumb on the seat.

Jess adjusted the seat so her knees weren't pressed quite so hard up against the dashboard, then fastened her seat belt. The click ricocheted off the walls in the silent space. "Thanks for the ride. Sorry you got stuck with me," she muttered.

Vivienne shrugged. "Whatever. It's fine." She started

the car and punched a few buttons on the display screen. "What kind of music do you like?"

"Anything. Except country."

Vivienne's mouth pinched. "All I listen to is country."

Of course. Jess added *listens to country* to Vivienne's long list of faults. "Whatever you want is fine."

Vivienne shoulder-checked and pulled onto the road. "There's got to be some country artist you like."

"The closest I get to country is Backyard Chickens."

"What? You have backyard chickens?"

Jess snorted. "No, Backyard Chickens is a band. They're from LA. They're playing in Sunside in a couple weeks, actually."

"And they're country?"

"No, they're folk rock. . . . I just meant that their name was sort of . . ." *Two hours and fifty-nine minutes to go. Just kill me.*

"Ah. Well . . ." Vivienne shrugged and turned on a Top-40 satellite-radio station. One of the ubiquitous radio hits that played constantly in the volleyball pavilion filled the air.

Jess took a drink of water.

"So how did you miss the bus?" Vivienne asked as they took a ramp for the highway.

"I wish I had a better reason than I slept in."

"Ouch." Vivienne checked her mirror as they merged. "Up late last night?"

"Yeah." It felt awkward to leave it there, so Jess kept talking. "Venus and Mars are really close together right now, so . . ." She stared at the passing gray buildings, wishing she wasn't such a dork.

Vivienne looked at her sharply. "You were stargazing?"

"I know, I know, I'm a nerd."

"No, it's just that—" A text message from Winston popped up on the display. "Read message," Vivienne said.

Jess blinked. "You want me to—?" but before Jess could finish her question, the car started talking.

"Message from Winston. 'Did you pick up Jessica okay?' Would you like to reply?"

"Yes," Vivienne told her car. "'Yup, I have her.' Send."

Jess could hear the resentment in Vivienne's reply. She shifted uncomfortably. It wasn't like she *wanted* to be there.

Vivienne slowed in the thickening highway traffic, tapping her glossy nails on the steering wheel in time with the music.

The silence between them got louder. "How come you're driving separately?" Jess asked.

"I have some family in Horn Beach. I'm going to stay an extra night."

"Oh, that's nice."

"Yeah."

The car slowed further. More silence. *God.* Jess wondered what else she could possibly say without resorting to commenting on the traffic.

Then Vivienne asked a question out of nowhere. "Why does Tania call you 'Button'?"

Jess blinked. That was . . . unexpected. And also a question she didn't want to answer. "Um . . . I don't really know. It's just dumb."

"Come on, you can tell me."

Jess twisted her fingers together, the silence growing even more awkward. She tried to think of some innocuous lie to tell Vivienne. . . . *I have a button collection? Fuck.* Or, on second thought, they were going slow enough now that

Jess could probably roll out of the car without any major injuries.

Vivienne kept talking. "I thought maybe it was, like . . . cause you're 'cute as a button' or something."

The words hit Jess hard, crashed right into her broad, broad shoulders and six-foot-two frame. A frame her mom always called "big-boned" or "husky." *"Cute as a button." Sure.* She clenched her jaw. "You don't have to be mean."

Vivienne furrowed her eyebrows. "I'm not being mean."

"Oh right, as if anyone would say *I* . . ." Jess waved up and down her giant body. ". . . am 'cute as a button.'" She bit her lip so she wouldn't say more. Stupid to lay out any vulnerabilities for Vivienne like that, or point out how her huge frame barely fit in the front seat.

"I . . ." Vivienne faded into silence. "Sorry. I was just curious. I didn't mean it that way."

"Could you . . . You know what?" Jess pushed the many strands of hair escaping from her disaster bun behind her ears and tried to find a coherent sentence from the jumble of words swirling up her throat through the emotions. "I'm actually really tired and I need to, like, just zone out for a bit. Do you mind if I sleep?"

Vivienne snapped her gum, eyes on the road ahead. "Yeah, fine. Whatever. You can recline your seat if you want."

"Great." Jess balled up her sweatshirt under her head and leaned against the window, pointedly not putting her seat back. Vivienne wasn't going to tell her what to do.

It was very uncomfortable. Not that it mattered. Given her sleep-in that morning, there was no way she'd actually fall asleep. But sitting wedged up against the window with a cramp in her neck was better than talking to Vivienne.

Until she had to pee.

Jess cracked her eyes open to check the time. They had been on the road for a little over an hour. She considered . . . Maybe she could hold it until Vivienne needed to stop? But ten minutes later she knew there was no waiting.

She sat up, biting back a groan at the twinge in her neck. "I, uh . . . I have to pee."

Vivienne shot a glance at her. "What?"

"I have to pee?" Jess repeated, wondering what could possibly be confusing about that.

Vivienne sighed. "Are you sure?"

"What are you talking about, am I sure? Yes, I'm sure."

"Fine. I'll pull over when I can."

"Thanks." Jess tried not to make it sound sarcastic.

"All those cars I just passed . . ." Vivienne mumbled to herself.

Jess didn't know what to say, as if it were somehow her fault the human bladder had limited capacity. She crossed her arms and legs and studied the approaching signs.

When an ARCO station finally loomed, Vivienne sighed and signaled their exit. The parking lot was packed, so Vivienne pulled up to the front door and didn't say anything as Jess fumbled with her seat belt and scrambled in to find the bathroom. Still cranky about being scolded for needing to pee, she took her time at the mirror trying to make her hair a little more presentable.

When she came back out, Vivienne was pumping gas.

Jess put her hands in her pockets and watched her. She looked a bit like a commercial for women's razors or something, in her pink romper, leaning against the shiny car, one golden leg propped against the wheel. "I thought you didn't want to stop?"

"Well, we're stopped now. Might as well make it worth it. Do you want to grab a coffee or anything?"

"Am I allowed to have tea in your car?"

"Why wouldn't you be allowed to have tea?"

"It's, like . . . pristine."

Vivienne raised an eyebrow. "Are you planning to spill it?"

"No."

"You can have tea."

"All right. You want me to grab anything for you?"

"Can you get me a French vanilla coffee and some sort of pastry—a muffin or banana bread or something?"

"Banana bread?"

"Yeah."

"I actually have banana bread." Jess pointed at her tote. "That I made."

"You made it?"

"Yes."

"And you'll share it with me?" There was a teasing lilt to Vivienne's voice, like it was so funny.

Jess shrugged. "If you want some."

"I do."

"Okay, so just a French vanilla then?"

"And . . . some gum. And can you get me a scratcher?"

"A scratcher?"

"Yeah, just like a dollar one. I'm feeling lucky."

Jess's head was spinning at all the words. This had to be the most she'd ever heard Vivienne talk at once, certainly the most she'd said directly to Jess. "Those things are such a waste of money."

Vivienne snapped her gum. "Can't win if you don't play."

Jess supposed there was some metaphor somewhere there, but she was starting to get a headache. "Anything else?"

"A Gatorade."

"Flavor?"

"Surprise me."

Vivienne's tank was almost full by this point. Jess suddenly realized she'd have to chip in. "Okay. And . . . let me know what I owe you for gas."

"Nothing." Vivienne waved an airy hand. "I was driving anyway."

"But I—"

"It's fine, Jess. You can buy me my snacks."

The way Vivienne said her name, like they were friends, annoyed her. Because they were not friends at all. Jess headed back inside, elbowing her way through the crowd to the drink cooler.

She pondered the rows of brightly colored bottles. Honestly, what kind of psycho left Gatorade flavor up to chance? Everyone knew lemon-lime or grape were the best flavors. Jess selected a yellow one for herself, then chose blue for Vivienne, to match her car.

The smell of the coffee machine brewing a French vanilla was enticing, enough so that she hit the button again to make a second one. Jess didn't normally drink hot coffee, but these things hardly counted. She arrived at the counter with her four beverages and scooped up two packs of peppermint gum. "Could I get a scratcher too, please?" she asked when it was her turn.

"Which one?" The cashier, a woman around Jess's age, was pretty, with short hair, freckles, and wide eyes. Her name tag read BETH.

"Hmm . . ." Jess leaned over to examine the tickets in the display case until a colorful design caught her eye. "I guess this 'Lucky Lolly' one."

"Good choice." Beth pulled a ticket from the case, then reached to remove an actual red lollipop from a stand on the counter. "Here," she said, handing them both directly to Jess, their fingers brushing. Beth held Jess's eyes for a moment. "On the house. For luck."

"Oh, thanks," Jess said. She stared back at Beth, whose mouth was curling in a smile. Jess's cheeks flushed as she smiled back. Beth was *very* pretty. There was no way she was flirting . . . was there?

She gave Jess the total and fluttered her eyelashes. "Do you want a bag?"

"No, I'm good, thanks." Jess paid with cash and fumbled trying to put the change back into her wallet.

Beth waited patiently while Jess loaded her purchases into her tote. "You have a great day," she said, eyes flicking over Jess's cleavage, then back to her face.

"You too," Jess stammered, fairly certain that it was flirting.

She left the store with a backward glance at Beth, who was still smiling at her. Jess's cheeks heated further.

Vivienne had just finished cleaning her windshield. She snapped the wipers back in place and threw out a paper towel. "What?" she said when she saw Jess's face.

"Nothing." Jess got into the front seat, coffees carefully balanced, one on top of the other. She busied herself putting the cups in the holders and passing Vivienne her Gatorade, gum, and scratch ticket, willing the flush in her face to fade.

"All right, if you say so. . . ." Vivienne opened her

Gatorade, took a long swallow—Jess braced herself for a complaint about the flavor that didn't come—and put it in the cupholder in her door. She tucked the gum and ticket in the console, and started the car. "You got that banana bread?"

"Yeah." Jess handed her a slice from the bundle in her tote.

"Thanks." She took a bite, then put the car into gear. "It's yummy."

"I like to bake."

They pulled back onto the freeway. "See? This. This is what I'm talking about," Vivienne mumbled through her next bite, glaring at a semi. "I passed this guy twenty minutes ago."

"So, pass him again." Jess took a sip of her French vanilla. As expected, it was both awful and delicious.

"That's not the point." Vivienne passed the semi but then groaned when she saw another slowdown ahead. She rested her elbow on the windowsill, head to palm.

Jess got a text from Tania. **You surviving?**

Jess tilted her phone away from Vivienne, just in case. **I suppose. I think I just got hit on.**

By Vivienne?

What??? No! Gross. By a hot cashier at the gas station.

Nice! Did you get her number?

Have you ever known me to get anyone's number?

"Where are they at?" Vivienne interrupted, nodding at Jess's phone.

"Who?"

"The bus. Isn't that Tania?"

Tania sent back the wonky-faced emoji.

Jess narrowed her eyes. "Why do you assume I'm texting with Tania? I have other friends. I could have a girlfriend."

Vivienne hit the brakes as a big, obnoxious pickup truck tried to force its way in front of her. "What the fuck! Merge at the sign, ass. . . ." She shook her head and took a sip of her coffee. "Do you?"

"Do I what?"

Vivienne sighed like a long-suffering high school English teacher. "Have a girlfriend?"

Jess took a sip of her own, pissed at herself for even bringing it up. "No."

"So . . ." The smile was evident in her voice. "Where's the bus at?"

Jess scowled. "I'll ask." **Where are you guys?**

Just passed Pacific Glade, Tania reported. **Traffic is brutal.**

Jess relayed the information to Vivienne.

"Ugh. Great." Vivienne took another swig of coffee. "This is painful."

Hard agree. "Aren't you going to have to pee in, like, half an hour after all those liquids?"

Vivienne quirked her eyebrow, then downed another mouthful. "I have a strong bladder."

"Good for you." Jess pulled her own piece of banana bread out, careful to eat it over her bag so no crumbs ended up loose in the car. She took only the smallest sip of coffee with it. If she had to pee again before Vivienne, she might be forced to go in her empty cup.

A song that Jess detested came on the radio.

"Ugh, I hate this song." Vivienne hit a button and switched to the eighties station. "Hold On" by Wilson Phillips filled the air. Vivienne immediately started singing along. She had a lovely voice—gentle and in tune.

Jess kind of wanted to sing too, but she was a terrible singer. She tapped the beat on her thigh instead.

"Sorry, I can't resist singing this song," Vivienne explained during a musical interlude. "It's on the eighties station every ten minutes but I'm not mad about it."

"Yeah, it's pretty good," Jess said in a bored voice, not wanting to admit she also loved it.

The song ended right as they came to a complete stop on the highway. Vivienne made a frustrated noise. "God, at this rate we're barely going to have time to warm up. Lee and I have the early game."

Jess held back an eye roll. "Couple minutes of pepper and I'm sure you'll be fine."

"What do you mean?"

"I mean you can still beat everyone without a proper warm-up."

Vivienne gave her a side-eye. "We need a good warm-up."

Jess let out a humorless huff. "Not like it even matters if you win or not. You have a six-point cushion."

"Eight. And it matters." Vivienne's voice was crisp.

"It does?"

"Of course it does. Performing our best every match matters." She said it like she was explaining to a five-year-old.

Jess fiddled with her Gatorade lid. "Well, I'm fucked then."

There were a few beats of silence, then Vivienne responded. "Your wins will come. You're just on a cold streak. I really think you—"

"I didn't ask," Jess snapped. The words flew out of her. She actually *would* throw herself from a moving car before she'd listen to Vivienne's opinion on her losing streak.

"Jesus. Fine." A car honked behind them. "Asshole," Vivienne muttered.

Jess thought about apologizing for snapping at her, but the words would not leave her lips. Even the simplest conversation with Vivienne seemed to go wrong. So instead, she balled up her sweatshirt against the window again, closed her eyes, breathed in the vanilla, and pretended to sleep for the rest of the trip.

6

Wins: 3
Losses: 12 (or, if you count the car ride, 13)

> ***Ace*: A serve no one even touches before it hits the ground. Kind of embarrassing/awesome, depending on which side of the net you're on.**

> ***Wipe off*: When a hitter uses your block against you and "wipes" the ball off your hands and out of bounds, so they get the point. Also embarrassing/awesome.**

"Read message."

Jess bolted up at the sound of Vivienne's voice, then hissed at the stab of pain in her neck. "Wha—?"

The car began to speak. "Message from Lee. 'Hey, are you guys almost here?' Would you like to reply?"

"Yes. 'Ten minutes out.' Send." Vivienne shot Jess a look. "How was your nap?"

Jess rubbed her neck. "Fuck." Maybe she had started to doze after all. . . .

Vivienne flipped her hair. "I told you to put your seat back."

A waft of vanilla reached Jess's nose as she dropped her hand to her lap. "I'm fine." She looked out the window, blinking, trying to orient herself. They were sitting at a traffic light in Horn Beach, another Southern California tourist town, a little smaller and more faded than Sunside in the daytime, but at night the main drag closed to cars and lit up with twinkling lights and neon signs. Pedestrians filled the space, on the hunt for vibrant photo ops, cheap highballs, and the throb of an irresistible bass line.

Vivienne pointed out of her window as they began to move. "That's my aunt's house. Where I'm staying."

Jess ducked her head to get a better view. The only house visible was up on the hill, and "house" was startlingly inaccurate. "Villa" was the word that came to mind. Terracotta tiles, beige stucco turrets, tall windows overlooking the Pacific . . . "Wow."

"Yeah, it's nice."

"What does your aunt do?" Probably didn't play beach volleyball and work on the midway at an amusement park.

"She's a romance author."

"Really? What's her name?"

"Veronica Doyle."

It took a second to register, then she screeched, "*Veronica Doyle is your aunt?*"

Vivienne winced at the volume. "Yes . . . You know her work?"

Heart racing, Jess dug into her tote and pulled out *Queen in Shining Armor* to wave at Vivienne. "She's only my favorite romance author!"

"Oh, that's cool. Yeah, her stuff is great."

Jess wanted to ask a hundred questions about Veronica Doyle but she tried to be normal instead. "And what does your uncle do?"

"He's some sort of copyright lawyer for an entertainment conglomerate." Vivienne glanced up at the house again as the light turned green. "They're doing all right."

"I'd say."

Jess craned her neck to stare at Veronica Doyle's house until it disappeared around a corner, then she sat back in her seat again, stroking the cover of *Queen in Shining Armor*.

Vivienne turned the music up—country now. Jess let her have this one without complaint because she was too busy wondering if Veronica Doyle would ever come to one of Vivienne's games—

"I'll tell you what," Vivienne said, interrupting Jess's train of thought. "If you win your match today, I'll make sure to introduce you to Veronica. I'll see if we can go for lunch with her or something."

Jess blinked as she processed the words. "Have lunch with . . ." Her stomach flipped. *"Are you serious?"*

"Yup. And if *I* win, you have to bake me a loaf of banana bread."

Jess scoffed. "If you introduce me to Veronica Doyle, I'll bake you a loaf of banana bread after every win for the rest of the fucking season."

Vivienne chuckled. "That's a lot of bananas."

If I win . . . Jess's stomach continued its dance. Was this Vivienne's way of psyching her out before her match? She shook her head. "No, I can't handle the pressure. I can't have meeting *Veronica Doyle* riding on this game."

"Jess." Vivienne sighed. "It's just for fun. I'm not trying to put pressure on you." Then she added under her breath, "God knows you do enough of that yourself."

Jess chewed her lip, mind too busy racing to respond. *Veronica Doyle*. She stroked her book cover again. She couldn't pass this up. "Okay. Deal," she decided as they pulled into the sports complex. The Sunside bus was parked along the curb, the players milling around and collecting their gear.

Vivienne pulled into a spot, then turned to Jess and offered her hand. "Deal."

They shook on it, and a buzz of nerves shot up Jess's arm. "Deal," she repeated.

Eager to escape the confines of the car, Jess groaned as she unfolded her legs and climbed out. Winston waved from the sidewalk, looking relieved to see them. They met again at the trunk to collect their bags. Vivienne only removed a duffel, the same as Jess. The rest of her luggage stayed in the car.

Jess forced herself to make eye contact. Maybe she'd assumed the worst of Vivienne. "Thanks for the ride. And the bet."

Vivienne's lashes went on forever, framing her deep, dark eyes. "You're welcome. I—"

"There you are!" Lee pounced on Vivienne. "Was worried you'd get stuck in traffic."

Vivienne hugged her back. "We made it."

Lee pulled Vivienne away, arm around her shoulders, chattering about something funny that happened on the bus.

Jess shook her head to clear the vanilla scent lingering in her nostrils and visions of Veronica Doyle and looked for Tania in the crowd. They had a match to win.

Vivienne and Lee had the early one o'clock game time. There was another set of matches at three, Jess and Tania played at five, and the final matches that night were at seven. Unless they were on the court or grabbing food, the players always hung out in the bleachers, so there wasn't anything for Jess to do besides sit in the stands and watch Vivienne warm up.

She moved like a panther, so smooth and sure, compact and muscle-y. Any time Jess saw a video of herself playing, it was like watching a giraffe lurch around the court. Or a stork, maybe. Awkward and gangly. Her shoulders were always a little hunched too, like she had bad posture, and her nose looked so much bigger from the side.

Vivienne's smaller stature never seemed to hold her back. She could tear around the court with ease, and jump high enough to be an effective attacker. Sure, she didn't record many stuff blocks, but she had Lee for that. If anything, her lack of imposing height actually helped her—lulled opponents into a false sense of security. How could that pretty little thing be anything to worry about? And then Vivienne embarrassed them by placing shots in any particular square inch of court she so desired while they flailed after it.

The match started with an ace jump serve from Vivienne. Jess huffed a dry laugh. There was no way anyone was going to take the league title away from them. And she would undoubtedly be handing over a loaf of banana bread for this win.

The Horn Beach team put up a fight, though. The blocker shut Vivienne down twice in a row—glee and jealousy battled inside Jess—and, for the first time, a flicker of something crossed Vivienne's face. . . . Anger? Frustration, maybe.

Vivienne called a time-out and she and Lee huddled on the side. It was a stifling day, hot for the end of May, no breeze. Vivienne squirted her water bottle over her head, but it still didn't mess up her ponytail.

Jess tried to read their lips, but Lee, who was doing most of the talking, was facing away from her. Vivienne wiped her face and shook her head, mouth a thin line. Then she nodded and took another drink. They low-fived and headed back out onto the court.

When the game resumed, the other team served to Vivienne again. She passed to Lee, who gave her a good set. Jess held her breath, fully expecting Vivienne to avoid the block with a safe roll shot. Instead, she approached at full speed, turned her body in the air, and swung as hard as she could into the side of the block. The ball went off the blocker's hands and into the stands. Point for Vivienne and Lee.

Lee pumped her fist but Vivienne's face was all business.

It was a sweet play, Jess had to admit. She almost never went for the wipe off. It was too risky. A couple inches short one way and you got stuff-blocked. Mess up in the other direction, and you cannoned the ball right out of bounds.

But Vivienne did it perfectly. Of course.

And the smirk on her face as she went back to serve indicated that she knew it.

That wipe was the turning point. Vivienne and Lee won the match in straight sets, 21–18 and 21–15. They grinned and hugged at the end, giving each other's butt a smack. Lee's laugh carried to the stands.

Tania stood and stretched. "We should probably have some food now before we need to get going."

Jess heard Tania but was still watching Vivienne and Lee. They shook hands with the other team and signed the scorecard. The sweat on their skin sparkled. Jess tried to remember how many overripe bananas she had in the freezer.

"Jess!"

She snapped out of her daze. "Yeah! Yes. Sorry. Okay, let's go grab something."

They picked up protein smoothies from the café, then went to put on their matching white two-pieces. Jess attempted a smooth ponytail six times before giving up and accepting an almost-smooth one. On their way out to the court for warm-up, she caught a glimpse of Vivienne emerging wet from the shower, wrapped in her buttercup-yellow towel that Jess had to begrudgingly admit complemented her skin tone perfectly.

Just before game time, Vivienne appeared back in the stands, right in Jess's line of sight, wearing a stylish gray-and-white-striped tank dress with a drawstring waist. She looked like she belonged in a summer catalog, not like she had just commanded the volleyball court for an hour. The other girls gathered around her and Lee in a very "tell me more, tell me more" kind of way. Jess noticed that a team's win percentage directly correlated with the number of fawning attendants they had.

Jess and Tania had no attendants.

"Jess?"

"Yeah?"

"I said, 'Are you ready?'"

"Yes. Sorry. I'm ready."

Tania gave her a "get your head in the game" look, which was fair.

They slapped hands and took to the court for perhaps the biggest game of Jess's life, given what was riding on it. At least she had made the bet when they were playing a beatable team—and it happened to be a team she especially enjoyed beating. In Jess and Tania's first game against them two years ago, they'd gotten a point Jess scored taken away by protesting to the ref. That was their MO: always playing the victim, with muttered comments and complaints about the ref's calls. They wore red bottoms and yellow tops, and Jess amused herself by referring to them in her head as Tweedledee and Tweedledum.

Sure enough, two points into the game, tied at one, Tweedledee made a noise of protest at Tania's set. It was a borderline carry, but not a blatant missed call.

Jess scored a point off the hit. "Nice set," she said to Tania, loud enough for them to hear across the net.

Tania rolled her eyes. "Thanks, Button."

Their opponents made sour faces. "Don't worry about it," Dum said to Dee at the same obvious volume. "Just play our game."

"If your game is making passive-aggressive comments for the ref to hear," Jess muttered to Tania, "then you've already nailed it."

"What you're going to do," Tania said with a look, "is not let them get to you and stick to *our* game."

"But they're so—"

Tania made a "what-are-you-gonna-do?" gesture. "I know."

A flash of Vivienne's black hair from the stands caught Jess's eye. She appeared to be watching their huddle. Jess nodded. "Let's crush them."

"Let's."

They high-fived and the battle was on.

They got a few points ahead with some tough serving, but then the Tweedles bitched about another call and slowed the game back down when the ref was forced to remove the whistle from his mouth and give them a warning.

Jess missed her serve after the pause and the Tweedles

pulled even again, then ahead by two. Jess and Tania battled back and the game teeter-tottered that way until it was tied at nineteen. Jess tried not to stare at the score. All they had to do was get two points in a row. She took a deep breath.

Dum served to Jess. She passed to Tania, then waited for her set. It was a little tight to the net, which meant she didn't have many attack options.

Jess jumped. All she could see in front of her was Tweedledee's hands. She thought about rolling the ball to the deep corner, but then she got another idea. She turned and smashed it off of Dee's outer hand for her own wipe off.

"Yes!" Jess cheered when the ball hit the ground.

Tania whooped and hugged her. "Sweet wipe!"

Jess went back to serve, heart racing. They were up 20–19. Only one more point to win the first set. She jump-served, aiming for a back corner, trying to make Dum move out of her comfort zone. Dum scooted back but didn't get far enough and made a bad pass. Dee chased it down and tried to loft the second touch up into the air to give Dum a chance to attack, but it was too far behind her. She cranked it into the net.

Jess exhaled in a whoosh. A win. But only halfway to meeting Veronica Doyle.

Jess and Tania hugged. The Sunside girls cheered from the stands.

"Yes, Jess," Tania said. "Beauty serve."

"Thanks, T." Jess couldn't hide the smile on her face as they changed sides and took a breather in the shade.

"We've got this." Tania nodded and sucked back some water. "I have a good feeling."

Jess stretched her shoulders, searching for that same

confidence inside. She wasn't sure it was there. But, "Me, too," she said, tossing her water bottle into their basket. "Let's fucking go."

The Tweedles continued to whine in the second set. Tied at eight, they were arguing with the ref about a net touch while Jess and Tania stood, hands on hips, waiting.

"This is ridiculous," Tania muttered.

Jess nodded, attention wandering into the stands. Her gaze met Vivienne's. Vivienne rolled her eyes in a "Can you believe this nonsense?" look. The corner of Jess's mouth twitched involuntarily. "Yes, it is. Let's fucking kill them."

And they did. Jess felt invincible, with two stuff blocks, four kills, and two more aces. Each point fired her up even more for the next one.

They won 21–15. Jess fell to her knees after her winning hit, laughing.

"Yes, girl!" Tania cried, diving to her knees next to Jess for a hug.

She knew it was just one small win in the standings, but . . . she won her bet with Vivienne. She looked up into the bleachers to the cheering Sunside teams. Vivienne was clapping. She gave Jess a meaningful nod. Jess had to grin back. This was worth a thousand loaves of banana bread.

Tania stood and hauled Jess to her feet. "You played amazing."

Jess's veins buzzed. "Thanks. So did you." She brushed the sand off and went to shake hands with the pouting Tweedles.

"Good game," Jess said across the net to Dee.

"Good game," Dee replied, squinting toward the ref. "You got some lucky calls."

Jess had to laugh. "So did you. That's how the game goes, right?"

Tania cut off Dee's reply. "See you guys in Sunside next time." She slung her arm around Jess and they headed off to the locker room.

Her shower was a pleasant affair, as she hummed to herself and breathed in the lavender shower gel aroma. Afterward, she changed into her standard uniform—jean shorts and a tank top—and spritzed herself with her favorite summery scent—pink dragonfruit and Brazilian jasmine.

Jess and Tania grabbed shrimp tacos from a food truck and climbed back into the stands to watch the rest of the seven o'clock match.

Chrissy stood to greet them. "Nice win, ladies!" She hugged Jess and Tania, careful not to jostle their tacos. Jess realized she was waiting for Vivienne to congratulate them or acknowledge their bet in some way, but Vivienne was deep in conversation with Lee over red plastic cups and couldn't spare a glance. Jess shook off the twinge of disappointment—maybe after their ride today she was expecting Vivienne to be a little more friendly, but she wasn't going to let it bring her down.

"Thanks," Jess replied to Chrissy, grinning.

They ate and laughed and cheered—although the Sunside team was getting their asses handed to them by Horn Beach. One of the players from Horn Beach caught Jess's eye—a supercute woman with bright eyes and medium-length blonde hair that was tip-dyed blue.

"What are you feeling tonight? Pub? Dancing?" Tania asked as the match wrapped up. "I think a bunch of the girls are going out to Bernie's."

Jess would usually say "pub," but maybe it was the adrenaline of the win that spurred her to say, "Bar. I feel like dancing."

"Bernie's it is."

Bernie's Booty, a ridiculous name, was on the main strip, ostensibly pirate-themed, in the way that Hooters was owl-themed. The servers—men, women, and others alike—all wore booty shorts with swashbuckler boots, striped shirts, and pirate hats. Netting hung from the ceiling, an animatronic parrot squawked from its perch above the bar, and every time someone threw a tip into the treasure chest, the bartender rang a ship's bell.

It seemed like every volleyball player was there—from Sunside and Horn Beach—along with half the town and its tourists. Jess and Tania made their way through the crowd to the bar to get a drink. Chrissy, Shay, and a few others were already on the dance floor. Vivienne and Lee hovered by the edge, still talking intensely.

"Come dance!" Chrissy cried once she saw Jess and Tania pausing nearby with their drinks.

Jess allowed Chrissy to pull her onto the dance floor. A few songs later, sweaty and laughing, Jess couldn't remember feeling this good in a long time.

Then she saw that cute woman with blue hair at the bar.

Her hair was down and parted on one side, strands teasing over her face in a carefree manner. Her short, floaty dress—if it was even long enough to qualify as a dress—left gorgeous legs available for admiration.

"Go talk to her," Tania said.

Jess startled. "What? Who?"

"The hottie with the blue hair you checked out all through her game. I think her name is Skye."

"I wasn't checking her out," Jess protested. "I was . . . admiring her form."

"Uh-huh. Then go talk to the girl with the great form."

Jess took a gulp of her beer, picturing it in her head. It didn't end well. "Nah, I . . . I wouldn't know what to say."

"Okay—and I'm sorry if this is too obvious, but it's hard to know with you—you could try 'Hey, nice game today.'"

"And then what?"

"Y—" Tania paused, shaking her head. "You're kidding, right?"

Jess grimaced. "Kind of."

"Listen. You look hot tonight. Didn't you say a cashier hit on you this morning?"

Jess stood a little taller, remembering her free lollipop. "Yeah."

"And you just had an amazing game. You're a total badass. Skye is *lucky* if you talk to her."

Jess had to laugh. "Stop."

"I mean it. Go."

Jess took a deep breath. Okay. She could do this. She headed over.

Skye was leaning against the railing, waiting for the bartender.

"Hey," Jess said, loud enough to be heard over the music.

Skye turned. Her face lit up. "Hey."

Jess licked her lips. "I like your hair."

"Oh, thanks." Skye smiled and ran her hand through her blue streaks.

"I'm Jess."

"I know."

Jess's eyebrows jumped up her forehead. "You know?"

"Yeah." Skye's smile turned shy. "I asked around."

Something swirled through Jess's gut. "Oh?"

"I'm Skye."

Now it was Jess's turn to be a little shy. "I know."

Skye laughed. "Good to hear."

The buzzing in Jess's veins was back. "Can I buy you a drink, Skye?"

7

Wins: 4! (or maybe even 5??)
Losses: 12

> ***Mind game*: Messing with your opponent mentally. . . . Making them second-guess, overanalyze, or just in general think about what a dick you are instead of volleyball.**

Skye's gaze took in all of Jess's seventy-four inches, lights pulsing, music thumping around them. Now her grin was sly. "I would *love* a drink."

Skye asked the bartender for a margarita on the rocks, so Jess chose the same, then they squeezed through the mass of bodies to a ledge overlooking the dance floor.

"Cheers." Jess tapped their glasses together.

"Cheers." Skye took a sip without breaking eye contact.

Jess swallowed. "You played great today."

"Thanks." Skye propped both her elbows against the ledge. It made her back arch, in the most appealing way. She looked up at Jess through her lashes. "So did you."

"Thank you." Jess took a drink, worried the encounter was already teetering over from promising into awkward. She searched for something to say that would keep it where it was.

But there was no need to worry. Skye rescued it. "Would you like to dance?"

Jess nearly slumped with relief. "Sure." They moved to join the sweaty, gyrating crowd.

Jess knew she wasn't sexy on the dance floor like some women, but she had a decent sense of rhythm and didn't think she embarrassed herself too much.

But Skye? Skye was one of the sexy ones. Her hair tossed in that perfect only-in-commercials way, gaze sultry, while her hips churned in a hypnotic sway. . . . Jess had trouble tearing her eyes off of them, in fact. Skye danced closer and closer to her, until it was natural for Jess to slide her fingers around—

An elbow jabbed her right in the ribs. "Ouch!" Jess turned. The elbow was, of course, attached to Vivienne.

"Oh, sorry—Button! It's you!" A *drunk* Vivienne. Her eyes were hazy and a strand of hair was actually out of place across her forehead. She swayed, then leaned in and touched Jess's arm. "I am so sorry. Do you think your elbow will be okay?" She smelled like a soon-to-be-fired baker—vanilla and tequila.

"*My* elbow? You're the one who elbowed me." Jess had to shout above the music.

Vivienne snickered. "You know, you're right. My elbow. I hope *my* elbow is okay."

Skye, meanwhile, had stopped dancing and was watching the exchange with interest. "Vivienne, is it?" she interjected, extending a hand to shake. "I've heard so much about you."

Vivienne did her best to focus on Skye without acknowledging her waiting hand. "Have you, now? I'm afraid I have no idea who you are."

Jess rolled her eyes. *Classic Vivienne.* "This is Skye. She played the last match today."

"How lovely to meet you," Vivienne said with over-enunciated syllables. "I'm Vivienne." Now she took Skye's hand for a dainty shake.

"I guess we've covered that," Jess muttered. Over Vivienne's head, she made brief eye contact with Lee, who was watching Vivienne with an amused look.

"It was great to meet you," Skye said, "but Jess and I are dancing, if you don't mind."

Vivienne narrowed her eyes. "I assure you, I do not mind in the slightest. Watch out for her elbows. She's very tall."

"For fuck's sake, it wasn't my—" Jess started, but Vivienne was already out of earshot, looping an arm around Lee and laughing. "God, what a nightmare," she mumbled.

"What?" Skye smiled and gulped the rest of her drink.

"Oh, nothing," Jess said. "Forget about her."

"Forget about who?" Skye put her hands on Jess's hips and started dancing again, and with her body close, moving to the rhythm, Jess forgot all about Vivienne, too.

Two drinks later, a slow song came on. Skye tilted her head and raised her eyebrows in question. Jess stepped closer and slid her arms around Skye's waist in answer.

Skye took hold of Jess's shoulders. "I'm really glad I met you tonight."

Goose bumps swept over Jess's skin. "Me, too."

Skye leaned into Jess's chest and rested her head on her shoulder.

Jess held her tighter, hands drifting on their own to rest at the top of Skye's sexy butt.

They swayed together, a tingle building inside Jess's ribcage. Skye was sweet and hot, there was no doubt about that, and she seemed to be enjoying the attention, and maybe even Jess's company. Did Jess dare to hope that she, too, could be graced by the magic of Horny Beach?

"Do you want to go back to my place?" Skye whispered when the song ended.

A pulse of desire throbbed low in Jess's gut. "Yes." She quickly found Tania in the crowd while Skye went to the bathroom.

Tania, sweaty and a bit drunk herself, was dancing with Chrissy and a few of the others.

"Hey, I'm heading out with Skye," Jess said into her ear.

Tania flung an arm around her and squeezed her shoulders. "That's my girl."

Jess's cheeks, already hot from the dancing and drinking, heated further. "Leave a key for me at the front desk?"

Tania nodded with a knowing grin. "Take your time, Button."

Face aflame, Jess went to collect Skye. "Let's go," she said, taking Skye's hand and lacing their fingers together.

They spilled out the front door onto the sidewalk, laughing as they bumped into each other. Even in the warm evening, the fresh air was still a delight after the hot, cramped bar.

Skye tugged Jess's hand toward the ocean. "Let's walk along the beach. My place is just down there."

It was a romantic setting, that was for sure. Jess's heart raced as they walked, trying to take in the sight. Skye was so beautiful in the moonlight, with the purple sand, black water, and silver pinpricks of light sweeping across the sky. Her hair danced in the breeze, and her laugh was like music, drifting up to the stars.

Jess stopped, pulled Skye closer, and kissed her.

Skye made a happy noise and wasted no time wrapping her arms around Jess as she kissed her back.

"Mmm, I was waiting for you to do that," Skye whispered when they pulled their lips apart.

"Yeah?" Jess's heart pounded. "Can I do it again?"

"Yes, but . . ." Skye pressed their lips together and plastered her body right up against Jess's. "I'm going to need you to do a lot more than that. My place is just up here. . . ."

Skye turned and skipped, laughing, away from the shore and up a wooden path that ran between two condos. Jess followed.

Skye's apartment building was a block from the beach, and the second her door closed behind them, she was all over Jess. A deep, wet kiss, then Skye peeled Jess's tank top off and tossed it behind her.

"Is this okay?" she asked, fingers resting on the button to Jess's jean shorts. "God, I want you so bad."

"Yes," Jess breathed, lifting Skye's dress and sliding her hands underneath it. She floated the dress right over Skye's head and let it drift to the ground. Skye wasn't wearing a bra—a fact Jess was well aware of already—and now in the dark hallway she looked so good it hurt.

She picked Skye up and carried her to her bedroom.

Skye rolled over in the tangled sheets and let out a happy moan. "God, that was good."

Jess kissed her bare shoulder. "Agreed."

Skye raised her arms above her head and stretched. "Too bad I have a game tomorrow. . . ."

"Oh." Jess processed the words for a moment. "You want me to go?"

"I don't *want* you to go. . . . But you probably should, so I can get some sleep. Or else . . ." Skye kissed her again, a reminder of how easy it would be to lose the entire night.

"Mmm . . . Fair enough." Jess slipped off the bed and collected her underwear and shorts from the floor.

Skye reached for her phone from her bedside table. "What's your number?"

Jess told her while she stepped into her shorts.

Skye sent Jess a text—**It's Skye**, with a blue heart emoji—then propped her head up with her hand. "You know what, I take it back, you should stay." She reached out her other hand with a pout. "Please."

Jess laughed and retrieved her bra from the dresser where it had landed. "You do need some sleep. It's fine."

Skye rolled onto her stomach, feet kicking idly in the air. "You don't have a game tomorrow?"

"Nope. Only a couple of the Sunside teams do."

"So you can watch me play?"

"For sure." Jess looked for her tank top for a few seconds, then remembered it was in the hallway.

"Do you want me to call you a cab?" Skye asked.

"Nah, I can walk. It's not far."

"Okay. I'll see you tomorrow then."

"See you tomorrow." Jess leaned down for one more kiss, then found her tank top on the way out. She pulled it on and slipped out of the front door, trying not to think about leaving a gorgeous, naked woman behind.

Meandering down the beach, Jess felt lighter than she had in months. A win on the court and off, the smell of a beautiful girl still on her skin. . . . Maybe this was shaping up to be an awesome summer. At the hotel, she paused outside the front door to admire the stars for a moment.

On one of the balconies a few floors above, someone else stood, gazing at the stars, too. Jess gave into the impulse to wave up at them. She felt like being friendly to all the world. The figure didn't wave back, but disappeared into their room just as a shooting star streaked across the sky. Jess smiled up at the night. *Definitely the start of an amazing summer.*

Jess stared at the coffee maker, squinting against the bright light, head pounding. *Where the fuck does the pod go?*

The door to their room opened and Tania stuck her head in. "Jess? Oh good, you're up! I was worried you were going to miss the matches."

Jess tried to focus on her, but left one eye screwed shut. "What time is it?"

"Twelve thirty. Half an hour until game time."

"Twelve thirty? Damn."

"What time did you get back? It must have been after three."

"Four," Jess admitted.

Tania grinned. "So it went well with Skye?"

A flush crept over her cheeks, as usual. "Yeah."

Tania shook her hips in a mini celebration dance. "You want to tell me all about it?"

Jess covered her face with her hands. "No," she replied, her voice muffled.

Tania laughed. "Just checking. 'Kay, I'm heading over to watch the matches. See you there?"

"See you there."

Jess gave up on the coffee and dragged herself into the shower. She smiled at the tiled wall, shivering in the steaming water, remembering Skye's legs and gentle hands and the noises she made. . . . She imagined the shy smile Skye might give her when she saw her watching, imagined their sweet goodbye kiss in the parking lot before she got on the bus. . . . Jess spent longer than normal drying her hair and applying a bit of makeup that, to be honest, she normally wouldn't have bothered with.

After collecting an iced coffee and some egg bites from the café, Jess found Tania and the Sunside crew watching the one o'clock match already underway. Skye and her partner were playing . . . Vivienne and Lee.

Vivienne showed no signs of being smashed last night . . . but for all Jess knew, she could have cut herself off early and drank several gallons of electrolytes before bed. They were up against Skye's team 3–1.

"Who won the first set?" Jess asked, settling into her seat with her breakfast.

"Viv and Lee—21–17."

"Crap."

Tania raised her eyebrow. "Switched alliances already? One night of sweet, sweet—"

"Girl!" Jess protested, trying not to laugh. "There're no alliances. I don't have to cheer for the Sunside team."

Tania snickered. "Horny Beach, it is."

Jess crossed her legs and ignored her, taking a pointed sip of iced coffee.

Skye dropped in a roll shot for a point. Jess made a point of cheering. She realized it was a mistake, though, when Chrissy swiveled her head around. "You're cheering against Viv and Lee?" she asked.

"It's not that I'm cheering *against* Vivienne and Lee. . . . I'm just cheering for Skye."

Chrissy pinched her eyebrows together. "Why are you cheering for Skye?"

"Yes, why are you cheering for Skye?" Tania said, propping her chin on her hands in mock fascination.

Jess glared at Tania. "I just . . . met her last night . . . and she's . . . very nice."

Then the confusion lifted from Chrissy's face. "Ohhh, right! I saw you dancing with her at Bernie's."

"Yes, they did a lot of *dancing*," Tania said helpfully.

Chrissy continued to chatter, oblivious to Tania's innuendo. "Well, I won't tell Viv and Lee that you aren't cheering for them. I don't think they'd like that."

Jess gave Chrissy a noncommittal half smile and turned her attention to her egg bites. *As if Vivienne would give a fuck,* she thought to herself.

At that point the set was tied 5–5. Jess continued to root for Skye . . . but silently.

When they were down 8–10, Vivienne and Lee called a time-out.

They had a lightning-quick chat and were ready to go again, all business, before Skye and her partner had even had a chance to grab their water bottles. Jess had to admire the subtle mind game. And it worked. Skye missed her next serve, then Vivienne scored three points in a row off hers.

They took charge after that. Vivienne and Lee won 21–14. They exchanged high-fives and easy grins after the final point. Jess frowned. She now owed Vivienne two loaves of banana bread for her wins. She definitely didn't have enough bananas in her freezer for that.

Skye looked pretty upset about the loss, tossing her water bottle into her bag with more force than necessary and not making eye contact with anyone.

Jess sat glued to her seat. Probably not the time to go talk to her. But she watched Skye collect her stuff from the bench, just in case she looked her way.

She didn't, though, and vanished into the locker room, still scowling. Okay, yes, she would wait until after.

"You gonna go talk to her?" Tania asked, reading her mind.

"Er . . . yeah. I think so."

"You think so?"

"Kind of awkward, hanging around, waiting for her to come out of the locker room."

Tania shook her head. "It's not awkward."

"I'll make it awkward."

"Well . . . it's certainly a possibility with you"—she dodged a swat from Jess—"but I have faith in your ability to say hi in a normal way."

"We'll see."

"I'm going to go grab a snack before we leave. You want anything?"

"I'm good, thanks."

"I'll see you on the bus?"

The stands thinned out as Jess waited, most Sunside players trickling toward the parking lot. They'd leave as soon as the girls who had just played were ready.

Vivienne and Lee emerged from the locker room before Skye did . . . and Vivienne was in a ridiculously stunning strapless sky-blue dress and shiny silver heels. . . . Jess blinked, confused. Why on earth was she so—Oh, she was heading to her aunt and uncle's ritzy house. There was probably a dress code for dinner, with five different kinds of forks and waiters in tuxedos and all that.

Jess watched her strut out, all Sandra Bullock in *Miss*

Congeniality. She even tossed her hair and put on sunglasses.

Still no Skye. When the other Sunside players emerged and made their way to the parking lot, Jess stood. She was the only one left in the stands. The bus would be leaving any minute.

She made her way to the parking lot with one last, lingering glance at the locker room door. The Sunside players were loading the bus—minus Vivienne, of course, who was leaning on her Mercedes again like a fashion model. Why didn't she just hop in her fancy car and drive off to Veronica Doyle's fancy house? No, she had to put on a show in the parking lot first. Jess consoled herself with the fact that at least she didn't have to get back in that car.

She climbed onto the bus and flopped into a seat near the front. Normally, she'd go sit by Tania, but she wasn't up for a bunch more questions. Jess dug through her tote for her phone and found the red lollipop first. She unwrapped it and popped it into her mouth, then grabbed her phone. It made sense to send Skye a goodbye text, didn't it? Or should she wait?

The cherry flavor dissolved over her tongue, tingling her taste buds. The heated look Beth gave her flashed behind her eyes. Jess pushed the lollipop to the side of her mouth and sat up straighter. Enough with these stupid games. It wasn't high school anymore, even if the league drama occasionally felt like it.

Hey, sorry I missed you after the game. That was a close one. I was rooting for you! It was so nice to meet you, and hopefully we can talk soon. *Send*. Then she read it again and panicked—way too dorky, much too needy. This would scare off Skye for sure. Should she edit the text? No, Skye would be able to see it had been edited, and then Jess would look even more desperate. And dorky slash needy, etc. It was too late now. All she could do was wait. She stared at her phone in vain for a while until her lollipop was gone, then she drifted off to sleep, rattling along the California coast.

Fleming was thrilled to see her. The wiener threw himself at Jess's legs until she scooped him up and peppered him with kisses. He wiggled with ecstasy, little pink tongue searching for her face. "I missed you, too," Jess said.

Nelson leaned on the doorframe. "How was Horny Beach?"

"Great." Jess put Fleming down and stroked his head a few times while his tail motored. "We won our match."

"And?"

"And what?" She tried to keep a neutral face as she looked up at him, but failed.

Nelson hooted. "Yeah, you did! Come on in for a drink and tell me all about it."

"There's not much to tell. . . . We met, we danced, we went back to her place. . . ."

"Mm-hmm, mm-hmm, are you going to see her again soon?"

"I don't know . . . we didn't make any plans or anything."

Nelson sighed at her hopelessness. "You got her number, right?"

"Yeah." Jess's fingers twitched with the urge to check her phone.

He raised his eyebrow. "Do not overthink this."

"I'm not overthinking anything! I already texted her."

"And?"

"And she hasn't replied yet."

Nelson held out his palm. "Let me see what you sent her."

"No!"

"Why not?"

"Because then I'll definitely overthink! You'll just tell me why it was wrong."

"Jess. Help me help you."

"Nelson. I'm good. Just let me handle it."

He made a skeptical noise.

"I'll let you know what happens, okay? I promise."

Nelson sighed and rubbed his head. "Girl, you do you. But when you want my help . . ."

She kissed his cheek. "I know where to find you."

"Have a good night, Jess."

"Oh, wait . . . do you have any overripe bananas?"

Bananas in hand, Jess took Fleming home and checked her phone the second she closed the door. Still nothing. She read her message to Skye again.

Hey, sorry I missed you after the game. Did it sound like she was annoyed at Skye for not coming to find her?

That was a close one. She shouldn't have brought up their loss.

I was rooting for you! God, who said "rooting"?

It was so nice to meet you. Sounded like she was talking to someone's grandparents.

And hopefully we can talk soon. Desperate. Whiny. Putting too much pressure on her.

Why did she have to be such a loser? Why did she always have to be so awkward and look like she was trying so hard?

Her phone buzzed.

She nearly dropped it, heart in her throat. But it wasn't Skye. It was . . . Vivienne?

"What the fuck?" she said out loud, swiping to read the message.

My aunt wants your banana bread recipe.

Then, **Please**, as an afterthought.

Jess sat on her couch, trying to slow her heartbeat. **What? Why does Veronica Doyle want my banana bread recipe?**

I told her how good it was. Shit, it's not like a family secret, is it? Are you going to be all weird about it? Because it's a sacred sewing circle recipe passed down from your great-great-great-grandmother that can only be known by your very tall offspring?

A laugh bubbled up in Jess's throat before she could stop it. **It's not a secret. One sec.** She sent Vivienne the link to the recipe she used.

Thanks. Aunt Veronica will be very happy. And she says she'd love to meet us for lunch after a game. I'm supposed to check with her assistant, so I'll get back to you with some dates.

Jess squeed to herself and forgave Vivienne for being an asshole the night before. Mostly. **I am available any time! And, I'll have your banana bread for you on Saturday.**

Sweet, thanks. Also . . . I won ten bucks on my scratcher. Told you I was feeling lucky!

Jess pursed her lips. No one had ever slept with Vivienne then ghosted her, that was for sure. Everything always went her way. **I will accept cash for my half,** Jess replied.

No way, this is my win.

My lawyers will be in touch.

Vivienne sent a laughing emoji, which Jess was not expecting. Then, **See you Saturday.**

See you then. Have fun with your family.

Jess stared at her phone. *"See you then."* That was strange enough on its own, then Jess had gone and added *"Have fun."* It wasn't like she and Vivienne ever talked or hung out, and she certainly had no interest in starting.

But it was nice to know Vivienne liked her banana bread.

8

Wins: 4
Losses: 12
Texts from Skye: 0

> ***Phaser*: A miss-hit that has no spin or finesse whatsoever, just goes flying out of bounds in an embarrassing and cannonball-like failure.**

Still no reply from Skye.

"Okay, that's weird, right?" Jess said to Tania the next morning at the gym. "To say nothing at all?"

Tania breathed through her chest presses. "It is a bit weird. But maybe it's like that thing where you get a text and you're in the middle of something, so you can't reply, then it just slips your mind?"

"Yeah, but . . ." Jess chewed her lip. "You wouldn't do that for a text you were really excited about . . . would you?"

Tania shrugged as she exhaled. "Maybe."

"Ugh." Jess did another halfhearted bicep curl.

"Give it a day and then maybe try once more."

"And say what? 'Hey, it's me, the woman you just hooked up with, sad and desperate, hoping you're not ghosting me?'"

"Maybe not . . . exactly that?"

Jess kicked at a rubber mat. "This is what I get for talking to cool women. Rejection."

"You have not been rejected!"

Jess raised her eyebrow at her.

"Yet."

"Ugggh."

"Listen, we play Sonja and Jonesy tomorrow. Let's focus on that. We've got to build off our Horny Beach win."

"Right." Jess nodded, stuffing down the thought of rejection . . . for now. "Right. What's our game plan?"

Saturday morning, there was still nothing from Skye. Jess knew she would never be able to focus on the match with the festering wound of the unanswered text.

Time to pull off the Band-Aid.

She sat at her small kitchen table with a bowl of oatmeal. **Hey, I don't want to bother you, but . . .** No, delete. **Hi Skye! I just wanted to make sure you got my message. . . .** Nooooo. Delete. **Hey, how's your weekend going? . . .** Maybe? Neutral. A tad boring perhaps, but . . . neutral. Neutral was good. Here she was, casual, expecting nothing beyond relaxed chit-chat.

She hit send.

Jess's leg jittered under the table as she ate her oatmeal on autopilot. No response.

She brushed her teeth, packed her bag, including the two foil-wrapped loaves she had made for Vivienne the night before, and walked to the pavilion. No response.

Jess got changed, then found Tania in the stands watching the match ahead of them, already in her uniform. Jess sat next to her, chewing her nails. No response.

"You okay, Button?" Tania asked when she saw Jess's face. "You look . . . extra white."

"I texted her."

"What?" Tania gasped. "When?"

Jess checked the time. "Forty-seven minutes ago."

Tania scrubbed her face. "Shit."

"I shouldn't have texted before our game."

"Well, since you said it first . . . yeah, you shouldn't have texted before our game."

"Fuck."

"Listen. Do you think you can do me a favor and not check your phone at all until after?"

Jess scrunched her face up. "Ummm . . ."

"You can do it." Tania scooted closer and took her hand. "Look, Viv and Lee are losing."

That was, admittedly, rather interesting. Jess turned her attention to the court. The fact that the match was still going on meant it had gone to a third and deciding set. Vivienne was scowling, her face a dark cloud.

Very interesting.

They were down 13–14. The match was on the line. Their opponents, from North Bay and not far ahead of Jess and Tania in the rankings, were clearly playing an incredible game. They sent over a tough float serve. Vivienne made a shaky pass, then waited for Lee's set, the tension in her limbs visible. Her approach was strange, sluggish, like she was underwater. Vivienne hit a phaser out the back line. Way out.

Game over.

They lost.

Jess wanted to celebrate, but . . . she couldn't. Vivienne just looked so sad. Utter devastation, like her favorite person had died. But only for a second, then her face switched back to pissed off.

"Let's go." Tania stood and hauled Jess to her feet.

"Yeah," Jess said, trying to read Vivienne's lips, but having no luck.

They reached the sand and hovered by the players' bench, waiting for Vivienne and Lee to vacate it. Vivienne's face was warped in a scowl.

Jess slipped the banana bread out of her bag. "Hi," she said, tentative.

After a pause long enough to suggest she had no desire to respond, Vivienne growled, "Hey."

Jess searched for what to say. "Tough game" or "good try" would be awkward. Actually, maybe it was best to avoid mentioning the game at all. "Um, this is for you." She held out the foil bundles.

Vivienne's face didn't move a hair from her scowl. "Oh. Thanks." She took them and stuffed them into her duffel. "Why two?"

"Oh, um, remember I said I'd bake you banana bread for every win?" Jess's face flushed. Their friendly bet in the car seemed a million miles away, and Vivienne could not be less interested in banana bread at the moment.

"Right."

Jess shifted in the silence, wondering how to end this conversation. Vivienne was clearly taking losing hard. "Well . . . at least you're still first in the league." Then she cursed herself internally. *The plan was not to mention the game, Jess. God.*

Vivienne looked at her like she was stupid. "What's with you?"

Jess folded her arms awkwardly across her middle. "What do you mean?"

"Why are you so obsessed with winning and losing?"

The question nearly knocked Jess over. "What are you talking about? I'm n—"

"You are."

Jess sputtered. "You're the one who made the bet with me."

Vivienne rolled her eyes and shouldered her bag. "I don't care if I win or lose, Jess. I care how I play. And I played like shit."

"You didn't . . . I don't . . ." Jess trailed off, words suffocated by the injustice of Vivienne telling her she was obsessed.

Vivienne waited for her to finish, then, when it was apparent she wasn't going to, huffed and stormed away.

Jess dropped her duffel on the bench, irritation squeezing her throat. "Easy for someone to say winning and losing doesn't matter when they almost always win," she muttered to herself as Vivienne's angry form disappeared into the locker room. "And, please, as if she doesn't care about her record."

"What's that?" Tania, who had been chatting with the scorekeeper and missed the exchange, asked.

"Nothing, I—" Jess's phone buzzed in her hand, right as she was about to tuck it into her bag.

They were due to start their warm-up. . . . She shouldn't even look at it. . . . But . . .

It was a message.

From Skye.

Jess read it, heart in her throat.

"No, don't—!" Tania cried when she saw Jess on her phone, but it was too late.

Hey Jess. It was really nice hanging out with you, but I've realized that I'm not in a place where I can be in a relationship right now. I need to focus on myself. All the best!

Jess sank onto the bench and read the words again, pulse racing. She read them one more time.

Tania tucked a ball under her arm with a grimace. "What'd she say?"

Wordless, she handed her phone to Tania.

Tania was silent for a moment, then . . . "Oh . . . Jess."

"Yeah."

"'Focus on myself'? That is some bullshit. Also . . . 'hang out with you'? . . . To be clear, you guys . . . ?"

"We did."

"Fuck. I'm so sorry."

Jess shook her head. "My text literally just asked how it was going. I got dumped without even being in a relationship."

Tania made a dismissive gesture. "Fuck her, Jess. Seriously. She obviously has her own issues to deal with. You don't want any of that anyway."

Jess nodded, blinking fiercely against the tears threatening to fall.

The ref blew his whistle to start their official warm-up time.

"Okay." Tania took Jess's hands to pull her to her feet. "I know you feel like shit right now, but we're not going to let an asshole like Skye get in our heads. Okay? We're not going to let her affect this match."

Jess's legs felt hollow. "Right." What had she done to repel Skye? Their night together had been so good. . . . Everything went perfect, really. Although . . . Skye had asked her to leave. . . . Was that an obvious sign she was getting rejected that she'd been too stupid to see? She realized Tania was staring at her expectantly. "Right," Jess said again, hoping to convince herself and Tania in equal measure. "I'm fine. I've got this."

She did not have it.

They lost. Badly.

Tania didn't even try to talk about the game when they sat on the bench after. "Are you going to reply to her at all?"

Jess wiped her forehead with a towel. "I don't know . . . I don't think so? I mean, what could I say?"

"The middle finger emoji is nice."

Jess let out a half-amused huff. "Maybe . . ."

"Seriously, you should tell her to fuck off. Such a dick move."

A thought hit Jess like a truck, flattening her lungs. "Oh my God. . . . Oh my *God*. Horn Beach is coming here in a couple weeks. I'm going to have to see her! . . . Fucking hell, *do we play her?*"

Tania's jaw dropped. "Shit. I think maybe we do."

"Oh God," Jess groaned. "Just end me now." She pressed her palm over her eyes. "You think there's any chance I could bribe Winston to change the schedule?" As nice as Winston was, she already knew there was no chance.

The team that was playing next hovered nearby, waiting for Jess's crisis to pass so they could sit on the bench. Jess stood and chucked her stuff into her bag, then followed Tania toward the locker room.

"It'll be fine," Tania assured her. "We'll just . . . beat her."

"Oh, is that all?"

"We will. We have to."

"Hey . . ." Jess ran her fingers through her sweaty hair. "Thanks for not being mad about the game."

"It's fine." Tania waved the apology away. "It's just volleyball."

Jess had to laugh, or else she'd cry.

Not that she was excited to put on her neon-green shirt and go to work, but the last few days had been occupied with either volleyball or staring at her phone, and maybe a few hours of ring toss was exactly what she needed to clear her head.

It helped that it was a busy day on the midway, a steady stream of customers to manage, prizes to hand out, and rings to collect. But as her shift wound down, a sense of dread built in her gut, knowing that she would soon have to face the real world again.

Until her favorite customer arrived.

"Jess!" Troy toasted her with his giant cup of soda. "Winston told me about your amazing game at Horn Beach! It sounds like things have been going great for everyone. Well, except for Viv and Lee losing today."

She nodded and handed Troy his rings. "It had to happen eventually, I guess."

"But you won one, right? That must feel good." He scored on the center bottle with his first throw.

The win in Horn Beach felt like it had happened years ago. Did she feel good? No. She felt rejected. Alone. Not lovable.

Because it wasn't just Skye, if she was being honest. Since Phoenix, she hadn't had *any* serious relationships. A few dates, a few hookups, but nothing that ever went anywhere. The other women didn't like her enough. They "didn't feel an authentic connection," or "were still processing some things" with their ex, or, now, needed to "focus on" themselves.

Troy tossed another ring, hand steady. Direct hit. He didn't seem to mind waiting for her reply.

What if she never found a life partner? She tried to answer Troy's question but asked her own instead. "How did you and Sunny end up together?"

He held up a ring, poised to toss it, but didn't actually throw it. "Depends on your definition of 'together.' We were friends in high school, and everyone but us knew we liked each other. She asked me to prom."

Jess nodded. "So . . . you've never had to worry about not being able to find anyone."

Teddy frowned thoughtfully and tossed the ring. Miss. He turned to study her. "It's hard, isn't it, to put yourself out there and hope someone sees that little piece of their soul in you?"

Jess blinked over watery eyes. "Especially when no one ever wants you."

Troy shook his head. "That cannot be true." He hit his next two shots. "Cannot be."

"Why would you say that?"

"I've known you for two seasons now, and you are a beautiful soul, inside and out. That very first day, you brought cookies for the entire league. You are professional and kind, and I know how much you care about the game. And here is the thing—all of that's true whether you have a partner or not. You are a whole, complete person on your own. Don't forget that."

Again with the tears. She sniffled and searched for a

tissue under the counter. "You know, you're a really good team manager."

"Everything will work out for you, Jess. Trust me." He scored with his remaining rings.

"Twenty-five points." Her voice was still a little watery. She handed him a ticket.

He tucked it in his pocket. "Trust me," he said again. He collected his soda and waved, heading off to find his Sunny.

Jess leaned her hip on the counter. The sun was hanging low over the horizon, glinting off the water. A waft of the buttery popcorn smell from the nearest cart hit her.

Her phone buzzed. A text from Vivienne, of all people. **Hey, thanks for the banana bread, I already ate a whole loaf.** Then another text came in.

The Saturday Losers Club is going to Maggie's for drinks. You and Tania in?

Jess bristled. **I thought it didn't matter if you won or lost?**

It doesn't, but if I lose at least I can go get shit-faced.

Jess imagined having to put up with Vivienne all night and decided she'd had enough of beautiful women walking all over her for now. **I'll pass.**

Aw, come on. You can talk about my win–loss record all you want.

Jess's thumbs hovered over the keyboard. Did she tell Vivienne she just got dumped and wanted to go sulk in her bathtub with a mug of tea and a bag of animal crackers? **I really don't feel like going out. Long day at work,** she said instead.

Boring.

Jess clenched her jaw. She could hear the word in Vivienne's snooty, judgmental tone. What did Vivienne want from her, anyway? They weren't even friends. They actively disliked each other, even. **Then I guess I'm boring.**

Vivienne sent the thumbs-up emoji. What the fuck did that mean? Jesus, she was sick of women right now. Time to go pick up her dog.

Of course she forgot that she had promised Nelson an update on the Skye situation.

"Oh no," Nelson said when he saw her face.

It was not lost on Jess that the people she was closest to read her face like a book. She didn't even need to say anything.

"Don't worry about it, baby girl." Nelson handed Fleming over. "You don't need a woman to complete you."

Jess sighed. "That's what everyone keeps saying. Still sucks." She also noticed that her friends seemed to have much more confidence in her than she had in herself. Too bad they were deluded.

She took Fleming home and was just settling into her bubble bath with Bianca Collazo's Pacific League game on her phone when it buzzed. She narrowly saved it from plunging into the soapy depths and opened the text. It was a photo from Vivienne—a selfie of her, Lee, and Chrissy. It was angled from up high and right down into Vivienne's cleavage. She was smiling in a rather seductive way, lips hardly curling, eyes lidded. . . . She looked fucking hot and it was extremely annoying. Jess wasn't sure how she was supposed to reply. She sent back a thumbs-up, lobbed her phone out of reach, and sank down deep into the bubbles.

9

Wins: 4
Losses: 13

> ***Tape*: The band of fabric along the top of the net. It sort of looks like a strip of tape, I guess. I don't know.**
>
> ***Ice the server*: Calling a time-out right before someone is about to serve. It messes with their head and makes them more likely to miss the serve after the time-out. Works more often than you'd expect.**

When Jess woke the next morning, there was a brief window of blissful nothingness, a sweet, empty Sunday stretching ahead of her, and then *everything* crashed over her in a dark wave, the kind that tossed you off your feet and sent water up your nose, then rushed back to the sea, leaving you breathless and battered, sand down your shirt and seaweed in your hair.

Jess hadn't replied to Skye's rejection text because she hadn't known what to say, but now, looking at it again, she wondered if that made her even more pathetic.

Hey Jess. It was really nice hanging out with you, but I've realized that I'm not in a place where I can be in a relationship right now. I need to focus on myself. All the best!

All the best.

What an absolutely . . . bitch-ass thing to say.

All the best to you too!!! Jess smashed with her thumbs, hoping her true feelings came through with all the exclamation marks. But then she sighed and deleted it. **Okay, take care,** she typed instead. She rubbed her forehead and swiped out of the chat without sending anything.

There was another message from Vivienne waiting. This time it was a picture of a whole crowd of them at the bar, hoisting green shots. Vivienne's tongue was out, licking a drop off the rim of her glass. Jess stared at the tongue longer than she should have. She didn't like the way that tongue made her feel. **We did a shot for you,** the caption read. **Everyone says you have to come next time.**

Jess scoffed. She didn't believe that for a second. Surface-level, she got along with everyone, but she knew that, aside from Tania, no one really cared if she was there or not, unless they needed something off a really high shelf. With another look at Vivienne's long, pink tongue, Jess pushed back her covers and teetered out of bed to the bathroom. Fleming needed a walk.

When they came back after a trip around the block, the jar of shells winking in the sunlight caught her attention. Getting dumped was so distracting, she forgot to track yesterday's loss. "See, I'm not obsessed with winning and losing, Vivienne," she muttered as she took a shell from the win jar and put it into the loss jar. Thirteen shells in there now. Four wins, and forty-three games to go. There was still plenty of time to turn the season around. "Right, Fleming?"

Fleming huffed a doggy sigh and wandered over to his water dish for a few halfhearted laps. He didn't seem convinced.

And rightly so.

Jess fell into a funk that Fleming must have been able to smell coming. Over the next few days, she still did all the things she needed to do—worked, bought more bananas, walked Fleming, met Tania at the gym . . . but it was like there was a veil over the sunshine, the world shadowed around her. She stayed up late with her telescope, thinking that might snap her out of her fog, but thick clouds drifted by and she only caught a few sorry glimpses of the quarter moon before giving up and going to bed.

Even the next chapter of *Queen in Shining Armor* didn't help, despite Queen Andromeda revealing herself to the rival queen at the masquerade.

Every night, she tossed and turned in tangled sheets and hardly slept.

Thursday, game day, Jess woke up with a splitting headache. "Fuck," she muttered, reaching for her glass of water.

Fleming trotted over, his beloved stuffed crab in his mouth.

"Hi, baby." Jess sat up and scratched his head. "Ugh. I don't have it in me today, Fleming. Can I just stay in bed all day?"

He dropped his crab and studied her with a cocked head.

"I know. You're right." She sighed. "I'll get up. Tania will be waiting for me."

Fleming yipped.

"And a walk, of course. I would never forget."

When Jess arrived in the locker room before their match, Tania was peering into a mirror, smoothing her bun. Her face pinched with concern as soon as she saw Jess. "Are you okay? You look like . . . Are you okay?"

Jess massaged her eyes. "Thank you for not finishing that sentence with 'shit.'"

"Rough night?"

"Rough week. Haven't been sleeping great. I have such a headache."

"You want some ibuprofen or something?" Tania moved to rifle through her locker.

Jess waved her off, setting her bag down. "I took some already. I'll be fine once we get going."

"Okay." Tania studied her, chewing the inside of one cheek.

"What?"

"Nothing."

"*What*?"

"Nothing, amiga." Tania smacked her butt. "Let's go win this game."

Their opponent was another Sunside team—Billi and Raya—who were feisty, loud, and a lot of fun to play. Well, normally they were, but Jess's world was still muffled, and their antics didn't make her smile as much as usual. As the match began, the more the energy swirled and flowed around Billi and Raya, the more it drained from Jess and Tania. The noisy pair built a quick lead, with lots of laughing and smart-assed quips.

Tania called a time-out at 1–6. "We've got to get some momentum going over here," she muttered in their huddle. "They're really cheating inside on defense—let's go for the line, okay? And listen, they're both hitting right at the tape. You can block them."

The frustration in her voice was hard to miss. And Tania never got frustrated. Jess nodded and gave herself a shake. "Okay, right. Got it."

Fortunately, Tania's time-out paid dividends right away and iced Raya's next serve. Tania went back to the line for her turn and ripped a great jumper down the middle. Billi made an okay pass to Raya, then tore in for their hit.

Block this, Jess. She jumped and reached as hard as she could into Billi's attacking space with two big, solid hands.

She stuffed Billi, hard. The ball smashed off her palms with a satisfying *thunk* and slammed straight into the sand. The familiar thrill of a stuff block was there, but still muted.

Tania charged in and hugged her. "Sweet block, Button."

Jess nodded and kicked the ball toward the linesperson. "Thanks."

Billi studied her from across the net. "Jess, if you don't smile soon, I'm gonna get Raya to flash you her boobs."

Raya called from farther back in the court, "I'm not flashing my boobs, Billi."

Billi half turned. "Why not? They're nice boobs."

Raya gasped. "Nice? How *dare* you."

Billi brushed the sand off their ass and went back to get ready for Tania's next serve. "Sorry. I meant to say they're exquisite."

"Hmph." Raya pouted. "That's better."

A grin finally cracked Jess's face.

Billi threw her a quick wink before the ref blew her whistle and Tania sent her next serve over.

Jess blocked Billi again.

"Fucking hell, Jess!" Billi laughed. "Did you grow?"

"Try hitting around her," Raya called helpfully.

Billi flipped her a cheerful middle finger.

Raya blew a kiss back.

Jess's smile grew. The score was 3–6. They were catching up.

But then Tania's next serve went straight into the net and was accompanied by a small hiss of pain.

Jess's head jerked around at the sound. "You okay?"

Tania rubbed her right shoulder, grimacing. "Yeah. My shoulder's just been bugging me lately."

"You need a time-out?"

"Nah." Tania rolled her shoulders. "Let's get a pass here."

Jess nodded and slapped her hand, but as they turned to face the next serve, Tania's brow remained furrowed.

"I thought maybe we were going to pull that one off," Tania muttered, tugging her hair elastic out.

"Yeah." Jess slumped next to her on the locker room bench and rubbed her face. She had thought so, too . . . but then Billi and Raya had adjusted to her block and she lost confidence in her ability to do anything at the net beyond jump around uselessly, and Tania's shoulder was clearly hurting, although she wouldn't admit it. Plus throw in a few unlucky breaks, and they lost a heartbreaker in the third, 12–15.

"Your shoulder okay?" Jess asked, watching Tania rub it.

"It'll be fine. I'll ice it tonight, go to PT in the morning." Tania paused, then asked, "Did you reply to Skye?"

"No . . . should I?"

"I don't know." Tania peeled her top off and wrapped herself in her towel. "Are you feeling okay about it?"

Jess took a swig of water. "I'm not feeling great about it."

"I know, Button. But maybe it is better to just move on."

"I'm trying."

Tania nodded. "I know you are." She removed her bottoms from underneath her towel and tossed them into her locker. "Hey, what time do you want to meet tomorrow?"

Jess blinked at her. "Tomorrow?" She was fairly confident they didn't have a game. . . .

Tania mumbled something in Spanish and rolled her eyes. "Tomorrow, Jess! The festival?"

It took a moment for Jess's brain to clunk into place, then she remembered. "Right! Tomorrow." The Sunside Surf and Sand Festival was on that weekend—a surfing competition in the mornings and live music after. "Uh, what time are we meeting again?"

"George and I are going to the surf competition before he has to be at the restaurant, then there's the music at five. Backyard Chickens, aren't you excited?" Tania nudged Jess in the ribs and Jess tried to give her a smile. Tania wasn't exactly a fan, but she liked watching the surfing and agreed to go with Jess since she loved the band so much. "We could meet at, like, four thirty? Grab some food first?"

"Sounds good."

When they left the locker room, Tania's family was hanging around waiting for her.

"Jess!" She melted into Tía Diana's warm hug. "Dinner at my house Tuesday! You'll be there?"

"You bet. Thanks, Tía."

Diana kissed her cheek. "I'm making your favorite."

Jess squeezed her again, towering over the petite woman. "You know anything you make is my favorite. Can't wait."

"You want to stay to watch?" Tania gestured at the court where Chrissy and Shay's match was getting underway.

Jess looked at the group of other players hanging in the stands, Lee's laugh drifting over the crowd. And there was Vivienne, tossing her hair and looking as perfect as ever in the center. She just didn't have the energy for all those people right now. "Nah, I've got the early shift tomorrow. I should get home."

"You sure? Might be fun to . . . hang out for a bit."

Jess shook her head. "Let me know how your shoulder is doing. See you tomorrow, T."

They hugged, then Jess made her way down the sidewalk, to her dog, his stuffed crab, and their quiet apartment.

Jess worked Friday morning, then came home, showered, and put on her green bikini and jean shorts. She threw her phone, keys, and cash in her belt bag, then added ChapStick and gum, kissed Fleming on the head, and headed back out to meet Tania at a taco truck outside the festival.

They sat on wobbly folding chairs and inhaled their food while Tania chatted about her family—"My cousin Amaya is studying abroad in Madrid. I'm so jealous, I didn't get to go in college but she's begging us to visit. Oh, and when you come for dinner on Tuesday just ignore my cousin Marco. It seems he's got quite the crush on you"—then they scanned their tickets to get wristbands and made their way in.

The opening act looked young—a ragtag ska band comprised of a pack of twenty-year-olds in Hawaiian shirts—but they made up for their lack of life experience in enthusiasm and volume.

"I'll grab drinks," Tania yelled over the horns. "You want to snag some spots up front?"

Tania went to get in line at the beer tent while Jess pushed her way through the mass of bodies—another benefit of her height and wide shoulders.

The typical festival crowd gave way before her—university students in Birkenstocks, teenagers on their phones, and lots and lots of skin. She came up to a woman in a white bikini, applauding the ska band as they took their final bows, with incredible posture—confident and commanding—long, shiny black hair, and a pert nose. . . .

It was Vivienne.

"What are you doing here?" Jess blurted.

Vivienne made a slow, smooth turn, as if she knew Jess was there even before she spoke, her lips curled in a smirk. "You kidding me? Backyard Chickens? They're my favorite."

Jess put her hands on her hips. Of course Vivienne would mock her. "Mm-hmm. What are you really doing here?"

Vivienne shrugged, giving up the charade. "Lee wanted to come. Symphony is playing after them or something."

"There's a symphony playing?"

"No, the band is called Symphony."

"Oh. That's kind of a dumb name, isn't it?"

Vivienne smoothed her hair. "Well, it's no 'Backyard Chickens,' that's for sure."

Lee appeared, carrying two cans of hard seltzer. "Oh, hey, Jess." She handed one to Vivienne. Her partner, Toni, was with her.

Jess nodded at the two of them. "Hey, guys . . . and congratulations, Toni!" Jess's eyes flicked to Toni's midsection but she wasn't showing yet.

"Did you come with Tania?" Vivienne asked.

In answer, Tania appeared and handed Jess a beer as she greeted the others. "¡Arriba, abajo, al centro, pa' dentro!"

Tania chanted. They tapped their cans together in the middle of the circle.

Vivienne took a long pull of her seltzer and wiped a drop from her lip. "Thank God we don't have the early game tomorrow. You guys don't play till Sunday, right?" she asked Jess and Tania.

"That's right," Jess replied.

Vivienne was about to say something else, but her words were lost in the roar from the crowd as the Backyard Chickens appeared.

Jess raised her drink and whooped along with everyone else, skin tingling in anticipation. This was her fourth time seeing them live and each show only got better.

Four women took the stage—two white sisters with wavy ginger hair, and two Black sisters, one with her curly hair piled on her head in a faux-hawk and one with long braids. All four of them were beautiful, with glowing skin and huge smiles. Jess loved them all dearly, although Serama, the lead singer and the one with the faux-hawk, was her favorite.

"Hello Sunside!" Serama cried. She thumped the count on her guitar before they dove straight into "Sunday," a song about being by yourself and reflecting on what you really want from life.

Jess cheered again in response. The white bikini next to her caught her attention as Vivienne turned to raise an eyebrow.

"They're hot," Vivienne mouthed over the noise.

Jess's cheeks flushed as she nodded.

Vivienne cackled and raised her drink, too.

By the second time through the chorus of "Sunday," Vivienne was dancing. By the third, she was singing along.

Jess danced and sang along too, to every word of every song. It took her awhile to realize that the veil she'd been living under for the last week had vanished. The world was sharp and clear around her again. . . . The hum of Silkie's bass in her blood, the steady thump of Wyan's drums in time with her heart, the comfort of Fay's harmonies wrapping her in warmth. She swore Serama smiled right at her, eyes bright and sure. There was the odd whiff of vanilla underneath the smell of sunscreen, beer, and sweat.

And, every time Vivienne's shoulder brushed her skin, an electric current down her arm.

Jess sang and danced and drank and felt better than she had in a long time, perspiration gathering at her temples and in her cleavage, cheeks hurting from smiling. The only bad moment was when their set came to an end.

They left the stage with one last wave, Jess wistful and happy and warm.

Vivienne whistled after them, then gave Jess an approving nod. "Okay, I'll give it to you. The Backyard Chickens were pretty great."

Jess wiped a trickle of sweat from her forehead. "Told you."

"Are you guys going to stay for Symphony?" Vivienne's skin shimmered in the stage lights, a trail of stars dusting her curves.

"Yeah," Jess said, brain loose, veins buzzing. "Yeah, we can stay."

10

Wins: 4
Losses: 14

> ***Side-out*: Winning the serve back from the opponent. Desperately needed when the other team is on a roll.**

"I WANT THE OCAPUS!"

Jess grimaced but, with great effort, refrained from covering her ears as the red-faced child continued to screech about the stuffed sea creature.

"Sorry, bud," Jess said in what she hoped was a neutral tone. "You need a hundred points for that one."

His mom huffed. "This place is such a rip-off."

If you want the cheap toy that bad, go to a dollar store, Jess bit back. Instead she shrugged, wishing she had another ibuprofen on hand for her pounding head.

The mom held up the tickets they had. "What can he get with twenty?"

Jess waved her hand at the clearly marked display showing the available prizes.

Kazoo in hand a minute later, the boy finally left. Jess took a long drink from her water bottle and pressed a hand to her eyes.

Backyard Chickens had been magical, of course, and Symphony turned out to be great—four cuties with a definite Queen vibe, led by a captivating, sultry queer man, all having the time of their lives—although the details of the night had become fuzzier as it went on.

George had picked up her and Tania and dropped Jess at home. She remembered giving Fleming a handful of treats, then the next thing she knew, the sun was streaming brightly through her window and she was sprawled on her covers, still in her bikini.

Work was a shit show too, which didn't help her hangover. The Whac-A-Mole was broken and no one on-shift could fix it. Jess couldn't even get anyone on the phone who could come deal with it. Three kids threw up on the midway during the first two hours, and two people had just called in sick for the night shift, so Jess would have to fill in herself. The kid screeching about the octopus just about put her over the edge.

Are you free to pop over and take Fleming for a walk in the next couple hours? she texted Nelson during a break. **Need to cover a shift so I won't be home until after ten.**

I got you, Nelson replied.

Taking a moment, once again, to be so grateful for her neighbor, Jess tried calling another repair place on her way back to the ring toss, plugging her ear against the screams from the roller coaster.

An hour into her second shift, her phone buzzed with a text from Nelson. **We saw your friend Vivienne on our walk.**

She's not my friend, Jess replied automatically. **What was she doing?**

I didn't interrogate her, but she appeared to be out for a walk herself.

Weird. I've never seen her around my apartment before.

She loves Fleming. And, might I add, as somewhat of an expert myself, she's sexy as hell.

Not really.

Bitch, please.

She's . . . too perfect.

Yeah, gross, who wants perfect? Not me.

Glad Nelson couldn't see her laugh, Jess sent the eye-roll emoji. **Vivienne and I don't fit together. Trust me.**

I don't trust you, actually. Your lack of self-awareness is truly stunning.

All she had time to send was the middle-finger emoji as a pack of teens approached. Jess tucked her phone under the counter and gave them her work smile, just hoping no one else would throw up tonight.

On Sunday morning, after a quiet cup of tea out on the walkway, Jess blasted Backyard Chickens while she got ready to leave for her game, trying to summon the buzzing in her veins she'd felt at the concert—the buzzing that had been somewhat tempered by yesterday's hangover and midway vomit.

"I can do this," she said to herself in the mirror after she brushed her teeth. "I've *got* this." Her reflection smiled back tentatively, too-big nose and new zit included.

Fleming barked in agreement.

She sang while she packed her bag, kissed Fleming goodbye, popped in her earbuds, and walked to the pavilion, slipping Vivienne's three banana bread loaves from last week's wins into her locker when she arrived.

Jess's step faltered a little when she got out to the court

and saw the team from North Bay warming up already. Tall, agile, and covering vast stretches of sand in no time at all, it was no surprise that they were second in the league behind Vivienne and Lee. Jess's stomach fizzed.

"Pfft, they've got nothing," Tania muttered in her ear after another spectacular warm-up hit from their opponents.

Jess pushed her nerves down and gave Tania a smile. "Nothing we can't handle, anyway,"

Tania slapped her hand. "Yes, girl. Let's do this."

They came out strong. The other team was maybe expecting an easier match, and Jess and Tania went up 7–2. Their opponents called a time-out.

Tania rocked from foot to foot on the sideline. "Let's just keep doing what we're doing. They're going to go hard for the side-out now. Watch for a roll shot or something cheesy."

But there was nothing cheesy. One of the women went up and smashed the shit out of the ball around Jess's block. Tania dove but couldn't get there.

"Fuck," Tania said, dusting the sand off of her hands.

"Mm-hmm," Jess agreed. "You want me to block her cross?"

"Yeah, let's see if she can do that down the line."

She could, in fact, also smash the shit out of it down the line.

"Soooo," Jess said when they called the next time-out, now losing 7–8. "She's a pretty fucking good hitter."

"Pretty good," Tania gasped, clutching her water bottle. They'd had a few long rallies and she'd been diving full out for every hit, getting to some in time, but others . . . not so much.

But the usual flutter of panic was gone from Jess's rib

cage. They were playing well, it just happened that this was a really good team. "I can block her. I'm going to go hard line with everything I've got. But her shoulders tell where she's swinging, and, when she's rolling it instead, she looks to the spot first. Keep going for those digs. Come on, let's get this side-out."

They slapped hands, then Jess added another smack to Tania's butt when she turned, for extra luck.

Jess got the side-out off her next hit, but then so did the other team. Jess got a block, they scored an ace. The score teetered back and forth until it was tied at twenty.

It was Jess's serve.

"Go for it, Button," Tania called to her. "We've got nothing to lose."

Jess nodded and hammered a jump serve at the sideline next to the weaker hitter. She left it, thinking—or hoping—it was out, but Jess's serve clipped the outside of the line.

Tania whooped and ran to Jess for a high five. "Fuck, yes! Amazing serve. One more."

Jess smacked the logo and served again, aiming for the same spot. This time it would have been out, but the passer took it. Jess ran to her blocking position at the net, watching the hitter's shoulders, and knew she was aiming for a line shot.

Mistake, Jess thought as she loaded her quads, because she was all over this one. She jumped, thrust her hands over the net as hard as she could, then felt the reverberation all down her arms when the hitter swung right into her block. The ball fell straight to the sand.

Holy fuck. They won the first set.

Jess had barely landed by the time Tania wrapped her in a hug.

"Yes! What a fucking block!" she cried.

Jess laughed, the adrenaline screaming through her cells. The other team looked grim.

They came out hitting even harder in the second set.

Jess blocked what she could, and Tania dug up a lot of balls, but it wasn't quite enough. They were down by four quickly, and then five, and, while they sort of hung in there, they couldn't win enough of the long rallies, and they lost 15–21.

Jess and Tania sat on the bench, winded.

"We know we can beat them," Jess said while Tania squirted some water over her head.

"Yeah," Tania replied, but she was distracted.

"What's up?"

"Nothing, I just . . . I think I'm gonna get my shoulder taped up real quick." She turned to signal to the trainer waiting nearby. The trainer hustled over, bag of supplies on her shoulder. She and Tania conferred quickly, then the trainer pulled out a roll of kinesiology tape and started cleaning Tania's shoulder.

"Are you okay?" Jess asked, trying not to be overly worried.

Tania didn't look at her. "Fine, just a bit sore."

Jess nodded, biting back further questions, knowing they would only irritate Tania.

Once it was done, Tania stood and rolled her shoulder. "Thanks. Feels good."

Jess offered what she hoped was an encouraging smile and avoided staring at the tape job. She had to trust that Tania knew her limits.

They hit the court for the third and deciding game.

It was another tight one. They had pulled even to tie it at

thirteen, thanks to a big hit from Jess, when the other team called a time-out.

"Be on your toes here," Tania said. "They're gonna fight for this side-out. Watch for an attack on the second hit."

Jess nodded and went back to serve. She took a deep breath, smacked the ball's logo twice, and closed her eyes for a moment. She pictured the serve she wanted to send over. The only sound was the thudding of her heart.

She aimed to thread her jump serve down the middle, but closer to their slightly less-effective attacker, then hustled up to the net into blocking position. The pass was high and tight to the net. Jess watched the attacker, but kept an eye on the other one too, in case she got some ideas about that tight ball. Tania was right—the woman jumped to hit the second touch. Jess was ready to move and launched herself in the air to block her swing. She got a hand on it, not enough for a full block, but enough to send it up into a high arch above her.

She called Tania off the ball and spun around for the second touch, lofting a rainbow behind her for Tania to hit. But Tania didn't hit it, even though she had plenty of room for a good approach. Instead, she bumped it over, trying to put it deep, but it wasn't quite deep enough. The other side got to it and sent a perfect pass to the setter, which led to a perfect set, and a golden opportunity for their best hitter.

Fuck, Jess thought as she jumped, the fatigue in her thighs creeping into her awareness.

The hitter, showing no signs of fatigue, smoked the ball sharp crosscourt. Neither Jess nor Tania had any chance. That left them down 13–14. Match point for their opponent.

"Shit." Tania was slow to get to her feet, brushing off the sand.

Jess gave her a low five. "Just need a pass here. We can do this. One at a time."

They waited for the serve, hands on their knees, squinting into the sharp-angled afternoon sun.

Jess passed the serve without too much trouble, got a solid set from Tania, and hit it hard down the line. The defender struggled to control the dig and it went soaring high out the far side of the court. The other woman chased it down and brought it back with a wild one-armed swing, somehow, in a perfect arc right into position for the hitter. The woman jumped and cranked it. Jess blocked her, but the ball rebounded back nicely to the hitter, who popped it up for her partner. Her partner swung before Jess could jump again. Tania made a desperate dive for the ball but couldn't get to it.

They lost.

Jess rested her hands on her knees, winded.

Tania sat up and sighed.

The crowd showered them with fervent applause for their effort. Jess tried to ignore the two celebrating on the other side. She helped Tania up and patted her back. "Good job, T. You played great."

They shook hands—"Great match," the other two enthused, which made Jess more annoyed—signed the score sheet, and went to collect their stuff.

Chrissy was waiting to drop her bag on the bench. "You guys played so good!" She squeezed Jess's arm. "So close!"

"Thanks," Tania said flatly.

"Chrissy's right," Jess said once they got back to the locker room. "We did play great."

"I know. Just sucks." Tania pulled the tape off her shoulder and rolled it into a ball. She tossed it into the trash can. "I'm gonna skip our workout tomorrow, I think."

"Yeah? You okay?" Jess made sure not to stare at Tania's shoulder.

"Mm-hmm, I just feel like I need some extra rest. Take it easy tomorrow. George and I might go for a drive, find a quiet beach somewhere for a picnic. . . ."

"All right, rest up. Sounds like a nice day."

Tania nodded. They headed for the showers in silence.

When Jess came out of the shower, Tania was combing her hair in the mirror.

"You know, I think I'm going to soak in the hot tub for a bit," Jess said, digging through her locker for a clean swimsuit.

"'Kay," Tania replied without taking her eyes off her reflection.

"Are we still on for dinner at Diana's on Tuesday?" Jess asked, pulling on a one-piece underneath her towel.

"For sure." Tania finally found Jess's eyes in the mirror. "We'll pick you up. I'll text you."

"Okay. Have fun tomorrow." They hugged, then Jess headed down the hall for the hot tub. Happily, she discovered it was empty. She hung up her towel, turned on the jets, and sank into the steaming water.

The first five seconds in a hot tub were one of life's greatest pleasures, topped only by a *really* good orgasm, and maybe the first sip of a peanut butter frozen mocha. Jess liked hot tubs that were *too* hot, but in the best way, the pinpricks of heat reaching down into her core, her nervous system jumping to attention and screaming *I'm alive*. She shivered and sank into a seat.

When the initial wave of bliss faded, Jess tipped her head back on the edge of the tub and replayed the match in her head, fingers drifting idly through the water. Normally after a match she beat herself up about missed plays and botched opportunities but . . . this time she was pretty happy with her game. Focused, smart, sticking to the plan. . . . She did wish she hadn't felt so tired at the end. . . . Maybe it was time to revisit her workout routine. But the fact of the matter was they had played great against a great team. Maybe it was something to build off of. . . .

"Thanks for the banana bread."

Jess jolted up from her daze.

Of course. Of all people to interrupt her quiet hot tub time, it had to be Vivienne.

Vivienne in a small, strapless bikini in coral pink that glowed against her tan skin. She leaned in the doorway, hair up in a messy bun, but the kind Instagram models had, not the limp, sad kind that Jess always ended up with when she attempted the hairstyle.

"It's no problem. A bet's a bet."

Vivienne pushed herself off the doorframe and glided over to the tub. "Really hoped you'd take those fuckers down today."

Jess cleared her throat. "Me, too."

Vivienne slid into the water, goose bumps raising along her arms. "You guys played great, though." She leaned back in the seat across from Jess and closed her eyes.

"Not great enough," Jess mumbled, unsure why her instinct was to disagree. Vivienne's bikini didn't cover much. The way she was sitting, with her top just below the water level, gave the illusion she was naked. Jess tried not to stare at the swell of her breasts.

Vivienne cracked an eye open and gave Jess a look. "I thought we talked about this. How you play is more important than winning and losing."

Frustration tightened Jess's chest. It drove her fucking crazy the way Vivienne talked down to her, but there was no point in rehashing this same discussion . . . especially since Vivienne was probably right. Jess shrugged and settled back in her seat again, closing her eyes. She could still see Vivienne's breasts, though, the water swirling and bubbling around her wet, glistening—

"I saw Fleming yesterday."

Jess snapped her eyes open and kept them on Vivienne's face. "I heard."

Vivienne's eyes were still shut. "He's so sweet."

"Yeah." Her gaze flicked lower, just for a split second. She couldn't help it. "What kind of dogs do you like?"

"Oh, wieners, pugs, papillons . . . The smaller the better."

"Small is good," Jess said, trying not to look at Vivienne's breasts again.

"Where's his name from?"

Jess wrenched her eyes up and shrugged, even though Vivienne couldn't see her. Explaining Fleming's name was never worth it. "Nowhere. I just liked it."

"Hmmm." A low hum of contentment. Vivienne rocked her head from side to side, long neck stretching. The water surged up her collarbones, leaving a wet trail.

Jess was suddenly too hot. She lifted herself up onto the edge to cool down for a minute.

Vivienne looked up. "Oh, I finally worked it out with

Veronica's assistant. Can you do lunch three weeks from today?"

From this angle, her breasts were even more apparent, floating there on the surface. . . .

An image flashed in her mind—her hands touching, caressing . . .

"Yeah," Jess gasped, pulling herself the rest of the way out of the tub, the cooler air raising the hairs on her arms. "Sure. That works."

"Perfect." Vivienne studied Jess, dripping on the edge of the tub. "Are you all done?"

Jess's face burned. "Yup. All done."

"See you later," Vivienne said dreamily, closing her eyes again and resting her arms on the sides of the tub.

Jess mumbled something similar, grabbed her towel, and scurried back to the locker room.

What the fuck was that about? Stop it, Jess scolded herself, trying to shake the image from her mind.

She went for a cold shower.

11

Wins: 4, still
Losses: 15

> ***Sky ball*: If the rally isn't going well and you can't attack your third hit, instead of giving your opponent an easy ball, you launch it as high into the air as you can on its way over the net. Your opponent—now at the mercy of what the sun, wind, and acceleration due to gravity have done to the ball as it falls—will be disoriented and dizzy.**

Tía Diana lived with her family—husband and four kids—in an airy ranch-style house in the next town, about forty-five minutes away. Her sister Nina's house was just down the street, and anytime Jess had been to Diana's house, there were at least ten other people there. Jess had trouble keeping track of which of Tania's cousins were Diana's kids and which were Nina's, or who actually belonged to neither but was just there.

Tania hopped out of George's old truck carrying a foil-wrapped dish. "Mmm, I can already smell the carne asada."

Jess followed her onto the sidewalk, stomach growling. Dinner was early at Diana's, so she had skipped lunch.

George took the dish from Tania and patted his round tummy. "Gonna eat my bodyweight in guac."

Tania slid her arm around him. "So, the usual?" she teased.

He kissed the top of her head. "We both know Diana would be insulted if I didn't."

Tania and George met in college—their orders got mixed up at a bakery, an actual meet-cute—and had been together since. He was just as laid-back as Tania, and Jess envied their easy familiarity, casual touches, and inside jokes.

They went in without knocking and found Diana in the kitchen, hands sticky from the masa. The room was packed with people either trying to help, or pretending they were helping while stealing samples of food. The rest were on the deck out back, including most of the kids, eating and chatting over the music.

Diana wiped her hands and gave them hugs and kisses.

"I made those palmiers you liked," George said, handing over the dish.

"So sweet. Thank you, love." Diana pecked his cheek again. "And Jessica, look at you," She gave Jess an extra squeeze. "So beautiful."

Jess flushed. "Thanks so much for having me. Can I help with anything?"

"No, you three head outside and relax. Find yourself a drink." She pointed at a tub of bottles on the deck as she pushed Jess through the sliding door, all the while yelling at her son to get his butt in there and help.

They each grabbed a beer and searched for a pocket of space in the crowd. Jess smiled and nodded and greeted people along the way, confident she knew most of their names, although it was hard to keep the kids straight since they kept getting taller, and, on occasion, new ones appeared. She cooed appropriately over two of Tania's newest relatives, holding one for a bit at the insistence of the mother, while she eyed the food table over the baby's fuzzy head.

Tania noticed Jess's wandering gaze. "Here, my turn," she said, holding her hands out for the bundle.

Jess gave her a grateful look and passed the baby over, then made for the carne, with its mouth-watering aroma. As promised, George was already there loading guacamole onto his plate.

Jess had just finished collecting her food when a melodic voice spoke from behind. "Well, hello there, beautiful."

She turned.

Tania's cousin Marco grinned up at her from down by her collarbones—eighteen years old, big brown eyes, adorable floppy hair, and all the confidence in the world. He swept a dramatic bow. "Jess, I am, as always, in awe of your radiance."

Jess bit her lip trying not to laugh. "Still gay, Marco."

A pack of older cousins nearby burst into guffaws, hurling insults, chips, and empty cups at him in equal measure.

He dodged the detritus as best he could, laughing and swearing in Spanish.

Tania appeared, adding to the insults, and steered Jess away from him. "I'm so sorry. I told him not to bother you."

"It's fine. He's harmless." Jess half smiled. "I could use some of that confidence myself, actually."

A strange expression flitted over Tania's features as she took a drink.

Jess started to ask what that weird face was about but she was nearly barreled over by a pack of squealing children making a beeline for the paletas Nina had just put out. An uncle followed behind the herd, yelling at them to slow down and apologizing to Jess.

"It's fine," Jess said, as another kid skimmed her elbow and she nearly dropped her plate.

Tania stiffened. "Ah, fuck, my mom's here."

Tania's mom had appeared on the deck in her pantsuit, fresh from her office.

Jess frowned through a bite of food. "Is that not good?"

"She turned fifty last week, and the hints about grandchildren have reached unforeseen levels. I cannot handle any more of her opinions on my relationship or my childbearing years right now."

George joined them, with the largest heap of guacamole Jess had ever seen on a single person's plate.

Tania groaned.

"What?" George scooped another mouthful. "I know you aren't judging me, the way you attacked those cinnamon buns yesterday."

Tania sighed. "My mom will probably be able to tell you how avocados affect sperm count. Just ignore her."

George froze with another loaded chip halfway to this mouth. "She what, now?"

The crowd on the deck dwindled as the evening wound down. Jess took an armful of empty dishes inside and went to use the bathroom.

She was heading back down the hallway when she heard Diana's voice from the kitchen. "Sorry we couldn't make it to your game Sunday. How did it go?"

Tania replied. "We lost. Again."

Something in Tania's voice made Jess's feet stumble to a halt.

Diana clucked in disappointment over the clattering of plates going into the dishwasher.

A wry chuckle from Tania. "Yeah, we're in a rough patch."

Jess's breath caught in her throat. *But we played so well on Sunday. . . .*

More dishes rattling. "Is something wrong between the two of you?"

"No. No, things with Jess are fine. It's . . . She's needed a lot of pep talking lately, you know? It's been . . . kind of tiring."

Diana hummed. "I'm sure you'll be able to help her out of whatever she's going through."

Tania's reply was lost as the sliding door opened and Tania's uncle's voice joined them in the kitchen, hollering back outside at his kids to come help.

Then, before Jess could move, Tania rounded the corner. She slammed on her brakes when she saw Jess.

They stared at each other, eyes wide.

Before Jess could think about it, a question fell out of her mouth. "Do you blame me for losing?"

Tania's eyes got even wider. "What? No. Of course I don't."

"But, I've been . . . I need pep talks?"

Tania shrugged. "Lately, kind of."

Jess's stomach tightened. "Sorry, I didn't know I was dragging you down."

She expected Tania to deny the idea immediately, but there was a long, awkward pause before she replied. "You're not dragging me down, you've just been . . . a bit off."

Now Jess's stomach folded itself right into a knot. "I'm doing my best."

"I know you are, Jess. That's not what I—" Tania rubbed

her forehead. "Can we just forget this? It's fine, okay? I don't even know why I said that to Diana. I guess I was just looking for a reason why we can't fucking buy a win. I don't blame you."

"Okay." Jess felt like she should promise to do better, or something, but she didn't want to make promises she couldn't keep. "We really played great on Sunday. Let's try to build off that."

Tania gave an unconvincing nod. She looked like she had more to say.

"What?"

Tania scratched her ear. "We play Skye on Friday."

Jess's heart jumped. "We do? Already?"

"Yup." Tania studied her, like she was waiting for a freak-out.

Jess willed her heart to slow down and kept her voice even. "Well, that's fine. I can play against her."

Tania had never looked more skeptical. "Great."

"Great." Jess cleared her throat. "It's getting late, we should probably head out soon. Do you know if Diana needs any more help?" She slipped by Tania in the narrow hallway and went to see what she could find to do to keep her hands and mind busy . . . and absolutely definitely not freak out.

A glitch in the schedule meant Jess and Tania had no games Wednesday or Thursday, but played Friday, Saturday, and Sunday instead. Jess worked Wednesday, and kept busy Thursday catching up on laundry, cleaning her apartment—no matter how many times she vacuumed, there was always sand—and, of course, making another batch of banana bread, until by dinnertime she was quite frankly having trouble not thinking about having to face Skye on Friday.

"Hey Jess. It was really nice hanging out with you, but . . ."

"But . . ."

But you're boring. But you're awkward. But you're not pretty enough. But the three orgasms you gave me were just okay.

She had to get out. . . . Out of her head, and out of her apartment.

Maggie's was an easy choice. Live music and a drink or two would help her get out of her head. Jess hadn't talked to Tania since the awkward car ride home on Tuesday, but she told herself not to be weird and just see if Tania was free.

Hey, you want to meet at Maggie's for a bit? Jess set her phone on the bathroom counter and put on a touch of makeup while she waited for a reply.

Tania only took a minute to answer. **Can't tonight. George's sister is over for dinner. But I think Chrissy said a few of them would be there.**

Jess tried not to read anything into the decline. **Okay. See you tomorrow.**

As promised, a bunch of players were at the bar, milling around a few high-top tables near the stage, bobbing their heads to the music—an older woman with a guitar currently singing about her first kiss—and sharing a few baskets of sweet potato fries.

Jess's eyes immediately found Vivienne—like the central figure in a Renaissance painting, her loose hair tickling her clavicles in soft curves, the other girls gathered around her, bathing in her light. Vivienne and Lee had won again today, of course. Vivienne glowed with confidence.

Jess tracked down April and ordered a beer, then headed to join the crew.

Chrissy gave her a hug as soon as she saw her.

"How was your game?" Jess asked. She knew Chrissy and Shay had won their match.

"Oh, good!" Chrissy started to share a few details of their win, but Jess quickly lost focus when Vivienne climbed onto the stage.

The performer smiled as she finished the verse, then she vamped for a bit as she welcomed Vivienne. "What's your name, sweetheart?"

"Vivienne," she purred into the other mic, like she'd been doing this her whole life.

"You ready for the chorus, Vivienne?"

"I'll give it my best!" Vivienne said, the way a star might promise to do its best to twinkle.

Everyone look at me, Jess thought with a bitter sip of her beer. *Perfect Vivienne, gorgeous and put together all the time, and . . . Oh, huge shocker, also an amazing singer?*

"It was our first kiss," they sang together,

It was a slow kiss.
It was a drinking coffee underneath the stars kiss.
It was a soft lips, cool night, hot kiss.
It was a never let me go cause you're my life kiss.

The second time through most of the audience joined in too, Jess's toe tapping all on its own, then the singer took Vivienne's hand and lifted it high while the patrons of Maggie's cheered.

Vivienne was greeted by further applause and whistles when she rejoined the group, flushed and smug.

Jess tried to ignore her.

That got harder when Vivienne propped herself against the high-top next to Jess.

Vivienne leaned over to stage-whisper, giving Jess a healthy glimpse of deepened cleavage. "You know what the secret is to getting up there?"

Jess tried not to roll her eyes. "Picturing everyone naked?" she guessed, the old cliché.

Vivienne scoffed. "Nah. I imagine *I'm* naked."

"You . . ." An image flashed before her eyes of naked Vivienne onstage. She shook her head to clear it. "How does that help?"

Vivienne fanned herself with a coaster. "It gives me confidence, because I look damn good naked."

Jess couldn't help but laugh at the logic, despite herself. She pushed her hair back, and then her heart stuttered.

Her stomach dropped.

Her throat closed.

Because there, across the bar, looking beautiful and glowing in the light from the sunset spilling through the patio doors, was a woman in a gauzy white dress with blue hair.

Skye.

Fuck.

Jess ducked her head out of Skye's eyeline. *Fuck. Fuck. FUCK.* Her heart pounded, cheeks hot.

"What?" Vivienne swiveled her head around. "Who's—Oh, it's Skye." She turned back to look at Jess.

Jess tried to wipe whatever was showing from her expression, but she wasn't fast enough.

Vivienne furrowed her eyebrows for a second, then understanding swept across her face. "Ah. So . . . it didn't end well?"

Jess's cheeks burned. "No. No, it didn't." She fiddled with her drink. "She . . . well, she slept with me and then brushed me off." Her pulse hammered in her temple. She was about to either shrivel up and die or actually explode, it was hard to say which was more likely.

"Shit." Vivienne turned to peek at Skye again, chewing on her lip, then looked back at Jess. "Hey, just breathe. It's okay."

Apparently, Vivienne had realized Jess was panicking before she did. Tears threatened under Jess's eyelids. "We play her tomorrow," she scratched out. How was she supposed to actually face Skye on the court if she couldn't even handle seeing her in a bar?

"Right. Fuck."

Jess risked her own peek over the crowd, then her heart stopped entirely. "Oh my fucking God, she's coming over here."

Skye was locked on them like a tractor beam as she edged through the crowd.

Oh fuck oh fuck oh fuck.

Every cell in Jess's body screamed to run while at the same time was frozen in terror.

Vivienne took Jess's hand.

Jess stared at their interlocked fingers, confused. "What are you—?" Jess's instinct was to yank her hand away but, again . . . frozen.

"Just go with it," Vivienne whispered. She stepped closer and pressed her whole body up against Jess.

"Wha—?" But the rest of that sentence evaporated into the ether when the sensation hit her. Vivienne's warm weight on her torso. Vivienne's breasts swelling under Jess's. Vivienne's sweet vanilla scent filling her nostrils.

Vivienne's deep, dark eyes, only inches from hers, peering deep into her soul. *What the f—*

The corner of Vivienne's mouth lifted. "Is she watching?"

Skye was almost there, gaze determined. "Yes," Jess gasped.

Vivienne shifted even closer, her nose drifting under Jess's jaw. "Lean down so I can whisper sweet nothings in your ear."

A brief pause while Jess's brain lurched into gear. She dipped her head down.

"Close your eyes, like we're about to kiss. . . ." Vivienne's breath ghosted over Jess's cheek. Her hand was an ember, hot on Jess's hip.

Skye arrived. "Hi, Jess."

Forming words was difficult with Vivienne's body—hard and soft in all the right places—still fully pressed against her and her scent permeating the air.

Luckily, Vivienne was up to the task. She responded without even looking in Skye's direction. "Can we help you?"

Jess's eyes met Vivienne's again. They twinkled with delight. She was definitely enjoying fucking with Skye.

"Vivienne, right?" Skye said.

"Do I know you?" Vivienne drawled, in the most uninterested voice possible.

Jess risked a glance at Skye.

The tentative smile on Skye's face flickered. "Are you two . . . together?"

Finally, Vivienne turned the full force of her gaze on Skye.

Skye visibly shrank.

"Are we together?" Vivienne repeated, as if Skye was the dumbest person on Earth. "What do you think?"

Skye folded her arms, but it was defensive, not angry. "Look, I just want to talk to Jess."

Vivienne frowned, lips full and shimmering. Jess wondered if they were as soft as they looked. "Do you want to talk to this person, babe?"

Babe. "Um . . ." Did she want to talk to Skye? No . . . no, she fucking didn't, actually. But was that immature?

Vivienne now had her hands on both of Jess's hips. One of her thumbs started to circle.

Jess looked at Vivienne, trying to read her eyes. If anyone would know what the right call was, it was Vivienne. What would she do?

Jess took a deep breath, Vivienne's weight against her comforting. She looked at Skye. "Thanks, but I'm good."

Skye's face fell. "Yeah. I get it. Good luck tomorrow, I guess." She turned and began to push her way back through the crowd.

"I bet that felt fucking good," Vivienne murmured into her ear.

Jess shivered. It did. It felt really fucking good.

12

Wins: 4
Losses: 15

> ***Float*: A serve hit hard and flat, with no spin. Deceptively difficult to pass when it starts drifting.**

Vivienne peeled herself off of Jess in a sinuous wave, eyes tracking Skye's retreat. The air against her torso where Vivienne's body had been was sharp and cold. Vivienne's hands lingered on Jess's hips for an extra second, gaze flicking back to Jess. "Hope that was okay?"

The noise of the bar was muted around them.

Everything in Jess's brain was still vanilla and soft curves. "Uh, yeah, n—no, that was very . . . helpful."

Vivienne ran her hands over her own hips, straightening her dress. "In my experience, showing someone you've moved on is the best revenge."

"Yeah, I . . . Thanks." Jess licked her drying lips.

Vivienne waved her hand. "It was no problem. Kind of fun, actually."

Jess nodded, grateful the dim bar lighting disguised her flaming cheeks. She searched for something else to say and came up painfully short.

Right before the pause got awkward, Lee appeared with a tray of shots. "What's going on over here?" she asked, eyebrow raised.

Vivienne took a glass. "Just putting a Horny Beach in her place."

Lee lifted a shot, too. "Cheers to that."

"You having one?" Vivienne asked Jess.

Jess's gaze bounced around—the glimmering butterscotch liquid, Vivienne's expectant look, Lee's amused eyebrow . . . Vivienne's parted lips . . . "Nah." Jess shook her head. "Big game tomorrow."

"Fair enough. You're gonna fucking crush her, by the way." Vivienne toasted her.

Lee moved on with the tray and Chrissy appeared to exclaim over Vivienne's singing. Jess sipped her beer and forgot all about Skye.

"This is the best ponytail I have ever done," Jess muttered to her reflection, turning her head from side to side. Not a bump to be seen.

Tania's reflection appeared in the mirror. "Look at you, all ready to go."

Jess gave her hair one final pat. "I got here early." Her eyes had snapped open well before her alarm that morning, and she just felt . . . ready. She turned to face her partner. "How are you?"

"Fine. You?"

"Great."

Tania raised an eyebrow.

"I mean it," Jess insisted. "I'm great."

"You're not . . . nervous about seeing Skye?"

"Nope." Jess collected her bag from the bench and headed out the locker-room door whistling.

Tania scurried after her. "Nope?"

"Saw her last night, actually."

"You did? At Maggie's?"

"Yup."

"Did you . . . ? Jess!" Tania halted.

Jess paused and turned around. "What?"

"Would you stop for a second and tell me what happened! Did you talk to her?"

"Very briefly. Vivienne talked to her more, actually."

"Vivienne?"

Jess patted Tania's arm. "You don't need to worry about it. I'm good." She turned on her heel and continued her whistling all the way to their bench.

Tania followed her, sputtering.

Jess and Tania hit the court the instant their warm-up time began, but Skye's side was still empty. They were well into the hitting warm-up before Jess even noticed Skye had arrived. A brief twinge fluttered in her stomach, then she heard Vivienne's voice. *Can we help you?* Jess's lips twitched in a small smile.

Tania continued to flash her concerned glances, particularly as Jess and Skye shook hands before the match.

"Good luck," Jess said, meeting Skye's gaze straight on.

"Good luck," Skye replied. She looked away first.

Jess turned and slapped Tania's hands. "Let's fucking go."

Skye had first serve. She avoided eye contact as she readied herself at the back line.

Jess smiled.

Skye popped in an easy float that drifted right toward Jess. She gave Tania a great pass, then loaded up to crank a hit to the far deep corner. Skye dove for it but couldn't get there.

Point. Jess's smile grew. She scored two more points off her serve, then they sided out right away after Skye's partner missed her serve. They were up 8–2 when Skye called a time-out.

"Good start," Tania said before taking a drink.

"Mm-hmm," Jess agreed, her gaze wandering over the crowd. Lots of Tania's family were there, as usual, then Vivienne caught her eye. She held up heart hands and blew a kiss. Jess tried to control her grin before she took another gulp of water.

"What?"

"Nothing. Let's fucking crush them."

And they did. They won the first set 21–11, and the second 21–8.

Every cell in her body crackled with fire. She hadn't played a match that easy since, well, ever.

She shook hands with Skye feeling like she was Julia Roberts in *Pretty Woman*.

"Good game, Jess," Skye said with a small smile.

Big mistake. Jess smiled back. "Good game."

Once they were back in the locker room, Tania blinked at her. "Jesus. I have to be honest, I thought you'd be really rattled playing against Skye, but that was fucking lights-out volleyball."

Jess replied with two words she never thought she'd say together. "Vivienne helped."

"Vivienne? . . . Are you guys friends now?"

"No," Jess said quickly. "Not really."

"Not really? Sounds like a thaw to me."

Jess shrugged as she peeled off her uniform. "I guess she's not so bad. When she wants to be. I still think she has a huge head."

"Well, whatever Vivienne did . . . hopefully you can keep it rolling this weekend."

Jess hoped so, too.

They won Saturday too, in three sets. They lost Sunday, but it was another close one, a long, tight match. When she got home that night, Jess dropped a shell into her "loss" jar and sank into her tub, happy and tired. In a broader sense, going 2–1 on the weekend wasn't anything to write home about, but she felt better about volleyball than she had in a long time. Who knew getting brutally brushed off was the key to kick-starting her game? Well, that, and saving some major face, thanks to Vivienne.

Speaking of Vivienne, the bananas on the counter looked ready for baking.

"Open up. Take it!" Jess carefully placed an envelope in Fleming's mouth. "Good boy. Stay." She straightened Fleming's bow tie, knocked on Nelson's door, and scurried back to her apartment.

His door opened. There was a pause, then, "Oh, hello Mr. Fleming, sir. Fly bow tie, my man. What do you have there?" Another pause, then the sound of an envelope tearing. Nelson cleared his throat. "Fleming Buttercup Brandybuck of House McLaughlin, First of His Name, King of Apartment 202, the Growler, Lover of Stuffies, Cutest of Wieners, requests the honor of your presence. . . ." Nelson started to laugh and called toward Jess's door. "Yes, I can come for dinner tomorrow. You're too fucking adorable."

Jess popped her head out of her door. Nelson was holding Fleming and scratching under his chin.

"Does five work?" she asked.

"Dress code?"

"Fabulous."

"Girl." Nelson tossed an imaginary boa around his neck. "On it."

The next day, there was a sharp rap on Jess's door at five o'clock on the nose.

Nelson was decked out in shiny black thigh-high boots that disappeared under flowy black shorts and a loose white tank with a black double-breasted blazer. Purple eyeshadow and a top hat completed the look.

Jess kissed his cheek. "Even more fabulous than I could possibly have imagined."

Nelson whistled at Jess. "And what are you wearing? Give me a turn."

"Oh, this old thing?" Jess wore the one fancy dress she had, a short red sequined number. She bought it on clearance a while back, the last one in the store, and it happened to be in her size.

"Goddamn, your legs go on for about a mile and a half. You need to wear this more often."

"I've actually never worn this anywhere."

Nelson held up his hand. "You what?"

"The clerk talked me into buying it, but then every time I think about wearing it, I chicken out. It's too fancy."

Nelson shook his head. "Wear it to fucking McDonald's, look at you."

Jess flushed and accepted the bottle of sparkling wine and bouquet of daisies he carried. "I hope you're hungry. I made way too much."

Nelson scooped up Fleming, who was dancing around his feet demanding attention. "I am, in fact, famished. Let me at it."

Jess had spent most of her day off prepping dinner—honey Dijon chicken, her own homemade sauce, and a giant cucumber-avocado salad with crispy rice—plus chocolate–peanut butter squares for dessert. Simple, but delicious.

Once they had tucked in, Jess asked how things were going with Nelson's latest "gentleman caller."

"Not such a gentleman in bed last night, let me tell you."

Jess laughed. "Good for you."

Nelson took a pointed sip of his wine. "But what about you, miss?"

Jess shrugged and cut a piece of chicken. "Nothing to report, as usual."

"Nothing?"

"Nothing since Skye. . . . I played her on Friday, though, and beat her." Jess told him the whole story about running into Skye at the bar the night before the game and Vivienne saving her from a public and humiliating panic attack.

Nelson leaned back in his chair and raised an eyebrow. "I have to say . . . Vivienne's name sure comes up a lot."

"No, it doesn't."

"Please, she's all you talk about."

"I . . . What! No, I don't, I—"

Nelson snickered. "I might be just pushing your button a bit." He pointed his fork at her. "And you do have a Vivienne button."

Jess glowered. Thank God he didn't know about the banana bread. "I take back the dinner invite."

"Hmm." Nelson stuffed another forkful of salad into his mouth. "I'll say it again . . . You do you . . . but Vivienne . . . There might be a *reason* her name keeps coming up."

Jess served him another scoop of salad, ignoring the heat in her face, and changed the subject.

Like the good friend he was, Nelson let her.

They had the late game on Wednesday. Jess worked an early shift, then went home to shower and eat before heading back to the pavilion to watch the match before hers. Vivienne and Lee were playing Chrissy and Shay. Jess sat low down in the stands, near the entrance, so she could slip out when it was time for her to get ready.

Her eyes stayed on Vivienne throughout the match. So strong, so smooth . . . muscles rippling under glowing skin. Vivienne ran a ball down like a gazelle and brought it back into the court, the easiest thing in the world. She allowed Lee to give her an exuberant butt smack before she crushed a gorgeous jump serve. The usual irritation flared up Jess's throat when she thought about Vivienne, but . . . this time it was a bit different. Because "irritation" was the wrong word. It was . . . jealousy.

Wait . . . I'm . . . jealous of Vivienne?

Jess had been a quiet kid, labeled "Teacher's Pet" for most of her school career, with distant parents who didn't seem to mind that she spent more time with private tutors and volleyball coaches than with them. Always gawky, she was tall enough that she had made every volleyball team she'd tried out for, but her awkward frame hadn't always cooperated as she grew. She saw the eye rolls from the other girls when she didn't get to a ball fast enough, or touched the net on an unbalanced block jump. Girls she had never really fit in with. Girls she had always been jealous of—smaller, faster, more graceful . . . and conventionally pretty . . . like Vivienne.

An idea smacked Jess in the face as she watched Vivienne now. It wasn't just that Vivienne reminded her of Phoenix, the first person to break her heart. . . . Was she lumping Vivienne in with the girls she hadn't really fit in with? Was she just stewing in jealousy over how perfect Vivienne was, both on and off the court?

Was she being unfair to Vivienne this whole time?

Vivienne scored another point with a cleverly placed roll shot to win the first set.

Maybe she *was* being unfair.

Jess sat with that idea as the second set began. Once it was clear that Vivienne and Lee were going to win that one too, Jess headed for the locker room to get ready.

When she and Tania came out and headed for their bench, Vivienne didn't see her, just breezed right by and went to sign autographs for the kids who were hanging around.

"Vivienne, I love you!" one teenage girl cried, eyes practically heart-shaped. "Will you sign my ball?"

"Vivienne, you are so amazing!" her friend squealed. "We love you so much!"

Jess shook her head. Yes, maybe it was unfair of her to lump Vivienne in with the mean girls she'd encountered on every team she'd played on. And maybe she was just choking on jealousy. But . . . Vivienne lived in a different world. It was important to remember that.

Jess had a tight schedule on Saturday. She had an early afternoon game and an eight-hour shift right after. In fact, she was glad they had lost in two, or else she would have been late for work.

It was a busy day for the SoCal VL—lots of matches that day on all three courts, and the locker room was humming with the athletes milling around and chatting. Jess was just pulling on her shorts when her phone rang. It was Nelson.

"Hello?" Jess said, heart jumping, imagining bad news about Fleming.

"Hey, hon. Don't worry, Fleming is fine, but I got called into work. Big emergency, server meltdown, screaming CEOs, I won't bother you with the details. I had to leave Fleming in your apartment and head to the office. I took him for a quick walk and put out some food but I'll probably be gone for hours, maybe even the night."

"Okay, no worries. I'll figure it out. Good luck with the servers!" Jess hung up and put her hands on her hips. "Shit."

"What?" Tania asked, toweling her hair.

"Nelson had to leave for the office and I have an eight-hour shift starting in, like, twelve minutes. Is there any chance you'd be able to swing by and let Fleming out tonight?"

"Oh, sorry, wish I could help. George and I are heading straight to his niece's ballet recital, then to a big family dinner."

Argh. Who else could she ask? Chrissy, maybe.

"I'll do it." It was Vivienne, with wet hair, emerging from the crowd in a sundress.

"Um. Thanks, but that's . . ."

"That's what? I don't mind helping."

"It's too much to ask."

Vivienne rolled her eyes. "You didn't ask, I volunteered. I can go check on your dog. It's not a big deal. I don't have any plans today."

"Okay. Um. Thank you." Jess dug in her bag for her key. "Apartment 202. Can you head over around dinnertime and take him for a walk and give him a scoop of kibble? And, actually, you know what? You can grab your banana bread off the counter."

Vivienne's mouth twitched right as Lee walked by and clapped Jess on the shoulder.

"Jess!" Lee said. "Your banana bread is delicious. Thanks so much."

"Oh, er, you're welcome," Jess said to Lee's back as she continued on her way by, then she added a few more instructions as Vivienne nodded.

"Don't worry, I'll figure it out."

"Okay. Thanks. Thanks so much."

Jess hurried down the boardwalk, but her feet almost lurched to a halt when a thought occurred to her. *Fuck. Did I leave underwear on the floor?*

At just after seven a text arrived from Vivienne. A selfie of her and Fleming with the sunset behind them. Fleming's tongue was out in a doggy grin and Vivienne's hair was blowing over her sunglasses. She was smiling, too. It was a cute fucking picture. Jess sent a smiley face back. **Thank you so much! I owe you huge.**

No problem. I adore Fleming. Just let me know if you ever need me again.

I will.

How can I get your key back to you? Want me to swing by your work?

Oh God, no. No, no, no. The last thing she needed was Vivienne seeing her in her orange-and-neon-green travesty of a uniform up close. **No, you don't need to go out of your way. I can come by your place after, although it'll be pretty late.**

Tell you what . . . I'll be at Maggie's. Why don't you stop by when you get off?

After a match and an eight-hour shift, her bed would be calling her hard, but Maggie's seemed like the easiest of the non-uniformed options. **Sure. I'll be there just after eleven.**

When Jess arrived at Maggie's, Vivienne was at their usual table, eyes lit up as she told some tale to a rapt crowd. They burst out laughing as Jess approached. She hesitated, feeling awkward as she intruded.

But Vivienne saw her. "Oh, hey!" She fished the key out of her purse and handed it over. "Fleming is such a darling. And your place is nice."

"Oh, thanks." And hopefully underwear-free. "It's small but I like it."

"Are you going to stay for a drink?" Vivienne asked.

"Nah. Long day. But thanks again."

"Like I said, just let me know if you ever need me. And don't forget—lunch with Veronica next Sunday."

Jess nodded and left Vivienne to her audience.

When she got home, the banana bread was gone, and

she could swear there was a whiff of vanilla in her apartment.

And, yup. A thong lying right in the middle of the floor.

Jess stared into the depths of her locker, dismayed and dripping wet. Like an idiot, she had forgotten to pack clothes to change into after her match.

"You almost ready to go?" Vivienne appeared next to her, looking like a flower fresh from the meadow in a short white sundress covered in daisies, hair floating over her bare shoulders. "Veronica hates waiting."

"I forgot to bring something nicer to wear." Jess had spent the morning in a tizzy of excitement over finally meeting Veronica Doyle and baking banana bread—she was five weeks into paying off their bet, had lost track of how many loaves she had given Vivienne, and was starting to wonder if she could buy bananas wholesale. And in the kerfuffle, had forgotten to bring anything to change into aside from the ratty tank and shorts she wore to the pavilion. "All I have is this." She held up the offending pieces of clothing.

"Oh." Vivienne chewed her bottom lip, teeth white against the rosy pink. "Hmm." She put her hands on her hips and studied Jess, then a lightbulb went off. "Actually, you know what? Hang on . . ." Vivienne opened her locker and started digging. "Yes! I have an extra dress." She held up a bit of gray fabric. "It's not super fancy, but it'll do."

Jess raised a skeptical eyebrow. "Dress? Where's the bottom half?" That scrap of fabric wouldn't even cover her belly button.

Vivienne's mouth curled. "It's long on me. It'll be fine." She tossed it at Jess. "At least try it on. Come on, you don't want to keep Veronica Doyle waiting, do you?"

Aunt Veronica—around fifty, with the same thick, shining black hair, pert nose, and dense lashes as Vivienne—was the most effortlessly glamorous person Jess had ever met. In a tailored red suit-dress, with a designer handbag and sunglasses perched atop her head, she rested her hip against a giant, shiny black SUV in the parking lot, cell phone pressed to her ear. "Immediately no," she was saying as they approached. "*Immediately* no." She saw them and fluttered her fingers. "I have to go, Lina. But please express my extreme and emphatic resistance to his suggestion. I could never . . . Mm-hmm . . . Correct. Okay, talk later." She hung up and stuffed her phone in her purse. "Vivienne, love! Aren't you just as gorgeous as ever? And this must be Jess, the banana bread girl."

Jess swallowed hard with a dry mouth and tugged at the hem of Vivienne's dress that was scandalously short on her, even though Vivienne insisted it was fine, and ignored the fact that her favorite author had just called her "the banana bread girl." "It's so nice to meet you, Mrs. Doyle. I'm a huge fan. I loved *Queen in Shining Armor*. All your books, really. Especially *Constellation Prize.* You're brilliant."

Veronica glanced at Vivienne with a quick look. Cheeks pink, Vivienne looked away. Jess hoped she wasn't embarrassing her too much by fangirling.

"Oh, you are too kind. And please, call me Veronica." Veronica's phone rang from the depths of her purse. She ignored it. "Shall we go?" She opened the back door and waved them in. "It's on me."

"I can't believe I met Veronica Doyle." Jess and Vivienne waved to Veronica's SUV as it pulled out of the pavilion parking lot. "She is so fucking cool." Jess had even made her laugh—laugh!—at the story behind Jess and Vivienne's bet.

Vivienne nodded. "Yeah, she is." She hadn't said much at lunch, letting Jess fangirl out to Veronica's effervescent storytelling.

"Thank you so much for arranging that. Best bet I ever made."

Vivienne shrugged a perfectly tanned shoulder. "It was my pleasure."

Jess struggled to explain how much that lunch had meant to her without spewing her particular brand of awkward all over Vivienne. "I feel like I owe you so much more than banana bread."

"I've actually been meaning to talk to you about that. . . ." Vivienne chewed her lip for a moment. "I don't think you owe me any more banana bread."

A stab of worry that she had done something wrong hit Jess's gut. "What do you mean?"

"It's . . . I think you've more than upheld your end of the bet. You got to meet Veronica, and my freezer is full. Don't get me wrong," Vivienne added hurriedly when Jess's dismay must have shown on her face. "I love it. But you've made me so many loaves. I'm sort of all stocked up for now and . . . you can stop."

So stupid, Jess scolded herself. *Of course it was too much.* "Oh. Okay. Yeah, I guess you won . . . a lot."

Vivienne stepped closer and put her hand on Jess's forearm for a second. "I really love it, though."

"Okay, well . . ." Jess's gaze rested on the spot Vivienne had touched. "If you ever decide you want some more . . ."

Vivienne gave her a small smile. "I know where to find you."

It grew quiet while they stared at each other until Jess bobbed her head. "I guess I'll see you later. Thanks again for lunch."

"Yup, see you later."

Jess gave Vivienne a half wave, and turned to begin her walk home. Her instinct was to be embarrassed about how she had misread the banana bread situation, but Vivienne had been nice enough to smooth it over by assuring her she loved it. And, thanks to Vivienne, she'd just spent two hours living the glamorous lunching life with a famous author. Maybe Vivienne wasn't so bad after all.

Then the realization hit her that she was still wearing Vivienne's dress. "Oh—" She whirled around on the sidewalk. Vivienne was standing exactly where she had been, staring after Jess. Vivienne startled, eyes wide.

"Er . . ." Jess pointed at herself. "Your dress . . . I can go change. . . ."

Vivienne shook her head, cheeks pink and gaze bouncing down to Jess's legs and back. "You know what? Keep it. It looks much better on you."

"Okay, um, thanks. If you're sure . . ."

Vivienne nodded. "Very sure."

Jess waved again and turned to keep walking, wondering if Vivienne's eyes were on her still . . . and wondering why she liked that idea so much.

13

Wins: 10
Losses: 20
Mothers who get their assistants to call instead of picking up the phone themselves: 1

***Hiatus*: A break. I hope.**

Jess's phone rang. The display read MARION'S ASSISTANT.

She sighed and paused her workout to answer, wondering if it would be the same person as last time, or someone new. "Hi, this is Jess."

"Oh, hello. Jessica McLaughlin?"

"That's me."

"This is Trent, Marion McLaughlin's assistant."

Someone new, then. "Hi, Trent. What can I do for you? Or rather, my mom?"

"Your mother asked me to confirm plans for when you're in town later this week."

"I already forwarded my flight and hotel details and the tournament info."

"Yes, I received those, thank you. Your mother also asked if you would like to have dinner with her and your father Thursday night when you arrive."

"Uh . . ." Probably rude to say no. "Sure?"

"Excellent. I'll send you a confirmation. Oh, and your mother requested that I pass on a reminder to wear a dress to dinner."

Jess bit back a few choice swear words. It wasn't Trent's

fault, after all. Poor, unfortunate Trent. She made a vague noise instead. "Thanks, Trent. Talk soon. Buh-bye." She hung up and rubbed her brow. Marion McLaughlin, brilliant and driven, was best in small doses, and, quite frankly, she was still digesting the dose from Christmas.

But it was too late for second thoughts now. At the beginning of every July, the SoCal VL took a two-week hiatus, and most of the teams found a tournament to enter for a chance at some prize money. This year, they were heading to Vancouver, Jess's hometown.

Jess always had mixed feelings about going back to Vancouver. Mainly because her mother was every high-powered corporate lawyer cliché in one—conservative blazers, clacking heels . . . and a ruthless and undying need to be in control of every detail of her life at all times. Jess had much more in common with her dad, Gerard—also brilliant, but in a quiet, thoughtful way. So quiet that, even when they lived in the same house, it felt like they would go weeks without having an actual conversation . . . except on the occasional clear night, when they'd go up to the roof and stargaze with her dad's old telescope. Neither Marion nor Gerard had played volleyball or were even especially tall, although Marion had several towering cousins.

Volleyball had given Jess an anchor in her teenage years—a place to be that wasn't an empty house, a place where people would notice if she was there or not. Her parents never really "got" the volleyball thing, but that was fine. Jess certainly never saw the appeal of drowning in paperwork, pacing the study all night, barking into the phone about contingent liability and adhesion contracts.

And despite feeling iffy about seeing her mom again,

and as much as she loved the California sunshine, nothing gave her a thrill like the view of downtown Vancouver on a clear sunny day, the city skyline dwarfed by the jagged, snow-capped North Shore Mountains jutting into an impossibly blue sky . . . next to the lush green of Stanley Park and deep blue of Burrard Inlet . . . there was no view like it in the world.

So when Winston forwarded information about the True North Invitational, Jess signed up, took a deep breath, and told her mom—or rather, her assistant—she'd be there.

And really, a break from worrying about their league win–loss record sounded good at this point. She'd had a bit of a breakthrough with the Skye match and they had managed to grit out a few more wins in the past couple weeks, but they were still in quite the hole, and it was going to take a lot more than an even record to climb out of it. Maybe the fresh Vancouver air and a few days of fun was just what she needed going into the second half of the season.

When the plane rolled to a stop at YVR, Jess toggled off Airplane Mode, waited for her phone to connect, then sent her mom a text.

Landed.

Welcome, darling! How was the flight?

Fine.

Lovely. We'll see you at the beach tomorrow! Your father and I should be able to make it for your match at five.

Jess could almost smell her mother's perfume swirling around her. **I thought we were having dinner tonight?**

Shoot, sorry, no. Vincent was supposed to contact you.

Who's Vincent?

My new assistant. Between you and me, I'm not sure he's going to work out.

Oh Trent. Good try, buddy. **No, never heard anything from Vincent.**

I'll be sure to speak with him. We're in court this week and it's a disaster. I'm afraid we'll be at work for several more hours. But you keep the reservation. Maybe Tania and another friend will want to join you? I left my card on file. Our treat.

All right. I'll ask. Thanks.

Lovely. See you tomorrow!

Lovely. Jess sighed and turned to Tania. "You want to go to dinner at Fanque's on my parents?"

"What?" Tania did not do well on planes. Face white, she gripped the armrest, even though they were firmly on the ground and, in fact, no longer moving at all.

"My parents bailed on me but I still have a reservation at this fancy steak house downtown. It's near the hotel."

Now Tania took on a shade of green. "Sorry, man. I just want to go to bed."

"Yeah, I figured. I guess I'll cancel it." Jess opened a web browser to look for the restaurant's number.

Chrissy's head popped up from the seat ahead of them. "Did you say Fanque's?"

"Yeah?"

"Oh my God, I've been getting all these ads for Vancouver restaurants and I saw one about Fanque's olive-fed Wagyu steak. It looks *amazing*."

"You want to come with me? My parents are paying."

Chrissy gasped. "For real?"

Vivienne's head appeared in the aisle. "Um . . . how many is the reservation for?"

Jess blinked at her. "Three . . . You want to come?"

"If you're sure your parents don't mind buying me Wagyu steak, count me the fuck in."

Dinner with Vivienne . . . ? "Okay, sure. But one rule. No dresses."

Jess wore dressy shorts, a flattering tank, and flat sandals. Vivienne toyed with the "no dresses" rule in a skirt, but it was hard to be mad at a plunging, lacey white top and a lavender skirt that looked like heaven against her tanned legs.

They met in the lobby and walked the three blocks from their hotel to the restaurant. It was weird that she was suddenly "hanging out" with Vivienne, but Chrissy was the perfect person to have along because she could chatter away about anything, so there were no awkward pauses.

Fanque's was in an old building on Seymour—sandstone with scarlet awnings, and all dark chestnut inside. It was the kind of place where you ordered your steak and sides separately, and the cheapest cut was nearly a hundred dollars.

"Don't be shy," Jess told them as they perused the menus. "Order what you like."

Vivienne's dark eyes flashed with desire. "I cannot decide. I want it all."

"Why don't we try a few different cuts and share?"

Vivienne snapped her menu closed. "Brilliant."

The meal was ridiculously perfect—Wagyu filet mignon, porterhouse, and New York strip, with mushrooms, creamed spinach, and multiple kinds of potatoes.

Jess hadn't been so full in years. "How are we supposed to play tomorrow?" She groaned, patting her stomach. "I ate way too much."

"Worth it, though." Vivienne sighed. "That was good fucking steak. Please thank your parents profusely for me."

"Me t—" Chrissy gasped and clutched Jess's forearm. "Oh my God, you guys! It's Rebekkah de Bex!"

"Who?" Jess and Vivienne said in unison, looking in the direction Chrissy was staring.

"You know! Rebekkah de Bex! She's the star of *Vancouver Vixens: Working Hard for the Money*. That reality show about the rich wives who got nothing in the divorce and had to find jobs?"

"I *don't* know, actually . . ." Jess muttered.

The three of them continued to stare. It was immediately obvious who Rebekkah was—a woman in her forties trying desperately to look twenty-seven in a slinky white dress and a seasonally inappropriate fuzzy fur wrap, fawning over a much older man.

"Looks like working hard wasn't for her," Vivienne said as Rebekkah's loud laugh reached them.

"I have to go talk to her!" Chrissy said. "Will one of you come with me?"

"Uh, no," Jess said.

"*Hell* no," Vivienne added, swirling the wine in her glass.

Chrissy stood and squared her shoulders. "Well, I'm doing it."

Vivienne raised her drink. "Go for it."

They watched Chrissy slink over, giving encouraging waves when she hesitated and shot them a nervous look.

She paused at the table and waited until Rebekkah looked up at her. Whatever Chrissy said was the right thing, because Rebekkah's face lit up with a dazzling smile. She pulled a chair out and invited Chrissy to sit down.

Chrissy threw them a delighted grin. Jess and Vivienne

toasted her, then turned back to the table, chuckling to themselves.

"I guess Chrissy's made a friend," Vivienne said.

They smiled as a silence fell over the table. Jess missed Chrissy already. She cleared her throat. "So. Is this your first time in Vancouver?"

"Yup. Yours?"

"Uh, no. I grew up here."

"You did? Wait . . . are you *Canadian*?"

Jess had to laugh at the wonder Vivienne managed to imbue in one word. "I have dual citizenship."

"So your family still lives here then?"

"My parents do, yup. They are, in fact, not far from us right now. Their law firm is just down the street—McLaughlin and McLaughlin." Vivienne made a face and Jess had to huff a laugh. "I know, it doesn't really roll off the tongue, does it?"

"Why couldn't they come for dinner?"

Jess shrugged. "Busy with work."

"Hmm." Vivienne splashed the remainder of the wine into their glasses. "When's the last time you saw them?"

Jess turned to see how Chrissy was doing. The older gentleman poured her a glass of champagne while the three of them laughed uproariously. "I went to visit at Christmas."

"They're going to come watch you play at least, right?"

"My mom said they'd make it to my match tomorrow, but . . . we'll see. Cancelling dinner plans and missing my games is nothing new for them." And even though she was used to it, even though she was a full-grown adult . . . it still stung.

Vivienne nodded thoughtfully and swirled her glass some more.

"Do you see your family much?" Jess asked. "Where do they live?"

"Not much. They're still in New York, mostly. But my mom is actually from LA, so her family is here, and my sister, Scarlett, ended up moving out here, too."

"Is Veronica Doyle your mom's sister?"

"Yup, older."

Maybe it was the wine, but Jess had to poke. "It seems like you and Veronica Doyle are pretty close."

Vivienne cranked her eyebrow. "Okay, first of all, please just call her Veronica."

Jess flushed. "Right. Sorry."

Vivienne sipped her wine. "I've always felt a connection to her. She dedicated one of her books to me."

"She did?" Jess's eyes bulged. "No way! Which one?"

"Uh . . ." Vivienne bit her lip. "It's one of her early ones. . . ."

"*Constellation Prize*?"

Vivienne nodded, impressed. "Yes, that was it."

Rebekkah's shrill laugh reached them again. They turned to look. Rebekkah rubbed Chrissy's arm, and the man's hand had vanished under the table.

"Oh, fuck." Vivienne laughed her low, breathy laugh, then tossed back the rest of her wine. "I think an extraction is required."

Jess nodded and polished off her wine, too. "I'll get the bill, you get Chrissy."

Vivienne blew out a breath. "No problem." She swayed over, hips turned up to full power. Jess turned to find their server, confident that whatever Vivienne set her mind to, she would do.

Sure enough, by the time Jess was signing for her parents' card, Vivienne was steering Chrissy toward the door.

"Thanks," Chrissy said. "I didn't know how to get out of there! I didn't think she'd be quite so . . . friendly."

Vivienne patted Chrissy's arm. "I got you. You're too adorable for your own good."

Something twinged in Jess's chest. Something like . . . jealousy? That was weird. . . . Was she jealous of Chrissy, too? Fortunately, the feeling eased when Vivienne let go of Chrissy's arm.

Wait . . . what?

"Jess?" Vivienne's voice intruded.

Jess startled out of her thoughts. "Sorry?"

"I said, anytime your parents bail on you for dinner, I'm there."

"Right. Yeah, for sure."

Vivienne bumped her with her hip. "I guess we should get to bed? When is your first match tomorrow, Chrissy?"

They chatted about the tournament and potential competition for the short walk back to the hotel. The air had cooled more than they were used to, but it was still a pleasant July evening for strolling along a bustling sidewalk under twinkling city lights.

Back at the hotel, Chrissy hugged them both in the elevator. Her floor was first. "Thank you again so much, Jess! Good night!" she cried, waving at them as the doors closed.

Jess's floor was next. "Drink some water," Vivienne said, "and get some good sleep."

The idea of a hug flitted through Jess's brain—Chrissy had hugged them both, after all, although Chrissy was a certified hugger—but in the time it took to consider the idea, it was too late. The doors would close again in a second. Jess locked her gaze onto Vivienne's. Her stomach jumped. "I will. You too."

Vivienne fluttered her fingers as the doors slid shut, lips curled in a soft smile.

The hallway spun around Jess for a brief moment as she stared at the closed elevator. *What the fuck.*

Too much wine.

Jess dug out her key and tiptoed into her room, careful not to disturb Tania's sleeping form as she got ready for bed. She chugged the rest of her water, then filled up her bottle again before she slid under her covers.

Images from the evening replayed behind her eyes. Vivienne's long, graceful arm reaching for the wine. The tilt of Vivienne's head sending her shining hair sliding over her collarbones. Her mouth closing over her fork . . .

Despite Tania's long, even breaths, Jess couldn't sleep. She grabbed her phone and searched for Vivienne's dedication in *Constellation Prize*. It read, *To my beautiful Vivienne—Never be afraid of the dark. Your truth is in the stars.*

The tournament was at Spanish Banks, a long, sandy beach on English Bay, the North Shore Mountains still doing their majestic thing in the background.

Match play didn't start until Friday afternoon, giving teams a chance to travel that morning. Chrissy and Shay had the first game at one, so the rest of the Sunside teams gathered to watch. The atmosphere was relaxed, with lots of good-natured ribbing and catcalling as they warmed up.

Chrissy and Shay made quick work of a local team, then

the crew stayed to watch the match after, cheering on a Northern California team against one from Texas.

When the first set was over, Jess hopped up and brushed the sand off her shorts. "I'm heading to the concession. Anyone want anything?"

"A Gatorade?" Tania asked. "And . . . see if they have a fruit cup or something?"

"You got it." Jess fell into step with Vivienne, who appeared to also be heading to the concession.

"Have a good sleep?" Jess asked. "Or did you hear all those sirens at two AM?"

"Ugh," Vivienne groaned. "Yeah, it was brutal. I could not fall back asleep. Although that might also have had something to do with the eight pounds of steak I ate."

Jess laughed. "Might have." They got in line at one of the concession trucks offering smoothies. Jess ordered a pineapple mango protein smoothie for herself, and a fruit cup and Gatorade for Tania.

Vivienne ordered blueberry banana. "Don't mix our drinks up," she said as they shuffled over to the pickup counter. "I'm allergic to pineapple."

"You are? I didn't know that."

"How would you?" Vivienne said. There was an odd note to her voice.

Jess glanced at her but Vivienne was still studying the menu board through her big sunglasses. "Right. Well, I'll be careful."

Vivienne and Lee played next. When it was their turn to warm up, Vivienne peeled off her tank dress and tossed it onto her bag.

Jess's stomach twisted. Goddamn. The word "goddess"

came to mind. Strong limbs, glowing skin, confident stance, laughing at something Lee said as she pulled her hair back into a perfect ponytail. Jess imagined every person on the beach stopping to admire her, and Vivienne knowing it was happening and soaking in every last drop of the attention.

Jess looked away, slurping the last of her smoothie, cheeks hot in the sunshine. Yes, Vivienne was objectively beautiful, no question about that. It was only natural Jess would admire her.

But the pull Jess was feeling . . . the way her chest tightened a little when Vivienne looked at her, the humming in Jess's veins when Vivienne was near. . . . That was something else entirely. Something she wasn't quite ready to think about yet.

14

Wins/Losses: On hiatus

> ***Roof*: See "stuff block," but also makes for a fun word to cheer.**

Vivienne and Lee handled the team from Toronto, no problem.

Vivienne was as in-the-zone as ever, jaw set and determined, eyes narrowed and focused. She and Lee had a quick word at a time-out, sand shading Vivienne's left butt cheek and extending down her thigh. Jess's hand twitched at the idea of wiping it off.

The Sunside crew hooted and hollered at every point, and it wasn't long until Jess noticed a few more rowdy spectators had gathered around the court. She wasn't the only one appreciating Vivienne's . . . form. Even the ref seemed to be getting into it—he totally stole a second glance at Vivienne's ass when she bent over to brush off her shins.

Tania startled Jess when she leaned over to talk into her ear. "They're probably going to win this whole tournament."

"Oh—Yeah." Vivienne crushed a kill right through the hapless blocker's hands. "Probably."

When it was almost time for their match, Jess and Tania waded through the sea of nets and sweaty bodies until they found the right court. Jess scanned the rows toward the parking lot. Still no sign of her parents. For half a second, she thought about texting them, but what was the point? They were either already on their way, or they weren't.

After their warm-up, the ref blew her whistle to start the match. One last look around. Still no parents.

Their opponents were local, young, and, quite frankly, looked a little bit terrified to be playing a team from the storied SoCal VL.

They shook hands—Jess tried not to grin at their wide eyes—then she and Tania huddled briefly.

Tania tightened her ponytail. "We're not going easy on them."

"I know."

"Don't feel sorry for them. They entered this division knowing the caliber of teams they'd have to play."

"I know."

Tania slapped Jess's hands. "Let's do this, Button."

The kids had a lot of trouble with Jess's jump serve. They were losing by seven points when they called a time-out, but it didn't help much. Jess and Tania won the set 21–5. The Sunside players that had gathered whistled while Jess and Tania went to grab some water.

And there was Jess's mom waiting at the sideline . . . in heels. At the beach.

"Oh—Hi, Mom."

"Darling! How are you?" Marion kissed her cheek. "It's awfully hot today, isn't it?"

Jess had actually found the day refreshing compared to Southern California in July, plus it was not nearly so humid, but her mom wasn't exactly beach-ready in a pencil skirt and blazer, so she agreed. "Mm-hmm. Glad you could make it. Where's Dad?"

"Parking. He'll be here in a minute."

Vivienne stood up from where the Sunside crew had gathered and inched over to Jess and Marion. "Hi," Vivienne said, extending her hand. "You must be Jess's mom."

Jess's manners kicked in. "Mom, this is Vivienne. Vivienne, this is my mom, Marion."

Vivienne shook her hand like they were securing a million-dollar deal. "It's nice to meet you, Marion. I wanted to thank you for dinner last night."

"Oh, did you get to go with Jessica?" Marion reclaimed her hand. "How nice."

"Yes, it was lucky for me that you were too busy." Vivienne was smiling perfectly politely, but the context was clear. *Your daughter came all the way from California . . . and you bailed on her.*

Marion's smile faltered for a half a second while Jess tried to keep her expression neutral.

"Yes, well . . . we were in court . . ." Marion trailed off, which was notable because Marion always finished her sentences.

Vivienne turned her smile up a notch to dazzling. "But you made it to Jess's court. That's great."

Jess covered her snort with a cough while a thrill swirled in her stomach.

Marion narrowed her eyes slightly and tried to smile back. "Indeed."

"Well . . . I'll let you two visit. Again, so nice to meet Jess's family." Vivienne waggled her fingers and exited gracefully.

The ref blew her whistle.

"Okay . . ." Jess tore her gaze from Vivienne and looked at her mom again. "Um, I've gotta go play the second set."

"Yes, of course. Good luck."

Jess jogged back to Tania, who was waiting on the court.

"How's Marion?" Tania asked.

"Oh, you know. The same."

"Nice pumps."

"Yup."

They started the second set with Jess absolutely roofing the other hitter for a point. The Sunside spectators howled. She couldn't help but look at her mom, who applauded politely. Her dad was there a few points later. Gerard had at least removed his jacket and tie and rolled up his sleeves. He was even carrying his dress shoes and socks in one hand.

Jess and Tania didn't let up and they won the second set 21–6.

"Good game," Jess said, shaking their opponents' hands.

"Not really," one of them replied with a laugh.

"You guys did fine," Jess said. "Just keep at it."

They thanked her, then Jess packed up her stuff and told Tania she was going to go say hi to her parents. She went to join them at the end of the court. Beads of sweat shone daintily in Marion's hairline.

Gerard held out his arms. "Hello, Star Girl."

"Hi, Dad." She smiled at the childhood nickname and hugged him a little longer than she normally would have, melting into his familiar scent of old books and aftershave.

"Great game," Gerard said. "You crushed them."

Jess shrugged. "They're young. That'll probably be our easiest match."

"Still. Great blocks."

"Yes, well done," Marion chimed in. "You've improved since we last saw you play."

Well, yeah, it's been two years, Jess wanted to say. Instead she just nodded. "How'd court go today?"

Marion sighed and lifted a foot, tsking at the sand stuck to the heel of her shoe. "Not our best day. We have a lot of work to do this weekend."

"That's too bad."

"Mmm." Marion examined her other shoe. "We should probably get back. Everyone will be waiting for us." She patted her husband's arm. "Go get the car, Gerard."

"But you just got here," Jess blurted. "I've only had a chance to say two words to Dad."

Marion twisted her mouth into a patronizing frown. "We can't let our team down. Just like you wouldn't want to let Tania down out there."

Jess nearly rolled her eyes right out of her head, but managed to bite back a sarcastic *Thanks for explaining teamwork to me.*

Gerard gave Jess a small smile. "Bye, Star Girl. Take care."

"You too, Dad."

He hugged her again and turned to trudge back to the parking lot.

"So . . ." Marion said after a small but awkward pause. "You're halfway through the season now, is that correct?"

"Yup."

"And how are things going?"

"We're ten and twenty." Jess shrugged. "Not great, but

we're coming out of a rough patch. Not sure we'll make playoffs, though."

"I'm sure you'll figure it out, darling."

If only that sentiment came from Marion's belief in her abilities, and not her desire to wrap up the conversation. "Well . . . I should go. There's a shuttle back to the hotel leaving in a couple minutes."

Marion gave her a brisk smile. "It was lovely to see you. Congratulations again on winning your match."

Jess hesitated a moment before asking, "Do you think you'll make it to any other games this weekend?"

A furrow appeared between Marion's immaculate brows. "I would love to, but we have a rebuttal witness we need to depose tomorrow."

Jess nodded. "Right." This was not the least bit surprising.

"We'll try. Do let me know how your schedule develops."

"I will."

"And maybe you'll make it back up here before Christmas?"

"I'm pretty busy until the end of the season. But you guys can always come visit?" They hadn't made it to a SoCal VL game since early in her first year, but she kept repeating her invitation, even if it would never be acted upon.

"Perhaps we can see how the fall shapes up." Marion kissed her cheek. "Oh—I suppose we could give you a ride back to your hotel? We're heading that way."

Jess gestured at the Sunside crowd that had gathered, waiting for her. Not technically a team, but it felt like one. "Thanks. I'll go with them."

"Of course. We'll talk soon, darling."

"Bye, Mom." Jess turned and headed back to the group.

Vivienne saw her approaching and raised an eyebrow. "Families, am I right?"

They watched Marion pick her way to the parking lot. She flinched when a ball bounced past her.

Jess sighed. "Yup."

"Fleming . . . Fleming! Come say hi to Mommy."

Fleming's adorable face filled her screen.

"Hi, baby," Jess cooed. "How's my special guy?"

"He's good," Nelson supplied from the background. "Pissed off a Siamese on our walk and barked at Mrs. Horowitz, so, you know. The usual."

"That's my boy."

Nelson scooped up Fleming and held him so Jess could see both of them now. "How did your match go?"

"Good! We won."

"That's what I like to hear."

"And how are you?"

"Oh, fine. This little wiener keeps me good company."

"The only wiener I've ever loved."

Nelson snorted. "I cannot say the same."

A text from Chrissy popped up on the screen. **Time to go!!!!**

"I've gotta run," Jess said. "We're heading to the tournament social."

Nelson blew her a kiss. "Have fun. Don't be too well-behaved. See if you can get some."

"Right." Jess rolled her eyes, blew a kiss back, then hung up and eyed Tania, sprawled on her bed in her underwear. "Are you sure you don't want to come?"

Tania rolled over to reply. "Nah. I'm gonna ice my shoulder and call George."

"Okay. Have fun. Don't wait up."

"I never do."

It had been a long time since Jess had seen so many gorgeous women in one place. The club hosting the social was packed with all types—tall, short, butch, femme, and everyone in between. The room hummed with energy, all eyes bright and roaming.

"Let's get drinks!" Chrissy yelled into Jess's ear over the thumping lesbian pop music. She took her hand and pulled her into the crowd toward one of the bars.

Chrissy bought the first round of the tournament's signature cocktail, a cosmo-ball-iton, and, since they were already there, to save time, Lee bought the next and carried the tray with them to a high-top table.

The drinks went down smoothly as Jess watched her crew banter and talk shit about the day's matches.

Jess was into her second drink when a tall woman with short hair and a muscular frame—undoubtedly a volleyball player—ambled up and leaned on the table next to her. "Hey. I saw you playing today." She had a Quebecois accent.

Jess's eyebrows climbed as she resisted the urge to look around and see who else she might be talking to. "Me?"

"Yes, you. You played great." The woman's intense gray-blue eyes studied her over the rim of her beer bottle as she took a sip.

"Oh." Jess admired the woman's biceps. "Thanks."

"I'm Justine."

"Jess."

"Where are you from, Jess?"

"Sunside, California. Between San Francisco and LA. You?"

"Ah, the SoCal VL, eh? Nice. I'm from Trois-Rivières, Quebec league."

Jess nodded and sipped her cosmo-ball-iton. She nearly choked on it when Justine leaned closer and murmured in her ear, "You want to get out of here? My hotel is not far and I have my own room."

The offer made her heart jump and cheeks flush . . . and think about Skye. Jess blinked as she cleared her throat. "Wow. Um." She looked over at her crew. Lee was doing an impression of their ref from today, drooling over Vivienne, much to Vivienne's amusement. Chrissy, who might have done some pre-drinking in her hotel room, had her arms around Shay and Billi and was loudly declaring her love for them. "I think I'm going to stay with my friends. But thanks."

Justine shrugged and smiled, giving Jess a toast with her beer. "Your loss."

Jess took another drink, pulse still thrumming, as Justine moved on through the crowd.

Chrissy tripped over. "And you!" she cried, throwing her arm around Jess's shoulders. "I love you, Jess!"

"I love you too, Chrissy."

Vivienne suddenly made eye contact with Jess and gave an affectionate eye roll at Chrissy's drunken confessions.

Jess smiled back, pretty sure Justine was wrong. No, she didn't think it was a loss to stay here.

Saturday morning came with a few regrets about the night before. Tania had already gone down for breakfast when Jess cracked her eyes open. She jumped in the shower, then hit the breakfast bar by the lobby to grab some oatmeal and coffee on the way out, which helped. The shuttle ride to the beach was a quiet affair, since most of the athletes had had a late night at the social and were hiding behind their sunglasses, sipping coffee and downing ibuprofen.

Admittedly, the first match started slow for Jess. It took her a few points to clear her head, giving the other team the advantage they needed. Jess and Tania lost the first set, but they recovered and won the match in three. Unfortunately, their next game followed right after. It was hotter than the day before, the sand burning Jess's feet as they slogged to the next court.

"You okay?" Tania asked when Jess sat down next to the court to crack open a Gatorade.

"Yeah, just tired."

"I'll bet."

Their next opponent was easily the strongest team in their pool, besides them . . . maybe. On a good day.

Today was not a good day. They lost the match in three long, intense sets.

Fortunately, their record was good enough to finish second in the pool and make the top flight for playoffs the next day.

They went to watch Chrissy's next match, and then Vivienne and Lee's, who had, of course, won all of their games.

Once the pool play was wrapped up for the day, they all trooped back onto the shuttle.

"Do you guys want to grab some dinner?" Vivienne asked the group as she examined her nails, frowning at a chip. They were a pearl color now.

Jess agreed, along with Tania, Lee, and Chrissy.

"Where's good?" Vivienne asked.

Jess realized the question was directed at her. "Um, the Orca Club isn't far. They'll probably have the PVL game on."

"Sounds great."

The Orca Club was packed and the PVL game was indeed on—Bianca Collazo dove for a ball across twenty huge television screens. And, somehow, even in July, the Canadians had found a hockey game to air on the other screens.

The host made a show of swiping a tablet as they waited by the entrance. "It'll be about a thirty-minute wait, unless you can grab a seat at the bar. . . ." They craned their neck to look. "Actually, five spots just opened up if you want to wait for your table there."

It was a tight fit for the five of them. Somehow Jess ended up on the end of the row next to Vivienne, their knees bumping together and a hint of vanilla in the air.

They ordered drinks—a Corona for Jess—and cheered for Bianca tearing around the court. Tania had actually played against her—Tania's first year in the league was Bianca's last before the pro league—and she never missed watching any of Bianca's games.

Jess's phone buzzed. A text from MARION'S ASSISTANT.

No, she didn't. . . . She read the message. **Your mother asked me to let you know that unfortunately they will not be able to attend—**

Jess swiped the window closed and set her phone on the bar. She bit her lip, somehow both shocked and not at all that Marion had her assistant send that message.

As if she had read her mind, Vivienne suddenly leaned forward and studied Jess over their drinks. "So. Tell me more about your family. No brothers or sisters?"

Jess blinked and gripped her beer bottle. "Nope. It's

just me. And there's not much to tell. My parents were . . . are . . . busy. I'm used to them not being around." She took a long pull of her Corona.

"I'm sorry." Vivienne said it quietly, words almost lost amidst the bar noise, but her expression spoke loud enough.

"It's fine. I mean . . . it's hard to complain when I know a lot of kids were worse off than me."

"No." Vivienne lifted her hand like she was going to put it on Jess's arm, but she rested it on the bar again. "You don't need to compare your experiences to anyone else's. It must have been hard having absent parents."

Jess's throat tightened too much to speak, so she just nodded and drained the rest of her beer. She hardly ever talked about her parents—they just weren't a part of her day-to-day life—and it felt a little strange to be sharing more with Vivienne, of all people. But she had handled Marion McLaughlin with ease, and was now continuing to show interest in Jess's family.

"Could I get another Corona, please?" Jess asked the bartender.

"Make it two," Vivienne added. She studied Jess again. "That sort of explains it."

"Explains what?"

"Why you are how you are."

Vivienne said it playfully, but her gaze pierced Jess's soul. She tried not to shiver and wished her new drink would arrive. "And how am I?" Jess dared to ask.

Vivienne shrugged and finished her cocktail. "A hard shell over a marshmallow center."

Jess was horrified to feel the temperature of her face climbing. "What about you?" she asked, desperate to change the subject. "Is your family close?"

Vivienne blew out a breath. "Growing up, I would say too close, if anything. Always someone in your business, offering their opinions. We don't talk as much now. Everyone's pretty busy."

"You said you had a sister . . . Scarlett?"

"Yup. And a brother, both older." Her face pinched for a moment. "I'm the baby. And they never let me forget it."

Jess wanted to ask what she meant, but the host approached to interrupt them. "There's a table ready for you if you'd like to move, or you're welcome to stay here."

"Do you guys just want to stay?" Lee asked, without tearing her eyes off the screen. The game was tied at seventeen in the first set.

Vivienne nodded. "I'm good here."

"Me, too," Chrissy added.

Tania, sitting at the other end, sniffed at the sticky bar. "I'd rather get a table . . . Jess?"

"Er . . ." Vivienne's knee brushed hers and didn't move away. "I'm fine here," Jess said.

A look of annoyance flashed over Tania's face. "Fine."

"We're good, thanks. We'll stay," Vivienne said to the host.

The bartender dropped off their beers. Vivienne tapped her bottle to Jess's before she tipped her head back and took a drink, throat long and golden.

Jess copied her with a deep drink of her own and put her parents firmly out of her mind. *Good? Maybe not. But getting better.*

15

Wins: Serious team bonding
Losses: Whatever's up with Tania's vibes

Digger: One who "digs" a hit from the other team, or gets the ball up in the air and in control for the setter. (Or, in life, one who digs a hole.)

After dinner, they piled back onto the sidewalk, joining the crowds enjoying a gorgeous summer night in downtown Vancouver.

"So . . ." Lee threw her arms around Vivienne and Chrissy. "Where are we going now?"

"Going?" Tania asked.

"I dunno, like dancing or something fun," Lee said, wiggling her hips.

Tania shook her head. "Not me. I'm ready for bed."

The rest of them looked at Jess.

"Uh . . ." She ignored Tania's sour expression and thought about where they could go. "There's a club nearby on Granville that's usually a good time."

"Done." Vivienne decided for all of them, which Jess was grateful for. There was nothing worse than the endless loops of indecision when traveling with a group.

"Do we get a cab or can we walk?" Chrissy wondered.

"Probably just as easy to walk—" Jess started to say until Tania interrupted her.

"I thought you said you were so tired?"

"Um . . ."

Vivienne steered Lee and Chrissy away. "Er, let's go make a wish on that fountain." She hauled them a few steps down the sidewalk so Jess and Tania could talk.

Jess turned to face her partner. "I *was* tired." Irritation prickled in her chest. She already had one uptight mother, and that was enough. "I'm not now."

Tania narrowed her eyes, then spun on her heel. "All right, fine. Night, you guys," she called to the others, marching off down the sidewalk. The hotel was visible from there, just a couple blocks away, and the sidewalk was full of people, so Jess wasn't worried about Tania walking by herself . . . but she was a little worried about the abrupt departure and the angry set of Tania's shoulders.

Vivienne bounced over, holding on to Chrissy's hand. She grabbed Jess's hand too, and whooped, "Let's go!"

Chrissy laughed and twirled under Vivienne's arm.

Vivienne squeezed Jess's hand.

Jess squeezed it back and lifted her gaze. There were no stars visible, but the city lights twinkled all the same.

Tania didn't slip quietly out of bed on Sunday like she had the day before. Sunday, she flicked on a lamp and fumbled with the coffee maker, then clattered around in the bathroom with the door open.

Jess groaned. Not enough sleep. They had returned from the bar at one—not too late . . . but not exactly early either. And now it was only seven. The shuttle didn't leave until eight—plenty of time for a bit more shut-eye. She rolled over and buried her head under her pillow.

The pillow didn't help. Just when she was wondering how much noise Tania could possibly make putting her hair in a ponytail, Tania's phone rang. "Hola, mamá. ¿Qué pasa? . . . Sí . . . Sí." She started chattering away in Spanish.

Jess pushed her pillow aside and sat up with a sigh. Guess she was getting up now, too. She collected her clothes from her suitcase and was about to snark something in Tania's direction about the noise—the classic *Need a hammer?* came to mind—but before she could say anything, the door to the room opened and thumped closed.

"Hmph." Jess's reflection in the bathroom mirror frowned back at her. She looked pretty rough, hair tangled and frizzy, dark circles under her eyes—from smeared mascara or lack of sleep or both, it was hard to say. She had a quick shower, brushed her teeth, and headed downstairs for breakfast. Tania was nowhere to be seen, but Lee and Shay were there, plus Vivienne, who was wearing large sunglasses in the dining room. Jess joined them with her oatmeal and coffee.

"Morning," Jess said. "How's everyone?"

She was met with unenthusiastic mumbles from Lee and Vivienne.

Shay snorted. "Couldn't get Chrissy out of bed." They checked the time on their phone. "She told me she only needs five minutes. I'm supposed to grab her a banana."

Jess grinned at Vivienne. "Nice sunglasses."

Vivienne took a dainty sip of her coffee. "Not sure why the lights are cranked up so high in here. It's breakfast, not open-heart surgery."

After they ate, they went back to their rooms to collect their luggage—Tania had already cleared out her stuff—

then headed out to meet the shuttle. Jess found Tania sitting in their usual spot.

She dropped into the seat next to Tania. "Morning."

Tania, headphones on and scrolling her phone, didn't reply.

"Hey," Jess said again, tapping her arm. "Morning."

Tania glanced at her. "Morning."

"What's up? You okay?"

"Yeah. Fine." Tania sat up straighter and gave her a perfunctory smile. "How are you? Ready to go?"

"Yup." Jess held up her coffee. "Thought a bit of extra caffeine wouldn't hurt, though."

"Yeah, probably not." Tania went back to her phone.

Jess tipped her head back and closed her eyes against the bright sun, willing her growing headache away and hoping Tania would be less cranky once their match started.

Sunday was forecast to be even hotter than the day before, and the sand heated quickly under their feet during warm-up. But Jess barely noticed because her head was now fully pounding.

"One sec," she said to Tania, trotting over to her bag to dig for ibuprofen.

Tania put her hands on her hips. "Warm-up's almost over."

"I know." Jess swallowed a pill with a mouthful of water. "I'm ready."

Butterflies tickled Jess's stomach when the ref blew her whistle to start the match. Maybe it was the Sunside crew watching her . . . maybe it was the extra round of shooters last night before they left the bar. . . . Either way, she took a deep breath and shook out her limbs, doing her best to ignore her stomach and focus on the task at hand.

Fortunately, the other team seemed a little sleepy too, so if Jess was half a step slower, or jumped an inch or two lower, she got away with it. They won the match in two sets that shouldn't have been so close, but at least they walked away with a win.

Billi and Raya played next. Tania was still quiet while they watched, but Jess was happy to sit in silence nursing her hangover until it was time for their quarterfinal.

This opponent didn't look sleepy.

Jess thought her first hit was going to score a point, but somehow the digger moved with superhuman speed and got the ball up. Tania dug the next hit, then the other team dug hers. The rally went on and on, until finally the other team sent over a weak roll shot that neither Jess nor Tania could get to. Jess rested her hands on her knees, out of breath after the first point. *Fuck.* If every rally was even half that long, she was in massive trouble.

"Okay." Tania slapped her hand. "We've got the next one."

They did, but barely, after another long rally that ended when an off-balance attack from Jess hit the tape and just trickled over. It was one of those games. They managed to eke out a 21–19 win, but at the expense of Jess's legs. She just couldn't keep up in the second, and they lost 15–21.

Jess sat down to rest before the third set, stretching out her hamstrings and chugging some more Gatorade.

"I really don't want to lose in the quarterfinal," Tania said.

"Let's win then," Jess said, swallowing a groan from the dull ache in her quads.

The battle continued. Tania missed two serves, but the other team started slow, and a couple lucky balls helped Jess and Tania tie the third set at thirteen.

Jess went back to serve, willing her heart rate to slow down. She took a deep breath and smacked the logo. *Just get it in.*

And her serve made it, but they passed it no problem and sent a vicious attack back over the net. Tania dove and got a knuckle on the ball, enough to give it a little bit more height, but it carried on out the back of the court. Jess took two steps after it until she realized there was no chasing that one down. She was out of gas. 13–14.

Jess slapped Tania's hand and got ready for the next serve.

"We need one good pass," Tania muttered, her voice flat.

They served to Tania, who put the ball up for Jess nice and high, although a little too far back. Jess gave Tania a decent set—not the best ever, but still very hittable. Tania stayed on her feet and bumped the ball short just over the net. The blocker had peeled off when she saw Tania wasn't swinging and barely had to move to lob the ball up to her partner, who went ahead and crushed it back at them.

Jess jumped, but it wasn't enough. The ball grazed the tip of her middle finger and continued on its way to the back line, where it landed for the final point.

The other team let out cries of victory and jumped around while Jess and Tania could do nothing but watch them and swallow the loss.

"Fuck." Jess sighed and went to shake hands and congratulate the winners, then plopped on the sand and took a swig of water. "Phew. That was a tough match."

"Yeah." Tania wiped her face with a towel, muffling her

next words. "Maybe if you hadn't gone partying again last night you wouldn't have missed that last one."

Jess was sure she had to have heard her wrong. "Sorry?"

Tania dropped the towel onto her bag and sighed. "It's pretty hard to go out two nights in a row and still play your best."

Jess's brain stalled. Tania had never been so blatantly critical of her before. Then again, at Tía Diana's . . . "I didn't think I played that terrible."

"I didn't say you were *terrible*."

"Pretty sure you just blamed the loss on me."

Tania shrugged. "Some points anyway."

"How many points did we lose 'cause of your shoulder, you think?" Jess regretted the words as soon as they were out of her mouth, except Tania didn't look hurt, just pissed.

"My shoulder is fine."

"Tania. It's obviously bothering you."

"The only thing bothering me right now is you." Tania scooped up her bag and stormed off toward the bathrooms.

Jess sat there, stunned, the conflict churning her stomach. She and Tania had never really fought before.

"You okay, Jess?" Chrissy stood in front of her, sweaty and disheveled after her match, face a picture of concern.

"Um . . . I guess. I . . . Tania just stormed off. . . ." Jess gestured helplessly.

"Ooh." Chrissy cringed. "Yeah, she seemed kind of pissed when you wanted to go out again last night."

"Do you think I should go after her?"

"You know Tania better than me, but . . . she might just need time to cool off."

"Yeah, maybe." She sure hoped so, anyway.

Chrissy offered Jess her hand. "Here, come watch my

semifinal. We're playing that team from Berkeley. We'll need all the support we can get."

Chrissy wasn't wrong. The team from Berkeley was pretty scary. They were currently sitting at the top of the Northern California league, and even their names—Athena and Faith—instilled fear. Chrissy and Shay put up a valiant fight, but lost in two. There was no denying it—Athena and Faith were bigger, faster, and stronger.

And now Vivienne and Lee had to play them in the tournament final.

They executed their usual flawless warm-up while the crowd grew rowdier around them. Athena and Faith were stiff competition and the battle was heated. Vivienne and Lee managed to just edge them out the first set 21–19, with lots of smart shots and fast feet, chasing down just about any ball they needed to. But Athena and Faith came out swinging even harder in the second, determined to overpower Vivienne and Lee at the net, and won the second set 21–17.

The Sunside group hooted and hollered as the third set started, along with all the other fans Vivienne and Lee had picked up over the weekend. Somehow, they seemed to shift into an even higher gear, serving tougher to try and force weaker passes. But it wasn't quite enough, and they lost a heartbreaker 14–16 when Athena ripped a final jump serve that just caught the outside of the line. Jess let out the breath she had been holding and mirrored the scowl on Vivienne's face.

After the match and medal ceremony, Jess went up to a still-cranky Vivienne. The red-and-white ribbon nestled between her breasts.

Jess tried not to stare. "Nice medal."

Vivienne lifted it off her chest and looked at it. "Silver sucks."

"It'll suck less tomorrow. You guys played great."

Vivienne shrugged. "We could have played better."

"They're a big team."

Vivienne put her hand on her hip and squinted up at Jess, lips in a playful quirk. "Are you calling me short?"

"I would never." Jess resisted the urge to pat her head. "I'm just calling them tall."

Vivienne stepped closer and tipped her head back. "You're taller." Vivienne's lips were tilted toward her, so close and plump. . . .

Jess tried to swallow with a dry throat and remember what they were talking about. "Yes, well . . . not tall is also . . . good."

Chrissy appeared and threw her arms around Vivienne. "Good job, Viv! You guys played so well."

"Thanks, Chrissy." Vivienne hugged her back. "We tried."

"Hey, second place is awesome! You should be proud." She held up her phone. "I just heard from our driver. He wants to head to the airport pretty quick. You guys ready to go?"

For some reason Jess looked at Vivienne . . . who was looking back.

"Ready," they said at the same time.

Tania had slipped into the back of the crowd and watched the final match from a distance, then she sat way at the rear of the shuttle, so Jess let her be. And Tania was clearly ignoring her through the whole process of check-in, security, and finding their gate at the airport. She had her headphones on and didn't look Jess's way once.

Tania was even up for the challenge of ignoring Jess when she was sitting *right next to her* on the plane. All through the safety demonstration, taxiing, and takeoff, her trusty headphones remained in place and, for good measure, now her nose was in a book. The silence ate away at Jess's sanity.

When the seat-belt sign turned off, she couldn't take it anymore.

She tapped Tania's arm and waited for her to remove her headphones. "Can we talk?"

Tania gave her a go-ahead gesture. "Talk."

Jess sighed. "Yeah, okay, I wasn't at my best today."

Tania raised an eyebrow. "Mm-hmm."

"But look . . . we were never going to win this whole tournament anyway. What's wrong with having fun?"

Tania shut her book. "We might have won it."

Jess made a disbelieving noise. "Against Vivienne and Lee or Athena and Faith? You've seen them play, right?"

"That's just your problem, Jess," Tania said, shaking her head.

Jess's defenses prickled. "What's my problem?"

"Your lack of self-confidence!" Tania spat. "You're just as good as anyone in our league, if not better. But you have this dumb—"

"Dumb?"

"—this *dumb* perception that you're lesser, for some reason, and I need you to snap the fuck out of it."

Jess reeled back in her seat like Tania had smacked her. "I don't—"

"You *do*. And look . . ." Tania paused and smoothed her

book cover while she searched for words. "You had fun going out with the girls. That's great. That's because you fit in with them. They *like* you. We all do."

Jess opened her mouth, ready to argue about how much she did or did not fit in, but Tania held up her hand.

"Not to mention Skye, the gas-station cashier, and, apparently, a French lady at the social on Friday. . . ."

Jess closed her mouth, losing track of what her argument actually was.

"So let's recap," Tania continued, getting louder as her momentum built. "You're an incredibly talented volleyball player, and people like you. You have no reason not to be so confident it oozes out of your pores. You should be fucking *insufferable* on the court. Other teams should *hate* you for it. But you act like you don't belong here and it's starting to really piss me off."

Jess was frozen, a little terrified that Tania was listing reasons she didn't want to play with her anymore.

Tania met Jess's gaze head-on. She wasn't done yet. "So when we get back to Sunside, it would be nice if you could *put all those fucking pieces together* and play like the hot shit you are."

Jess sat in it for a minute, relieved that Tania had said "we" and flattered at all the compliments . . . but a little simmer of hurt still slipped out, because Tania clearly felt like Jess was letting her down. Jess raised her eyebrow. "Yeah? Speaking of pieces, how's your shoulder?"

Tania looked down at her book for a second. Her mouth twitched. When she looked up, she was full-on grinning. "That's the exact kind of attitude I want out of you, actually. And I told you . . . my shoulder is fine."

"Are you sure? You'd tell me the truth if it was serious, right?"

"Of course I would. You're my partner."

Jess had to grin back, eyes prickling as multiple emotions washed over her. "Tania."

"What?"

"I love you." Jess slid her arms around her and hugged her tight.

"I love you too, dummy." Tania hugged back. "I just wish you'd believe in yourself as much as I do."

Jess sniffled into her shoulder. "I'm sorry I partied too much."

Tania rubbed her back. "It's okay. Just . . . find the balance. Yeah?"

"Yeah." Jess pulled away and wiped her eyes. "Yeah. I hear you. Thank you."

"Great." Tania smiled and patted her hand. "Let's get a drink."

"Ugh, not me. I'm still hungover."

Tania stared at her for a second, then a laugh burst out of her. "Fuck you. *I'm* getting a drink."

16

Wins: 10
Losses: 20

> *Approach*: **As in "spike approach," the set of steps you take and your arm swing as you jump and hit the ball. Harder than it looks, hitting a moving target while moving yourself.**

"Oozing confidence," Jess's reflection said. "*Oozing*."

She blinked at her image, looking for the positives. She turned to the side and flexed. "Nice pipes. Great boobs." She skipped over her nose. "Pretty eyes."

Fleming sat at her feet and huffed.

Jess bent to scratch his head. "Fake it till you make it, right, pup?"

She startled when her self–pep talk got interrupted by a hammering at her door.

"Jess! Hurry up!" came Nelson's muffled voice.

Jess opened the door to reveal Nelson wearing nothing but sandals, a tight neon-green bathing suit, and clearly some sort of oil that set his skin to shining.

She leaned on the doorframe, lips quirking. "Yes, sir? Is there some sort of swimsuit emergency with which you require assistance?"

Nelson held out his hands and peered around her. "I need Fleming early today. There's an absolute snack walking toward the beach with two corgis."

Jess gasped in mock indignation. "You'd use my precious baby to get laid?"

"Without even blinking. Let's go." Nelson reached inside the door to grab Fleming's leash off the hook.

Laughing, Jess scooped up Fleming, kissed him on the head, and handed him over to Nelson. "Good luck, darling."

"Thanks!" he cried over his shoulder, already hustling toward the stairs. "See you after your game! And good luck to you too, baby girl!"

The July break had come to an end, and today was their first match since the Vancouver Incident. Jess and Tania had trained hard this week, both eager to get back on the court. Halfway through the season with twenty losses and only ten wins, they had some work to do if they were going to make the playoffs in September. That work began today against Chrissy and Shay.

Jess arrived at the pavilion right as George and Tania were pulling into the parking lot.

"Button!" Tania cried, hanging out of the window.

"T!" Jess called back. She waited for Tania to climb from the truck and bounce over to the sidewalk.

Tania hugged her. "I'm so ready. Are you ready?"

"Never *been* more ready. Hey, George," Jess said when he joined them. "How are things?"

"George got promoted to sous-chef!" Tania exclaimed, grabbing his chin and kissing his cheek. "I'm telling you because he hates to brag."

George turned pink and hunched his shoulders. "It's not a big deal."

"It is a big deal! Pay raise, better hours. . . ." She held her hands over her head. ". . . and, like, a *giant* hat."

Jess laughed at Tania's miming. "Congratulations, George! That's great."

"I'm making dinner tonight to celebrate—my world-famous barbecue ribs and corn bread. You should come!"

"Oh, that sounds great! As long as you don't mind cooking for another person?"

George grinned at her. "Nah, we'd love to have you, Jess. Now you guys better get going. Tania's been vibrating all morning, and if she doesn't get her hands on a volleyball in the next few minutes, I think she might actually explode."

"Mine!" Jess cried when Shay's serve floated over the net, right in between them. She passed the ball to Tania, who set her up beautifully. Jess approached hard as Chrissy lined up to block her down the line. Jess decided to thread the needle and go for a line shot anyway. Shay's digging was too good today to throw a crosscourt shot anywhere near them. Jess's gamble paid off—her hit snuck past Chrissy's hand and landed right on the line.

"Yes!" Tania cheered. She gave Jess a high five. "*Fire.*"

Jess grinned. "Thanks."

Chrissy groaned through the net. "Jess! What a shot. I didn't think I left you any room."

"Barely. I got lucky."

"Nah, that's all skill." Tania smacked Jess's butt. "Now go crush your fucking serve, Button."

Jess and Tania won the match 21–18 and 21–15.

Chrissy wagged her head when they shook hands after the match. "You guys played awesome. Good game."

"Thanks." Jess tried not to smile too huge, but she felt amazing. It was only one match, but it was a good start.

On their way to the locker room, they stopped to high-five George and the rest of Tania's family, and signed a few autographs for the kids.

"My queen," someone said from a few rows above in the stands.

Jess looked up.

Marco approached, brandishing a bouquet of at least two dozen red roses.

Jess laughed and blushed at the same time. She opened her mouth to reply, but Tania got there first.

"Marco, you stupid motherf—" Tania bit her lip and eyed the kids hanging around. "Shut your goofy ass up, Marco. She's a *lesbian*. She doesn't want your f . . . frigging flowers."

Marco tilted his head and looked at Jess with pleading eyes. "Not even a little bi?"

"I'm gonna make you eat those flowers if you don't. . . ." Tania glared at him, leaving the threat hanging in the air.

Jess shook her head. "Sorry, no."

Tania scoffed. "Do not apologize to that moron."

Marco dropped his head and placed a hand over his broken heart. "I understand. I hope you will accept these flowers anyway as an apology." He held them out to Jess.

"Er, thanks." She collected them awkwardly.

"You are most welcome. And I'd like you to know that whoever you *are* interested in is one lucky woman."

"Thanks, Marco." Eager to disappear with her giant bouquet of roses, Jess turned to head to the locker room and almost collided with Vivienne. "Oh, sorry!"

Vivienne steadied her with a hand on her arm. "No worries. Nice flowers."

"Uh . . . yeah . . ." Jess rolled her eyes toward Marco in what she hoped was an explanatory manner. "Tania's cousin. . . ."

Vivienne looked at Marco. He waved. "Right. Men. Anyway, just wanted to say nice game. You guys played great."

"Thanks." Why was she feeling so awkward? She gripped the bouquet. "Do you like roses?"

"Do I like roses? Sure, who doesn't like roses?"

"Do you want some? Of these roses?"

Vivienne's eyebrows climbed her forehead. "Do I—Sure?"

"Uh . . . You know what, here." Jess thrust the bouquet at her. "Just take the whole thing. They're wrapped pretty tight, so I can't really . . ."

Vivienne laughed, sort of a surprised sound. "Thanks. They're lovely."

Jess caught Marco's eye. He winked at her.

"You're welcome. Uh, good luck on your match. I should go shower." Cheeks burning, she all but bolted for the locker room.

Tania caught up and put an arm around Jess. "You played great, Button."

"Thanks."

"Don't know what that mess was, though."

"What? What mess?"

Tania chuckled. "Nothing."

After they showered, Chrissy plopped down next to Jess on the bench. "Ooh, guys, guess what! We're all getting tattoos!"

"Who's 'we'?" Jess asked, toweling her hair off.

"Me, Shay, Vivienne, Lee . . . plus you two!"

"Oh, really?" Jess swapped an amused look with Tania.

"Yes! You know how Shay's partner owns a tattoo parlor? She said we could all come in one night and get some sort of volleyball tattoo!"

Shay nodded. "We can bring in food, play music. . . . It'll be so fun!"

Jess had thought about getting a volleyball tattoo before, but had never quite gotten around to it. Why not now? "Sure, I'm in!"

Chrissy clapped her hands. "Yay! Tania? You have to join."

"I'll come hang out for sure, but . . . let me think about the tattoo. My mom would flip out. Not sure it's worth it."

Jess tilted her head. "Maybe it'll make her forget about grandkids for a bit."

"Hmm . . . Good point. Tattoo it is!"

When Jess arrived at Tania and George's house for dinner—a nondescript bungalow they rented near the highway—she entered without knocking, as she'd been instructed to do many times. She followed the Spanish pop music coming from the kitchen at the back and found Tania and George dancing around, waving spatulas and other cooking utensils in the air.

"Jess!" Tania cried. "Dance with us!"

Laughing, Jess joined in, admiring the way George was able to slather more sauce on the ribs while keeping time with the music.

"Dinner is ready," he announced at the end of the song. "Please sit!"

Jess helped set the food out on the table—ribs, corn

bread, plus roasted veggies and potato-bacon salad—and salivated at the sight of it all. "George, I can't believe you made all this. It looks amazing."

George stacked a few half-racks of ribs onto his plate. "Cooking makes me happy . . . especially when she likes it." He gazed at Tania with heart eyes.

"Aw, mi bombón. . . ." She leaned over to kiss him.

Once her plate was loaded, Jess sampled the corn bread. "This is incredible," she said through her first bite.

"Isn't it the best?" Tania's phone buzzed next to her plate. She picked it up and frowned at it.

"Is that the doctor?" George asked.

Jess froze in the middle of her second bite. *The doctor?*

Tania shot George a tight-lipped look. "Yup. Just confirming my appointment."

"Everything okay?" Jess asked, watching the two of them exchange a glance.

"Yup." Tania smiled brightly. "Just need to get some bloodwork done to get on George's insurance. So . . . the corn bread's great, huh? Have you tried the ribs yet?"

"Not yet," Jess said, reassuring herself that Tania promised to tell her anything important. And she definitely would . . . right?

Ink Me Baby occupied the bottom floor of a converted house on the outskirts of downtown Sunside. Shay and Locke lived above the shop.

Tania had picked up Chrissy and Jess on her way. They climbed out of the truck, carefully balancing their potluck dishes. Tania made mini tacos, Chrissy carried a spinach dip, and Jess had made chocolate cupcakes for dessert.

Vivienne pulled up in her Mercedes at the same time with Lee next to her.

Vivienne sighed after she climbed out, looking from her takeout sushi platter to the other dishes. "Goddamnit. Did everyone else make theirs?"

Chrissy gently bumped her hip. "It looks like it."

Vivienne frowned, then shrugged and tossed her hair. "Oh well, good thing I'm amazing in bed."

An image flashed in Jess's mind—Vivienne lying in tangled sheets, moonlight slicing across her naked body. Her hair streaming across the pillow, back arched and eyes closed in passion—*fuck*. Jess's cheeks heated to a thousand degrees as she almost dropped her cupcakes.

"You okay there, Jess?" Tania asked when she noticed the wobble.

"I'm fine," Jess said with an embarrassing scratch to her voice. "I just felt . . . dizzy for a second."

"Oh no!" Chrissy eyed her with concern. "Are you nervous about getting a tattoo?"

"Er, yeah," Jess lied.

"There's really nothing to be nervous about." Chrissy smiled brightly. "This will be my third one and it's not that bad . . . mostly."

Shay unlocked the door when they saw them coming and waved them inside past the CLOSED sign. "Welcome, everyone! You can put the food on the counter over there. . . . And this is my partner, Locke. . . . I think you've all met her before?"

Locke—with olive skin, a purple pixie cut, a lip ring, and covered in beautiful, delicate nature-inspired tattoos—was fiddling with a tray of supplies next to a tattoo chair. She hugged everyone as Shay refreshed her on their names.

Vivienne looked around approvingly. "Thank you so much for doing this for us after hours. Very VIP."

"This is going to be so fun!" Chrissy agreed.

Two more people joined from the back of the shop. Locke introduced them. "This is Shelly and Lewis, the other artists who are working with us tonight." Shelly was in her forties, with pink hair, and Lewis looked young, maybe twenty, with more tattoos than even Locke. He was also quite petite and had to tilt his chin up to look at the volleyball players.

Locke surveyed the group. "Who are the first-timers again?"

Jess, Tania, and Vivienne put their hands up. For some reason, Jess was surprised to see Vivienne was new at this. She seemed like the type to have tattoos. Then again, Jess had seen Vivienne in a bikini a thousand times, and had glimpses of more in the locker room, so unless the tattoo was in a very private place, she would have noticed it before.

"We've taken a look at the designs you chose. They're all fairly simple, so each tattoo will take probably an hour or so. Which three want to start?"

"Me!" Chrissy jumped forward.

Lee also put up her hand.

"I'll go," Jess said.

Locke paired each of them with an artist and they sat to finalize their designs.

"So . . ." Locke slid a folder over to Jess. "I looked at the samples you sent me and read your ideas. What do you think about this?"

Jess had found a cool crescent-moon tattoo design, then had the idea to turn it into a crescent volleyball instead, with maybe a few stars sparkling around the outside.

Jess gasped when she saw Locke's drawing. "Locke!

Oh my God, it's perfect." It was even better than Jess had imagined—shaded and textured, a beautiful combination of crescent moon and volleyball. Goose bumps sprung up on her arms.

"Are you sure? A tattoo is forever. We can make any changes you want."

"I absolutely love it. You're brilliant."

Vivienne had come over to check out Locke's drawing. "Wow! That is gorgeous!"

"Isn't it?" Jess couldn't stop staring at it.

"I'm glad you like it. And do you still want it on your outer forearm?" Locke asked.

"Yes." Jess showed Locke right where she wanted it to go, close to her left elbow. She chose the spot so she would see it when she steadied her telescope.

"Okay. I'm going to make up the stencil. You can grab a few bites of food while you wait. Have some soda, get your blood sugar up. It'll keep you from feeling faint."

Jess headed over to the food and snarfed some spinach dip and a couple tacos, then selected a can of Coke from the mini fridge.

Vivienne had wandered over to a display of jewelry near the till. She crossed one leg over the other and gripped the counter. She was shaking.

Jess set her empty plate down and eased over to her. "Are you okay?" she asked quietly, almost reaching out to put a hand on Vivienne's arm.

Vivienne gave her an unconvincing smile. "Fine." Her knuckles were white. "Just a little nervous."

"Oh. Yeah, me too," Jess lied again.

Vivienne didn't buy it for a second. "You're not nervous."

"I am! I'm totally nervous about the . . ."

"The needle," Vivienne supplied.

"Yes! The needle. Hate needles. They're so . . . needly."

Vivienne huffed a small laugh. "*So* needly."

Jess wanted to say something helpful. "You don't have to go ahead with this if you don't want to."

"I know . . . I do want to, though. I've always wanted a tattoo."

"Just tell Locke that you're feeling nervous. I'm sure it's totally common and she'll know how to help you."

"I will." Vivienne nodded, then tried smiling again. "Thanks."

Jess smiled back at her, adding this information to her mental Vivienne file. *Afraid of needles. Kind of adorable when she's scared.*

"I'm ready for you, Jess," Locke called.

Jess gave Vivienne an encouraging nod, then went to sit in Locke's chair. She placed her arm on the table.

Locke prepped the area, then placed the stencil on Jess's forearm. "Here?"

"Perfect."

Jess was pleased to discover it didn't hurt too badly, more uncomfortable than painful, and it was pretty magical watching the design be permanently etched onto her skin.

The time passed quickly. Vivienne seemed to relax in the background. She collected a plate of food and chatted with Shay and Tania while the artists worked.

"I think we're done," Locke announced. "What do you think?"

Jess studied her new tattoo. Her two great loves, space

and volleyball, there forever. Jess's eyes stung. "It's incredible, Locke. Thank you so much!"

"You are so welcome." Locke wiped the area again and took a picture for her portfolio. Jess snapped a few pics, too.

The girls who weren't currently getting tattooed came over to admire it.

"It's gorgeous," Vivienne said. "Really beautiful."

"Thanks." Jess smiled, warmth running through her body.

Locke covered it with a clear protective layer while she gave Jess some aftercare instructions, then looked up at her next customer. "Your turn, Viv!"

Vivienne gulped and nodded.

"So you want just a simple volleyball, like Lee's?" Locke confirmed.

"Actually . . ." Vivienne chewed her lip. "Jess, I'm sorry if this is crazy, but I really, really love the design you got. Would you be mad if I got the same tattoo as you? On my back though, not in the same spot."

"Oh, um . . ." Vivienne would have the same tattoo as her? Was that weird? Or . . . was it weirder that she really liked that idea? "Yeah, that's fine, of course."

Locke frowned at Jess. "Are you okay, Jess? Your face is really red."

"Uh . . ." She put her hands to her cheeks. "Yeah, maybe I'm feeling a bit lightheaded."

Tania took hold of Jess's elbow and steered her toward another chair. "Here, sit down and finish your Coke. I'll bring you some more food."

Jess ducked her head and sat without protest.

When Locke was ready, Vivienne pulled off her tank

top, revealing a very small bikini top underneath, and lay down on the table. Her eyes were wide and wet and her limbs were shaking as Locke prepped the area and stuck on the stencil.

"Take a deep breath," Locke soothed her.

Jess hesitated for a second, then pulled her chair up next to Vivienne, took her hand, and squeezed. "You're okay. You can do this."

Vivienne squeezed back and blew out a breath.

Locke paused with the tattoo gun hovering over Vivienne's upper back near her right shoulder. "I'm going to start with a small line so you can see how it feels, okay?"

Vivienne twitched when the needle touched her skin.

"Easy . . ." Jess soothed. "You're okay."

"Will you distract me?" Vivienne whispered.

"Sure . . . Actually, I have a funny story I was going to tell you anyway. You know what Fleming did yesterday? When we got back from our walk, he had something in his mouth. But he wouldn't show me. I kept saying 'Fleming, drop it' but he'd just look at me, wagging his tail, with this piece of hot pink plastic sticking out of his mouth. So I finally grabbed his jaw and pried it out of his mouth . . . and it was a fucking mini vibrator!"

Locke lifted the tattoo gun as they all exclaimed.

"No way!" Vivienne said through her laughter.

"Swear to God!" Jess said.

"What did you do?"

"Well, I screamed and dropped it . . . and Fleming picked it up again and ran to try to hide it in his bed."

"Oh no!"

"I had to wrestle it away from him. . . . Then I washed my hands a hundred times."

"What about Fleming's mouth?"

"He's a dog, he eats garbage . . . or worse. I think he'll survive. But wait, I haven't told you the worst part yet. . . ."

"There's more?"

Jess nodded. "Mm-hmm. Later on, I saw my neighbor Mrs. Horowitz pacing around outside like she was looking for something she had dropped."

Vivienne cackled. "Noooo. Poor lady. I hope she has a backup. Or are you going to return it?"

Jess face-palmed. "It had teeth marks in it."

"Bad Fleming. You gotta be careful with your teeth." She raised a knowing eyebrow.

Jess snickered. "So true."

"Okay, no more funny stories, Jess!" Locke admonished. "Vivienne has to stay still."

"Sorry!" They were still holding hands. She updated Vivienne on the scores from the California leagues from the weekend, showed her a reel of cute dachshunds wearing hats, and summarized the plot of *Queen in Shining Armor*. The time flew by and, before they knew it, Locke was done.

Jess grinned at her. "You did it! And it looks amazing on you."

Vivienne sat up and looked in the mirror that Locke held up. "Oh, I love it. Thank you so much, Locke." Her gaze swung over to Jess. "And thank you. I don't think I would have been able to go through with it without you." Her voice was low and smoky and traveled through Jess's body in a shiver.

Jess's tongue was heavy in her mouth. "Sure you could have. You're the most confident person I know."

Vivienne studied Jess's face for a moment. "I'm really not."

"Well . . ." Vivienne's hair fell loose on her shoulders, highlighting her long, elegant neck. A hint of vanilla reached Jess's nose. She cleared her throat. "You fake it pretty good."

A small smile ghosted the corner of Vivienne's mouth. "'Fake it till you make it,' right?"

17

Wins: 14
Losses: 21

> ***Five hundred (or sometimes written ".500")*: A winning percentage of 50 percent, where a team has won and lost the same number of games. So you're not really winning, but you're not losing either. A classic glass at 50 percent capacity situation.**

After the victory against Chrissy and Shay, Jess and Tania had found a bit of a groove, winning three out of four matches through the end of July. Then August arrived, and with it, the specter of playoffs.

"Last year the cutoff for playoffs was four games above five hundred." Jess screwed the cap onto her nail polish. She and Tania were sitting on the rug on Jess's floor painting their toenails a matching seashell pink. "And right now we're seven under."

Tania shrugged without taking her eyes off of her toes. "All we can do is play our best. Also, you know I hate Playoff Math."

"I know. . . ." It was well-documented that Tania's soul began to shrivel every time Jess started running playoff scenarios. "Sorry."

"We still have so many games to go. Let's just win as many as we can. How's that for math?"

"Not that we have much of a chance against Vivienne and Lee tomorrow," Jess mumbled.

"Whatever." Tania blew on her wet polish. "They're human. They can't win every game."

"Well, they're sure giving it a go."

"So are we." Tania wiggled her toes. "And our feet are gonna look sexy as fuck while we do it."

"Looking sexy is important," Jess agreed. Her very helpful brain immediately delivered an image of Vivienne on the court in her bikini, brushing sand from her ass and smirking at a smart comment from Lee. Sweat glistened on her forehead, trapping a few wisps of black hair, while other strands lifted in the ocean breeze.

"Jess!"

"What? Sorry."

"I said, are you done with the topcoat?"

"Mm-hmm." Jess slid the bottle over to Tania.

"Let's hope you're a little more focused tomorrow, yeah?" Tania gave her a look, half reproving, half joking.

"I'm focused," Jess insisted. "I was just thinking about . . . smashing Vivienne."

Not exactly a lie.

It was not that beating Vivienne and Lee was impossible. As Tania pointed out, they were just people, and no one was perfect. But they were pretty damn close. They rarely made mistakes, and every point against them had to be earned.

Jess wiped the sweat off her brow after a long rally—she'd chased down an errant dig, jumped three times for a block and twice for a hit, and dove for a ball . . . and they'd lost the point. They were down 7–12 in the first game.

Tania called a time-out. They huddled on the sideline. "Lee is blocking line and Viv is digging cross. You need to make her work harder. Go deep, go short, go for the far sideline. . . . She's cheating inside, you've got to keep her honest."

"Right." Jess sucked down a gulp of water. "On it."

"Let's go." Tania smacked her butt. "You've got her."

On her next hit, Jess tried to act like she was winding up for a huge swing, staring hard at the far line, then she pulled up and doinked it sharp crosscourt, just over the net.

Vivienne tore after it in an impossibly fast blur. She dove, body stretched into one long line of muscle and speed, but the ball hit the sand a split second before she could get her fist under it.

Tania crowed. "That's what I'm talking about!"

Jess grinned and couldn't help sneaking a glance at Vivienne.

Vivienne was dusting sand off her abs, giving Jess a cool look of indifference . . . until a corner of her mouth twitched. "Nice shot, Jess."

Jess almost fell over. Vivienne never spoke to her opponents during the game. Never. "Thanks."

Vivienne pointed at her. "If you can pull it off again, I'll buy you a drink."

Jess lifted her eyebrow. "I'll take a margarita, please."

"We'll see." Vivienne raised a matching eyebrow and snapped her bikini bottom into place. Jess thought she got a glimpse of Vivienne's smile growing before she turned to slap Lee's hand and get ready for the next serve.

The battle continued at an even keel, until it was game point for Vivienne and Lee, 17–20. Tania called another time-out.

Jess tugged out her hair elastic and hastily fixed her ponytail while Tania chewed her lip. "We gotta keep doing what we're doing. Make it tough for them."

"We'd need five points in a row to win," Jess pointed out.

Tania glared at her. "So let's get five points in a row."

"I don't think—"

"Jessica." Tania's tone shut her down. "*Oozing confidence.* Remember?"

"Right. Okay, let's get five fucking points."

They slapped hands and got back on the court.

They scored one point, then another, thanks to flukey shots that hit the tape and just barely made it over, but Vivienne and Lee weren't having it. On Jess's next serve, Lee crushed a second ball that they had no chance of digging. First game done, 19–21.

Tania shifted her weight from side to side as she devoured a protein bar at their bench. "So close. So fucking close. Jess, we can beat them."

Jess nodded, gaze drifting over to Vivienne and Lee. Vivienne nodded and rolled her eyes at Lee. It looked like she said "I know."

Jess wondered what it was like in Vivienne's head. Did she feel unbeatable? Or did she go into games rife with self-doubt? Did she give herself pep talks? Or was it all easy for her, instinctual?

Either way, they'd have to find another gear to beat her and Lee.

Back on the court, the second set began with the same even back-and-forth.

Down 10–11 after losing another marathon rally, Jess rested her hands on her knees to catch her breath. "Goddamn."

Tania came over to pat her back. She was breathing hard, too. "We're holding them. We need this point."

Jess nodded and settled in to pass the next serve. Lee sent a rocket of a jump serve over to Jess. Tania set her. Jess went in hard like she was going to crank it crosscourt, hoping Vivienne would think she was actually planning to doink over an itty-bitty roll shot again. It worked . . . Vivienne crept forward a couple steps as Jess swung and she hit it hard and deep, aiming for the back corner. Vivienne was too far in and had to let the ball go over her, hoping it would be out. It landed just inside the line.

"Fuck, yes." Tania pumped her fist. "Just like that, Button. Keep her honest."

Eleven all.

At nineteen all, Lee called a time-out before Jess's serve.

Tania continued to rock back and forth on the sideline. "Make this serve. Don't let her get to you."

"I know."

Jess put her serve in, even if she had to take a touch of heat off it to make sure. Nothing worse than missing after the other team tried to ice you.

Vivienne passed it to Lee, then tried to chip her hit in short. Jess dug it, then peeled off the net to have enough room for a spike approach. She hoped she was messing with Vivienne's head enough to make her second-guess herself. Jess tried to telegraph that she was planning to just tap it over the net. Vivienne didn't move from her spot early this time and Jess's scheme worked. She rolled a tiny hit and Vivienne couldn't get there. Point.

Jess and Tania were up 20–19 . . . and Vivienne owed her a drink.

Jess served again. Lee attacked another second ball off

of Vivienne's pass. Tania dug it this time. Jess set her, but Tania hit it long. 20–20.

"Fuck," Tania spat.

Jess slapped her hand. "It's okay. Next one."

They didn't get the next one, but they did get the one after that, and tied it at 21.

They hugged quickly while they tried to catch their breaths. "Guess we're doing this the hard way," Tania said grimly.

Jess nodded. "Yup."

They won a point, then lost a point. Twenty-two all.

Jess's serve. She held the ball in front of her, arm quivering. She was tired. Her serve was a lollipop and Lee had a monster hit off it for a point.

Vivienne's serve now, for the match. She crushed a jump serve. *This is why she's a champion,* Jess had a fleeting half second to think before the ball crossed the net. Tania's pass wasn't great, heading out the back of the court. Jess chased it down and bumped it back in. Not the best second ball, but Tania was able to get a good swing at it. Lee blocked her. The ball hit the sand. Point. Game over.

They lost.

Jess bent over to catch her breath again.

Vivienne and Lee slapped hands and congratulated each other.

The crowd cheered, the league fans fully on board Vivienne and Lee's winning train.

"Fuck," Tania said.

"Yeah." Jess hugged her. "Good game, T."

"So fucking close."

"I know."

"We had them."

"Yup."

Tania sighed and wiped her brow. "Fuck."

"Yup."

They went to shake hands.

"Good game," Vivienne said, extending her hand for Jess.

Jess took her hand and met Vivienne's eyes. No pity. No derision. There was nothing there but respect. The other thing missing was the prickle in her stomach that usually came with a loss. "Good game."

After a few greetings and autographs in the stands, they rinsed the sand off and headed into the locker room. It was a busy place. Chrissy, Shay, Billi, and Raya were playing against each other next and were all in there getting ready.

"Hey, great match, guys!" Chrissy said. "You all going to Maggie's after?"

Jess had to work opening tomorrow. She was about to turn down the invite, but—

"We're going," Vivienne replied. She pointed her chin at Jess. "I owe this one a drink."

It was true. There was that drink. "Yeah, I can go for a bit."

Jess, Tania, Vivienne, and Lee trooped into the stands to watch the next match once they were dressed. Vivienne was in the cute tie-dyed pink romper she had worn for the drive to Horny Beach.

Billi and Raya edged Chrissy and Shay in the third 15–12, then once the four of them were changed, they collected a few other players and partners who were hanging around and headed to Maggie's.

Vivienne dissolved into the crowd as soon as they were in the door, then materialized again at the bar. Jess went to sit with the crew. When Vivienne reappeared, she handed

Jess a margarita on the rocks and tapped their glasses together. "Can't believe you got me again."

"Me neither. That was a tough match." Jess immediately wished she hadn't said that. Because it probably wasn't that hard for Vivienne.

But Vivienne nodded. "Very tough. You played great."

Not great enough, Jess wanted to say, but she didn't want to seem like a sore loser. "You too," she said instead. "Obviously."

Vivienne opened her mouth to reply, but Shay and Locke stood up at the head of the table and called for everyone's attention.

"We have an announcement," Shay said, threading their fingers through Locke's and pausing for dramatic effect.

They waited, Jess and Tania sharing a speculative look.

"We . . . have decided to get married." Shay and Locke beamed, Locke holding up her hand to display an amethyst ring.

The volleyball crowd cheered and squealed and covered the happy couple in hugs and kisses.

"We're gonna need some bubbly over here!" Vivienne called toward April, gripping Shay's hand.

"Tell us the story!" Chrissy cried.

"Well . . ." Locke turned to Shay and they shared a soft look. "We were walking on the beach after dinner yesterday, and we came up to this big heart on the sand made out of sea stones. I stopped to admire it, and when I turned around, Shay was kneeling in the sand."

More cheering and squealing.

"How did they ask?" Tania called.

Shay's round face flushed. "You all know I'm not much of a talker. . . ." They held up their hands and laughed as they were met with a deluge of sarcastic denials. "I told Locke that I've never been so happy as I am with her, and I want to be with her forever."

"And I said yes, of course." Locke leaned in to kiss Shay, eyes sparkling with joy.

"When are you going to have the wedding?" Lee asked.

"That's the thing." Shay's gaze swept over the group. "We want to keep it super small and simple . . . and do it in two weeks, before Locke's parents leave for Europe. But . . . we'll need your help."

"When they said 'help' I thought they meant, like, help making the decorations. Not *being* the decorations," Tania grumbled.

"They meant both I guess, to be fair," Jess said, settling into the front seat of Vivienne's Mercedes. Being the tallest in the group led to some perks. "I also think you're being a touch dramatic about clothes shopping."

"Come on, Tania! Shopping is fun!" Chrissy chirped from the back, where she was squished in next to Lee and Tania. "Don't you want to pick out something new and pretty to wear to the wedding?"

"No," Tania muttered.

Shay and Locke—along with recruiting everyone to help with jobs like food and flowers and picking up grandparents at the airport—had requested that they wear "nature-inspired" outfits to the wedding to tie into Locke's love of nature.

Jess knew there was nothing in her closet, or Tania's, that would do, so when Chrissy arranged a trip to the outlets, Jess signed her and Tania up, despite Tania's protests.

The first store Chrissy marched them into was not Jess's vibe at all, a little too flashy, but she trailed behind the others, watching Tania with amusement.

Tania held up the first dress she came across. "What about this?"

"It's fine, but . . . florals are maybe a little too obvious, don't you think?" Chrissy frowned and flipped through the rack.

Tania rubbed her forehead. "Chrissy, so help me. Ask me how much I care about florals being 'obvious.'"

"I mean, you can definitely go with flowers, if you want," Chrissy said. "But I was thinking something more fun, like a bird-of-paradise vibe."

Vivienne quirked an eyebrow. "Isn't bird-of-paradise a flower?"

Chrissy tapped her chin. "Is it?"

"It's both, I think," Jess chimed in. "The flowers look like birds."

"Okay, well, I guess I was thinking exotic bird, then." She held up a red-and-yellow number hemmed with dangling feathers.

Tania raised an eyebrow. "I'll stick with florals, thanks." She waved the blue-and-purple-flowered dress she was holding. "Where are the fitting rooms?"

"Tania, we've been in this store for seventeen seconds. You need to find a few options. . . ." Chrissy took Tania's arm and led her to the next rack.

Jess flipped through the hangers. Florals weren't really her thing either, but she certainly didn't want to look like a bird.

"Nothing catching your attention?" Vivienne asked, running her hand over the row of hangers.

Jess shrugged. "I don't really know what I'm looking for."

"I'll help you find something." Vivienne surveyed the store with a skeptical eye. "Yeah, nothing in here really screams 'Jess,' does it?"

"What does scream 'Jess'?" she had to ask.

Vivienne's face flickered. "Um." She bit her lip. "Something . . ." She yanked the nearest hanger off the rack and held it up, staring. ". . . with a lot of buckles? Or . . . No, maybe not."

Jess had to laugh. "Maybe not."

Jess didn't have any luck in the next store, or the one after that.

The fourth place had a big sale and was full of bargain hunters. Chrissy had already picked a dress but had made it her personal mission to see that Tania found the perfect outfit. Tania was putting on a show but Jess could tell she was secretly enjoying Chrissy dressing her up and fawning over her.

Just when Jess was about to give up on that store too, she spied a light blue sleeveless dress in her size with white swirls that reminded her of clouds. She snatched it up, then groaned when she saw the huge changeroom line. Resigned, she joined the queue.

Vivienne hopped in line right behind her, holding an armload of dresses in green, taupe, and yellow. "Ugh, this line is brutal." She shifted from foot to foot. "My feet hurt."

Chrissy scurried up to them. "Oh, there you guys are. Tania and Lee are buying something, then we're just going to pop over to the shoe store across the way, then we're thinking we'd grab some dinner?"

Jess's stomach growled. She hoped the blue dress fit. "I'm in."

"Perfect. I'm starving," Vivienne agreed.

They waved to Chrissy and shuffled forward an inch.

"God," Vivienne groaned. "I'm ready to just strip my clothes off right here to try these dresses on."

Jess tried to keep her face blank, but was now imagining Vivienne taking her clothes off. "Er . . ."

"Just kidding," Vivienne assured her. "For now. . . ."

"Just one item?" the salesperson said when Jess finally got to the front.

"Four," Vivienne said, scooting behind Jess. "We'll share."

Ummm . . . Jess's brain lurched.

Vivienne followed her into the changeroom. "That's fine, right? I just cannot wait another second."

"Yeah, sure." *We've changed together in the locker room a million times,* Jess reminded herself. Jess put her dress on the hook while Vivienne tossed hers onto the bench. Then Vivienne turned her back and whipped her tube top off. Jess stared at her naked back. Imagined her naked front. Vivienne picked up the green dress and started to pull it over her head.

Jess wrenched her eyes away and turned her back, fumbling to pull off her tank top accompanied by the sound of Vivienne unzipping her jean shorts.

"What do you think?" Vivienne asked a moment later.

Jess turned, holding the blue dress to her chest over her bra. Her heart fluttered. "Oh, that's pretty."

Vivienne turned to study herself in the mirror with a skeptical expression. "I'm going for a few notches above 'Oh, that's pretty.'"

"Er, I mean . . ." Surely Vivienne knew how gorgeous she looked in everything. Or nothing. "You look—"

"Nah, this one's not right." Vivienne whipped it off, not

turning around fast enough. Jess got an eyeful of breast. Her face warmed. She tried to pull the dress over her head but got tangled in the lining, all trapped elbows and staticky hair. She yanked it off again.

"What about this one?" Vivienne examined herself in the taupe dress. How did she get changed so quickly? "No, this is the worst shade ever on me. I thought it was a good nature color but I look like someone's eighth-grade shop project. Just a hunk of cheap wood."

"Oh, I—"

Vivienne tugged the taupe dress off.

Jess flushed and attempted to pull the blue dress over her head again. "Oh, sorry . . ." she mumbled when she bumped into Vivienne's warm shoulder, the contact leaving a trail of sparks down her arm.

"Do you need some help there?" Vivienne asked. Jess couldn't see anything but the white lining tangled around her head, but Vivienne sounded amused.

"Yes," Jess said, aware that her bra was fully in Vivienne's view.

Vivienne tugged at the dress in a few places until Jess's arms were freed and it fell down over her shoulders. She wiggled it into place and turned to look in the mirror.

"Oh, Jess. That's . . . perfect. It's like the sky."

Jess frowned at her reflection—her hair was a casualty of the wrestling match with the lining, and the dress was a bit short.

"And it shows off your arms so nicely," Vivienne continued. "And your waist. And . . . You *have* to get it."

"Really?" Maybe her arms did look nice. And her waist. Her stomach growled again. She'd have to hope Vivienne wasn't just being nice. "Okay. I'll get it."

"Perfect. I'm right behind you. I'm going to try on this yellow one, but if it doesn't work, I'll take the green."

Jess nodded and slipped out of the room, but her thoughts stayed with the way Vivienne looked at her in that dress.

About a week later, Jess opened her door at quarter to six on Monday morning to a scowling Vivienne.

"How did we get stuck with the flowers?" Vivienne grumbled.

But Jess's chuckle died in her throat, because Vivienne . . . Vivienne looked like she'd just rolled out of bed. The only makeup she had on was mascara smudged around her eyes. Her hair was wild, like the tide tossed against a rocky shore in a storm, and she was wearing . . . well, not much at all. Small, soft-looking, low-slung gray cotton shorts, and a loose pale pink tank top with, evidently, no bra underneath. Vivienne raked a hand through her hair, flashing a shadow of cleavage and the curve of her breast. And exposing toned golden abs. Vivienne scrunched her nose. "It's way too early."

Jess's gaze bounced around, wondering where it was safe to settle it. She went with Vivienne's plump lips. Which turned out to be a mistake. "Who knew florists got started so early in the morning?" she asked, heart thudding.

"Not me. No flowers at my wedding, I guess."

That was too bad, because if Jess were to imagine Vivienne at her wedding, she'd be showered in pink rose petals—

"You ready? We're supposed to be there right at six."

Jess grabbed her keys, grateful for the distraction. "I'm

ready." She locked the door and followed Vivienne down the stairs to a black SUV.

"No Mercedes today?" Jess asked.

"Not ideal for flower delivery. This is Locke's mom's." As they got in, Vivienne nodded at the cupholders in the middle. "I got you an iced coffee."

"Oh, perfect. Thanks."

The drive was quiet, both of them mostly focused on sipping their drinks and trying to wake up. They collected the flower order—a dozen buckets of roses in red, pink, yellow, orange, and white, plus greenery—then drove to Locke and Shay's place.

Locke, Shelly, and Lewis were waiting outside and helped them carry the buckets into the shop.

"So . . ." Locke displayed her flowery sketches on her tattoo table. "We're making an archway, centerpieces, and bouquets. Jess and Viv, can you two work on the arch? I'll do the bouquets and centerpieces with Shelly and Lewis."

"You bet." Vivienne toasted her with her coffee. "Don't worry about a thing."

Locke started sorting roses while Jess and Vivienne hovered over the table and studied the drawings.

"Have you ever made a flower arch before?" Vivienne muttered quietly enough that Locke couldn't hear.

"Nope."

Vivienne rubbed her forehead. "How did we get stuck with flowers again?"

"Well, we didn't want to cook. . . ."

"Oh. Right. I remember now." Vivienne whipped her phone out and leaned on her elbows. "There's gotta be something on YouTube. . . ." The curves of her breasts were visible down her top.

Jess glued her eyes to the phone screen as the video began to play.

"We can do this," Vivienne said when it was done. "Build the arch, attach the foam, and then, you know . . . stick a bunch of roses in."

Thank God for Vivienne's confidence.

They put the arch together with minimal trouble, but had a brief speed bump when they discovered that soaking the florist foam before attaching it to the frame meant it dripped all over them. Vivienne squawked when a drop fell in her eye. Rubbing it only smudged her mascara further.

They got back on track starting with the greenery base, then moved on to the roses.

But Jess struggled. She struggled, because every time Vivienne stretched up to jam a stem into the foam block, she revealed abs and hip bones and the hint of a nipple through her thin shirt as her breasts moved under the fabric.

"This looks pretty good, right?" Vivienne asked about an hour and a half in, stepping back to examine their work, hands on her hips. Jess was sitting on the ground, working on the bottom. She looked up at . . . Vivienne towering over her.

Jess's face heated while a throb of desire pulsed between her legs. *Are you fucking kidding, Jess? You're getting horny now? For Vivienne? You've gotta get it together, this is the dumbest—*

"Jess?"

"Yeah?" Jess gasped through her dry mouth.

"I said, do you think yellow here, or pink?"

"Pink," Jess said, eyeing Vivienne's tank top.

Vivienne studied the arch. She shifted, jutting a hip out. "Yeah?"

"Yeah. Definitely."

They paused their work here and there to help with deliveries—folding tables and chairs, ice, grandparents—and, when the arch was finally done, eased it out to the garden and down the flagstone path, setting it against the backdrop of palm leaves and weeping shrubs.

They stood under it, adjusting roses here and there, then turned to look at each other.

Vivienne had a smear of dirt on her nose and leaves stuck in her hair. "I'm ready to go back to bed."

"Going to bed sounds good." Jess cleared her throat. "Unfortunately, it's not time for sleeping quite yet. Um . . . You've got . . ." She took a step closer and pulled the leaf gently from Vivienne's hair.

"Thanks." Vivienne looked up at her.

Everything slowed. The garden beyond Vivienne blurred into green with smears of pink and orange. Vivienne's long lashes fluttered around wide, dark eyes.

"I . . ." Jess trailed off, unable to look away, not even sure what she had started to say. Her heart thudded against her rib cage.

"You guys, this looks amazing!" Locke squealed, appearing next to them. "You absolutely nailed it. Thank you so much!"

Vivienne smoothed her hair as the garden snapped back into focus. "It was no problem."

Jess nodded, wordless.

"Do you need help with anything else?" Vivienne asked.

"I don't think so. You two should head home to get ready."

"Yes," Jess said, relieved she managed to say a coherent word. "We should."

Vivienne dropped her off with a promise to pick her up again for the ceremony.

Jess had a shower and found a message from Tania waiting when she got out.

If I never see another mini taco . . .

Jess grinned. **How did food prep go?**

It was fine, actually. Lee is an amazing cook. How were flowers?

Good. I think the archway turned out really beautiful.

Nice! Want me and George to pick you up?

Vivienne said she'd give me a ride.

All right, see you there!

This time when Vivienne knocked on her door . . . the transformation was, to put it mildly, dramatic. Vivienne's hair was down in loose, rippling waves and she wore the yellow sundress, ruched around her breasts, legs glowing, lips shimmering.

"You look . . ." Jess's brain searched for the right words, but "so hot it hurts" seemed inappropriate. ". . . beautiful."

"Thank you. So do you."

Jess smoothed her blue dress. "Uh . . . not really. Not compared to you."

Vivienne took a step back and dragged her gaze up Jess's legs. "Nah, you're good."

Jess flushed as she locked the door behind her.

The wedding was a small affair. Shay's side was mostly SoCal VL friends, and Locke's side just her family, and they all fit in the garden around small tables draped in white tablecloths. Chrissy stood up with Shay as their best mate. It was unlike any wedding Jess had ever been to. She'd never wanted a marriage like her parents, all business and schedules, and after Phoenix, it was hard to imagine having a future with anyone. But if she could have a wedding like this . . .

The couple looked gorgeous underneath the flower arch, Shay in khaki shorts and a cream short-sleeved dress shirt, Locke in a light, lacy dress in the same shade. When they said their vows, Toni started sniffling, baby bump now gently visible under her flowered dress. Lee patted her hand. Jess's eyes slid over to Vivienne. She was sniffling, too. The corner of Jess's mouth curled. She reached into her bag and handed Vivienne a tissue.

"Thanks," Vivienne whispered, and dabbed at her eyes.

When Shay and Locke sat to sign the register, Jess leaned over to Vivienne, whose eyes were still wet. "I didn't take you for a wedding crier."

Vivienne delicately wiped at another tear. "There's a lot you don't know about me, Jess."

Yeah . . . I'm beginning to realize.

And she wanted to know more.

18

Wins: 24
Losses: 25

***Serve receive*: How you receive the serve. Duh.**

***Game in hand*: As playoffs approach, and every win counts, a team that has one more game left to play than another has an extra opportunity to climb the rankings with a win.**

"Here's to hitting five hundred!" Tania cried, with an inebriated softening to her consonants. "I can taste it!"

"What you've been tasting is tequila," Jess reminded her, dodging the amber liquid that sloshed from Tania's shot glass.

Tania was doing a solid job celebrating her birthday and their four-game winning streak—that brought them to within one game of five hundred—in equal measure.

"I taste victory, Jess! I taste a championship!" Tania crowed before downing her next shot.

Jess gave George a pointed look, motioning at Tania's empty water glass. George nodded resignedly and went to find a fresh pitcher.

Chrissy swallowed her own shot with equal gusto. "Come dance with me!" she cried, grabbing Tania's hand and pulling her onto the dance floor.

"Jess! Come on!" Tania lunged for Jess's hand on her way by, but missed.

"Just getting another drink," Jess called after them. "I'll be right there."

She headed over to the bar for a Corona, then was threading through the crowd trying to get back to their table when a loud voice and a familiar name cut through the bar noise.

"Ugh, I hate Vivienne. She's such a bitch."

Jess lurched to a halt, scanning for the source. She discovered, unsurprisingly, Tweedledum, one of the complainers from Horny Beach, drunk and talking way too loud to her partner.

"Right?" Tweedledee replied. "She thinks she's hot shit and I'm over it."

Jess smirked, trying to fight off a full-blown laugh. Vivienne and Lee had spanked the Tweedles hard today, 21–6 and 21–9.

Tweedledum made eye contact with Jess. Her face soured further at Jess's grin. "What?"

Jess blinked innocently. "What?"

"Why are you standing there staring at us?"

"Oh, it's nothing."

Dee chimed in. "Don't be shy, Jess. What's on your mind?"

Jess mulled for a second if it was worth getting into it. She decided it was. "I'd be bitter too, if Vivienne and Lee had just kicked my ass like that."

Dee and Dum's jaws dropped in unison.

Dum recovered first. She laughed and picked up her cocktail. "I'm trying to remember the last time you beat her."

Jess shrugged and took a slow drink of her beer, then swallowed and wiped her lip with her wrist. "It's true, I haven't, but . . . I'm not a little bitch when I lose."

Dee's lips flapped while she tried to swim through the indignation and find a retort, but then she noticed Jess's forearm. Her eyes widened. "Wait . . . do you have the same tattoo as Vivienne?"

"Oh my God, she does!" Dum crowed.

"What, are you trying to be like her? That's sad."

Jess laughed. Oh, those fuckers did not just go after her perfect tattoo. "Actually, I watched your match today, and what's sad is your serve receive." She lifted her beer in a mocking toast and took another drink.

Their expressions morphed from derision into outrage.

Dee sneered. "Whatever, Jess. Have fun being Vivienne's little wannabe."

Tania materialized at Jess's elbow and hurled an insult in Spanish at the Horny Beach team.

"Whoa, girl," Jess said, putting an arm around Tania before she could lunge toward them. "It's fine."

Tania continued to rant at them in Spanish from the safety of Jess's grip.

"I know," Jess soothed. "They're not worth it. It's okay."

Dee stood, collecting her purse. "Let's get out of this shithole." Dum followed. They glared at Jess and Tania and retreated through the crowd toward the door.

"Yeah, you'd better leave!" Tania called after them. "Horny beaches."

Lee pulled up, eyebrow raised, with Vivienne right behind her. "Jesus, what was that about?" Lee asked.

"Nothing," Jess tried to say as Tania started babbling.

"They were talking shit about Vivienne, but Jess told them to fuck off."

Vivienne fluttered her eyelashes up at Jess. "You did?"

"I mean . . ." Jess swallowed hard, her cheeks heating. "Not in so many words."

"She shut them down so hard, it was incredible!" Tania gave a gleeful blow-by-blow recount of the events, with only slight drunken embellishments.

Vivienne's face glowed in the last light from the sunset spilling in the windows, half in shadow, half Aphrodite. "Thanks for having my back, Jess."

"I mean . . . of course—"

Tania threw her arms around Jess and Vivienne. "Sunside has to stick together!"

"Yeah, we do," Vivienne agreed quietly, not taking her eyes off of Jess.

Jess's stomach swooped. The way Vivienne was looking at her. . . . There was something soft and unguarded there instead of the usual glint and polish.

"Let's drink on it," Tania whooped. "Also, did someone mention cake?"

How are you feeling? Jess texted Tania the next morning. Well, late morning. She was making a bagel melt for lunch.

Ugh, Tania replied. **You should have made me drink water.**

Babe. George and I tried.

That's what he said, too. Thanks, though. I had so much fun.

You're welcome. Hope 27 is good to you.

So far 27 wants me to go back to bed.

Get some more sleep, T. See you tomorrow.

Jess ate her lunch, took Fleming for a walk, then headed into work.

It was a busy Sunday along the boardwalk. Roller skaters

weaved through the tourists posing for photos, the last hurrah of summer before the crowds thinned as October approached. Jess changed into her hideous uniform shirt and made her way to ring toss.

In a lull near the end of her shift, she put her hands in her pockets and leaned against the counter. Her gaze drifted along the beach to the lifeguard chair. There was Vivienne. It was hard to really see her, given the sun hat, sunglasses, and distance, but there was no mistaking her posture and golden skin, swimsuit a red blip against the blue, blue sky.

"Hi, Jess."

Jess jolted out of her thoughts to see Troy standing at the counter. "Oh, hey, Troy! You're back from vacation?"

"Yup. Family reunion in Atlanta. We had a great time. But how about you? I see you've been tearing it up out there."

Jess had to grin. "Yeah, we're on a bit of a roll."

Troy studied her for a moment, eyes narrowed. "I have to say . . . your energy is different."

Jess smoothed her hair self-consciously. "It is?"

"Yes." He rubbed his chin. "You've got this confidence. . . ."

A patch of warmth grew in Jess's chest. She'd definitely been feeling more confident, and if Troy noticed . . . "Tania and I figured some stuff out, and we've been winning a lot more. We have eleven games left, and if we win eight of them, we should make playoffs."

Troy nodded and placed his five dollars on the counter. "You can do it. I have no doubt."

Jess smiled and handed him his rings. Once his tosses were taken care of—twenty-five points—he tucked his ticket away. "Keep doing whatever it is you're doing, Jess. It's working for you."

As soon as he turned to leave, a flash of red on the edge of her vision caught Jess's attention. It was Vivienne, sprinting toward the ocean. A small crowd had gathered at the water's edge, and Jess lost Vivienne once she dove into the surf. Jess stood on tiptoe, as if that would help, watching the onlookers point and gesticulate.

A pack of teenagers arrived at her counter, quickly followed by a family with four kids, so even though she tried to steal a glance every couple of minutes, she missed what happened. The crowd at the shore grew, then dissipated, and Jess didn't get any more glimpses of the red swimsuit.

She texted Vivienne from the locker room as soon as her shift ended, just to check on her. **Hey, I saw you dash toward the water today. Everyone okay?**

Vivienne replied by the time Jess had changed out of her uniform. **Yeah, just some women got in over their heads and needed help.**

Glad it was nothing too serious. A question floated through her mind. She decided to ask. **Do you ever get scared when you're running into the ocean?**

Scared that I'm too late, maybe.

Jess shivered. **I couldn't imagine being responsible for someone's life like that.**

I try not to think of it like that . . . or I'm not sure I could do it either.

What was the scariest save you've ever had to make? They chatted about lifeguarding Jess's whole walk home, even when she almost tripped over a dog leash and nearly got clipped by a wobbly roller skater. She turned on one of Bianca's matches when she got home and they watched that together too, swapping volleyball stories from earlier in their careers and oohing and aahing over a commercial for Bianca's new athletic wear clothing line. Each time Jess's phone lit up with a notification, her heart skipped a beat.

I'd better get to bed, she finally said, well after the match had ended and her eyes had grown heavy. **I work opening tomorrow.**

Yeah, I should get some sleep, too. Good luck on Wednesday if I don't see you before then. I know you guys are going to hit 500.

Thanks. I hope so! Jess fell asleep smiling, muscled bodies in red swimsuits dancing through her dreams.

Vivienne was right. They won their next game and hit five hundred, bringing their win streak to five. The playoff push was official now. Playoff Math consumed Jess, much to Tania's dismay.

Leg day firmly on the back burner, Jess hunched over her phone and frowned at the standings. "Ten games left. Do you think we can win all ten? If we do, we'll make playoffs for sure . . . probably."

But then they lost the next game against a Horny Beach team. Tania's shoulder seemed sore, and the bounces weren't going their way. "It's fine," Jess said after, checking the day's results on their way into the locker room. "Nine games left, and Sonja and Jonesy lost today too, so even if we win eight out of nine we should be safe."

They won two more, then lost. "We're still at five hundred, but we only have six games left. We probably need to win five . . . unless Chrissy and Shay lose all of theirs, then maybe only four. But they won't lose all of them. . . . Now, if they *win* all of them . . ."

They lost again, then won the next two.

Jess sat bent over her tablet at her kitchen table. "So if

the Tweedles win today, and Sonja and Jonesy win, then we have to win all three remaining games. But if only one of them wins, we only need to win two. That's good, because our last match is against Vivienne and Lee. Wait, the Tweedles have a game in hand. . . ."

"Jessss," Tania groaned from the counter, where she was mashing avocado.

"Imagine being Vivienne and Lee right now? No pressure. They had a playoff spot locked up weeks ago."

Tania pinched the bridge of her nose. "Jess."

"Although they must feel pressure to win the whole thing."

"*Jess*."

"Yeah?"

"I'm *begging* . . ."

"Okay, you're right. I'm sorry." Jess resumed her task of chopping cilantro. "So . . . what's new with you?"

Tania chuckled. "Not much. George's aunt is visiting from Nova Scotia. Sounds like such a beautiful place. She keeps telling us to come visit."

"That's great."

"You're still doing Playoff Math in your head, aren't you?"

"No. Yes."

"Okay. That's it." Tania shook her head. "After we eat, I am getting your mind off of things."

"How?"

"You'll see."

Tania sent a few mysterious texts while they were eating, then she herded Jess out her front door.

"Am I dressed okay?" Jess asked as Tania grabbed Jess's keys from her to lock the door.

"Yup. Let's move."

"Where are we going?" Jess asked when Tania didn't stop at George's truck and they continued to march down the sidewalk toward the beach.

"Just walk."

Jess thought they were going to the pavilion at first, but they veered off course. It was almost like they were headed to . . . "The amusement park?" she said when the gates came into view.

"I know, I know, you work here. But when was the last time you had *fun* here?"

"Um . . ." Then she saw Chrissy waiting for them, and Shay, Billi, Raya, Lee . . . and Vivienne. Vivienne, achingly hot, with windblown hair, a white bikini top, and jean shorts. Jess tore her eyes off of Vivienne's long, smooth neck and muscled shoulders and grinned at the group.

"Welcome to Operation Fuck Playoffs!" Tania announced. "There are two rules this evening: No talking about volleyball—I mean it, Jessica—and have fun!"

They ran straight to the roller coaster and got seats right at the front, Jess squished in between Tania and Vivienne. Vivienne's skin was as warm as it was golden, and it gave Jess a shiver as it pressed to hers, ankles to shoulders. She screamed at the first drop, arms in the air, letting any pent-up anxiety spiral loose into the darkening California sky.

Jess chose a gold horse on the carousel because it reminded her of Vivienne's radiant skin. Vivienne sat next to her on a white horse with a pink mane. Billi and Raya fought over a purple horse, only pausing when Tania held up her phone to snap a group selfie.

After the carousel, they rode the giant swings, then the

roller coaster again. They played Whac-A-Mole and ring toss—Troy certainly made it look easier than it was, although Jess did manage to win a mini mermaid stuffie with black hair after a few tries. They had churros, popcorn, and frozen lemonade. And they laughed. They laughed until their sides hurt, laughed till they cried, laughed until the whole sky was a blanket of stars twinkling far above their heads, until the playoff math had dissolved away in adrenaline and midway bells, shared looks and pinkies brushing in the crowd, a head tilted back, a lazy smile, and a tongue licking a sparkle of sugar off a lip.

And the whole time, with Vivienne by her side, Jess felt her pull, like a comet around its sun, wondering how there was a time when she thought Vivienne was distant and cold.

"I can give you guys a ride," Vivienne said to Jess when they got to her Mercedes at the curb after the park closed. "It's on my way."

It's fine, we can walk, Jess was about to say, not wanting to make Vivienne go out of her way, but Tania jumped into the car and scrambled into the back seat.

"Oh, thanks," Jess said. "That would be great."

Jess rolled her window down and tipped her head back on her headrest, smiling in the breeze, the most relaxed she had felt in weeks. Then her mind drifted forward. "We play you on Saturday," she said to Vivienne at a red light.

"Jessica! No volleyball talk!" came from the back seat.

Vivienne cast a look sideways at Jess. "I know," she said softly.

"That game might decide if we make playoffs or not," Jess added, eyes closed.

"I know," Vivienne replied.

Tania grumbled from the back seat, but she had lost her steam.

"You won't let us win, right?" Jess asked.

Vivienne drummed her fingers on the steering wheel. "I would never."

"Good."

Jess and Tania waved goodbye to Vivienne from the curb, then Jess hugged Tania. "Thank you. I needed a night like this."

Tania hugged her back. "You're welcome. Sleep well tonight, Button."

"I will."

Jess set the mermaid stuffie with black hair on the shelf next to her jars of shells . . . twenty-nine wins, twenty-eight losses. And she did sleep very well indeed.

Friday, on the penultimate day of the regular season, Jess sat next to Tania on the bleachers. "Sonja and Jonesy won their match. . . ."

"And that means we have to beat Vivienne and Lee tomorrow to make playoffs," Tania finished.

Jess nodded and settled back into her seat. "So let's beat them."

19

Wins: 31
Losses: 28
Wins needed to make playoffs: 32
Matches left: 1

> ***First kill*: When you're such hot shit that you let the other team serve first, so you can score your first point off of a hit.**

Vivienne was almost naked when Jess and Tania arrived in the locker room. She had her black-and-gold bikini bottom in place and was just pulling the top on. Jess dropped her gaze, but not before she got a good eyeful, the image stark in her brain—Vivienne's muscles rippling under her tattoo, and her gently sloping breast and dark nipple. . . .

"Oh, hey," Vivienne said once her top was secured.

"Hey," Jess said, trying to shake certain thoughts out of her mind.

"Hey, Viv." Tania dumped her bag on a bench. "Ready to lose today?"

Vivienne pulled her hair back for a ponytail. "Someone's feeling confident."

Tania didn't reply, or least Jess didn't hear her, because the outline of Vivienne's nipple was still visible through the fabric. Jess's pulse jumped as she pictured it again, the memory morphing into fantasy . . . what her fingers could do, what her tongue might find—

Tania chuckled and patted Jess's shoulder. "Thankfully, she's not as dumb as she acts sometimes."

"Er, what?" Jess stammered, pressing cool fingers to her hot cheek.

Tania waved her hand. "The moment has passed us by, Button. Time to get your head in the game and out of . . . wherever it was." She raised a meaningful eyebrow at Jess.

Jess's face neared the temperature of the sun. "I'm fine. I'm . . ." She willed her eyes not to look at Vivienne. ". . . focused."

"Mm-hmm."

Vivienne picked up her bag and slid into her flip-flops. "Good luck, guys. I'll see you out there."

Jess stared hard at Tania so her gaze didn't accidentally wander to Vivienne's retreating curves. "Yup. Good luck."

Tania's expression was half concerned, half amused. "You okay? Your face is red."

"Fine. Just . . . excited."

"I'll bet you are."

"For the game!"

Tania snickered. "I have no doubt."

Jess pressed her lips together and changed the subject, refusing to acknowledge what Tania was hinting at. "Did you see the cable van on the way in? Guess we're televised."

"Perfect." Tania pulled her uniform out of her locker. "Some of my family couldn't make it. And now we can watch our victory over and over again, as many times as we want."

Jess let out a weak chuckle, but her stomach clenched. Tania was certainly acting confident to the extreme, but did she really believe it? Vivienne and Lee had set a SoCal VL record this season for win percentage. Were they really going to lose the last game of the season to a team scrabbling for the playoffs?

She supposed they were about to find out.

Warm-up was bumpy. Jess's stomach continued its dance, while a headache at the base of her skull started to bother her.

When Tania had the trainer over at their bench to massage her shoulder, Jess took a deep, calming breath. *Just another game, Jess. It's just another game.*

Vivienne and Lee won the coin toss and chose to receive the first serve. This was a power move, for sure. Everyone always picked serve when they won the coin toss, but Vivienne and Lee were so confident that they wanted first kill instead.

"We choose the other side," Tania responded.

Jess swallowed her chuckle. This call wasn't so much a power move as it was a dick move. Requesting a side switch to start the match was rarely done, unless forces of the sun or wind were significantly at play, but in the pavilion, neither was a major issue. Tania just wanted to make them move their stuff to the other bench.

Lee laughed with a sarcastic bow. "Fine, Tania. Take your side."

"Did you enjoy that?" Jess asked, settling onto their new bench.

Tania grinned. "I did, in fact. Now go make them pay for choosing to receive first."

The ref blew her whistle to start the match. They took to the court and shook hands under the net.

Vivienne met Jess's gaze and reached for her hand. "Good luck."

Everything but Vivienne went blurry. The crowd vanished. The heat of the sun faded. Vivienne's hand was elegant and smooth, nails shining black to match her uniform. Jess circled her thumb on the back of Vivienne's soft hand without meaning to. "Good luck."

Their eyes held another full second, until Tania smacked Jess's butt. "Your serve, Button."

The corner of Vivienne's mouth twitched as they turned their backs on each other.

Jess marched to the back line, ball in hand. She took a deep breath and closed her eyes for a moment. When she opened them, she made eye contact with Vivienne again. The tentative smile was gone. Now her smirk said "Let's see what you got." Jess thumped the logo, tossed the ball in the air at the whistle, and sent a rocket jump serve over, spinning away from Vivienne. For a fraction of a second, she thought Vivienne wasn't going to step into it far enough, but she did. Her pass wasn't terrific, and neither was Lee's resulting bump set.

Tania dug Vivienne's easy hit no problem, a perfect rainbow pass to Jess, who gave her a great set. Tania wanted that first point and she didn't hold back. She cranked one sharp cross past Lee's block and it slammed into the sand before Vivienne could get there.

First point.

"Yes!" Tania roared. "Who's got first kill now?"

Jess blocked Vivienne for the next point.

"Jess!" Tania crowed. "*Hell* yes!"

A spark in Jess's gut caught fire.

And the flames grew. It turned out, Jess and Tania showed up with their best volleyball of the season. Vivienne and Lee didn't roll over, by any means, but their energy drained away point by point while Jess's fire roared. Lee called a time-out once they were down 9–6. Vivienne's body language was more irritated than anything as she made her way off the court.

"Holy fuck." Tania squirted water over her head. Even for early October, it was still scorching hot in the direct sun.

Jess wiped her face with a towel. "Yeah."

"Just keep going, Button. I've got a good feeling about this."

Jess realized her nerves had vanished. Her headache had faded. She also had a very good feeling crackling inside of her.

And it continued. They won the first set 21–17.

"That's what I'm talking about," Tania hissed to Jess on their way back to their bench, pumping her fist. "*Yes.*"

Jess hadn't felt so alive in a long time. She was in the fucking zone. She felt like she couldn't lose a volleyball game ever again.

Vivienne and Lee huddled close together at their bench, talking with lots of nodding and hand slapping.

"Okay, they are going to come out *hard* this game," Tania said, wiping sweat from her brow. "We have to do whatever it takes to get the first point. We have to keep the momentum on our side."

Of course Jess knew that. That was the thing about volleyball . . . momentum changed all the time.

And Vivienne and Lee came out flying. They were champions, after all. They hit harder, they served tougher, they ran faster.

Jess could get a block touch on Vivienne's hit four times

but not five. Tania dug her six times but not seven. Vivienne and Lee chipped at the momentum they had built, and, despite Jess's best efforts to hold on, it slipped away one grain at a time, then a chunk, then an avalanche.

They lost 15–21.

"We know we can beat them. We just proved it." Tania chewed her protein bar furiously. "They're not robots, they can't be perfect forever."

Jess wasn't sure which of them Tania was trying to convince.

Tania continued. "I want you to mess with Viv's head again. Make her guess every time. Fuck with her as much as you can."

"I'll try."

Tania glared at her.

"I mean, yes. I'll do it." She gave Tania five. "I believe in us. Let's get this done."

Vivienne and Lee looked like they had the same plan—determined and unrelenting—but at least they were sweaty, too. Lee adjusted her visor and slapped Vivienne's butt in the most business-like way possible.

The third and deciding set began, with Jess and Tania's season riding on it.

Lee blocked for the first point, then Jess returned the favor. Tania dug an impossible ball, then Vivienne did, too. Jess chased down a shank she never thought she'd get to, but she did. It was one spectacular play after another, and the crowd ate it up. They roared in equal measure for all good plays, and every play was good.

Jess did her best to mess with Vivienne's head, moving her around the court as much as she could, trying to make her think one thing, then doing another.

It almost broke through Vivienne's facade, almost. After she misread a dig and shanked it into the stands, she clenched her fist and might have muttered a swear word.

The game continued at an even keel until, tied at twelve, Tania missed her serve. Now down 12–13, she called a time-out.

"What's up?" Jess asked.

Tania shook her head and found the tube she was looking for in the med kit. She squirted a dollop of ointment onto her shoulder and rubbed it in. The pungent smell tickled Jess's nostrils, and worry tickled at her brain.

"Just wanted to make Viv think before her next serve," Tania explained, without making eye contact.

Jess had to ask. "You sure your shoulder's okay?"

"It's fine. We need this side-out."

Jess nodded and drank some more Gatorade. Tania didn't need to tell her how crucial the next point was, and if she said she was fine . . . Jess had to trust her.

They went back out at the whistle. Vivienne walked slowly to the back line for her serve, head down. The sweat glimmered on her skin, limbs almost moving in slow motion as she caught the ball the linesperson tossed at her.

Jess waited, hands on her knees. The stands were quiet.

Vivienne drilled her serve at Tania, which was smart. She had no doubt seen Tania's ministrations to her shoulder.

Tania passed it, and, noticing Vivienne creeping forward in anticipation of a short shot, lobbed her hit deep. Vivienne turned and went after it. Jess held her breath. The ball was maybe heading out, and Vivienne was maybe not going to make it. Vivienne dove, but, midair, decided it was out and let it hit the sand.

The ball landed so, so close to the line. The rope didn't

obviously bounce, and Jess couldn't even tell if it was in or out. Every eye was on the line judge. She paused, then dramatically swung her flag downward to call it in.

Jess and Tania hollered and jumped into each other's arms. Tied at thirteen.

Vivienne and Lee took their time getting set for the next serve, throwing a few muttered words at each other in between hand slaps.

Jess's serve . . . maybe the biggest serve of her life. She shook out her limbs, took a breath, and smacked the logo. Nerves jittering again, her toss was a little low, but the ball made it over, spinning toward Vivienne. Jess ran to the net to block her, tired quads aching in protest. Vivienne tried to roll the ball short crosscourt, but Tania was all over it, popping it up nice and high. Jess bump set her, breath held as Tania approached. Tania swung hard line, with a sharp hiss of pain. Vivienne got her fist on it but wasn't able to control the ball, and it continued flying out the back of the court in a graceful arc. Lee chased it, but her desperate swing sent the ball soaring off into the stands.

Up 14–13. Match point.

"Yes!" Tania cried. She hugged Jess. "Fuck, yes. One more serve, Jess." She held Jess's shoulders. "Deep breath. You've got this."

Jess blew out the rest of her breath at the service line. A hush fell over the stands. She tossed the ball in the air and sent her serve over to Vivienne.

Vivienne passed it to Lee, cool as ice, then swung at Lee's set. It clipped the top of Jess's block, enough to slow it down for Tania to bump set her.

Jess took a quick look at the court. Vivienne was too far back. The short shot was there.

Jess jumped, swung big, then pulled up and popped it short and sharp, away from Lee's block.

Vivienne was after it, feet digging into the sand as she pushed off. She was so fast, always so fast. Vivienne ran, ponytail swinging. Three steps, four, she dove . . . and she couldn't get there. The ball hit the ground.

They won.

Tania jumped onto her, screaming. Or maybe Jess was the one screaming. It was hard to tell.

Vivienne stood up slowly, brushing the sand off her body. She looked down at her feet . . . but not before Jess saw a tiny curve of a smile.

Tania squeezed Jess hard enough to crack a rib and picked her up. "Yes! Yes, yes, yes! Jess, we did it!"

Jess's legs shook with exhaustion and elation when Tania set her down again. "Yeah, we fucking did!"

Tania threw her head back and hollered, "Playoffs, baby!"

They laughed, they cried, they hugged. Jess was so fucking proud of herself and Tania.

But Vivienne's little smile haunted her.

Maggie's was packed that night as the whole league celebrated the end of the regular season, with some getting a little silly if they'd qualified for playoffs . . . or if they hadn't.

Vivienne and Lee sat at one end of the table amidst their court of admirers. The number of wins they'd racked up this season was truly something to marvel at. Vivienne wore a simple white sundress that did insane things for her skin and legs and delicate clavicles. . . . Jess tried not to stare at her down the table but had had enough drinks for that to be a real challenge.

At one point, when she was not even aware she was staring, Vivienne suddenly looked over and made eye contact. Jess's heart jumped at being caught. But she couldn't look away. Vivienne's hair spilled over her shoulders like she was the damsel on the cover of a romance novel. They held eyes for a moment, then Vivienne picked up her drink and came over.

Jess's brain told her to panic. Sweat beaded on her hairline. Her mouth dried out. *But why? Why am I panicking?* she tried to ask her brain. Her brain did nothing but crank up her heart rate.

Vivienne tapped their glasses together as she sat, a vision in white. "Cheers. Congrats on a hell of a finish."

Jess's heart pounded harder. "Congrats on a hell of a season."

Vivienne took a sip of her margarita. "You guys played great today."

The thrill of the victory washed over Jess again, the sense of what she and Tania had accomplished . . . but . . . Vivienne's little smile . . . "Thanks. You did, too."

Vivienne shrugged and looked at her hands. "You beat us, though."

Jess snorted. "You finished first in the league by a mile, and broke a record for the most wins in a season. 'Amazing' barely covers it."

"Yeah, well . . ." Vivienne took another sip, gaze distant. "Not everyone would agree."

"Those people are assholes." Then Jess remembered what she had in her bag. She pulled out a foil bundle and handed it to Vivienne.

Vivienne shook herself and blinked, then let out a little laugh. "Banana bread! What's this for?"

Jess lifted a shoulder. "I thought it would be fitting if you beat us today, but . . . you deserve it anyway."

A grin took over Vivienne's face. "Thanks, Jess. That's really sweet of you. And my freezer stash was starting to get a little low. . . ." The opening notes of a Shania Twain song blasted through the air. Vivienne tucked the loaf into her bag, downed the rest of her drink, and stood. "Dance?" She held out her hand.

Jess froze. Dance? With . . . Vivienne?

Vivienne nodded her head at the dance floor. "Come on. Everyone's out there."

Jess stole a glance. Indeed, Chrissy, Shay, Billi, and a bunch of others were attempting to get a line dance going, laughing and pointing and tripping over each other. Jess finished her beer and took Vivienne's hand. Vivienne laced their fingers together, but only for a second, until they reached the crowd and had to find their place in the wobbly line, then she let go.

But even when they weren't touching, Jess was very aware of where Vivienne was. A current of electricity connected them, tingled when Vivienne came closer, and sparked when they made eye contact.

Vivienne danced like she played, smooth, strong, and confident, and Jess could not take her eyes off of her. They stepped and turned, grapevined and twirled.

And the current hummed.

It crackled under her skin like an itch, even when she got home, even still in the dark in her bed. She thought of Vivienne's dress hugging her body. She thought of Vivienne's bronze-colored nipple, and her bare breasts.

She thought of touching her, running her hands over every alluring curve, pressing her lips to Vivienne's lovely skin, until Jess moaned, her back arching, sparks turning her vision white in the dark.

20

Wins: 32
Losses: 28
Matches left to win the league championship: 4

> ***First round*: The top sixteen teams make the first round of playoffs. The winning eight play in the quarterfinals, top four is the semifinals, then it all comes down to the final two teams in the league championship match. No big deal.**

The league paused for a few days until playoffs started Friday. Jess and Tania's first-round matchup was in North Bay against the team that had finished second behind Vivienne and Lee.

"Be a good boy." Jess gave Fleming one more kiss when she dropped him off at Nelson's on Thursday afternoon.

"He'll be good enough, anyway," Nelson said, bending over to pat Fleming's head when Jess set him down. "Can't get in that much trouble when your legs are an inch long."

Jess handed Nelson a bag of dog treats. "Sunside Cable is airing all the playoff matches, so you guys can watch if you want."

"Of course. We're making 'Go Jess' signs later."

"You and Fleming are making signs?"

"Well, me, Fleming . . . and Ramón."

"Ramón? *Ramón?* Tell me more!"

Nelson studied his nails. "A lady doesn't kiss and tell."

"Maybe, but they f—"

"Ramón," Nelson interrupted, "is the lovely man I met with Fleming's assistance. Remember the snack with the corgis? Turns out he was more than a snack—he's a whole damn meal. And things have been . . . progressing."

"Progressing?" Jess squeezed his forearm. Nelson hadn't mentioned the actual name of a romantic interest in at least a year and a half. "Nelson, I'm so happy for you!"

Fleming barked. They both looked down at the pup wagging his tail.

"Does Fleming like Ramón?" Jess asked.

"He doesn't growl at him . . . too much."

"Sounds promising. When can I meet him?"

"He should be here when you pick up Fleming on Saturday." Nelson gave Jess a hug. "Good luck, love. You crush those North Bay fuckers, yeah?"

Jess laughed and hugged him back. "That's the plan."

"Maybe we didn't think this through. . . ." Jess paused her sunscreen application to frown at Tania. "We had to play the game of our lives to beat Vivienne and Lee . . . and now we're going to have to do it again for every single playoff match."

Tania shrugged and continued rubbing ointment into her shoulder. "Vivienne and Lee are the best team we'll have to face, by a mile. And if we can beat them, we can beat anyone."

Their first-round opponents had a similar vibe to Vivienne and Lee—scrappy, strong, and cool under pressure. Which was why it was such a surprise when Jess and Tania won the first set 21–13. Matches were best of five in the playoffs, though, so they still had two to go.

"That was a little too easy," Jess said as they returned to their bench between sets.

Tania's face was grim. "The next one won't be. They didn't take us seriously enough, but they won't make that mistake again."

Their opponents came out much stronger in the second, but Jess and Tania held on to eke them out 22–20.

"One more," Tania breathed during their next break. "Jess, we're doing it."

They won the next one, too. Jess could hardly believe it. No one would have bet on them beating the second-place team in straight sets.

Well, Tania might have.

"I love you!" Tania growled, grabbing Jess's face and kissing her cheek after the final point.

Jess laughed. "I love you, too."

Tania nodded firmly. "We're doing it. Let's fucking go."

Jess ignored the way Tania rubbed her shoulder.

They could have hit the road right after the match and made it back to Sunside by midnight, but the league paid for their room, so instead they chose to have a nice meal and a good sleep, heading home well rested the next morning.

They picked a Japanese place near their hotel and ordered enough food for ten people. Jess planned to eat all of it.

Once she had tucked away a yam roll and some tempura, Jess scrolled through the other playoff results. "Billi and Raya won in four! But, shit, Chrissy and Shay lost in five."

"Damn. That sucks," Tania groaned, adding more soy sauce to her dish.

Jess set her phone down and attacked her sashimi. There were more first-round games to be played Saturday and Sunday still, so they'd have to wait to find out who their quarter-final opponents would be. "So . . . three more matches to win SoCal."

Tania nodded. "We can do it."

"Yes, we can. . . . I really believe that."

"I know you do, Button. I'm so proud of you . . . and us, and how far we've come this season. It's been . . . it's been really special."

Jess picked up a piece of fish with her chopsticks as a thought surfaced. "You know . . . It might be time to retire that nickname."

Tania chuckled and raised her eyebrow. "Yeah?"

"I don't think it suits me anymore."

Tania pondered. "You know what . . . you're right. You've really outgrown it."

They ate silently for a few bites.

"I'll need a new nickname now, though," Jess said.

"We'll have to see what bubbles up. You can't force these things. Unless . . . What do you think about Bubbles?"

Jess glared at her as she chewed, then her phone buzzed. A text from Vivienne. **Fuck yeah! I watched your game, you guys crushed them.**

"Who's that?" Tania asked.

"Oh, sorry. Just Vivienne congratulating us." Jess fired a quick reply. **Thanks! Good luck tomorrow. We'll be there cheering for you.**

Tania looked like she was fighting to hold something back.

"What?" Jess asked.

"Nothing, it's just . . ." Tania set her chopsticks down. "You should have seen your face light up at that text."

Jess's cheeks flushed. "What are you talking about?"

"I wasn't sure I should say anything, but . . . Jess, do you . . . do you like Vivienne?"

An automatic denial jumped to position on her tongue, but the truth was . . . Tania had just asked her a question she hadn't been able to ask herself yet. A scary question. A question that might provide the answer to a lot of the heart-pounding, sweat-inducing feelings she'd been having lately.

When she didn't get a reply, Tania shrugged. "If you don't want to talk about it, I get it. . . ."

"It's not that, it's just . . ." Jess ran her hand through her hair. "I don't know. I haven't really let myself think about it. Because it's Vivienne. I thought I hated her for so long."

Tania nodded and sipped her water, giving Jess space to say more.

"I . . ." Jess tapped her chopsticks on her plate, trying to put the uncertainty she'd been avoiding into actual words. "Fuck. I'm definitely attracted to her. She's . . . well, she's fucking hot."

Tania nodded. "Gorgeous."

"But I . . . I don't think we'd go together." Or it was too scary to try, anyway. And that smile after their game . . . what had that even meant?

Tania tilted her head. "What do you mean?"

"She's like . . . stunningly beautiful, and perfect, and so confident, and a *star*. . . . Why would she want me?"

Tania's face flitted through several emotions before she settled on exasperation. "Jessica McLaughlin. Why would she . . . ? God, I want to smack you sometimes. I thought we were working on this confidence thing?"

"I *have* been more confident!" Jess protested.

"On the court I guess, sure, but . . . we need to expand the confidence off the court. Because you're actually fucking amazing, and totally beautiful and wonderful yourself."

"No." Jess shook her head. This automatic denial came out just fine. "Nothing like Vivienne."

"Vivienne is not perfect. No one is. Everyone has shit they're insecure about." Tania sighed and studied her. "You know . . . I've sort of been thinking that maybe Vivienne likes you, too."

"What?" Jess's heart leapt, then crashed back down again. "There's no way. What makes you say that?"

"Well . . ." Tania gestured toward Jess's phone. "She didn't text me."

"We're friends."

"I saw her pull you onto the dance floor at Maggie's."

"Everyone was dancing."

"Mm-hmm. I know you could argue until the cows come home, but it doesn't change the fact that I've definitely been getting a . . . vibe from her lately."

Jess allowed herself a second . . . imagined Vivienne liking her back, smiling up at her, taking her hand, tilting her lips up—"There's no way. She's way out of my league."

Tania sighed again. "You are literally and metaphorically in the same league."

They stared at each other for a moment, both recognizing the wall they had arrived at. Jess just couldn't believe there was any way someone as amazing as Vivienne would settle for someone as plain as her.

Jess smiled and picked up her water. "So . . . What are you and George going to get up to this winter?"

Tania inclined her head, accepting the back-burnering of their argument. "Not sure . . . George has some vacation saved up for the offseason. We thought about heading up to Nova Scotia to stay with his aunt, see some of the Maritimes maybe."

"Oh, nice. I've never been."

"You'll have to come visit."

"Visit? How long are you going for?"

"Awhile, probably? At least a month." Tania stole a piece of tempura off of Jess's plate.

"That would be fun."

"Will you head back up to Vancouver at some point?"

Jess shrugged. "Yeah, for Christmas, I guess. Marion likes to do things the way we've always done them. She'd be pissed if I missed it."

"Traditions are nice. Family is important."

Jess narrowed her eyes at Tania. "You're very philosophical tonight."

Tania smiled and dipped a piece of sushi into her soy sauce. "Maybe I am."

They chitchatted about Nova Scotia for a bit, but Jess's thoughts returned to Vivienne, and the question she had ignored for so long.

Do I like Vivienne?

Even Jess could appreciate that Ramón was smoking hot. Tall, with high cheekbones, radiant terra-cotta skin, and an easy, relaxed smile that immediately put her at ease.

"It's so nice to meet you, Jess," Ramón said, kissing both

cheeks. His Spanish accent was slow and warm, every syllable carefully rolled across his tongue on its way out.

"You too. Nelson never lets me meet his boyfriends."

"Oh, are we boyfriends?" Ramón said, turning his smile onto Nelson.

Nelson, uncharacteristically, froze. "Um."

"Ooh, my bad," Jess said, though she wasn't actually sorry.

Ramón chuckled. "Only if you are comfortable with the label, mi amor."

Nelson's shoulders relaxed. "Of course. Of course you're my boyfriend." He slid his hand onto the back of Ramón's neck and leaned over to kiss him.

Jess grinned.

Nelson saw her grin and rolled his eyes. "All right, take your damn dog. We have other things to do right now."

"It was really so nice to meet you, Ramón," Jess said as Nelson put Fleming in her arms and herded her out the door. "I'll have to have the two of you over sometime for—" Nelson, with a playful glower, closed the door in her face before she could finish. She chuckled and scratched Fleming's head. "Ah, young love. It's a beautiful thing, isn't it, Fleming?"

Fleming licked her chin in agreement.

She took Fleming for a walk, dumped out her duffel bag, did some laundry, and went for a short jog to shake the car ride out of her legs. After her shower, she got dressed and made herself a tuna melt. Most of the crew would be meeting at the pavilion that evening where Vivienne and Lee were playing the bottom-ranked team from Horny Beach . . . which happened to be Skye's.

It was funny to think how the last time she had watched

these teams play, she had been cheering for Skye. This time she'd be rooting for Vivienne with her whole heart.

Do I like Vivienne?

Jess wondered how many times her brain would ask that question without answering it.

When she arrived at the pavilion, Jess took a seat next to Chrissy in the stands as the warm-up was finishing.

"Hey, congrats on your win!" Chrissy said, pulling her in for a hug.

"Thanks. I'm sorry you guys didn't make it."

"Ah, it's okay." Chrissy shrugged and tossed her red hair back. "There's always next season!"

Jess's attention was drawn by Vivienne bending over to brush sand off her ankle. Jess admired the view, then flushed, thinking about the last time she had seen Vivienne, dancing at Maggie's in a sexy white dress, and the thoughts that had accompanied her into her dreams that night. . . .

"Let's go, Viv and Lee!" Chrissy hollered as the ref prepared to blow his whistle.

Jess applauded and joined the cheers, hoping no one noticed her red face.

Jess sent a text after the game. **Way to go. You guys make it look so easy.**

Vivienne replied right away. **Thanks. I quite enjoyed kicking Skye's ass.**

Jess chortled. **Lol, I'll bet. I enjoyed it, too.**

Good luck against Sonja and Jonesy on Wednesday! I know you can beat them.

Thanks. I hope so.

Vivienne was right again. They won their quarterfinal in four sets. Jess saw the court with a clarity she never had before. The game slowed down around her. When she jumped for a hit, she had all the time in the world to look around and decide where to put the ball. It was easy, and so much fun.

Fantastic game! Vivienne texted her after. **Through to the semis!**

Jess smiled at her phone. She kicked off her slippers and climbed into her bed, letting Fleming and his stuffed crab snuggle with her. **Yeah, I can't really believe it.**

You can't believe it? Why not?

Jess looked at the "loss" jar on her shelf, remembering how full it got so early in the season. **It's been a long road.**

Well, you're almost at the end. Only two matches to go.

It was funny that, if they won their semi, Vivienne would be waiting for her at the end of that road in the finals.

Vivienne.

Was Tania right? Was it really possible Vivienne liked Jess? Sure, they'd been texting a lot, but Vivienne had made no effort to see her or hang out since playoffs had started. Tania had said Vivienne had been giving off a vibe, but that was probably just Vivienne being Vivienne—used to moving through the world with smooth confidence, everything always going her way. Nothing at all like Jess. Besides, now wasn't the time to be asking these questions. They should both be focused on volleyball this week.

Her semifinal against Billi and Raya was next.

"Winner buys the shots?" Billi said, instead of "good luck," when they shook hands under the net.

"Yeah, we'd love to get you wasted tonight," Tania replied, grinning.

Billi shot finger guns at them with a wink, smacked Raya's butt, and the game was underway.

Billi and Raya were a solid team, and still with a sense of humor, even in the semis. Billi gave Raya good-natured shit for a missed hit, and tried to make Jess laugh before her serve. But nothing could throw Jess off her game.

They won the first set, lost the second in a close one, then won three and, for the match, number four. The sweat poured from her brow, her abs were sore, and she had sand wedged in every crevice of her body. But she was so fucking happy.

And now . . . they'd face Vivienne and Lee, again, in the final of the SoCal Beach Volleyball League.

You did it! Vivienne texted her that night. **Congratulations. You guys have had such an incredible run. Win or lose on Thursday, I hope you're so proud of yourself.**

Yeah, I am. I hope you're proud, too.

Vivienne didn't reply—*See? She doesn't like me*—so Jess went back to texting with Tania as they made a plan for the next few days.

They did all the right things that week—light cardio, foam rolling, yoga—and Tania sent Jess podcasts on mindfulness and performing under pressure.

Vivienne didn't text her at all, so Jess didn't text Vivienne. It was better that way, of course. She had important things to focus on.

The night before the final, Jess covered a shift until eight, then she walked home eyes up, hoping to catch some magic from the Orionids meteor shower. It was a perfect night for viewing—cloudless, and no moon. She spotted two shooting stars, faint streaks of light, and thought about taking her telescope up to the roof when she got home, but by the time she ate and took Fleming for a walk, it was too late. She had a big game tomorrow.

Except once she got into bed, she couldn't sleep. Too many thoughts crowded her head, each one demanding attention, then flitting away before it could take hold. Could they beat Vivienne again? Did Vivienne really like her? Did she like Vivienne? Could they actually work together as a couple? Jess tossed and turned and drank some more water. Covers off, covers back on.

Finally, she sat up, collected her keys, slipped on a sweater and flip-flops, and eased out of her front door quietly, not wanting to wake up Fleming. She had considered heading up to the roof to watch the meteor shower, but her feet needed to move. They took her down to the beach. The pavilion was dark, save for the security lights around the perimeter.

She walked past it and went down to the boardwalk, the noise from the surf changing from a whisper into a rumble. There were a few people here and there . . . a wandering couple holding hands, teenagers hooting from a park just down the way. But it was mostly dark and quiet—the perfect spot to lie down and take in the light—light that was billions of years old, combined with bright, transitory flashes of fire as meteors burned in the atmosphere.

Then she realized she wasn't the only one with this idea. . . . There was another person on the sand—a shadowed figure just above the high-water mark lying back on a blanket, dark hair spread out. . . . Jess's heart jumped.

It was Vivienne.

Vivienne. Here, like she was waiting for her.

Jess hesitated at the edge of the boardwalk. She didn't

want to intrude . . . but she must have made a noise, because suddenly Vivienne sat up and turned to look at her.

"Jess?" she said, squinting in the dark. "Is that you?"

Jess took off her flip-flops and made her way over, the sand cool against her feet, embarrassed that she had barged in. "Yeah. Sorry."

"Sorry for what?" Vivienne scooted over and patted the blanket next to her. "Sit."

"Sorry for interrupting."

"You are not interrupting. There's enough stars for the both of us." She lay down again.

Jess copied her, their bodies not touching, but only inches apart. She scanned the sky, waiting for a distant streak. "What are you doing here?"

Vivienne's shrug brushed her shoulder. "Same as you, I imagine. Couldn't sleep, wanted to stargaze for a bit. . . . I'm a bit of a space nerd."

Jess almost sat up again. Instead, she turned her head to look at Vivienne's profile. "What? You are?"

Vivienne looked back at her. "You are too, right?"

Jess frowned. "How did you know?"

"When I drove you to Horny Beach . . . you said you were up late because of Mars and Venus."

"Oh, right."

"Plus, your tattoo. It's a crescent moon volleyball. And . . . Fleming? Is he named after Williamina Fleming?"

Jess's jaw dropped.

Vivienne's eyes sparkled. "Ha, I fucking knew it! I love it. The woman who discovered the Horsehead Nebula. . . ."

Jess shook her head, processing this revelation. Her love of astronomy was such a big part of who she was. . . . "I can't believe you've heard of Williamina Fleming—Oooh!" Vivienne's gasp echoed Jess's as a brilliant silvery-white streak flashed above them.

"How many have you seen so far?" Jess asked in a whisper.

"Three."

"Four!" Jess pointed at another.

"So beautiful," Vivienne murmured.

The heat from Vivienne's body was like static, lifting the hairs on her arm. "Yeah." It was so strange to think that they would be facing each other across the net in just a few hours in the biggest game of Jess's life. Could they really beat Vivienne and Lee again?

Had they even beat them the first time?

It was a silly insecurity. Of course Vivienne wouldn't lose on purpose. But the question that had been niggling at the back of her brain burst out of Jess's mouth. "Did you let us win?"

Vivienne turned sharply to look at her. "What?"

"The last game of the season . . . We won when you didn't get to that ball. Did you let us win?"

Vivienne's face curdled like she'd bit into a lemon. "Did I let you win?"

"I'm sorry. I have to ask." Jess shrugged, palms sweating.

Vivienne stared at the sky, her silence loud and long. Then she spoke, voice flat. "I can't believe you would even ask me that."

Jess waited for an answer while her nerves continued to dance. "Did you?"

Vivienne looked at her again, eyes flashing. "Absolutely not, Jess! I already told you, I would never, ever throw a game."

"So you didn't miss that last ball on purpose?"

The anger darkening Vivienne's face faded into disappointment. "You don't know me at all, do you?"

It echoed in Jess's head. *You don't know me at all, do you?*

Did she know Vivienne? "I . . . I don't know. You just looked . . . happy when we won."

Vivienne huffed a small laugh. "I was happy, Jess. I was happy for *you*."

Jess's thoughts swirled, trying to make sense of what Vivienne was telling her, trying to sort out how much she did or did not know about Vivienne. She didn't know what Vivienne's parents were like, or her favorite color, or what she liked to eat for breakfast, no. But did she know if Vivienne was the kind of person who'd throw a game? If she was the kind of person who might smile for her opponent after a crushing defeat? Yes, she did know that. "So you . . ." Jess trailed off, unable to put any thoughts into a sentence.

"You got in my head, okay?" Vivienne fiddled with the blanket. "I second-guessed—and third-guessed myself, if I'm being honest—over and over in that match. You beat me, fair and square."

Jess studied her face . . . her beautiful, perfect face. Vivienne returned the gaze head-on. Her eyes were wide and clear . . . deep and dark . . . and easy to fall into. But there was only honesty in them. Maybe Jess didn't know Vivienne well in some ways, but in others . . . she very much did. "Okay." Jess nodded. "I'm sorry, I just had to check. I know you didn't."

The tension left Vivienne's face. "Okay."

Jess felt warm, even in the ocean breeze. Relaxed in a way she . . . really never had before. It felt good, to be able to ask such an embarrassing question, and for Vivienne to comfort her and still take her seriously. Really good.

They watched in silence for a few more minutes. The idea of holding Vivienne's hand crossed Jess's mind, but she could never actually go for it. "Why can't you sleep, do you think?"

Vivienne sighed. "Pressure to win, I guess."

Jess snorted. "You can't be that worried."

Vivienne turned her head and shot Jess a look. "What do you mean?"

"You guys are amazing. And you've beat us so many times."

"Well, as we just established, not last time."

"It's just . . . You're so good."

Vivienne went up on her elbows. "Are you kidding? Your team is on fire right now. And you're an amazing player, by the way—the way you see everything happening at the net. . . . Not to mention, everyone is terrified of your block."

Jess snorted again.

"They are!"

"You're not."

Vivienne wrenched both eyebrows up. "You think I'm not? Haven't you noticed I almost always roll shot past you?"

"I thought that was just 'cause you're short."

Vivienne's jaw dropped, then she burst out laughing. "I knew you were calling me short!"

The laugh was contagious. A giggle slipped out of Jess, too. "You are kind of short."

Vivienne gasped and shoved her. "I am not! You're just tall!"

"That doesn't make you any less short."

Vivienne's peal of laughter was music, in harmony with the stars, brighter than any burning meteor.

Once their giggles quieted, Jess tucked her hair behind her ear. "But for real. Why do you feel so much pressure to win?"

After a few beats of silence, Vivienne sat up and rested her chin on her knee with a sigh. "I have to win or I'm a complete failure."

Jess sat up, too. "Are you shitting me? In what world are you a failure? You . . . You're perfect."

Vivienne studied Jess a moment before she spoke again. "My brother is a cardiothoracic surgeon and my sister is a world-renowned child psychologist with a bestselling book. I'm a lifeguard who plays volleyball. I am the failure of the family."

Jess turned her words over in her head and something clicked. Vivienne, a shining star—the billion-year-old kind, not the meteors above pretending to be stars as they flashed and went out—thought she was a failure.

"You are . . . Vivienne . . . You're the most incredible person I know."

Vivienne rolled her eyes, but her mouth was soft. "Stop."

"You're smart, funny, determined, strong . . . beautiful. . . ."

Vivienne swung her gaze up to meet Jess's. "You think I'm beautiful?"

"You . . . You know you're gorgeous, all right? And all-around amazing. By any standards."

"Scarlett—"

"Your sister is great, I'm sure. But you . . ." The words dried in Jess's throat.

Vivienne shifted and blinked slowly, eyelashes thick and alluring.

"You're also great." Jess's next inhale was a shudder. The tension was too much. Her brain told her to run away before she could be rejected, before she could fuck everything up. Before Vivienne could look at her in disgust and horror, and she'd have to face her on the court tomorrow. Jess leaned back and cleared her throat. "But it's so late. We'd both better get some sleep."

Vivienne sighed. "Yeah, you're probably right."

They stood. Jess shook out the blanket for her and handed it over, their fingers touching.

"You want a ride?" Vivienne asked when they got to her car.

The panic welled in Jess's chest again. "That's okay. I'll walk."

Vivienne still looked sad, though, eyes wide and dark in the shadows, and Jess couldn't leave her like that.

"You're great," she said again as Vivienne opened her door. "Whether you win tomorrow or not."

"Thank you, Jess. That means a lot to me. . . . And I need you to know . . ." Vivienne paused, studying her feet before she looked up with a devious grin. "I *am* going to win."

A spark of adrenaline ignited in Jess's gut. She grinned back. "We'll see."

21

Wins: 35
Losses: 28
Matches left to win the league championship: 1

> ***Dive lines*: A grueling ball-less conditioning drill run at indoor volleyball practices, often as a punishment for lackluster performance, involving sprinting and diving over and over again, until your lungs are burning and your muscles are begging for mercy.**

Outside, the cameras were rolling. The crowd hummed. Jess listened to the buzz, a small bit of that old panic rising in her chest. She took a deep breath and stepped back into the locker room.

The trainer was taping up Tania's shoulder, a neat black crisscross.

"What did they say at PT?" Jess asked once they were alone in the locker room.

Tania shrugged and avoided eye contact, digging in her bag. "Oh, you know. Just getting older. Overuse. I'll be fine with a bit of rest."

"Okay . . . Just don't do anything stupid. Winning a match is not worth wrecking your shoulder."

"It's fine." Tania looked up and tossed Jess a protein bar. "Here, try this one. New flavor."

"Thanks." Jess pretended to read the label while she chewed her lip. She really hoped Tania wasn't in more pain than she was letting on, but at this point all she could do was trust her partner and get through this match.

Every seat in the stands was packed, their VL friends all hollering when they stepped onto the court.

Jess took a deep breath and looked across the net at Vivienne.

Vivienne's nails, gold again, sparkled against the black-and-white volleyball in her hands. But Jess quickly forgot about fingernails when Vivienne's jump serve came screaming at them.

Tied at ten, in the fifth and deciding set of the league championship match, Jess and Tania were playing lights out, but, as expected, so were Vivienne and Lee. The crowd was on their feet, roaring after every play, a sound that lifted Jess and carried her from point to agonizing point.

Tania's shoulder was clearly hurting, but when Jess had tried to bring it up after the third set, Tania just shrugged her off and took some more ibuprofen. And now, only a few points to go.

Jess dove to get to Vivienne's serve, sand flying, then scrambled to her feet as Tania chased down the pass and popped it up. Jess jumped, took a look, and decided to go for a wipe off Lee's imposing block.

In a blur, Vivienne dove and got a knuckle on it, but the ball continued on its way into the stands. Lee took a step like she was going to go after it, then grimaced and bent over, out of breath. Vivienne huddled with her for a second, a stripe of sand up one side of her body, before she called a time-out.

Tania dumped a water bottle over her head at their bench. "Four more fucking points, Jess."

Jess nodded and bit back a repeat of "How's your shoulder?" "We've got this," she said instead, cracking open another Gatorade.

They high-fived and returned to the court. Vivienne and Lee were still talking, hidden by the umbrella pulled low over their bench. They didn't get back out until the ref blew her whistle, then they settled in for Tania's serve, faces hard and focused.

Tania served to Vivienne. Jess readied her block, studying Vivienne's approach. They jumped together. Jess squeezed her abs and pushed her hands over the net into Vivienne's space as hard as she could. Vivienne rolled it over her block, deep to the corner. Tania chased it and dug it up high in the air over the end line. Jess ran to lob the ball back into the court. With a grunt, Tania jumped and hit it over. Lee's hands came out of nowhere and blocked the ball. Both of them were too far away to get to it before it hit the sand. Jess wiped the sweat from her brow. Tied at eleven.

Jess waited while Lee got set for her serve, hands on her hips, lifting her head in search of a breeze. The crowd rumbled around her.

Lee's serve was a weak float, drifting gently over the net. Maybe nerves were getting to her, or maybe she was tired. Jess passed it, eager for Tania's set, then crushed a hit. 12–11. Her pulse thrummed in her ears.

Jess's turn to serve. She walked slowly to the end line, trying to calm her heart rate, and, with a deep breath, sent it over to Lee. Lee's subsequent hit just clipped the tape and trickled over, impossible to get to. Twelve-all.

"Fuck." Tania massaged her shoulder.

"Three more." Jess low-fived her. A feeling buzzed in her chest, like everything she had ever learned got her to this moment. Every drill, every set of dive lines, every workout, every win . . . and every loss. It had all made her who she was, a fucking superstar, who was going to win this game. She wanted the fucking ball. Wanted it like her lungs wanted air.

Vivienne's serve again. Her face was as focused and in-the-zone as Jess had ever seen it. They made eye contact, but Vivienne's expression didn't waver. She served tough, right down the middle of the court. Jess passed it, then rolled one short past Lee's block. Vivienne made an impossible dive and dug it up, then scrambled to her feet. Lee bump set her and Vivienne rolled her own short one. Jess dove and popped it up. Another hit, another dig.

The rally went on, crossing the net four more times. Jess was winded, her quads twitching. She gathered what she had left and jumped for a block. Lee hit an awkward off-speed ball, looping it just over Jess's hands. She tried to turn and play it as she landed but couldn't make it. Tania didn't have enough gas in the tank to get there either.

Down 12–13.

They were out of time-outs, so they took their time getting into position. Tania made a show of cleaning her sunglasses, giving them a chance to catch their breath.

Vivienne went back for another serve. Jess made eye contact for a half second as Vivienne turned. And right there, in the middle of one of the biggest, most important moments of her life, the only thought in her stupid head was *God, she's breathtaking.* A goddess, really. Eyes dark and flashing, body strong and golden. Sweaty, covered in sand, ready to strike down her enemies. Jess couldn't help it. She smiled.

Vivienne's eyes met hers again, right as she raised the ball to toss it. Her arm hitched and she gave herself a terrible toss, way too low, and she cranked her serve into the top of the net. Her curse made it to Jess's ears.

Tania tried not to smile too broadly when they slapped hands. Thirteen-all.

The crowd in the bleachers seethed and bounced, stomping their feet and waving signs, a fever pitch of anticipation for the champion being crowned in a matter of minutes.

Tania's serve. She put in an easy ball and Jess didn't blame her. They *had* to get that one in, and Tania's shoulder was shit, if they were both being honest. Vivienne passed it and fucking smoked her hit so hard around Jess's block that Tania didn't have a chance. Clearly, the goddess was still pissed about her missed serve.

They were down 13–14. Match point. The rumble of the crowd climbed, waiting for what could be the last serve.

Lee went back to serve, expression deadly serious.

"This is our kill, Jess," Tania murmured.

Jess nodded and wiped her brow, then rested her hands on her knees, waiting for the serve.

Lee served to Tania. She hit a decent ball over but Vivienne got to it and dug it up no problem and doinked a short one back. Jess lobbed it up, then jumped hard for a hit. Lee got a touch on the block, sending the ball straight up high and close to the net. Vivienne went for the attack.

The crowd disappeared. There was nothing but Vivienne and the ball.

Jess jumped, straining to push her hands over the net.

Vivienne slammed it straight into her block. It spun off Jess's fingers, falling toward the line in slow motion . . . Jess held her breath . . . and it landed . . . out.

They lost.

Vivienne and Lee jumped into each other's arms, screaming and laughing, the cheer from the crowd like the roar of an ocean wave crashing over her head.

It was over.

Jess's eyes stung as the disappointment flooded her lungs and stole whatever air was remaining. They hadn't made it. They had failed. So close, but not enough. But then she looked at Vivienne and was able to suck in a breath again. Vivienne's perfect face, alight with joy, eyes dancing.

Tania hugged her. "I'm so proud of you, Jess."

"I'm proud of you, too," Jess said into Tania's bad shoulder.

Tania sniffled as they pulled apart, eyes wet.

Jess rubbed her arm. "Aw, T. Don't cry."

"I'm not crying 'cause we lost. I'm just crying because I love you."

Jess laughed and hugged her again. "It's okay. Next season is going to be amazing. We're going to come out so strong."

Tania smiled and nodded, wiping her eyes, lips pressed together.

They went to shake hands under the net. Lee's face was drenched in sweat, and Vivienne's ponytail was the messiest Jess had ever seen it, stray pieces hanging out everywhere.

"Congratulations," Jess said to Vivienne. "You guys deserved to win. You played amazing."

Vivienne squeezed her hand. "Thanks, Jess. You could have won just as easily. That was an incredible match."

Jess shook Lee's hand, then watched as Vivienne and Lee hugged again and waved at the cheering crowd.

There was a brief ceremony where Winston, the league manager, and a representative of the VL board congratulated both teams on the match and recognized Jess and Tania's second-place finish with silver medals. Jess looked down at the silver on her chest and felt a swell of pride. They'd fought uphill the last half of the season and played the volleyball of their lives to make it to the final. They fell short of the championship, but getting here was an accomplishment to be proud of.

Tania held her hand and squeezed.

Next came the gold medals and league trophy for Vivienne and Lee. They hefted the hardware between them, a glowing tableau in the pavilion lights. They deserved to win. A championship for champions.

The first day of the offseason was always a bit strange, the rhythms of life abruptly different, the thing that had always held the center now gone and, after the intensity and pressure of the playoffs, the absence felt even larger this year. Jess allowed herself to laze in bed for a bit when she woke up, scrolling her phone and scratching Fleming's head, then she took her tea outside to extend her slow start before heading into work for an afternoon shift. When she walked by the pavilion, she got a glimpse of Lee and Vivienne practicing in preparation for the state final, rolling through their usual efficient warm-up pepper. No rest for champions, it seemed.

Jess filled her week with everything she'd been putting off in the race to finals, like deep-cleaning her kitchen—how was there sand in the oven?—and taking Fleming to get groomed, on top of her usual hours at work. She was on her way home from a short morning shift when she came across Chrissy and Shay hanging out on the picnic tables outside the pavilion.

"Jess! Oh my God!" Chrissy cried when she saw her. She jumped off the table to clutch Jess's arm, her fingers cold from her cup of lemonade.

"What's up?" Jess asked. Chrissy was vibrating with news.

"Shay and I were practicing with Viv and Lee this morning, but Lee had to leave in a panic. Toni's having some complications and I guess she's being airlifted to a neonatal hospital in LA."

Jess's stomach flipped. "Shit. Is she all right? The baby? She still has, like, a month to go, doesn't she?"

Shay chimed in. "Five weeks left. Lee said something about them being overly cautious, but I don't know. Vivienne drove her to the hospital to meet Toni."

"Oh, wow. That's scary. I hope everyone is okay." Jess sat next to them on the bench and pondered the panic the parents-to-be must be feeling. Then another thought occurred to her. "Wait, what about the final? It's four days away."

Chrissy shook her head. "I don't think Lee will be playing in it."

Jess furrowed her brow. "I guess not."

Another voice interrupted. "Jess?"

Jess turned around.

Winston had popped his head out the front door of the league office. "Do you have a moment?"

"Sure." With a shrug at Chrissy and Shay, she followed

him inside, mind humming. What could he want? Would she and Tania go to the state champs instead? No, that wasn't fair to Vivienne. Maybe he needed some other favor. . . . Maybe they were able to delay the championship until Lee could play again and they needed someone to train with Vivienne in the meantime. . . . Because . . . he wasn't going to ask Jess to *play* with Vivienne . . . was he?

"Have a seat, Jess," Winston said, gesturing to an empty chair across from his desk. Troy was waiting in the other chair, flipping through a coil-bound notebook. He gave her a reassuring smile.

"Wow, this is such a shock. So scary for Lee and Toni," Jess said, settling into her seat. "I can't believe it."

"Our thoughts are certainly with them," Winston agreed. "But Lee just texted me to confirm that she will be unable to play in the state final. It sounds like they'll be keeping Toni in the hospital in LA until their baby is born, and Lee is going to stay with her."

Jess sat in Winston's pause until she wanted to shake the next sentence out of him. "So . . . ? What happens now?" *Why am I here?*

Winston straightened a stack of papers on his desk. "There is a rule, in the case of a medical emergency or other extreme circumstance, that a player from the second-place team may compete in the affected athlete's place."

It took Jess a second to remember that she was on the second-place team. "Are you saying . . . ?"

"Yes. We are inviting you to join Vivienne for the state final."

"Me?" Jess leaned back in her chair, mind spinning. "But . . . what about Tania? Shouldn't she get a chance to play in that game?"

Winston and Troy exchanged a look. "You are a natural fit for Vivienne. Tania and Vivienne have too many of the same strengths. We need your height."

It was true, of course. They had to have a blocker to have any chance. But still . . . "I can't just abandon Tania."

"You're not abandoning her. Her season was already over."

"But . . ." Now the room was spinning along with her brain. "What if Vivienne and I win? Does that qualify me for the pro circuit? And what about Tania and Lee?"

"If you were to win, the board would have to make a ruling, based on the specific circumstances. And you would all need to make some decisions, of course. But for now, we just need a partner for Vivienne on Saturday."

Vivienne. "Does Vivienne even want to play with me?"

They shared another look. "We're following league procedure. If Vivienne wants to play in the final, this is what's happening."

"Um . . ." Jess rubbed her forehead. "Can I just have some time to process this?"

Winston shifted in his chair. "Sure, but Jess . . . We'll need to confirm before the end of the day tomorrow."

Jess sat across the table from Tania with her mug of tea, stomach churning. As soon as she left Winston's office, she had texted Tania the news about Lee and asked if she was free to meet. She didn't remember much of the walk to the coffee shop.

Tania blew on her decaf and looked at Jess expectantly.

Jess could barely force the words out. She stared at her

hands as she began to speak, afraid of what she'd see on Tania's face. "So, I met with Winston and . . . they . . ." She took a deep breath. "They want me to play in the finals with Vivienne."

It took Tania a moment to process. "Oh."

"Yeah." Jess forced herself to look up.

She had prepared herself for tears or anger, not the dazzling smile that stretched across Tania's face. "Jess! That's amazing!"

"It is?"

"Of course it is."

"But . . . What if Vivienne and I win and they offer me a spot in the circuit?"

Tania laughed. "Why are you saying 'what if' like it's a bad thing? That's your dream!"

Jess tried to make sense of Tania's joy. "But I can't leave you."

Tania's smile softened. "Oh, Jess. You're sweet to think of me. . . ."

"Of course I would think of you. You're my partner. We're partners."

"Jess." Tania took her hand across the table. "It's funny, I was struggling with how to tell you this. . . ."

Jess's stomach flipped. "Tell me what?"

Tania's gaze met hers. "I'm retiring. This was my last season."

A shock wave swept over Jess. "What?"

"Yeah."

"You're . . . *retiring*?"

"Yes. I think it's time. George and I want to do some traveling—and who wants to go to the Maritimes in the winter? Plus, my shoulder . . . It's been tough for me to admit, but I think it's done. Or at least, according to my doctor, it needs more time to heal than just the offseason."

"Your *doctor*? You were seeing a doctor about your shoulder and didn't . . . Why didn't you tell me before now?"

Tania sighed. "Honestly, I'm not sure I fully decided until right now. Because I just didn't know how to. I've been absolutely drowning in guilt at the idea of leaving you . . . but this is perfect! You and Vivienne are gonna win the whole fucking thing."

Everything shifted for Jess, knowing that she wouldn't be abandoning Tania. But . . . "But what about Lee?"

Tanya shrugged. "Maybe she'll be done, too. She's a parent now."

"But . . . What if Vivienne doesn't want to play with me?"

"How many more 'buts' you got in there, Jess?"

Jess covered her face. "So many."

"Look, life is messy. Shit happens. Nothing ever goes according to plan. But this is an incredible opportunity. Yes, it sucks for Lee to miss it. And it could get complicated if . . . when . . . you win. But that's not really your problem. All you need to do now is go fucking kick ass with Vivienne."

Jess shook her head slowly, mind racing. Playing in the finals was certainly a dream, having a shot at the pro circuit . . . but in all the times she'd dreamed about it, she'd never once been next to Vivienne. And poor Lee. Her heart must be broken.

Tania sipped her coffee. "What does Vivienne think about all this?"

"I don't know." Jess rubbed her forehead. "I'm afraid to ask."

"I'm sure once she gets over the shock, she'll be psyched to play with you. Although . . ."

Jess raised her eyebrow. "Although what?"

"I'm just saying . . . If you guys *do* have feelings for each other, maybe wait until after the final to act on them."

Jess rolled her eyes. "I'm not gonna suddenly hit on Vivienne moments before the state championship, Tania."

"All right." Tania lifted her mug with a coy smile. "Just saying."

As soon as Tania hopped into her truck, Jess texted Vivienne. **Hey . . . can we talk?**

About volleyball, she added hastily.

She walked home, and Vivienne hadn't replied by the time she arrived. Should she message again?

Do you know how Toni's doing? she typed, then paused. *Send? Don't send? Send.*

Three dots this time, then Vivienne replied. **What do you want to talk about?**

Jess blinked at her screen. Wasn't it obvious? **Playing together in the finals. Maybe we could meet at Maggie's?**

We don't need to meet. This is how it works. If you want to play, then I'll play with you.

Jess sank onto her bed, a weight settling in her stomach. Vivienne didn't want to play with her but was too polite to say it. Jess had clearly imagined the connection they'd had under the meteor shower. And Tania had no idea what she was talking about. Maybe she should step aside. Maybe Lee would decide she could play after all, and Jess didn't even have to get involved.

Okay, was all she replied and, fortunately, she didn't

have too much time to stew over it, because the midway assistant manager called her in a panic, and she reluctantly agreed to head back into work to cover a late shift.

But even once she took her spot behind the ring toss counter, questions and scenarios and doubts still crowded her head. Vivienne and Lee . . . trophies and hospitals—

"You look like someone deep in thought."

She startled out of her thought hurricane and found Troy watching her. "Oh hey, Troy. Yeah, I guess you could say that."

He leaned against the counter, arms crossed. "This is a fantastic opportunity for you, Jess."

"I guess, but . . ." Jess tucked her hair behind her ear. "I don't think Vivienne wants to play with me."

"What makes you say that?"

"I sort of reached out and she shut me down."

"You 'sort of reached out'?"

"I asked if she wanted to talk. She said there was nothing to talk about."

Troy frowned and scratched his chin. "I think she's grieving a little. For Lee. For their partnership. For their dreams and plans."

"Oh."

"Nothing to do with you, Jess, or what you can offer her. She'll get there; she might just need some time to adjust."

"Right . . ."

Troy put his money on the counter, ten bucks instead of five this time. "I'm feeling lucky today."

He racked up forty points with a sure and steady hand.

Jess wrote up his points and handed the ticket over, but instead of tucking it into his pocket like normal, he pulled out a wad of tickets. He added the new one to the stack and set them on the counter. "I believe I have enough."

Jess gasped. "You do?" She flipped through the slips, giving a cursory count. "You do."

They both stared up at the giant toasted-marshmallow teddy. He looked ready to be adopted.

Jess grabbed her giant hook and reached up to haul the big guy down. "Here you go," she said, plopping him on the counter in front of his new owner.

Troy beamed. "Thank you, Jess. Sunny is going to love this." He stroked the bear's big head, then hoisted it into his arms. "Good things take time, Jess. Give her time."

Jess knocked on Vivienne's door the next morning holding two iced coffees. She'd texted the night before asking if she could stop by in the morning and drop something off. Vivienne had finally replied late—Jess was still awake because her racing brain wouldn't let her sleep—with her address and a terse **Sure**.

Vivienne's bungalow was small, but clean and modern with a metal roof, white board-and-batten siding, and low-maintenance landscaping, with all rock and native plants.

She opened her door.

Jess had never seen her look so . . . vulnerable. In a tank top and sweatpants, hair up in a messy bun, no makeup . . . lost, and beautiful. Jess wanted to pull her into her arms and comfort her. "Hey." Jess cleared her throat and held out a cup instead. "I brought you a coffee."

Vivienne studied her and shifted her weight.

Jess waited.

"Thanks," Vivienne finally said. She took the drink.

Jess stared awkwardly, not sure what to do next.

Vivienne rolled her eyes, but a smile cracked the corner of her mouth at the same time. "Come in." She held the screen door open.

Jess blew out a breath. "Phew. I let my Uber driver leave." She followed Vivienne inside.

It was nothing like Jess had been expecting . . . something a little sleeker, maybe, mostly gray and white. But this was art and texture, nature and interior design, all mashed up into one exceptionally lovely home. She tried not to gawk too obviously as she took it in. The walls were moss green, some covered in matching wallpaper with gold embossing. A lighter green button-tufted couch sat on one side of the open space. A row of wooden stools lined the kitchen peninsula. But what really grabbed her eye—what made her stop and stare, in fact—was the back wall of the house, mostly glass doors, that looked out at a rich green backyard—palm trees, vines, a small rock-lined pond. . . . Her own private jungle-garden oasis.

Jess's jaw dropped. "Wow. *Wow*. This is . . . gorgeous."

Then she noticed the three mugs and two glasses on the coffee table. Socks crumpled on the floor by the couch, a sweater and a bra thrown over the back of it. A stack of bowls by the sink.

Jess suddenly realized it was very quiet. Vivienne was sipping her coffee and watching Jess stare. Jess flinched and put her hand on her face. "Oh, God. Sorry. I was just . . . taking it all in. Really, your place is stunning."

"Mm-hmm." Vivienne stuffed the bra behind a cushion, kicked the socks under the couch, and slid the collection of cups to one side of the coffee table. "It's been a rough couple of days." She sat on her couch, tucking a bare foot underneath her, and gestured for Jess to join her.

Jess sat next to her and took a sip herself. "So . . . how are Toni and baby doing?"

"They're okay. Toni's blood pressure spiked and they're keeping a close eye on the baby. They might need to induce in the next few days."

"And . . . how's Lee feeling about . . . this?"

Vivienne looked at her hands. "I mean, she's mostly just concerned with Toni and her baby . . . but I know part of her is pretty devastated that she's missing the final."

Jess nodded and bit her lip. "I'm sure she is."

"It's not fair," Vivienne said quietly.

"I know, it's not." Jess resisted the urge to touch Vivienne's arm. "You guys worked so hard. It was such an amazing season."

"Yeah."

"I'm sorry."

Vivienne looked up, straight into Jess's eyes. "It's okay. We just need a healthy mom and baby, right?"

"Right." Jess clutched her cup, even though it was freezing her fingers. "Do you . . . I don't . . . Fuck. I'm sorry. Vivienne . . . do you *want* to play with me?"

Vivienne scrunched her nose, like the question was silly. "Of course I do."

"You do?"

"Yeah, Jess. I have a state championship to win. And . . . I think we'll be great together."

"Oh." Jess's heart fluttered, relief sweeping over her. "I think so, too."

Vivienne smiled—still a little sad—and sipped her drink. "But we'll need to work hard, get into the same rhythm. We only have a couple days. Are you free now?"

"Now?"

Vivienne blinked her big eyes at her. "Now."

"Yeah, I'm free now."

Vivienne went to change into practice clothes while Jess snooped her bookshelves—quite an impressive astronomy section. She imagined pulling Carl Sagan off the shelf and curling up in the jungle garden next to the burbling pond.

"What does Lee think about us playing together?" Jess asked as they were getting into Vivienne's car.

"She'd rather it be her, of course, but she thinks we'll be a great pair."

Jess nodded, a weight lifting from her shoulders. "I'll let Winston know that I'm in."

Vivienne started the car, then pushed back a chunk of hair that had fallen over her eye. A waft of vanilla hit Jess's nose. "You didn't tell him yet?"

Again, the urge to touch Vivienne's hand overwhelmed her. "I wanted to make sure you were okay with it first."

Vivienne smiled, a big one this time, igniting a sparkle deep in her eyes. "I'm okay with it."

22

New partners: 1

> *Pickup game*: **Casual, spontaneous game, made up of whoever's there. Just casual. Super casual.**

Training with Vivienne was strange. Jess was so used to Tania's routine, Tania's banter, Tania's preferences. In two days, Jess had learned that Vivienne would only use black hair elastics, there always had to be a cooler on the sideline, because she liked ice water, and if she said "one more," she meant five more reps . . . at least.

Chrissy and Shay joined them on the second day to help run some drills. They were three hours in, and Jess's legs were feeling it.

"One more," Vivienne said for the seventh time that drill, tossing a ball to Chrissy.

Jess tried to muffle her sigh. "Yeah."

Vivienne folded her arms. "What's with the sigh?"

"Nothing, it's just . . . Have you ever noticed that you say 'one more' and do, like, ten more?"

Vivienne grinned. "What, you need a rest?"

"I'm good if you're good." Jess sniffed. "I just think precision of language is important."

Vivienne shook her head, still grinning, and nodded at Chrissy to send the ball over.

Jess was tired, though. Her thighs refused to move in time to get the next short ball Chrissy tossed.

"Man, tall girls are slow sometimes." Vivienne flicked a speck off her arm and examined her nails.

Jess climbed to her feet, brushing sand off her torso, and put her hands on her hips, lips tight.

Vivienne laughed. "Are you always this cranky during training?"

"I'm not cranky. I'm just . . ."

"What? Am I pushing your buttons?" Vivienne's eyes widened. "Wait a second. . . . Is that where 'Button' came from?"

Jess sighed, reluctant to spill. "Yes. Tania says I let people push my buttons, okay? But we decided I've outgrown that nickname now."

"Oh, have you?"

"Yes, I have."

"Hmm. Well, you'll need a new nickname."

"I'm open to suggestions."

"J-Money?"

"Hard no."

"J-Dog?" Chrissy suggested from across the net.

"No!"

Vivienne tapped her chin. "Stretch?"

Jess scowled. "What are you, a boy from my fourth-grade class?"

Chrissy tried again. "Messy Jessy?"

"What did I ever do to you, Chrissy?"

"Anyway," Vivienne said, waving her hand, "it's a work in progress. We'll think of something." She picked up the ball and dusted it off. "One more?"

Jess slid into the hot tub with a low groan of appreciation. She had earned this soak.

Vivienne came in reading her phone. "Looks like Aunt Veronica is throwing us a party!"

"A party? What kind of party?"

Vivienne rolled her eyes. "A birthday party, of course. There'll be a clown making balloon animals and pin-the-tail-on-the-donkey. . . ." She paused at Jess's confusion. "A cocktail party, Jess! Sort of a 'good luck in the finals' thing. Tomorrow night at her place in Horn Beach."

"A cocktail party?" Jess suffered a flashback from when she was twelve and her mom started making her attend their client receptions to project a wholesome family image. It was a real fight when she went through her black lipstick phase. "What do I wear to a cocktail party at Veronica Doyle's house?"

"Something fancy. A dress-to-impress-type situation."

"How fancy?"

"Why, do you have a wide selection of ball gowns?"

"Zero ball gowns, in fact. And only one thing with sequins."

"Sounds perfect."

"I don't know. . . ."

"How about I give you a ride home and come take a look at your closet?"

"Sure . . . and best of luck to you."

They showered and stopped for tacos, and it was dark by the time they got back to Jess's place, save for the waxing crescent moon bright in the sky.

"You want some tea or something?" Jess asked on their way in, dropping her keys on the shelf by the door.

"Sure, tea sounds good." Vivienne followed her in and looked around. "Your place is great."

Jess shrugged and went to turn the kettle on, stepping over the pile of clothes on the floor. "It's small. Not as nice as yours."

Vivienne made a dismissive noise. "I like yours better. It feels like . . . you." She wandered over to the shelves by the window and examined Jess's knickknacks. "These shells are pretty. Wait . . . are these the shells you stole off the beach?"

"Yeah. Those are my win–loss shells."

Vivienne turned to face her. "I'm sorry. . . . Your what, now?"

"Um . . ." Jess sensed she was about to be in trouble. "I start off the season with sixty shells in the 'win' jar, and then every match we lose, I move one into the 'loss' jar. . . ." She trailed off at the expression on Vivienne's face.

Vivienne pointed at the jar. "So, these shells are all your losses?"

"Yes." Jess didn't like the gleam in Vivienne's eyes.

"These shells right here?" Vivienne picked up the jar.

"Yeah— What are you doing?"

Vivienne tucked the jar under her arm and marched out the front door.

"Vivienne!" Jess scrambled to turn off the kettle, grab her keys, and lock the door behind her. Vivienne was already halfway down the next block by the time she caught up. "Vivienne! Where are you going?"

Vivienne didn't slow down—didn't even look at her. "A jar full of losses. Honestly, Jess . . ."

Jess had to laugh at the determined expression on Vivienne's face. "What are you doing with my shells?"

Vivienne refused to answer, only kicked her flip-flops off at the edge of the boardwalk and continued her march down to the water. It wasn't until she was knee-deep in the Pacific Ocean that she stopped.

Jess halted at the water's edge. "Vivienne, seriously. What are you doing?"

Vivienne finally looked at her—held eye contact while she reached into the jar, plucked out a single shell, held it up for Jess to see, then tossed it into the surf.

"Hey, that's my shell!"

"Mm-hmm." A second shell joined the first.

"Vivienne! Stop!" Jess chewed her lip and eyed the dark water at her feet.

Vivienne pulled out another one and held it up. "Your turn." The wind whipped her black hair across her face in shadowed lines, her eyes gleaming bright.

Jess hesitated one more second then followed her in, gasping at the cold. "You're crazy. This is fucking freezing."

Vivienne handed Jess the shell. "Here. Toss it."

A wave washed over Jess's knees. The ocean hummed all around her. "I . . ." *I can't,* she wanted to say, but . . . she couldn't say why not.

Vivienne stepped closer. Her eyes were deeper than the ocean. "Go ahead."

Jess hesitated, her gaze bouncing between the shining white curve in her hand and Vivienne's steady conviction . . . then threw the shell as far as she could. It disappeared into the black, lost before it hit the water.

Vivienne tossed her head back and let out a whoop.

Jess reached into the jar, grabbed a handful, and flung the whole thing into the night. A laugh bubbled up and joined the shells.

Vivienne laughed, too. "Right?"

Jess took the jar from Vivienne.

"Wait!" Vivienne removed one shell and pressed it into Jess's hand. "Here. Keep one."

Jess tucked that shell into her pocket, then heaved the remaining losses out into the swirling salt water.

Vivienne howled again. Jess howled, too.

She had completely forgotten she was afraid of the ocean.

Later, wrapped in blankets to drive off the chill of the late October ocean, they sipped their tea while they sat on Jess's love seat. Their knees touched, a low hum under her skin that she was constantly aware of.

Jess held her mug tightly, willing the heat to transfer into her fingers faster. "So, we're going to drive all the way to Horny Beach tomorrow for a cocktail party? Who's even going to be there?"

Vivienne shrugged a shoulder. "Mostly my mom's family—aunts and uncles, some cousins—and family friends. . . . My sister might even show, if she can make time in her extremely busy and successful life. . . . Getting her to leave Brentwood is always a challenge. But I was thinking we could make a day of it. There's this beach court near Veronica's place I used to play at all the time when I was younger. I bet we could find some decent matches there. It'll be a fun day."

"Okay, if you think so," Jess agreed, even though . . . A mansion full of Vivienne's family?

Not so much "fun" as it was absolutely terrifying.

It was funny thinking about the last time Vivienne drove her to Horny Beach. Awkward silences, worrying about crumbs, country music . . .

This time Vivienne played Backyard Chickens, and they laughed and chatted easily the whole way. Jess never once thought about needing to roll when she hit the ground. Vivienne tried to lay out her mother's family tree for her, listing the people Jess would be meeting.

"But your parents won't be here?" Jess asked once she thought she had the aunts and uncles straight.

"No. . . . My mom moved to New York for my dad after college. My brother lives there, too. Scarlett relocated her practice to LA once her book became a bestseller. I think she's trying to work Veronica's connections for a streaming deal, to be honest."

They pulled into a small lot next to two beach volleyball courts. Veronica's place towered above them on the hill. Battles raged on both courts, with a range of players from their late teens into their thirties and forties.

Vivienne and Jess climbed out of the car, stretched, and sat on the logs that ringed the parking lot, watching.

When a match finished, the victorious team—two men in their mid- to late thirties, blond, tanned, and toned—approached them. "You two up for a game?" one of them asked.

Jess and Vivienne stood.

"We sure are," Vivienne replied.

"I'm Sawyer and this is Jayson." Sawyer sized up Jess's height and her and Vivienne's muscled physiques. "Are you any good?"

Vivienne shared a look with Jess. "Yeah. We're not bad."

Sawyer and Jayson were a solid team—had probably played in university, or had at least spent long hours on the beach courts—but they weren't *amazing* or anything. Which is why it was concerning when Jess and Vivienne were quickly down 0–3.

The first point they lost because they both stepped in to pass a seam serve.

"Shit, sorry," Vivienne said after they collided and the ball shanked wildly away. "You've got seam."

The second point they lost because Jess's set wasn't great—Vivienne liked them farther off the net than Tania, and Jayson stuff-blocked her on a tight ball. The third point they lost because Sawyer rolled a short ball over Jess's block and she turned to dig it—a ball Tania would have known she was going to take—and she ran into Vivienne, who had barreled in to get it.

"Fuck," Vivienne said.

"Yeah," Jess agreed.

"Okay . . ." Vivienne scrunched her adorable little nose at the horizon for a second before she spoke. "Here's what we're going to do. We're going to communicate our asses off. Call for every touch. Who's got it, where you want it. Everything. Okay?"

Jess nodded. "Okay." They slapped hands.

It went better from there, but it still felt . . . unnatural, like they were two pieces of a puzzle that weren't meant to snap together. Still, they managed to scratch out a win, 21–19 and 21–17.

The four of them sat on the logs with their water bottles after, letting a group of teens have the court.

"You guys don't play in the pros, do you?" Sawyer asked.

"Not yet," Vivienne said.

"The SoCal VL, then?"

Vivienne nodded.

"I told you!" Sawyer said to Jayson, then he turned back to the women. "I thought I recognized you. But I don't remember you two playing together. . . ."

"We're a new partnership," Vivienne explained. "Last minute. We've got the state final on Saturday and we're just getting used to playing together."

"New partnership? How new?" Jayson pointed between them. "You have matching tattoos. . . ."

Jess touched her tattoo on reflex at the same time Vivienne touched hers. They exchanged a smile.

Vivienne replied. "Oh. Well . . . We've been friends awhile."

A blush rose in Jess's cheeks. She looked at her feet. Hearing Vivienne call her a "friend" felt really, really good.

Sawyer shook his head. "You guys are fucking awesome. You've totally got this. Just trust each other."

"How long have you two been playing together?" Vivienne asked.

The men smiled at each other. "Three years now?" Jayson said. "We were both looking for a doubles partner . . . and we fell in love by the end of our first match."

"*Before* the match," Sawyer corrected. "As soon as I saw him."

Jayson squeezed his knee. "We got married last year."

"Aw, congratulations. How is it, playing with your husband?" Vivienne wondered.

"It's the best, honestly," Jayson replied. "We barely need to talk, we just know what the other one will do. Completely in the groove, you know? We love it."

"If only we could jump into that groove," Vivienne said.

"Maybe you two should start going out," Jayson joked.

Jess almost choked on her water.

Vivienne offered a polite if strained laugh and jumped to her feet. "You know, we'd better get going. We've got a party to get to."

Jayson and Sawyer stood, too.

"Good luck in the final!" Sawyer said.

"We'll be watching and cheering you on," Jayson added. "Go get 'em."

Aunt Veronica looked like a character in a movie as she came to greet them in the foyer, gliding down the curved staircase, her long amethyst dress with a bold slit sweeping the ground behind her.

"Vivienne, love!" Veronica cried. She kissed Vivienne's cheek. "Thank you so much for fitting in my little party. And Jess, how nice to see you again!" She brushed her lips against Jess's cheek, too.

"You too," Jess said, flushing. "Your house is gorgeous. And I just saw the announcement for your next book! It looks amazing!" She bit her lip and forced herself to stop fangirling.

Veronica rested a hand on her chest. "Why thank you, Jess. Aren't you the sweetest? I'll send you home with some swag, do remind me tomorrow." Veronica turned and motioned for them to follow her up the stairs. "I'm afraid quarters are tight tonight—Scarlett's whole family is here, including the nanny—but I figured you two wouldn't mind sharing? The sapphire room is made up for you."

"Uh . . ." Vivienne's gaze slid sideways to Jess. "Yeah, we can share. Is that okay with you, Jess?"

"Um . . ." Sharing a bedroom? Jess had figured in a place this size, they'd have their own rooms. She hadn't considered other family members staying over, too. Was she actually going to share a *bed* with Vivienne? Her pajamas were pretty skimpy. . . . Her heart sped up, keeping time with her racing thoughts. "Yeah, of course."

"Fantastic— Oh, one moment please." Veronica fished a cell phone out of somewhere and took a call. "Lina? . . . Yes . . . No . . . No! *Absolutely* not."

Jess leaned over to whisper to Vivienne to cover the sound of her pounding heart. "The 'sapphire room'? That sounds like a strip club."

"You're not far off," Vivienne murmured back.

The sapphire room indeed featured sapphire-colored decor, plus shining crystals around the lamps and on the headboard. The bed was up on a platform that definitely seemed like a bit of a stage. There was even a mirror on the ceiling. Jess half expected a pole in the corner.

Call completed, Veronica held her arm out like a model on *The Price Is Right*. "One of you can use this en suite, the other can use mine. There are towels, robes, toiletries. . . . I need to go check in with the caterers, but do help yourself to whatever you need."

"We will," Vivienne assured her. "Is Uncle Milton around?"

"Oh, buried in paperwork in his office, of course. He swears he'll emerge in time for the party. We'll see." She waved her fingers and glided out the door.

It was very quiet in their bedroom for a long three seconds.

"Okay," Vivienne said briskly. She unzipped her suitcase. "You can get ready in here. I'll head to Veronica's bathroom." She retrieved her toiletry kit and bolted out the door.

Jess took a moment to stare at the bed she would apparently be sharing with Vivienne that evening—king size at least, but still. She found her dress in her suitcase and shook it out. After their dip in the ocean and mugs of tea, Vivienne had taken one look in Jess's closet and declared the red sequins the only option. But after her shower, standing in front of the full-length mirror in the sapphire guest bathroom, Jess wasn't so sure. It was so . . . flashy. Literally and metaphorically.

Maybe it was a mistake.

Maybe Veronica would have something more low-key she could wear . . . like her workout gear or something. Jess opened the door to see if Vivienne had returned.

She had.

She sat on the foot of the bed scrolling her phone in a white robe, opened dangerously low in the front, and with her leg sticking out all the way up to her hip. Jess jammed the brakes on, feeling like she had walked in on Vivienne naked.

Vivienne looked up and her jaw dropped. She mouthed something that Jess could have sworn was "damn." Then she cleared her throat. "Yes. Yes, that dress works just fine."

Jess smoothed it over her hips. "Are you sure? It's not too much?"

"It is . . . just the right amount. I mean . . . your legs . . ."

Jess's cheeks flushed. "Thank you. I just don't know what to do with my hair." She had blow-dried it, but otherwise was at a loss as to how to make it do anything at the level required for this dress at this event.

Vivienne stood and straightened her robe, covering up swaths of skin. "I can help if you like. I wanted to be a hairdresser for a while. Scarlett let me do her hair all the time. Here, sit at the vanity."

Once Jess was settled, Vivienne rested her hands lightly on Jess's shoulders. "What sort of hairstyle were you thinking of?"

"Not sure . . ." Jess studied her thin brown locks in the mirror. "I don't ever do anything exciting with it."

"Hmm . . ." Vivienne ran her fingers through Jess's hair the way that hairdressers do . . . but Jess had never ended up with full-body goose bumps when a hairdresser did it. "What if we put some waves in and went half-up, half-down?"

"Sure, that sounds great," Jess said through a dry mouth.

Vivienne went off to collect the supplies she needed, humming a Backyard Chickens song.

By the time Jess's hair was done, she was jelly on the inside. The soft, intimate touches, her scalp, her neck . . . If only she could just sit there all night getting her hair done, with Vivienne's fingertips gently tracing—

"Okay, I think I'm finished," Vivienne said, setting down the hairspray and stepping back. "What do you think?"

"I love it," Jess said, turning her head from side to side to admire her reflection.

"You look so beautiful," Vivienne said.

Jess, her cheeks almost as red as her dress, caught Vivienne's gaze in the mirror. "Thank you."

Jess nearly jumped out of her skin when Vivienne's phone buzzed.

Vivienne read her message. "Shit, Veronica says people are arriving. We'd better get moving."

Vivienne pulled a scrap of pink fabric out of her bag. Jess wasn't sure how it was going to cover her enough to attend a cocktail party, but that thought quickly flew from her head when she realized Vivienne was about to drop her robe right there in the middle of the room. Jess instructed her eyes to look away, but they didn't quite make it in time. . . . Although it turned out Vivienne did, in fact, have a sensible nude-colored bra and underwear on, appropriate to wear underneath what looked like sheer pink fabric. By some miracle, the dress did stretch over Vivienne's curves, in a very thin and clingy way, with glittering rhinestones here and there adding to the effect.

"You look really . . ." Jess forced herself to finish the sentence, lest she stand there like an idiot all night. ". . . really amazing."

"Thank you." Vivienne fluffed her hair and looped their arms together. "Are you ready?"

"Not at all."

"Perfect. Let's go."

23

Wins: 36
Losses: ??? Somewhere at the bottom of the Pacific

Pregame: **Light cardio, stretching, foam rolling . . . yoga . . . ice baths . . . more stretching . . . veggies and lean protein, lots of water, mindfulness, deep breaths . . . game tape of your opponents, positive self-talk . . . lots of sleep . . . deep breaths. Deep breaths. Deep breaths, Jess.**

An older mustached man in an ill-fitting sweater tore himself away from the cocktail shrimp to greet Vivienne. Then he noticed Jess. "Hello, Lee, nice to see you again."

Vivienne maintained her smile. "No, Uncle Lane, this isn't Lee. This is Jess."

"Jess?" He frowned at Jess. "I could have sworn your name was Lee."

"No," Vivienne explained patiently. "Lee is my . . . was my . . . partner. I mean, she *is* my partner. But she had a family emergency and she can't play in the final, so Jess stepped in."

Uncle Lane dunked a shrimp into the cocktail sauce. "Oh, dear. How terrible."

Vivienne shifted, hands clasped in front of her. "Well, for Lee, yes, but—"

"Do tell Lee I hope things are right as rain soon." Lane took a bite, splattering a glob of red sauce onto his sweater, gaze roaming the crowd in search of someone better to talk to.

"I will, Uncle Lane," Vivienne said as he wandered away with his shrimp. "Ugh, I'm sorry about him. I don't think he's ever watched a single game."

"It's fine," Jess said. Her stomach growled. "Let's get some food."

She was loading up her plate when another uncle arrived, this one balding, and dressed in a light gray linen suit.

"Jess, this is Veronica's husband, Uncle Milton," Vivienne introduced. "Uncle Milton, this is Jess."

"Thank you for having me," Jess said. "Your home is beautiful."

"Oh." Milton looked around like he had never been in this room before. "Yes, thank you. It does the trick."

Jess was about to tell him that her parents were also lawyers, but Milton puffed out his cheeks and shook his head. "Such a shame about Lee missing the final. You two had quite the season!"

"Yes, we did—" Vivienne started.

"Broke a record for games won, didn't you?"

"Er, yes, but—"

Uncle Milton examined the charcuterie board. "*Such* a shame."

Jess smiled blandly and took a bite of a baked salmon cake.

A furrow appeared between Vivienne's eyebrows. "Yes, Lee is sorry to miss it, but Jess and I are a great team."

Milton took a piece of each kind of cheese, then peered at Vivienne. "And there's no chance Lee will make it after all?"

"No. Nope. It'll be me and Jess on Saturday."

"Well. Best of luck to you. And do try the smoked Gouda, it's fantastic."

Vivienne gave him a forced smile. "Thanks."

Jess wanted to curl up under the table with the entire hunk of smoked Gouda. And that feeling didn't end with Uncle Lane or Uncle Milton.

The next confused uncle studied Jess over his glasses. "Who's this?"

Then an aunt put her hand on Vivienne's arm. "How awful."

A cousin glanced up from their phone. "Poor Lee."

Uncle Milton again. "What a shame."

"What a shame."

"*What* a *shame*."

Jess was having trouble swallowing her food, and the sparkling water didn't help.

"I'm gonna go to bed," she finally murmured to Vivienne after nearly two hours of being Not Lee. "I'm not feeling great."

"Oh. Yeah, sure." Vivienne immediately set her glass down on a side table. "I'll go with you."

"It's okay, you don't have to. You can stay with your family."

"No, it's fine. I haven't had a chance to talk to Scarlett yet and, trust me, it's actually better that way. Are you done with this?" Vivienne collected Jess's glass and placed it next to hers. "I'll just tell Veronica we're heading up."

"Really, you don't have to," Jess protested, but Vivienne had already dipped into the crowd to find her aunt.

Jess waited, smoothing her dress, smiling flatly in case anyone looked her way, itching to bolt, until Vivienne reappeared at her side. She took Jess's hand and pulled her out into the hall and up the stairs.

"What's wrong?" Vivienne asked as soon as she shut the sapphire-room door behind them.

Jess kicked off her flats and removed her lucky sunshine earrings. "Nothing. I'm sorry, I'm just tired."

"Jess." Vivienne waited, hands on her hips. "Come on. We agreed to communicate about everything, and that is not limited to the court."

Jess set her earrings on the vanity, alarmed to feel a prickle behind her eyes. She shook her head.

"Jess, come on. You can tell me anything. I promise."

"It's just . . ." Jess took a deep breath, trying not to cry. "I don't belong here, Vivienne."

Vivienne furrowed her eyebrows. "What are you talking about?"

Jess waved her hand at herself. "The dress. The party. You. Your shot at the pros. Lee should be here, not me."

Vivienne looked around, searching for words. "Jess . . ."

She had to say it. "I'm going to fuck this up for you."

"Jess. Stop."

Jess knew she *should* stop talking, but the ugly thoughts in her head clamored to come out, to be said aloud, to be more true. "And I know you think so, too."

Vivienne's eyes flashed. "If you could not put words in my mouth—"

"I'm not putting words in your mouth."

"You're not? Did I ever say that I wished Lee was here? Or that I didn't want to play with you?"

"I can tell what you're thinking."

"Ha!" Vivienne pushed her fingers through her hair.

"Jesus *Christ*, Jess, you've actually proven over and over again that you absolutely *cannot*."

"I'm *trying*, Vivienne. I—"

Vivienne grabbed her arm, fingers pressing into her skin.

Jess stared at Vivienne's hand and knew she'd gone too far, picking a fight with her teammate when it wasn't even her fault, but—

Before she could finish that thought, Vivienne went up on her tiptoes, put a hand under Jess's chin . . . and kissed her.

Everything exploded behind Jess's eyes, like a bomb flashed, like the whole world disintegrated into nothingness. The only thing left was Vivienne's lips on hers, sugary sweet.

It was the single greatest moment of Jess's life. Her body started to dissolve too, cotton-candy floss melting away.

She touched Vivienne's tongue with hers, slid her arm around Vivienne's waist, and put one hand into Vivienne's thick, shining hair.

Vivienne undid her completely when she groaned into Jess's mouth.

Jess couldn't think, couldn't put together anything coherent beyond how fucking hot Vivienne was and how fucking good it felt to kiss her and how she wanted more, more, more, more . . . more of her lips, more of her tongue, more of her smell, more of how good it felt to press against her—

Vivienne froze, body suddenly cold and rigid, then broke away, panting. "Fuck."

Jess was also panting . . . and also not thinking much beyond *fuck*.

Their eyes met. Vivienne's were wide and searching, but Jess didn't know what she was searching for.

"I'm so sorry." Vivienne touched the back of her hand to her mouth. "I should not have done that."

"I—" Jess tried to force the gears of her brain into motion while her body screamed *Yes, you should have.*

Vivienne covered her eyes. "That was so dumb."

Jess took hold of Vivienne's wrist and pulled her hand away from her eyes. "Maybe . . . Maybe not . . . How about one more? Just to make sure. . . ."

Vivienne's body softened, and her face lit up, but only for a flash, because then their lips met again.

Jess gasped at their next breath while Vivienne kissed along her neck, sliding her hand up Jess's rib cage until she was cupping one of Jess's breasts. *Vivienne Morris wants me* ran through her head. *This is happening.*

Jess groaned and leaned into the hand, burning with desire. "Could we, uh . . . Do you want to . . ." Jess flicked her gaze to their bed. Someone had turned down the sapphire duvet. She almost had to laugh.

"Yeah, I really fucking do . . . if you do?" Vivienne studied her, eyes darting around Jess's face, one swollen pink lip between her teeth.

Jess had never wanted anything more in her life. "Oh yes. Yes, I do."

The moonlight fell across Vivienne's form, curved over the swell of her breasts, dipped into her hips until the shadow won.

She was so beautiful that Jess was lightheaded.

"What?" Vivienne asked with a smile, rolling over to look at Jess head-on.

"Nothing, it's just . . ." Jess trailed her finger down Vivienne's arm.

"You can't believe we just had sex?"

"I can't believe we just had sex."

Vivienne laughed. "Me neither."

Jess scooted a little closer. "But it's fine. We're not going to let it get in the way of performing on Saturday, right?"

"Right. Of course." Vivienne waved her hand. "Obviously. We have a championship to win. It doesn't matter that we . . ." Her gaze traveled down Jess's naked torso and lingered between her legs. "That we . . ."

The corner of Jess's mouth twitched. "That we . . . ?"

Vivienne rolled on top of her. "I forget."

Jess drifted from asleep to awake when the mattress shifted under her and a footstep creaked on the floor. She reached for the form that was next to her in her dreams, wrapped in scents of vanilla and musk and . . . Vivienne.

Vivienne.

Jess's eyes flew wide open. *Holy fuck.*

Vivienne was not in the bed next to her, but the bathroom door was closed and light shone around its edges. Sunlight attempted to poke between the curtains.

Moments from the night before came rushing back and flooded Jess's brain. Every glorious inch of Vivienne's body under her fingers and lips and tongue, writhing and panting. . . . Bringing Vivienne to the edge and then sending her crashing over it again and again. . . . Jess's cheeks heated at the memory and then so did her—

Vivienne opened the bathroom door, hair tousled and impossibly sexy in an oversize Veronica Doyle–branded T-shirt. She sat on the end of the bed and tucked her hair behind her ear in a very shy, un-Vivienne-like way. "Hey."

Jess smoothed her own hair, suddenly aware of how naked she was. "Hey."

"How are you?" Vivienne twisted her fingers in the duvet.

No sense in holding back. They were in it now. "I'm . . . fantastic. How are you?"

"Also fantastic."

Jess breathed a sigh of relief as Vivienne's T-shirt neck slipped down her shoulder. Vivienne pulled it back up.

"Okay—" she started to say at the same time Jess said, "So—"

They both stopped, bashful.

"You go," Jess said.

"Um, I was going to say . . ." More duvet twisting. ". . . that last night was really fun—"

"Really fun," Jess agreed. *Okay, maybe chill a little, Jess.*

Vivienne's lips curled. "But— Saturday is such a huge day, you know?"

"Oh . . . Yeah. Totally."

"And, as much fun as this was, maybe we need to, like . . . not think about it until after the game."

"Mm-hmm." Jess imagined freeing Vivienne's shoulder from the T-shirt again and leaving a trail of kisses along her soft, soft skin. "Yeah, for sure. You're right."

"Okay." Vivienne looked relieved. "Good. Good, we need to focus. On volleyball."

"Of course we do."

Vivienne nodded. "Great." Then she stood, back to normal Vivienne. "I'll go find another shower. You can use this one. Veronica said breakfast was at eight thirty."

"Okay," Jess said.

Vivienne was almost out the door when she stopped, hand on the knob. "Wait, sorry . . . what was it you were going to say?"

I want you. I'm obsessed with you. That was the most amazing sex I've ever had. I want to have more sex just like that. How about right now? "Er, just . . . Yeah, the same thing, basically."

Vivienne smiled, soft again for one second, then she was gone down the hall.

The kitchen hummed with activity. A continental breakfast buffet was laid out on the island and people were up and down from the long farm table collecting plates of food. Smaller children who hadn't been at the party the night before pelted around, and the whole room smelled of coffee and fresh-baked pastries.

A woman in screaming red lipstick who looked like Vivienne, except she was rounder and with paler skin, sat at the table next to a baby in a high chair and a pouting toddler rolling grapes off her pink plastic plate. "Oh, Vivienne, there you are," she clipped with an accent that was much more Manhattan than California. "Interesting choice to miss your own party."

"Scarlett." Vivienne gave her a gruesome smile. "Shoot, are you having trouble telling time again? The party started at seven."

"I had to put my *children* to bed first, Vivienne. In case you didn't know, 'responsibilities' are—"

"'Responsibilities'? Didn't you bring your nanny?"

Aunt Veronica swooped in between them with a platter of chocolate croissants. "Oh, that's quite enough of that, my beautiful nieces. 'Thank you for coming to the party, Scarlett.' 'Good luck in your big game, Vivienne.' You should try basic manners sometime. Honestly." Then she saw Jess. "Are you feeling better today, love? I hope you're not getting sick before the big game."

"Oh . . . Yes, I'm feeling *much* better, thank you," Jess said, avoiding Vivienne's eyes.

"Excellent! Here, have a croissant. Oh, I found a few books to send home with you. . . ." She nodded her chin in the direction of a wet bar, where two canvas Veronica Doyle book bags sat stuffed until overflowing. "I found some merch for you, too. There're stickers and shirts and such. . . ."

Jess's jaw dropped at the haul. It looked like a special-edition cover of *Queen in Shining Armor* poking out. And, no . . . Surely that wasn't an advance copy of the sequel, *Up All Knight*? "Wow, that's . . . that's amazing, thank you. So kind of you." Her fingers itched to dig into the stash.

"See?" Veronica raised a pointed eyebrow at Vivienne and Scarlett, who were still glaring at each other. "Basic manners."

"So that was Scarlett," Vivienne said as soon as they got in her car.

"It was nice of her to come?" Jess tried.

Vivienne punched the ignition button with extra force.

"Was it? Was it 'nice'? Or was it just another chance for her to feel superior to me?"

That this incredible, bold, brilliant, beautiful woman could feel inferior to anyone on earth . . . Jess curled her lips. "That explains it."

Vivienne raised her eyebrow. "Explains what?"

"Why you are how you are."

Vivienne started to grin despite herself. "And how am I?"

"You said I'm a hard shell with a marshmallow center . . . You're a kitten inside a cactus. And Scarlett doesn't hold a candle to you, Vivienne."

Vivienne dipped her head, cheeks maybe flushing pink, and turned the music on. "Thank you," she mumbled.

They didn't talk much on the drive home aside from their pregame plan—an easy workout today, watching game tape of their opponents after dinner over video chat, and a light practice tomorrow. Otherwise, Vivienne sang along to the music in a quiet, absent-minded way.

When they arrived back at Jess's apartment, Vivienne got out and opened up the trunk for her. "Okay, well. Enjoy your workout. Video chat at seven?"

"See you then."

Vivienne handed Jess her bag. Their fingers touched. "Make sure you get a good sleep. Drink lots of water."

Jess wanted to lean over and kiss her. Instead, she just nodded and admired the long lines of Vivienne's neck. "I will."

Jess waved goodbye as Vivienne climbed back into the car.

The memory of Vivienne's body in her hands, so soft and hard, strong and gentle, accompanied Jess as she climbed the stairs and knocked on Nelson's door. The taste of her, the smell of her—

"Girl." Nelson stroked Fleming's head and raised a knowing eyebrow. "Tell me."

Jess's face burned. "Uh."

Nelson hooted. *"Jessicaaaa!* Hell yes!"

"I . . . uh . . . Can I have my dog?"

"Nuh-uh." Nelson pulled Fleming closer. "I'm gonna need more information. Details for dog."

"Um . . ." Jess scratched her head. "We just . . . We sort of hooked up."

Nelson wagged a finger. "That is not a detail."

Jess gave in, raising clenched fists. "It was fucking amazing, okay? It was so good. She was . . . She's just . . ."

Nelson put a hand on his chest. "Oh, holy shit. Did you go and fall in love with her?"

"No! No! . . . No, I didn't fall in love with her! We're not even talking about it, okay? We hooked up, and now we're focusing on the game, and that's fine. It's fine. We'll sort it out later, after the final."

Nelson stared at her for a moment, then thrust Fleming into her arms. "Take the dog. Good lord. Take your dog, go home, and call her."

Jess collected Fleming, dodging his pink tongue. "I can't call her! We're not talking about it."

Nelson leaned on the doorframe and rubbed his forehead. "Jess. If you had seen your face when I opened this door. You think you're going to be able to play volleyball with her in front of the world, with all of this sexual tension between the two of you? When all you can think about is grabbing her and—"

"Yes," Jess yelped before he could finish that thought. "Yes, I can play with her. It's going to be fine."

"Right. So you said." He tilted his head. "Listen. I care

about you, Jess. Do what you need to do, okay? Do what feels right for you."

"I will." Jess leaned forward and kissed his cheek. "I promise. Thanks."

Fleming got a few more licks in on their way home before Jess unlocked her door and set him on the floor.

I should text her. Should I text her?

But no. She had other things to do. She fed Fleming, made herself a sandwich for lunch, and was about to search the laundry pile for workout gear when her phone buzzed.

Her heart leapt. But it was just Tania. A pang of guilt stabbed her chest. She had barely spoken to Tania since agreeing to play in the final.

How's it going, Button? (Sorry, I had to use it one more time.) How have things been with Vivienne?

Jess's thumbs hovered.

It felt wrong not to tell Tania, but she wasn't sure she had the strength to withstand the phone call and thousand-million questions that would follow. Plus, with Vivienne so unsure about it, who knew where things would end up? She already had Nelson offering his opinions, and she didn't want to tell Tania anything now if Vivienne decided to pretend nothing had ever happened after the game.

Good, she replied. **A little bumpy at times but overall I'd say we're connecting.**

I knew you guys would figure it out. Have you done your workout yet today? Want some company?

If she saw Tania in person, she'd have to tell her. She felt terrible lying, but . . . **Just started it actually. But thanks.**

Okay. Well, get some rest. You guys have got this. We're gonna be cheering for you so loud on Saturday. Marco is making a sign. Don't worry, the rule was I had to approve it.

Jess had to laugh. **Love you, T.**

Love you, too.

Jess hurried to change into her workout clothes so her lie became more true, then went for a short jog and did some stretching and foam rolling.

After a shower, she roasted a few chicken breasts and ate one with a quinoa salad. Then, at seven o'clock on the nose, she clicked the video-chat invite Vivienne had sent her and cued up the videos of their opponents' playoff matches. When Vivienne's face filled the screen, Jess's heart swelled in a rapid and concerning way.

Early Friday afternoon, they met at the pavilion for a light practice. Vivienne was all business, so Jess was too, even though it was hard not to think about Vivienne sprawled under her in the moonlight, putty in her hands.

"We're ready," Vivienne said when practice ended. "I've got a good feeling about this."

Jess also had feelings . . . she just wasn't sure if they were good or not.

24

Wins: I slept with Vivienne.
Losses: But does she want to sleep with me again? How am I supposed to forget about that? What if she wants to pretend it never happened? Oh God, how am I supposed to play volleyball with her now?

> ***Free ball*: Sending an easy ball over the net instead of an attack. A gift from your opponents. A chance to shape the next play however you want.**

Jess got to the pavilion early Saturday, when it was still deserted, aside from Winston and the custodian tasked with opening up the building.

She was a disaster.

She'd barely slept the night before, Vivienne invading her every thought.

"Until after the game" Vivienne had said. "After the game" was only a few hours away. What would Vivienne say after the game? *We should kiss some more? We should never have kissed?* Maybe she wouldn't say anything at all. Maybe she hoped Jess had forgotten all about it.

As if she could.

As if the night with Vivienne wasn't burned into her brain for the rest of her life, on permanent display behind her eyes, complete with floodlights and red velvet ropes.

"Jess!"

Jess screeched to a halt. She had almost crashed headlong into Troy on her way into the locker room. "Shit, sorry. Hi, Troy."

Troy shifted his armload of binders. "Hey. Are you okay?"

"Oh, yeah, fine. I'm fine. Just . . . you know. Nervous."

Troy nodded and looked like he was debating saying something. "I saw you guys training yesterday. Everything going okay?"

"What do you mean?"

"Oh, don't get me wrong, you guys looked great, I just felt like . . . you looked a bit uncomfortable at times, and I was worried about you and Vivienne together."

Jess tried to keep from laughing. *I'm worried about me and Vivienne together too, Troy,* she wanted to say. Instead she shrugged. "You know, it's hard to play with someone for years and then suddenly have a new partner for such a huge match. But it's fine. We're fine."

The binders started to slide. Troy bobbled the stack. "All right, then. Good luck, Jess. You know we'll all be pulling for you."

"Thanks." Jess watched him walk away, rolling the lie around in her head. Because it wasn't fine at all.

She had never been so un-fine before a match in her life.

By the time she had changed into Lee's uniform—it was a little small but there wasn't time to order her a new one—and pulled her hair up, she had decided to say something to Vivienne. She had to let out the turmoil in her head. It was the only option. Maybe Vivienne would be horrified, maybe she would be angry, but Jess just could not play in a match this huge with an entire section of her brain dedicated to the sounds Vivienne made as she came undone. She had to tell her—*I can't stop thinking about you. I really hope you want to kiss me again. Can I kiss you right now?*

When Jess heard rapid footsteps approaching, she turned to face Vivienne, heart in her throat.

Vivienne rounded the corner at full speed, beaming, eyes bright. "Jess! Guess what! Toni and Lee had their baby!"

Jess gasped. "What! That's amazing! Everyone's doing okay?"

Vivienne squished her in a celebratory hug. "Yeah, the baby's pretty small but she's okay. She'll be in the NICU for a bit."

"Oh, that's such great news."

"Look at her . . ." Vivienne dug her phone out of her bag and showed Jess a photo of an itsy-bitsy bright pink baby with wide black eyes and a look of bewilderment.

"Aw, she's precious. Do they have a name yet?"

"Yeah, it's . . ." Vivienne choked up, tears filling her eyes. "It's Vivienne."

Jess's jaw dropped. "Oh my God, that's . . . that's the sweetest."

"I know." Vivienne put a hand over her mouth, crying in earnest now. "I can't believe it."

"Well . . . they couldn't have picked a better person to name her after."

Before Jess knew it, she was hugging Vivienne again, Vivienne's tears wet on Jess's shoulder. So . . . now was not the time to ask for another kiss, probably.

Vivienne sniffled. "I just can't wait to cuddle that little baby."

"I'll bet." Jess squeezed Vivienne's arms and went to find her a tissue.

"Fuck . . . Okay. Enough of that. I have to focus." Vivienne dabbed her tears away. "*We* need to focus."

"Yeah." Jess smiled and handed her another tissue. Vivienne was so fucking cute. Just a big mushball under her cool exterior. "You want to review our match plan?"

"Yes." Vivienne's game face switched on. "Let's do that."

Vivienne got ready quickly, then they sat down cross-legged facing each other on the benches, notebooks in hand, reviewing what they had planned.

Jess glanced at the time when they were done. "We should head out th—" She stopped and cocked her head. "Do you hear that?"

"Hear what?" But then Vivienne picked up on it, too.

As they walked out of the locker room, it grew—a rumble, like the surf rolling in.

They stepped out into the pavilion lights, and the rumble turned into a roar. The stands were packed. Vivienne and Jess turned in a slow circle, taking in the sea of cheering faces surrounding them.

Chrissy, Shay, Locke, Billi, Raya, even Skye, the whole VL crew, shaking pom-poms and screaming their names.

There was Tania and George, Tía Diana and Tania's entire extended family, plus . . . yup, Marco with a sign—I LOVE YOU, JESS! and in smaller letters underneath, RESPECTFULLY AND PLATONICALLY. He beamed when Jess waved at him. Tania rolled her eyes.

Nelson was there with Ramón, waving a dachshund stuffie and a GO JESS! sign in the air.

Aunt Veronica, Uncle Milton, and Uncle Lane were at the front of a group cheering in "Team Vivienne" shirts, and even Scarlett showed up with her family. Vivienne's eyes widened in shock, but a smile crept over her face as she waved at them.

April and a bunch of the staff from Maggie's whistled and hooted from the very front row.

A wave of goose bumps swept over Jess's skin as her eyes prickled. Looking at all the faces, it hit her hard—the realization that all those people were there for her, to support her, to cheer for her . . . and she was a hot mess, teetering on the brink of total collapse.

Vivienne took Jess's hand and squeezed it. "Wow."

Jess's heart clenched. No matter what she was feeling, she had a job to do. A job for Vivienne, but also, a job for herself. She squeezed back.

The first step was warming up. Their opponents were already at it—Faith and Athena, the NorCal team that beat Vivienne and Lee in the final in Vancouver. They were much scarier when they were right there across the net. Faith was almost Jess's height, Puerto Rican, muscular, and tough. Athena, a little bit shorter but not much, had shining umber skin, razor-sharp cheekbones, and hit the ball harder than anyone Jess had ever played against.

Jess tried to ignore them and turn her attention to Vivienne. . . . The way she was so locked in. The way her eyes smoked with intensity, with determination and focus, the set of her jaw and shoulders . . . and muscular arms and . . . *fuck.*

Jess shook her head. She was running out of places to look. *Volleyball, Jessica.*

It was hard to settle into a groove for warm-up with her thoughts doing their best to escape their constraints. By the time they lined up for the match, Jess was vibrating with the effort of keeping them contained.

"And now," the announcer boomed, after introducing

the officials, "representing the Southern California Beach Volleyball League, wearing number one, Vivienne Morris."

Vivienne jogged to the end line, waving as the crowd cheered.

"And number two," the announcer continued, "Jessica McLaughlin."

Jess took a deep breath and joined her. They high-fived. Jess shifted her weight from foot to foot as the announcer introduced Athena and Faith. There were some cheers for them, and polite applause, but they definitely had home court advantage. Jess was happy it was SoCal's turn to host the state final this year.

After the anthem, they shook hands, then, having lost the coin toss, readied themselves to receive the serve.

Athena was up first.

It was a tough one, as expected, but Jess made a good pass and took a quick look at the other side waiting for Vivienne's set.

Jess got a kill with a shot over Faith's block to the back corner. The crowd roared.

Vivienne slapped her hands. "Fuck, yes, Jess. Do that again."

She had said those exact words in the sapphire room.

Jess tried to shake that thought out of her head on her way back to serve. Her toss was too far behind her and she had to lob an easy serve over. Athena cranked it back at them for a point of their own. Tied at one.

When she should have been noticing where Faith's eyes went before her serve, Jess noticed the way Vivienne adjusted her bikini bottom to loosen the sand trapped there. Faith scored an ace on the seam between them.

The set continued that way. They scored a point, but

then Vivienne ran her fingernail along her browline to scoop back a stray hair and Jess missed the next block—small mental mistakes that made her half a second too slow. The crowd's energy started to fade. They gave up the next point, and then another.

They lost the first set 14–21.

Vivienne cracked a Gatorade. "Not the start we wanted, but we're okay. We're fine. Right?"

"Right," Jess lied, when what she wanted to say was, *I'm the reason we're losing this match.*

Jess's focus continued to splinter. What if Vivienne decided she did want to be with her, but then a week later realized she was way out of Jess's league? What if they both got a circuit invite and they had to play together as exes? They lost the second set 13–21 and the energy in the pavilion had flattened.

Down two sets to none, they sat on their bench in silence, punctuated by the squirt of water bottles.

Jess clenched her jaw, frustration piling up. This could not be it for Vivienne after the stellar season she'd had—losing in the championship final in three straight sets. And she didn't want to be the reason Vivienne's star crashed and burned like that.

There had to be more. She had to find a way to calm her mind, to get the job done. To be there for Vivienne. There had to be a way she could snap out of it.

Jess made a decision. She put her water bottle down. "When you kissed me, what were you thinking?"

Vivienne gave her a look that went from surprised to amused. "I was thinking that I really wanted to kiss you."

"What made you actually do it?"

Vivienne shrugged and wiped a drop of water from her

lip. "I don't know, I guess I just thought . . . fuck it. I'm gonna do it."

"Were you worried about getting rejected?"

Vivienne's lips quirked. "Yeah, a little, but in that moment I didn't really care. Getting rejected was not as bad as not kissing you."

Jess only hesitated for half of a second before she put her hand on top of Vivienne's. "That's sort of how I feel right now. There is nothing as bad as not kissing you."

Jess waited while Vivienne's eyes lit up and her smile grew. One heartbeat. Two. Finally, Vivienne spoke. "You want to kiss me?"

Jess's heart thudded against her rib cage. "So badly. I sort of feel like I *have* to, in fact."

Vivienne turned her hand over and laced their fingers together.

Jess's heart rate accelerated.

"I want to kiss you, too," Vivienne admitted. "I don't know if you noticed, but I'm a mess out there. Kissing you is kind of all I can think about."

Jess realized she had swayed closer to Vivienne. "I think we should go for it."

Vivienne looked around at the sea of faces. "Like . . . right now?"

"Yes. Right now. And after the game, but especially now."

"Everyone will see."

"Yup."

Vivienne tipped forward and murmured, "Fuck yeah. Let's do it."

Jess touched their lips together, and the stars began to sing. Vivienne's lower lip fit between hers like it was made to be nowhere else. Her lips were so soft, and so sweet, and the kiss flooded Jess's body with euphoria and clarity and calmness, with the sense that this was exactly the right thing. In the back of her mind she heard wolf whistles and cheers from the crowd.

Their lips shifted and they kissed again. Joy zinged through Jess's body and bubbled up her throat. She pulled away and laughed. "Viv . . ."

Vivienne stared at her. "You called me Viv."

Jess grinned. "Let's go win this fucking thing."

Vivienne's smile . . . it was magic, brighter and more dazzling than a thousand shooting stars. She stood and pulled Jess to her feet. "Let's go win this fucking thing."

The crowd roared as they stepped back onto the court.

Jess turned to find Tania in the sea of faces.

Tania was beaming, hands clasped to her chest. She whooped when their gazes met. "GO GET THIS, JESS!" she hollered over the voices.

Jess grinned back.

She and Vivienne slapped hands. She adjusted her ponytail and took her position at the net, ready for Vivienne's serve. She smiled.

Vivienne's serve split Athena and Faith down the middle. Ace.

Her next serve hit the sideline on Faith's weaker side. Ace.

Jess hugged her. "This is a good game plan. You got nineteen more aces in you?"

Vivienne slapped her butt. "I got a few."

Jess was so happy she wanted to burst. She jumped a mile in the air and blocked Athena. She jumped even higher—nothing up there but her and the stars—and scored another kill. They were winning 7–2 when Athena and Faith called a time-out.

They sat on their bench and grinned at each other.

Jess had to laugh. "This is fun."

"Yes, it is." Vivienne shook her head. "But we should stay focused. Athena and Faith will be more ready now. They're not going to go down without a fight."

Jess raised an eyebrow. "Can I make a joke about going down?"

Vivienne's gaze swept over Jess in a way that made her feel naked . . . and she loved it. "You can do anything you want . . . tonight."

Jess shivered. "God, you're sexy."

Vivienne patted her hand. "You can tell me about it later."

Back on the court, they kept the momentum going and won the third set 21–12.

Vivienne unwrapped a protein bar. "You hungry? You should eat something—some *food*, I mean."

Jess grinned. "I'm good for now."

"Athena and Faith are pissed. They're going to come out full force. You ready?"

"I can literally do anything right now, Viv."

Vivienne wrinkled her nose. "You're adorable."

Jess could have flown in that moment. "Not as adorable as you."

Athena and Faith *were* pissed. They fought hard. The game was closer this time, but Jess and Viv still won 21–18.

They hugged after the last point. "Amazing," Vivienne breathed into her ear. "You're . . . a meteor, blazing across the sky, Jess. You're the moon, the sun, and all the stars."

She paused and pulled back to touch Jess's tattoo. "That's it. That's your nickname."

"What is?"

"You're light itself. I'm going to call you Starshine."

A warmth spread from the center of Jess's chest, through her body, tingling her fingertips and heating her cheeks. Words failed her.

Vivienne blinked, eyes wide and dark. "No matter how this game goes . . . thank you for playing with me." She kissed her again.

Jess kissed back, ready to catch a shooting star with her bare hands if Vivienne asked.

"We've got this," Vivienne said. "We prepared. We know their rhythm. We know that when the game is close, Athena is going to roll shot. We know that Faith likes to go short on her third serve. We know that Faith hits the second ball if it's tight. But they don't know anything about how we play together. We can beat them."

Athena and Faith, faces hard, settled in to pass Vivienne's serve in the fifth and deciding set.

Jess gave Viv her blocking signal and admired the bomb Vivienne sent over the net. Athena hit one hard back and Vivienne's dig was a little tight to the net.

"Hit it," Vivienne said, low and fast.

Jess jumped without a blocker and crushed the ball sharp cross. Athena dove but had no chance.

"Fuck yes." Vivienne hugged her. "Love that, Starshine."

Athena scored the next point when she looped it over Jess's block to the far corner and Vivienne couldn't quite get there.

"So close," Jess said, giving Vivienne five. "You'll get

the next one." And she did. Vivienne was like the whirlwind around the court, picking up absolutely everything.

The battle was tight, but they edged ahead 14–13 with another tough serve from Vivienne. Match point serve for her now. A hush fell over the crowd as Vivienne tossed the ball in the air.

It was a rocket, and Faith had to send over a free ball.

Jess passed it to Viv and went in for the attack. Faith blocked her. Vivienne dug it up and Jess hit it again. Athena dove to get a fist on it and scrambled to her feet. Faith bump set her and Athena went hard for the kill. Jess jumped, watched Athena's shoulders, and pressed her hands hard over the net. The thrill of connecting with the hit reverberated into her core as the ball smashed straight down in the sand.

They won.

Vivienne whooped, Jess roared, and they jumped into each other's arms, laughing and crying.

The crowd lost its collective mind, screaming and jumping and tossing hats and popcorn in the air. The earth shook. The moon trembled. Confetti cannons went off and filled the pavilion with pastel stars.

Jess pulled Vivienne into her, nose in her neck, breathed her in, sweat and sand, vanilla and the sky. "You did it, Viv."

Vivienne shook her head. "We did it."

"No, it was your focus, all season. You worked so hard. I'm so proud of you." Winston and Troy stood on the sideline carrying a trophy and a tray of medals but Jess ignored them. "The game's over now so . . . I'm going to kiss you again."

Their lips met while their family and friends cheered,

over the rumble of the ocean, over the singing of the stars.

Two days later, they had only left Jess's apartment to walk Fleming. They had barely left Jess's bed at all, really.

Curled up together, Viv traced Jess's hand splayed on her stomach, her hair tickling Jess's arm.

Jess was deliriously happy. The last forty-eight hours had been a dream.

Partying at Maggie's with Vivienne's hand in hers. Even better, falling into bed with Vivienne after, kisses hot and frantic. Waking up together the next morning, kisses slow and methodical. Vivienne's taste on her tongue, Vivienne's legs and vanilla smell wrapped around her in equal measure . . . everything she had ever wanted, right there in the bed next to her.

Well, almost everything . . .

"What if you get the pro invite and I don't?" Jess whispered.

"You'll get an invite." Vivienne kissed her bare shoulder. "You played lights out."

Jess didn't know what she'd do if Vivienne had to be on the road half the year in the Pacific League. Fortunately, she had the immediate distraction of Vivienne's rumbling stomach to worry about instead.

"You want something to eat?" Jess fished around on the floor for her own Veronica Doyle T-shirt to pull on.

"Sure." Vivienne rolled over to watch Jess get up and dig through the fridge.

It was slim pickings in there. They'd really have to go grocery shopping soon. Jess got to work on omelets.

"Oh, Veronica says congratulations," Vivienne informed her.

Jess plopped a frying pan on the stove. "Veronica Doyle does?"

"You're such a dork." Vivienne laughed. "Yes, Veronica Doyle said we were amazing. And . . . Okay, I have to tell you something. You know *Constellation Prize*, the book dedicated to me?"

Jess paused, egg in hand, and turned to face Vivienne, who was chewing on her lip. "Of course."

"And you know Cleo, the main character?"

Oh, did she ever. Sexy, daring Cleo, Jess's first gay crush. "I do. . . ." she said, wondering where Viv was going with this.

"Well, I didn't say anything at first, because it's sort of embarrassing . . . but . . ."

Jess had to smile at Vivienne wringing her fingers together, topless and tangled in the blankets, hair a mess. "But?"

"Veronica based Cleo off of me. Cleo is me. I just wanted to tell you because I didn't want it to be weird and—"

Vivienne was cut off by Jess's lips on hers.

Later, when Vivienne's stomach was *really* growling, Jess got back to the eggs. Fleming trundled up his ramp and snuggled into the warm spot Jess had just vacated.

"Wow, if I'd known how much you'd like hearing about Cleo, I would have told you a lot earlier." Viv scratched Fleming's head, all smug, and picked up her phone. Then she lurched up, sending the pup back to his feet. He glared at her. "Oh my God. Jess. We got an email from California Volleyball." Vivienne grabbed a pillow and clutched it to her chest. "Jess! I can't read it."

Jess snatched her own phone from the counter and

opened her email. There it was. California Volleyball. She clicked on it, heart in her throat.

"'Dear Jessica,'" she read aloud. "'We are pleased to offer you and your partner Vivienne Morris entry into the Pacific Professional Beach Volleyball League—'"

Vivienne screamed and flew out of the bed wearing only her underwear. They jumped up and down together in the kitchen, hugging and laughing while Fleming barked.

"Wait, wait." Vivienne gasped, wiping her eyes. "Wait . . . read the rest. Does it say anything about Lee?"

Jess scanned the rest of the email, then picked out a sentence to read. "'Given the circumstances, we would also like to extend an invitation to Lee—'"

Vivienne's phone rang, interrupting her renewed screeching. "It's Lee!" She answered it. "Lee! Hi! . . . Yes, we just got the email too, I . . . I know . . . Congratulations to you, too. But first, how is baby Vivienne doing?" Vivienne found one of Jess's zippered hoodies on the floor and shimmied into it while she listened.

Jess went back to chopping peppers and onions, clutching the knife, dizzy from the major life moments coming at her . . . and considering who would be Vivienne's partner on the court. Jess would have to step aside and let Lee take her spot back, both the right and painful thing to do.

"Aw, that's so great," Vivienne continued. "So not too much longer until you're home then? . . . Awesome. I can't wait to see all three of you." She laughed. "I know . . . Oh, she's just making me breakfast. Or lunch? What time is it?" She laughed again. "So . . . the invites . . . Can you believe— Oh. Oh, sure." She put her phone down. "Lee wants to talk to both of us." She tapped the button. "Okay, you're on speaker. What's up?"

"Hey, Jess," Lee said, her normally loud voice thin through the phone. "I just wanted to let both of you know . . . I've decided that I'm not going to be joining the circuit."

"What?" Vivienne said, sharing a look with Jess.

Jess's heart lifted.

"It's not something I ever really wanted, you know?" Lee continued. "It was never my dream. I'm happy in Sunside playing in the VL. And especially now that I have a baby. This is the place for me."

"Oh, Lee." Vivienne took Jess's hand. "Are you sure?"

"One hundred percent. But I'm so happy for you two. You make an amazing team, and you're going to have so much fun touring together."

Vivienne nodded, eyes misty. She squeezed Jess's hand, then they chatted a bit more while Jess finished making the omelets, mind spinning with visions of her and Viv together in a stadium full of fans, partners both off and on the court.

When Viv hung up, she came over to wrap herself around Jess, head tucking right under Jess's chin, like she was always meant to fit there.

"You did it, Jess," Vivienne whispered. "I'm so proud of you."

Jess hugged her harder, taking a deep breath of vanilla. "We did it together."

Vivienne nodded and sniffled.

Jess leaned back to get a look at Viv's face. "Hey . . . are you okay?"

"Yeah. Yeah, I'm great." She wiped a tear. "I'm super excited for you . . . for us. It's just . . . it's a little weird to think that I'll never play with Lee again. But . . ." She scrunched her nose in that adorable way she had. "I can't wait to play more with you."

Jess tilted her head down to kiss her. "I feel the same way about Tania. It'll be strange, but we'll figure it out together."

Once they finished their omelets, they walked Fleming, shared a soapy shower, then snuggled up in Jess's bed again to watch a movie on her laptop.

"We really need to get groceries tomorrow, though," Jess murmured as the title card appeared.

Vivienne suddenly reached to click pause and sat up. "Jess . . . now that we're going to be partners, officially, I need to be honest with you."

Oh God. Jess's heart skipped a beat, then started to thump. She braced herself for bad news.

Vivienne took a deep breath. "When I kissed you . . ."

Jess held her breath. . . . *I don't know what I was thinking. . . . I made a mistake.*

"I wasn't just trying to hook up. It wasn't *only* that I wanted to kiss you."

Jess forced herself to breathe. "You weren't? What were you trying to do?"

Vivienne laughed, although it was more of a wheezing exhale. "Jess . . . I . . . like you. A lot. And the last couple days . . . Well, it's clear to me that I have some pretty big feelings for you."

"You . . . do?"

Vivienne covered her eyes. "And I wasn't going to push anything, *ever*, because you clearly hated me for so long."

Vivienne . . . had big feelings for her? "I didn't always hate you."

Vivienne snorted. "Yes, you did."

"Well, you hated me, too."

"Never."

Jess sorted through her memories, the cutting remarks, the haughty looks, all the hair tossing. "What about the time you—"

Vivienne held up her hand and interrupted. "I promise you . . . anytime I said something bitchy or rude, I was literally just trying to flirt or be funny and failed miserably. Whenever I was around you, nothing came out right. I didn't think I would ever win you over. But then . . . I don't know. Things started to change a little . . . and you kissed me back after the party, and here we are now and . . ."

Another memory floated up for Jess. "That time I got to the locker room and you were practically naked . . ."

Vivienne batted her eyelashes.

Jess gasped. "Were you trying to entice me with your nakedness?"

"Don't be dense, of course I was. Did it work?"

"Work? It nearly killed me."

Vivienne snickered. "Excellent."

Jess took Vivienne's hand and kissed her fingers. "I have big feelings too, Vivienne. And if I 'hated' you, it was only masking the fact that I was obsessed with you." Her lips moved up Vivienne's arm.

"So you definitely don't hate me now?" Vivienne asked, as Jess kissed her shoulder.

"Mm-mm," Jess mumbled into her skin. Then her lips reached Vivienne's neck.

"Jess," Vivienne moaned, turning every bone in Jess's body to liquid.

Jess kissed her, soft and slow—showed Vivienne how much she didn't hate her, how much she had never hated her. How much she wanted her . . . for always.

Epilogue

TEN MONTHS LATER,

AUSTIN, TEXAS

Vivienne threw her hands in the air in the ref's direction. "Are you fucking kidding me? That was such a carry!"

"Viv . . ." Jess touched Vivienne's arm. "It's okay."

"But . . . she practically caught it. . . ." Vivienne trailed off, expression pained.

Jess gave her a low five. "We need a pass now. Come on, refocus."

"Okay. Okay, you're right." Vivienne smiled at her. One of her small, private smiles.

A thrill ran down Jess's spine, like it did every time it hit her. This was her reality now—playing professional volleyball with the love of her life. The competition in the Pacific League was intense, but so was her connection with Vivienne.

The ball kissed off of Jess's forearms on the next serve—a

perfect pass. Vivienne set the ball right where Jess liked it and she cranked it down the line for a point.

"Yes!" Vivienne smacked her butt. "Great hit, Starshine."

"Great set, V."

Vivienne served for match point, a wicked jumper that curved at least four feet to the side before it hit the sand for the win.

Jess and Vivienne whooped and jumped into each other's arms.

"We just beat Bianca Collazo," Jess murmured into Vivienne's ear.

Vivienne squeezed her. "First time of many."

Bianca, brow dripping with sweat, shook their hands under the net with a smile. "Great match, ladies. Congratulations on making the playoffs your first year, too."

"Thank you," Jess said, trying not to wheeze. She still wasn't used to mixing with so many famous faces, especially not the one that had been taped up in her locker for three years.

"You two want to grab some dinner with us?" Bianca asked, like it was the most normal thing in the world.

Jess's jaw flapped.

Vivienne stepped in smoothly. "We have an early flight home tomorrow, but sure. That would be great."

Jess nodded and forced out a word. "Great."

Waiting at the gate in the airport the next morning, Vivienne slumped in her seat, resting her head on Jess's shoulder. Jess fished out the last piece of the homemade banana bread from her bag and they split it as Jess replayed the events from dinner the night before in her mind. A teenage girl had approached them while they lingered over dessert, knew all their names, and asked them for autographs. Jess signed the girl's shirt, right between Vivienne and Bianca's signatures.

Jess smiled, wondering what awkward, gangly fourteen-year-old Jess in black lipstick would think about her now.

Vivienne's phone buzzed. "Scarlett says great game," she told Jess. "She says the whole family watched, and now my niece wants to be a professional beach volleyball player when she grows up."

"Can we get them all tickets for our LA game, you think?" Jess asked.

Vivienne kissed Jess's shoulder. "That's a great idea."

Jess sent a text to Troy, who was their manager now, then scrolled through her socials as the gate filled up around them. "Oh my God, Viv, look at Baby Vivienne! She had her first dip in the ocean yesterday!"

Viv sat up, instantly awake. "Let me see! Aw, she is the cuuutest! I can't wait to see her tomorrow. Make sure we remember to bring the onesie we got her from Vegas." Vivienne scrolled through the photos, cooing like the doting aunt she was, then handed Jess her phone back and settled against her shoulder again.

Jess threaded their fingers together, studying the new dachshund tattoo on her inner wrist. She missed Fleming so much when they were traveling for games, but at least he was happy boarding with Nelson, Ramón, and his two sweet corgis, Pedro and Pascal.

When boarding was announced for their flight, Jess stood and helped Vivienne to her feet. "Ready to go home?"

Jess had been a bit sad to say goodbye to her apartment, although it was made easier when Nelson announced he was moving out, too. And Vivienne had made her feel nothing but welcome in her green bungalow, adding shelves in the living room for Jess's books and knickknacks. Her jars were filled with sand now, with one shell resting on top.

When it was time to leave for dinner, Jess went to check on Vivienne's progress and found her applying mascara at her vanity, hair up, neck so elegant and tempting.

Jess kissed the galaxy tattoo on the back of Vivienne's neck. "Honestly, if I had known how long it takes you to get ready . . ."

"You'd have what? Not have moved in with me?" Vivienne put the lid on her mascara and turned on her stool to blink prettily up at Jess.

Jess forgot what she was going to say at the sight of those dark eyes. She took Vivienne's hand, pulled her to her feet, and wrapped her hands around Vivienne's waist. "You look beautiful."

"Thank you." Vivienne kissed her. "So do you."

Jess deepened the kiss, breathing in the vanilla and sliding her fingers under the straps of Vivienne's dress.

"Easy," Vivienne murmured against her lips. "Or you're going to be the one making us late for dinner. And I'll throw you right under the bus, I don't even care."

Jess groaned.

Vivienne tossed her lipstick into her clutch and snapped it closed. "Come on, Nelson and Ramón are waiting!"

Maggie's was packed, a hot August night, but April had saved their favorite table for them, and added a photo of Jess and Viv at their first pro match on the wall above.

"You'll have to sign that later," April told them with a wink when she took their drink orders.

Nelson and Ramón arrived a few minutes later—"How can someone with no hair take so long to get ready?" Ramón wondered—and, after hugs and kisses all around, they sat and began the important work of catching up with friends.

"How did the move go?" Jess asked, with a grateful sip of her Corona. They tasted better at Maggie's somehow.

Nelson sighed. "Mrs. Horowitz told me she's glad to see Fleming go, but I think secretly she'll miss him. She gave me some doggy treats for him on the way out."

"Have you heard from Tania and George?"

"Yes, they landed safely in Madrid. They said to say thank you again for all the advice you gave them, Ramón."

"And you guys have already qualified for playoffs? That's incredible!"

"Give me the behind-the-scenes dirt. Who is sleeping with who on the circuit?"

"Did I tell you what happened when Fleming tried to play with Pedro's favorite toy?"

The evening flew by with laughter and stories, Vivienne's knee against hers under the table, and a warmth building in Jess's chest that made her feel more like herself than ever before.

Late that night, Jess and Vivienne climbed out of their Uber and started up the path to the front door. Jess tugged Vivienne's arm to make her pause. "Wait." Jess tilted her head back to take in the sky.

Vivienne took hold of Jess's arm with her other hand and looked up with her.

No moon, just stars spilling across the black. A satellite blipped in a slow arc above Venus.

They held each other in silence. A meteor flashed in the atmosphere. They gasped together.

Jess looked at Vivienne and tucked a stray piece of hair behind her ear. "I love you."

The starlight in Vivienne's eyes was as steady as the light billions of years old crossing the cosmos to reach them now. She smiled. "I love you, too."

Hand in hand, they turned to head up the walk and into their home.

Acknowledgments

Writing a book is impossible to do alone, and this one was even more of a team effort than my first four. I am deeply grateful to the people who have been the Tania to my Jess. My editor, Grace Gay, continues to be an absolute delight to work with. I don't know how I got so lucky to have her on my team. Grace, thank you for caring about this book so much and pushing me to make it better. I owe you about a million loaves of banana bread.

Hanna Kubicka, a continent and an ocean away from me, but still so close, somehow continues to find the time to lend her brilliant brain to my work. Reading her notes on my chapters is one of my life's greatest pleasures. Andrew Padgett, so generous and funny, read this book about as many times as I did, and never failed to offer brilliant suggestions (the wiener joke is his) and obsess over the details like it was his own. John, the greatest cheerleader in the world, who can always find the bright side, and has designed the most gorgeous website for me: jmoffattwrites.com. The idea for this book was also sparked while chatting with him when he suggested a story about lifeguards who fall in love playing beach volleyball.

I am so lucky to have online-turned-real-life friend Rebekah Rodriguez-Lynn, who lives in Southern California and offered me so many fantastic suggestions about the life and culture there. (Any remaining inaccuracies are due to me and my artistic license.) Bex, I love that our online friendship has morphed into the real world. Looking forward to our next glass of wine.

Stephanie Jameson, my Vancouver expert, who, with 168 caps for Team Canada in field hockey, also happens to know a thing or two about high-performance athletics, and never failed to immediately reply to all my texts with hyper-specific details.

Thank you to my agent, Jordy Albert, and early readers of *Bump, Set, Sparks*, Chip Pons and Matthew Hubbard, for their kind words. To the wonderful team at St. Martin's Griffin—Zoë Miller, Austin Adams, Meryl Levavi, Ervin Serrano, Chrisinda Lynch, Brant Janeway, Janna Dokos, and John Morrone. They are the most kind and helpful people. I am so grateful to them, and anyone I may have inadvertently missed.

Thank you to Alice Bellandi, the Italian judo athlete who won a gold medal at the 2024 Paris Olympics and immediately ran to kiss her girlfriend on the sidelines. Thank you to soccer legend Megan Rapinoe, who said "You can't win a championship without gay players." Thank you to my parents, who took me on so many camping trips along the Pacific coast. Thank you to Space Camp at the U.S. Space & Rocket Center in Huntsville, Alabama, and Honeywell, who sponsored me, and all the people I met while I was there, especially astronaut Story Musgrave, who further stoked my love of space. Thank you to my volleyball coaches and teammates over the years, especially my East Kelowna Hall team. I miss you all so much. Thank you for being the absolute best to play with.

Thank you to my husband, children, and dad, who have helped me carve time into our busy life for writing, and to all my friends and family who continue to be excited about my books. See you all at the release party!

And finally, thank you for reading *Bump, Set, Sparks*! I hope it made you smile.

About the Author

Jennifer Moffatt believes that there are so many more romantic stories to tell than the ones that have traditionally been lined up on bookstore shelves, and she plans to write as many of them as she can. Her short stories have appeared in multiple anthologies and literary magazines. Jennifer loves hot summers and potato chips and lives with her family in British Columbia, Canada. She can be found on Instagram: @jmoffattwrites and her website jmoffattwrites.com.